D0265607

Knowsley Library Service

...ake you feel nostalgic for your own past, for those feverish ...en fear and elation were pretty much the same thing'
Rachel Cooke *Observer*

'Not since *One Day* have I stayed up so late reading a book, but Rona Jaffe's *The Best of Everything* has me gripped . . .' Laura Craik, *Evening Standard*

'One of Don's first bed companions in series one of *Mad Men* is not another woman, but *The Best of Everything*, this 1958 novel by Rona Jaffe . . . It is a world of typing pools and tie-wearing at all times; of whiskey drinking and womanising; a world in which secretaries grope their way towards feminism with difficulty and bosses grope their secretaries with ease . . . As Draper himself might say: fascinating' *The Times*

'This stirring, evocative novel tells it exactly as it was' Fay Weldon

'Decades before *Sex and the City*, Jaffe recorded the minutiae of women's lives and broke powerful taboos' Joan Smith, *Independent*

'This is a novel that believes in the power of fiction to influence, inspire, transform . . . Jaffe's heroines are able to test the boundaries. They are changed by what they experience. But – and here comes the big difference from today's commercial fiction for women – so is the world'
Viv Groskop, *Telegraph*

'I absolutely loved this . . . what a great novel' Lizzie Noble

'A classic of its kind. The dialogue is real, the people are real. Most career girls, past or present, will respond with the shock of authenticity' *Saturday Review*

'It will ring a bell with anyone who has lived in New York at a time of life when the city looks like a vast crackerjack box of amorous possibilities. It has mountains of merit' *New York World-Telegram*

'Rona Jaffe will have you believing that very shocking things do happen in New York bars and apartments. This is a story that should be read by girls with dramatic ideas about New York, parents with qualms about their daughters' ideas, and men with baffling questions about girls' minds' *Cleveland Press*

'An exuberant and readable book. Miss Jaffe is an artful and persuasive storyteller. It almost will certainly ruffle many a male ego' *Spokane Chronicle*

'Such is the author's skill that this story of five girls is unmistakably the story of someone you know' *The Boston Globe*

'Any employer reading these pages will make a mental note to check up on what the girls in his office do after lunch, and with whom' *New York Post*

ABOUT THE AUTHOR

Rona Jaffe (1931–2005) was the author of sixteen books, including the bestselling and internationally acclaimed novels *The Road Taken*, *The Cousins*, *The Last Chance*, *Five Women* and *The Best of Everything*. She also founded the Rona Jaffe Foundation (www.ronajaffefoundation.org), which presents annual awards to promising women writers of literary fiction, poetry and creative non-fiction.

RONA JAFFE

The Best of Everything

PENGUIN BOOKS

PENGUIN CLASSICS

Published by the Penguin Group
Penguin Books Ltd, 80 Strand, London WC2R ORL, England
Penguin Group (USA) Inc., 375 Hudson Street, New York, New York 10014, USA
Penguin Group (Canada), 90 Eglinton Avenue East, Suite 700, Toronto, Ontario, Canada M4P 2Y3
(a division of Pearson Penguin Canada Inc.)
Penguin Ireland, 25 St Stephen's Green, Dublin 2, Ireland (a division of Penguin Books Ltd)
Penguin Group (Australia), 250 Camberwell Road, Camberwell, Victoria 3124, Australia
(a division of Pearson Australia Group Pty Ltd)
Penguin Books India Pvt Ltd, 11 Community Centre, Panchsheel Park, New Delhi – 110 017, India
Penguin Group (NZ), 67 Apollo Drive, Rosedale, Auckland 0632, New Zealand
(a division of Pearson New Zealand Ltd)
Penguin Books (South Africa) (Pty) Ltd, 24 Sturdee Avenue, Rosebank, Johannesburg 2196, South Africa

Penguin Books Ltd, Registered Offices: 80 Strand, London WC2R ORL, England

www.penguin.com

First published in the United States of America by Simon & Schuster 1958
First published in Great Britain by Lowe and Brydone (Printers) Ltd 1959
Published in the United States of America in Penguin Books 2005
Published in Penguin Classics 2011

006

Copyright © Rona Jaffe, 1958
All rights reserved

The moral right of the author has been asserted

Set in Dante MT Std
Typeset by Palimpsest Book Production Limited, Falkirk, Stirlingshire
Printed in Great Britain by Clays Ltd, St Ives plc

Except in the United States of America, this book is sold subject
to the condition that it shall not, by way of trade or otherwise, be lent,
re-sold, hired out, or otherwise circulated without the publisher's
prior consent in any form of binding or cover other than that in
which it is published and without a similar condition including this
condition being imposed on the subsequent purchaser

ISBN: 978-0-141-19631-2

www.greenpenguin.co.uk

MIX
Paper from
responsible sources
FSC
www.fsc.org   FSC™ C018179

Penguin Books is committed to a sustainable
future for our business, our readers and our planet.
This book is made from Forest Stewardship
Council™ certified paper.

ALWAYS LEARNING   **PEARSON**

For Phyllis, Bob, Jay, Jerry and Jack

YOU DESERVE
THE BEST OF EVERYTHING
The best job, the best surroundings,
The best pay, the best contacts.

From an ad in *The New York Times*

Foreword

The way all this happened sounds itself like a novel. I was a young struggling writer in New York City in the 1950s who had been practicing her craft since she was two and a half. I used to send stories to *The New Yorker* when I was nine, and they would come right back. The editors thought I was an adult who couldn't write.

After graduating from Radcliffe at nineteen, I worked at a publishing company, Fawcett Publications, for almost four years, rising from filing clerk to associate editor. While there, I finally had several stories published in national magazines, and eventually quit my job to write full time, hoping to complete a novel. I had no money and was still living with my parents.

One day, I was visiting the offices of Simon & Schuster to see my college friend, Phyllis Levy, who was then the secretary to the editor-in-chief, Jack Goodman. Jerry Wald, the famous Hollywood producer, happened to be there meeting with her boss. Goodman said to Wald, 'Rona's going to write a hell of a novel some day.'

'And we're going to publish it,' Phyllis added.

Wald, who was in town scouting for properties to option, said, 'I'm looking for a modern-day *Kitty Foyle*. A book about working girls in New York.' Out of curiosity, I went to the library and read the novel by Christopher Morley, which had been made into the 1940 movie starring Ginger Rogers. I thought it was dumb. I said to myself: He doesn't know anything about women. I know about women. And I work in an office. Still I let the matter drop, until I went to Hollywood on vacation with Phyllis, and Jerry invited us to lunch. I wanted to say something interesting to him, so I casually remarked, 'I'm going to write that working-girl book.' He replied that he was going to produce it.

On the train back from California, coming into New York, I had the vision of the beginning for the book, which is all 'the hundreds and hundreds of girls' walking to work. I came up with the title that morning, too, a phrase I remembered from a *New York Times* help-wanted ad that began: You Deserve the Best of Everything.

I didn't know if the things that happened to my friends and me were an anomaly, so I interviewed fifty women to see if they'd had the same experiences, with the men and the jobs and all the things nobody spoke about in polite company. Back then, people didn't talk about not being a virgin. They didn't talk about going out with married men. They didn't talk about abortion. They didn't talk about sexual harassment, which had no name in those days. But after interviewing these women, I realized that all these issues were part of their lives too. I thought that if I could help one young woman sitting in her tiny apartment thinking she was all alone and a bad girl, then the book would be worthwhile. I had no idea what a chord it would strike for millions.

Jack Goodman died suddenly of a heart attack, and was replaced by Simon & Schuster's rising young star Robert Gottlieb. He told me to 'look back in horror and write,' and so I did. We spoke on the phone regularly, and I'd tell him what I was going to work on every day. Meanwhile, Jerry Wald was doing a huge publicity campaign for a book I hadn't written and he hadn't read, so it was a surreal and rather nerve-racking time.

I wrote, obsessed, every day for five months and five days, on a manual typewriter, until the 775-page manuscript was finished and the two fingers I used to type with were bleeding under the nails. I was proud of the fact that my publisher made no revisions except for grammar and spelling. And because I hadn't made a carbon copy, and since we didn't have copying machines then, they had to send the manuscript out to a typing service to make copies. My first indication that the book would be a success was when I spoke with the women from the typing service who had gotten hold of my phone number. Because the publisher was in a hurry, they had to hire a team of typists who were each given only a portion of the manuscript to work on. The girls had gotten so caught up in the chapters they were working on, they couldn't wait for the finished book to find out what happened next. Instead, they would ring me. At the time I thought: There's my audience.

The book was published less than a year after I left my parents, got my own apartment, and began it. I was twenty-six.

As soon as *The Best of Everything* was published, it was a huge bestseller. Women would show up at book signings with their well-worn office copy asking me to inscribe it to 'all the girls on the forty-ninth floor.' To this day women come up to me and say that the book changed their lives. After they read it, they decided to come to New York and work in publishing. I was a little surprised, because I had thought *The Best of Everything* was a cautionary tale. But of course an exciting life, even if very difficult, is better than a dull one, even if it changes you forever.

There was so much publicity and it all happened so fast that the situation felt completely unreal. Interviews and photos of me were in the newspapers constantly, and I was even sent to Hollywood several times to help with the movie. Standing in front of a bookstore, I would look into the window at all the copies of my first novel, with my picture on the front cover, and wonder what I would think of this suddenly celebrated person if I weren't her. The one thing that was clear, though, was that I was now a professional author with a career ahead of me.

The honesty of *The Best of Everything* paved the way for other authors. And in many ways it's as relevant today as it was then. Some things have stayed the same and some have come back. *The Best of Everything* is a sociological document but it's also about change: how your dreams change, how your life changes, how each thing that happens to you changes something else.

And that doesn't change.

RONA JAFFE 2005

I

You see them every morning at a quarter to nine, rushing out of the maw of the subway tunnel, filing out of Grand Central Station, crossing Lexington and Park and Madison and Fifth avenues, the hundreds and hundreds of girls. Some of them look eager and some look resentful, and some of them look as if they haven't left their beds yet. Some of them have been up since six-thirty in the morning, the ones who commute from Brooklyn and Yonkers and New Jersey and Staten Island and Connecticut. They carry the morning newspapers and overstuffed handbags. Some of them are wearing pink or chartreuse fuzzy overcoats and five-year-old ankle-strap shoes and have their hair up in pin curls underneath kerchiefs. Some of them are wearing chic black suits (maybe last year's but who can tell?) and kid gloves and are carrying their lunches in violet-sprigged Bonwit Teller paper bags. None of them has enough money.

At eight-forty-five Wednesday morning, January second, 1952, a twenty-year-old girl named Caroline Bender came out of Grand Central Station and headed west and uptown toward Radio City. She was a more than pretty girl with dark hair and light eyes and a face with a good deal of softness and intelligence in it. She was wearing a gray tweed suit, which had been her dress-up suit in college, and was carrying a small attaché case, which contained a wallet with five dollars in it, a book of commuter tickets, some make-up, and three magazines entitled respectively *The Cross*, *My Secret Life*, and *America's Woman*.

It was one of those cold, foggy midwinter mornings in New York, the kind that makes you think of lung ailments. Caroline hurried along with the rest of the crowd, hardly noticing anybody, nervous and frightened and slightly elated. It was her first day at the first job she had ever had in her life, and she did not consider herself basically a career girl. Last year, looking ahead to this damp day in January, she had thought she would be married. Since she'd had a fiancé it seemed logical. Now she had no fiancé and no one she was interested in, and the new job was more than an economic convenience, it was an emotional necessity. She wasn't sure that being a secretary in a typing pool could possibly be engrossing, but she was going to have to make it so. Otherwise she would have time to think, and would remember too much . . .

Fabian Publications occupied five air-conditioned floors in one of the modern buildings in Radio City. On this first week of the new year the annual hiring had just been completed. Three secretaries had left the typing pool, one to get married, the other two for better jobs. Three new secretaries had been hired to start on Wednesday, the second of January. One of these was Caroline Bender.

It was five minutes before nine when Caroline reached the floor where the typing pool was located, and she was surprised to find the large room dark and all the typewriters still neatly covered. She had been afraid she would be late, and now she was the first one. She found the switch that turned on the ceiling lights and prowled around waiting for someone to appear. There was a large center room with rows of desks for the secretaries, and on the edges of this room were the closed doors of the offices for editors. Tinsel Christmas bells and red bows were still taped to some of the doors, looking bedraggled and sad now that the season was over.

She looked into several of the offices and saw that they seemed to progress in order of the occupant's importance from small tile-floored cubicles with two desks, to larger ones with one desk, and finally to two large offices with carpet on the floor, leather lounging chairs, and wood-paneled walls. From the books and magazines lying around in them she could see that one of these belonged to the editor of Derby Books and the other to the editor of *The Cross*.

She heard voices then in the main room, and the sound of laughter and greetings. Stricken with a sudden attack of shyness, she came slowly out of the editor's office.

It was nine o'clock and the room was suddenly filling up with girls, none of whom noticed her presence at all. The teletype operator was combing her hair out of its pin curls, one of the typists was going from desk to desk collecting empty glass jars and taking coffee orders. Covers were being pulled off typewriters, coats hung up, newspapers spread out on desks to be read, and as each new arrival came in she was greeted with delighted cries. It sounded as though they had all been separated from one another for four weeks, not four days. Caroline didn't know which desk was hers and she was afraid to sit at someone else's, so she kept standing, watching, and feeling for the first time that morning that she was an outsider at a private club.

A lone man came in then, briskly, with an amused, rather self-conscious look, as if he were intruding on a ladies' tea. At the sight of him some of the girls sat up and tried to look more businesslike. He was in his late forties, of medium height but wiry so that he looked smaller, with a pale, dissipated face that looked even more ravaged because there were signs that it had once been very handsome. He stopped at the water fountain and drank for a long time, then he straightened up and went on into one of the editors' offices. He was wearing a camel's-hair coat with a large cigarette burn on the lapel.

'Who's that?' Caroline asked the girl nearest her.

'Mr Rice, editor of *The Cross*. You're new, aren't you?' the girl said. 'My name is Mary Agnes.'

'I'm Caroline.'

'I hope you like it here,' Mary Agnes said. She was a thin, plain-looking girl with wavy dark hair, and she wore a black wool skirt and a transparent white nylon blouse. She was extremely flat-chested.

'I hope so too,' Caroline said.

'Well, you can have either of those two desks over there if you want to put anything away. You'll be working for Miss Farrow this week, because her secretary quit on her. She usually comes in around ten o'clock. She'll take you around and introduce you to everybody. Would you like some coffee?'

'I'd love some,' Caroline said. She put her attaché case and gloves into the drawer of one of the empty desks and hung her jacket over the back of the chair.

Mary Agnes waved over the girl who was taking coffee orders. 'Brenda, this is Caroline.'

'Hi,' Brenda said. She was a plump, quite pretty blonde, but when she smiled there was a tooth conspicuously absent on either side, giving her the look of a werewolf. 'How do you want your coffee? You'd better take it in a jar instead of a paper container.'

'Thank you,' Caroline said.

Brenda walked back to her desk with a twitch of her hips. 'Watch out for her,' Mary Agnes said conspiratorially when she was out of earshot. 'She makes you pay for the coffee and the jar, and then she gives back the jars and keeps all the deposit money. Don't let her get away with it.'

'I'll try not to,' Caroline said.

'Do you have a key to the ladies' room?'

'No.'

'Well, you can use mine until you get one. Just ask. Did you notice her teeth?'

'Whose?'

'Brenda's. She's engaged to be married and she's having all her bad teeth pulled so her husband will have to pay for the new ones. Did you ever hear of such a thing?' Mary Agnes giggled and began putting sheets of carbon paper and letter paper into the roller of her typewriter.

'What's Mr Rice – is that his name? What's he like?' asked Caroline. She liked camel's-hair coats on men, they reminded her of *The Front Page*.

A genuinely stricken look of piety came over Mary Agnes' plain face. 'It's very sad,' she said. 'I always feel sorry for a person like him. I wish somebody could help him.'

'What's the matter with him?'

'Wait till you read that magazine he puts out. It will sicken you.'

'You mean he writes that stuff because he believes it, is that it?'

'Worse,' said Mary Agnes. 'He writes it because he doesn't believe in anything. Those articles he writes sound very pious but they're just a lot of words. I feel sorry for the poor souls who believe them, but I feel sorrier for Mr Rice. I often think he must be very lonely.' She smiled ruefully. 'Well, don't get me started on Mr Rice's lack of faith, it's a subject I feel very strongly about and right now I've got to get these letters typed.'

'Maybe you and I can have lunch together,' Caroline suggested.

'Oh, that would have been fun . . . but I can't. I always have lunch with my boy friend. That is, some days he brings his lunch up here and eats it with me, and some days I bring my sandwiches downtown and eat them with him. He works downtown in a furniture factory. We're saving up to get married. We're getting married a year from this coming June.'

'That's a long time from now,' Caroline said.

'I know,' Mary Agnes said matter-of-factly. 'But it could have been even longer.'

'I certainly wish you luck,' Caroline said. She went over to her desk and sat down. She'd come here to get away from thoughts of marriage, and the first two girls she had met were engaged. Well, she would clean out the drawers of this desk, and then Miss What's-her-name would arrive and give her more work probably than she could handle, nervous as she was on her first day, and soon her mind would be so filled with office problems that there would be no room for remembering things she shouldn't.

She had a mental list now of things she had to keep out of her mind, but it was hard because they were everyday things for anyone else and they kept cropping up. Boys named Eddie. Paris. Almost any Noel Coward song. Three or four particular restaurants. Any book or story by F. Scott Fitzgerald. Chianti. W. B. Yeats. Steamships going to Europe. Steamships coming back from Europe.

She didn't really want to forget all of it, because it had all meant happiness at the time it happened. She only wanted to be able someday to remember without finding it painful. That was the trick, to keep all the good things from the past and cast away the ones that hurt.

She had been a junior at Radcliffe when she met Eddie Harris. He was a senior at Harvard. He was a marvelous, funny, appealing-looking boy, he played jazz piano, he read books none of the others had even heard of, he had a sense of humor that could keep her laughing for hours. He had moody spells too, when he walked around his room in a turtleneck sweater and khaki pants and bare feet and played Noel Coward songs on the phonograph and wouldn't talk to anyone but her for days. He got all A's in school with a minimum of study, it seemed, and his family had money. She couldn't really believe it was happening to her, a girl of eighteen who had never met a boy she cared about at all, and now Eddie Harris was in love with her and she adored him.

She was quite sure that she loved him more than he loved her, but he was a man, after all, and men had other things to worry about.

They planned to get married the autumn after he was graduated from Harvard. Meanwhile she was to go to summer school and get her diploma. It was something her parents insisted upon, she was only nineteen then and they told her she would regret it someday if she had gone this far toward a degree and then given it up. Girls of nineteen didn't have to rush into marriage, they told her, although they were as pleased about her engagement to Eddie as she was. Eddie encouraged her, and of course she would do anything he wanted, although she couldn't really see how another few months of classes could make any difference when simply being near Eddie made her so much more aware of everything she read and heard and saw that she felt like a different person. College was supposed to make you think, wasn't it? Well, Eddie made her think, and what she really wanted out of life was to be a good and interesting wife for him and make him happy, not cram down another hundred lines of Shakespeare.

Anyway, she went to summer school. And Eddie's parents sent him to Europe for a graduation present. She thought it would have been nicer if they had waited and then let Eddie and her go there on their honeymoon, but the thought struck her as so self-ish that she didn't even mention it to him. There had been a big boom in world travel at Harvard and Radcliffe in those years; everyone went. Travel was a new experience for their generation those early years after the war, and Caroline had already grown tired of the constant cocktail-party conversation which consisted mainly of place-dropping. She kept her mouth shut and everyone said to her, 'You've been to Europe, of course, haven't you?' She thought the college boys who ran to Paris and then sat around in cafés looking for American girls whom they had known at home were very funny. She knew Eddie would get a lot more out of his trip than that.

When she saw him off on the ship she gave him a bottle of champagne and a brave smile, although all the time they were kissing goodbye she wanted to cry out, 'Take me with you, don't go alone.' He told her it would be only six weeks, that the time would go quickly, that he would think of her all the time. He told her, 'Miss me a little' (smiling), when they both knew he meant she should miss him a great deal, and that she would whether he told her to or not. On the deck he discovered the parents of a girl he had known years ago when he was in prep school, Helen Lowe, and he latched onto the father. See, his smile said comfortingly to Caroline as the ship pulled away from the harbor, here I am with this nice middle-aged man, see how well I'm keeping out of trouble.

Helen had been on the ship too, she had been down in her stateroom with four of her classmates from Sarah Lawrence getting drunk together. She was a tall, slim, bosomy girl with the kind of ash-blonde hair that looks almost gray and was not a really popular color until several years later. She had a white French poodle and she had taken French lessons before she left on the ship.

When the six weeks were finally over, a letter arrived for Caroline on the day Eddie's ship came in to New York without him.

'I don't know how to tell you this,' the letter began. 'This is the fourth time I've tried to write you about it, the other three efforts I've torn up.' He sounded rather sorry for himself because he had to tell her. He probably thought, What a mess, what a mess. How much easier to declare love than to withdraw it, especially from someone you still like very much. He sounded even sorrier for himself and his unpleasant predicament than he was for her, who only had to read what he had written and see her future and her happiness shatter quietly around her.

Eddie had always hated anything unpleasant. Perhaps he thought marriage to Helen Lowe would solve everything, she was sophisticated and poised and intelligent and pretty, and her father owned oil wells. You couldn't say much against oil wells. Or perhaps he had been just like those other lonely college boys in Paris sitting in the cafés (or in his case on shipboard) looking for a familiar face. Perhaps Caroline had overestimated him. So Helen and her parents accompanied him back on the ship to America, and a month later there was a monstrously expensive wedding in Dallas.

Having finished summer school, Caroline did not have another term of college to help her occupy herself, so she took a business and shorthand course and the day after she was graduated she took the first job she was offered. It didn't make much difference to her, really, as long as it was something from nine to five, which meant eight hours less to think about herself. She was rather glad, however, when it turned out to be a job in publishing. She bought three of the Fabian magazines and read them from cover to cover the night before her first day at Fabian, and she couldn't make up her mind who seemed more startling – the people who read such trash or the people who published it. The strange thing was, though, that lately whenever she read a story with a happy ending she found herself crying.

'You're the new secretary? I'm Amanda Farrow.'

Caroline jumped to her feet, shaking off her daydream. The woman in front of her desk was in her late thirties, tall and slim with bright copper hair pulled back into a chignon. She was cool and polished and fashionably dressed. She even wore a little hat, two fluffy feathers really, with a tiny black veil. 'My name's Caroline Bender.'

'You can come into my office in a moment. Number nine.'

She watched Amanda Farrow disappear into Office Nine and then found a shorthand pad and some pencils in the drawer of her new desk. From her investigation in the early morning Caroline knew that Amanda Farrow's office was one of the executive ones, one rank lower than the offices with carpets. She saw the overhead lights go on in Number nine and waited a moment more, then opened the door and went in.

Amanda Farrow was seated behind her large desk. She was still wearing her hat, and she was busy applying nail polish to her fingernails. There was a large filing cabinet against one wall, and two armchairs in front of the desk.

'First you can order me some coffee, black with sugar,' Amanda Farrow said. 'All the filing to be done is in this box here. My secretary left last week and the place is a mess. The mail comes four times a day, you open it, and anything that requires a personal answer goes in this box. Some of the letters you can answer yourself, if they're from cranks, for instance. But show me everything you write before you send it out. Do you have a Social Security card?'

'Not yet.'

'Well, you'll have to get it on your lunch hour. Mr Fabian is very strict about employees working without their Social Security cards. You get one hour for lunch and I want you back here on time so you can answer my phone. Oh, and if you have time you can pick up a box of dusting powder for me at Saks.'

Caroline was beginning to dislike this woman, she talked so fast it was hard to follow her. She sat down in one of the armchairs beside Amanda Farrow's desk and picked up the telephone receiver to dial the coffee shop.

'Not here!' Miss Farrow said in annoyance, capping her bottle of nail polish. 'You use *your* phone outside. You always answer my telephone at your desk and say 'Miss Farrow's office.' After you've ordered my coffee you can come back in here and take some dictation.'

Caroline hurried back to her desk, called the coffee shop, went back to take dictation, was interrupted in her filing to take another letter, was interrupted in her typing of the letters to do more filing. Amanda Farrow seemed to have anything but an orderly mind; the minute she thought of something she wanted to have done immediately she thought of something else she wanted done more immediately. Every time the phone rang Caroline had to run out of the office, if she was filing, and answer it at her own desk. Once in a while Miss Farrow would stroll out of her office and come to peer over Caroline's shoulder. The first time she did this it made Caroline so nervous she made two mistakes.

'I thought you were supposed to be a good typist,' Miss Farrow said.

At twelve noon on the dot, having been in the office two hours, Miss Farrow went out to lunch.

'How do you like your new boss?' Mary Agnes asked.

'I hope she's only going to be my temporary boss,' Caroline said worriedly.

'She's had twelve secretaries in three years,' Mary Agnes said. She took a sandwich wrapped in brown paper out of her desk drawer and put on a white Orlon sweater with glass beads sewn on it. 'Come on, I'll ride you down in the elevator.'

'Can you tell me where I can get a Social Security card?'

'There's a place two blocks from here. You'd better eat first, it will take you *hours* to get one.'

'Oh, but I only have an hour for lunch,' Caroline said.

'She doesn't come back until three-thirty. She'll never know. Just get back by three.'

'How does she get any work done?' Caroline asked. 'Or is that a naïve question?'

'Executives don't do the work,' Mary Agnes said. 'The higher up you get the less you have to do. Until you're the top man, and then you have to make decisions, and that's hard. It's the ones just under the top who have the best deal.'

When Mary Agnes had gone off in the direction of the subway

Caroline strolled down Fifth Avenue looking around. Everyone seemed to be in a hurry to get somewhere, meet someone, do something. The girls trying to do some hasty lunch-hour shopping in the department stores, the messengers shuffling along to get the envelope or the package to its destination before the recipient went out to lunch, the executives rushing to embrace that first Martini. On the steps of St Patrick's Cathedral were some tourists, focusing leather-encased cameras on each other, beaming in front of the historic architecture. A flock of pigeons rose up with a dry, snapping sound from the top step, like white wood shavings flung into the cold air. The sun had come out and everything was glittering.

Caroline was suddenly taken with excitement. It was her first day at a new job, she was going to make fifty dollars a week. It seemed like a fortune. She was still living with her parents, in Port Blair, New York, and she had almost no expenses except for clothes, lunches and commuter tickets. Perhaps by summer she would get a raise, and then she could rent an apartment in New York with another girl. There must be a hundred girls working at Fabian, she thought, and I'll certainly find someone I'll really like who'll want to share an apartment with me. She jostled her way along with the stream of people, blinking in the unexpected winter sunshine, and she realized that she had been smiling, because a delivery boy in a leather jacket grinned at her and said, 'Hi Beautiful.'

He thinks he's being so fresh, she thought; if I turned around and said, Hello, yourself, he'd probably faint. She laughed. She was still used to the friendly informality of a small college town, where in the fifteen minutes it took you to walk from the dorms to classes your face could get stiff from smiling greetings to all your casual acquaintances. And of course in Port Blair everyone knew everyone else, if not in person, then at least through gossip.

She found the grimy-looking gray building that housed the Social Security office and went upstairs. She realized that she had forgotten to stop for lunch, but she was too excited to eat anyway.

The small room was crowded with people, sitting dully in rows of straight-backed wooden chairs. She took her place at the end of the line and looked around.

What a group of unhappy-looking people! All of them looked as if they were waiting in line to pour out their troubles to Miss Lonelyhearts. Perhaps it was only because they had all been waiting in line for a long time, boredom has a tendency to bring out the worst in people's faces. She looked at their clothes. Most of them were frayed at the cuff and run down at the heel. It made her feel self-conscious with her raccoon collar and clean kid gloves. Where were all the happy, comfortably off people? Didn't they work? Or were the people in this room the ones who had not worked for a long time? Perhaps she had come to the Social Security office for failures, and there was another one uptown or downtown for successes.

I'll never look like that, she thought firmly. No matter what, I'll never let myself look like that. As long as I have to work, I'm going to get something out of it. These people look as if they have – just jobs. They don't look as if they particularly like their work, they look as if they can't help themselves. I don't want to look like them, I want my job to be one of the happy things in my life.

'Next,' said the bored man behind the counter. The line moved up one. It's like musical chairs, Caroline thought, except no one is having a good time and they all want to get out of here soon so they won't be fired. She looked at her watch and began to glance through a leaflet the woman ahead of her had left on her chair.

Protect your future, the leaflet said. Sixty-five years old for women. It seemed so long away. Caroline could hardly imagine what she would be like at twenty-five. Last year, even six months ago, she had been sure. Now the future was a mystery. She wondered whether it could ever be for her the same thing it once was going to be.

She came back to her desk at two o'clock with her lunch in a paper bag, her Social Security card in her wallet, and Miss Farrow's dusting powder (gift-wrapped) in a gold-and-white-striped box. Mary Agnes was sitting at her own desk, looking contented. Brenda was talking animatedly on the telephone, making use of the office to save on her personal phone bill. The desk next to Caroline's, which had been unoccupied that morning, now bore a straw handbag with flowers sewn on it and a pair of white cotton gloves with a hole in one of the fingers.

'Hi,' Mary Agnes said. 'Did you get everything all right?'

'Yes,' said Caroline. 'Is Miss Farrow back yet?'

'Are you kidding?'

She sat down at her desk and began to eat her sandwich. The coffee container had already leaked through the bottom of the bag and now was making rings on her new blotter. Looking at them, she began to feel as if she'd been at this desk for a long time.

'The third new girl finally came,' Mary Agnes said, gesturing toward the other desk. 'She told Mr Rice she was sick this morning and he was very nice about it. But she told *me* that she forgot to set her alarm clock! Can you imagine such a scatterbrain? I was up all night the day before I went to my first job.'

'Oh, is it her first job too?'

'Yes, and she's only been in New York for a few weeks. She comes from Springs, Colorado. She just got out of junior college.'

Mary Agnes, the Louella Parsons of the thirty-fifth floor, Caroline thought.

'Her name is April Morrison,' Mary Agnes went on. 'That's a pretty name, isn't it – April. That's her with the long hair.'

She nodded toward a girl crossing the bullpen from one of the side offices to another, carrying a shorthand pad, one of the oddest girls Caroline had ever seen. April Morrison had an almost breathtakingly beautiful face, and she wore no make-up except for some pale-pink lipstick. But her hair, which was a tawny gold, cascaded down her back to the middle of her shoulder blades, thick and tangled, making her look like Rebecca of Sunnybrook Farm. She wore a shiny baby-blue gabardine suit. She had big blue eyes and freckles on her delicately sculptured nose, and Caroline almost expected to see her carrying a sunbonnet.

'It's lucky for her she hasn't got your job,' Mary Agnes

whispered, as April went into an office and closed the door. 'Miss Farrow would eat her alive.'

'Well, thank you,' Caroline said. 'You mean I look like I could hold my own against *Miss Farrow?*'

'You should be able to if anyone can. But if she asks you if you want to be promoted out of the typing pool to be her private secretary, say no, no, no.'

What would I ever have done without someone to give me tips and advice on my first day, Caroline thought gratefully.

'Were you ever her secretary?'

'Oh, I worked for her a few times from the pool, that's all. But everyone knows what a terror she is.'

'What were her regular secretaries like?'

'Sophisticated,' said Mary Agnes. 'Like you, a little. College graduates. Usually pretty. She always hires a secretary who has the qualities to make a successful career woman eventually and then she always hates the poor girl's guts.'

'I guess working for Miss Farrow is kind of like hell week for getting into a sorority, is that it?'

'Hey,' said Mary Agnes, 'that's cute.'

'Doesn't anyone else need a private secretary right now?'

'Uh-uh. All the other girls like their jobs. See, being a private secretary is a good deal around here because from there you can get into editorial work. If you're interested, that is. Me, I wouldn't want to be a reader, even though they pay seventy-five dollars a week to start. I like to read magazines but I wouldn't know where to *begin* to criticize them.'

I would, Caroline thought. I'd start with *My Secret Life* and tell them that 'My Two Days in an Attic with a Sex-Mad Criminal!' is the worst piece of trash I ever read. And I bet they'd sell more copies if they didn't have covers that people were ashamed to have lying around their living rooms.

'Look sharp,' Mary Agnes said, and bent over her work with a diligent expression. Miss Farrow, pink of cheek and long of breath, was walking dreamily toward her office. Caroline picked up the box of dusting powder and followed her.

'Here's your powder, Miss Farrow. I charged it to you.'

'What's the matter, didn't you have any money?' It was obvious that Miss Farrow's lunch-hour euphoria did not extend to her treatment of the office help.

'As a matter of fact, I didn't.'

Miss Farrow raised her eyebrows. 'That's funny. I thought, to look at you, that you were another one of those Vassar girls who wants to be an editor just because she majored in English.'

'Radcliffe. And I did major in English.' Caroline smiled.

'I suppose you think it's easy to be an editor.'

'I'm not even sure it's easy to be a secretary.'

Miss Farrow looked at her sharply to determine if she was being sarcastic or serious. Caroline tried to keep a very bland, amused and slightly humble expression on her face, and not to look frightened.

'It's not easy to be my secretary,' Miss Farrow said finally.

'I'll try to do the best I can until your regular secretary comes.'

'How much are you making now?'

'Fifty dollars a week.'

'No experience, eh?'

'I've just finished six weeks of a business and secretarial course. So my shorthand is better than a girl's who hasn't been working for a while.'

'Private secretaries start here at sixty-five, you know. Are you ambitious?' What a look of dislike and mistrust this woman has on her face, Caroline thought with surprise. What in the world does she think I might do to her?

'Well, sixty-five sounds a lot better than fifty,' Caroline answered gently.

The look of mistrust softened a little. 'I haven't looked for a permanent replacement for my other girl yet. Maybe I won't have to. We'll see if your typing improves.'

It will if you stop peering over my shoulder, Caroline thought. 'I have some letters at my desk for you to sign,' she said. 'I'll bring them in. Is that all for now?'

'Yes,' Miss Farrow said with a little half-smile. 'That's all for now.'

The rest of the afternoon went by as rapidly as the morning had, with Miss Farrow firing her disjointed commands and Caroline trying to follow them as well as she could. She felt like a girl who knows she is going to be invited to a dance by the football hero who also happens to be the notorious class wolf, and has to decide what she really wants. She didn't know what she wanted. A pleasant job, yes, but to be in a rut like Mary Agnes, no. Something in between would be ideal, but she was already beginning to realize that the working world was more complicated than she had ever dreamed. She knew that although right now she found the office routine exciting and tiring, that was only because it was new to her, and in a few weeks she would find it boring. Her mind wanted more creative work. But most important of all, if she found herself mired down in a job that bored her, she would be thinking about Eddie and what might have been, and that was what she had come here to escape.

At a quarter to five Miss Farrow came out of her office pulling on her gloves. 'There's an editorial report on my desk,' she said. 'Type it up for me, double-spaced. That's all for today unless you have some work left over. Good night.'

'Good night, Miss Farrow.'

'Ooh . . . what next?' Mary Agnes whispered in righteous indignation. 'She's the only editor who doesn't type her own reading reports. She's probably afraid she'll mess up her nail polish.'

Caroline laughed and went into Miss Farrow's office. It was already dark outside the huge window that made up the entire fourth wall, and through the opened blinds Caroline could see the lights of the city. She pulled up the blind and stood there for a moment. Every square of light was an office, and in every office all over the twilit city there were girls much like herself, happy or disappointed, ambitious or bored, covering their typewriters hastily and going off to meet people they loved, or delaying the minutes of departure because home meant the loneliness of a long dark night. Suddenly her throat hurt so that she could hardly swallow. She turned to Miss Farrow's desk and picked up the manuscript.

It was a heavy manuscript, of loose sheets of white typing paper held together with a thick rubber band. She leafed through the first few pages curiously. The top sheet was headed *Derby Books. Comment Sheet.*

She read Miss Farrow's comments, which had been scrawled in a large, ostentatious hand. It was a rave review: 'Clever writing, plot held me from beginning to end.' She typed the review neatly on a clean comment sheet and attached the typed copy to the manuscript. From St Patrick's outside, bells were chiming five o'clock.

Mary Agnes opened the office door and looked in. She was already wearing her sweater and coat and was carrying her purse. 'Good night, Caroline.'

'Good night.'

'Don't stay here all night. Ha-ha.' Mary Agnes waved and started to leave.

'Mary Agnes . . .'

'What?'

'Do you think it would be all right if I took this manuscript home with me tonight to read? I mean, are there any rules about it?'

'You want to *read* it? On your own time?'

'I think it would be exciting – to read a book that's this good, before it's even been published!'

Mary Agnes shrugged. 'Help yourself. There are some big red envelopes in that filing cabinet.'

'Thank you.'

'So long.'

The door shut and Caroline found an envelope and put the manuscript carefully into it. Then she gathered her things together and walked to the elevator. At five minutes past five the bullpen was empty; it had cleared out as rapidly as if an air-raid alarm had sounded. From a lone office down the hall she could hear the sound of a typewriter. It had been a long day, and she was just beginning to realize how tired she was. She remembered, riding down in the elevator, that Miss Farrow had never gotten around to taking her on the introduction tour Mary Agnes had promised. It didn't matter. She'd had quite an introduction anyway. And she could hardly wait to read the novel she'd found. She hugged the manuscript under her arm as she walked quickly to catch the five-twenty-nine.

2

New York is a city of constant architectural change, buildings being torn down, new ones being put up in their places, streets being torn up, fenced off, signs proclaiming politely Sorry! We are making way for a growing New York. Its inhabitants, more likely than not, live in recently converted houses – converted brownstones, converted whitestones, converted rococo mansions, all partitioned off into two- and three-room apartments and what is euphemistically called 'the one-and-a-half.' April Morrison, waking up in her new apartment at seven o'clock on a Thursday morning in January, lived in a 'one-and-a-half.' Her apartment building was a converted tenement, just north of Columbus Circle.

It was a walk-up apartment, three stories above what the landlord called a 'winter garden,' which was really a kind of small enclosed courtyard with metal chairs piled upside down on one another and going to rust, and a patch of dirt where someone might someday plant flowers. It consisted of one large room with a kitchen that was in a closet and a bed that came out of the wall and had an uncoiled spring that made her sleep in a fetal position. The uncoiled spring did not bother her sleep particularly, however, because April was an extremely relaxed and healthy girl. There was also a bathroom in this apartment, with a makeshift shower in the bathtub, and a fair-sized closet.

On this morning the moment her alarm clock went off April was out of bed and standing on her feet. The day before had been the first day of her first job in New York, and excited as she was she had forgotten to set her alarm and had gotten to the office at noon. It wasn't going to happen again.

Heating water for her instant coffee in a pot from the five-and-ten, April sang a little song she hadn't remembered in years. It was a song she had learned in Sunday school. Her two older sisters back home in Springs had both been Sunday-school teachers before their early marriages, and when April had announced that she wanted to go to dramatic school instead, they had laughed. After all, there were thousands of pretty girls with long gold hair who wanted to go to Hollywood, they had told her, and even though she'd always had the lead in the high-school plays, if she had any sense she would forget that nonsense in a hurry. 'Why?' her father had said. 'Why shouldn't April be an actress?' But fathers always thought their youngest daughters were rather special.

In junior college she had studied speech, ballet and singing, and, to appease the family, typing and shorthand. For a graduation present her parents gave her a train ticket to New York and five hundred dollars. She was to stay in New York for as long as the money lasted and do as she pleased – go to the theater, sight-see, go to museums, look up a high-school classmate of her mother's who had married a man from Brooklyn and had gone there to live. April arrived just after Thanksgiving and did all these things for three days. On the fourth day she read in the newspaper of a chorus call for girl dancers for a new musical. She went to it, with mingled hope and terror, had her turn with what seemed like at least five hundred other girls, and was told politely that she would hear. She never heard anything. At the end of the second week she had been in New York she answered a call for girl singers.

Most of the singers were quite unattractive, she noticed with private hope, they seemed much less pretty than the dancers had been. Why were the singers in shows never as pretty as the dancers? She discovered why very soon. With their trained voices, these girls did not have to be pretty, you could listen to them and you didn't have to look too closely. With her semi-trained voice (church choir and the two years at junior college) April didn't stand a chance. She was thanked for coming and told politely that she would hear. The next day she went to a chorus call at the Copacabana. At least she could walk straight.

When she got to the Copa she felt like a midget. All the girls were six feet tall, or at least they looked that large to her. April was five feet three in her bare feet. They didn't even ask her to show her legs, for which she was just as glad, because she decided at the last minute that she would never be able to explain it at home if she became a showgirl. Her parents thought all night-club chorus girls were kept women on the side.

What should she do? The five hundred dollars was not lasting as long as she had thought it would – there was that hansom-cab ride (who would have *thought* it would be so expensive?), and having a facial, and that bottle of perfume she couldn't help buying, and then all those taxis. She had a feeling the taxi drivers took her on a longer route than was absolutely necessary. She knew one thing, though. She was going to take the subway, and eat at the Automat, and stay in New York if it meant being a sales clerk at the five-and-ten. The hotel was too expensive, so she found this small apartment.

How she loved New York! She had never seen anything like it in her entire life. It wasn't as if she would die if she couldn't become an actress. Back home in Springs being an actress had seemed both glamorous and obtainable, because it had been part of a dream world. She had read all the plays of Eugene O'Neill and J. M. Barrie and Kaufman and Hart, and she had said the lines aloud in the privacy of her own room. That didn't give her any more right to be a successful actress, she realized, than cutting out recipes gave one a right to be a chef at the Waldorf. Being an actress had been part of a fantasy, a picture, which had included tall buildings in the blue twilight and the fountain in front of the Plaza, seeing Marlene Dietrich buying handkerchiefs at Bonwit's, and Frank Sinatra coming out of Lindy's, and beautiful women no one had ever heard of wearing white mink and diamonds and being escorted by handsome older men. The body of the fantasy was true, she was walking in it and looking at it, breathlessly. And the actress part of it? She hadn't realized until she had actually been walking past those tall buildings in the blue twilight how insignificant she really was. Where could she ever begin to attack a fortress like New York? She didn't even want to. She only wanted to stay there until she herself was part of it, one of those well-groomed, well-attended women, and she half realized that was a fantasy too. She only had to walk up the three flights to her dingy room to know what a fantasy it was. Nevertheless, she was very happy, and every moment brought something new and exciting. Nobody else back home had been rejected in person by Mr George Abbott.

An employment-agency ad in *The New York Times* interested her. She went to the agency, and was sent to Fabian Publications. She had wanted one of the ninety-dollar-a-week jobs, but this was her first, and she was told to take it and be glad for the experience. Everyone at home had read *My Secret Life* avidly in high school – she herself had outgrown it only three years before. To tell the truth she was quite thrilled to be working at the very source of a magazine which had helped build up much of her present misinformation. Her grandmother read *The Cross*, too. She wrote home about her new job immediately, and also broke the news that she was not coming back, at least not for a long time.

She drank her coffee standing up and dressed hastily. Here it was eight-thirty and she had been daydreaming again. As she emerged into the street she caught sight of her reflection in the window of a delicatessen next door to her apartment house. Her coat was too short – or was it? She remembered the girl in the tweed suit with the raccoon collar who had been working at the desk next to hers yesterday afternoon at Fabian. What a sophisticated-looking girl! Something about her looked – right. Was it the leather gloves? Perhaps white cotton gloves looked terrible in January. They were her best gloves, and so she had never given them a second thought. She looked down at them and noticed for the first time the hole in the finger. She pulled them off and stuffed them into her purse and walked quickly to the subway.

She was still rather frightened of the subway and never could bring herself to run for a train the way the other people did, for fear one of the huge doors would close on her and leave her half in and half out, screaming as the car bore her away to a mysterious and horrible death in the darkness of the tunnel. She watched the people scurrying and pushing one another as the sound of an approaching train grew louder, and she delayed for a moment in front of the change booth counting out her money for a token.

'Good morning,' she said pleasantly to the man behind the bars. He was one of the few people in New York whom she had seen more than once, and this gave her a rather friendly feeling toward him. She always said good morning to him, it made her feel less lonely.

'How are you today?'

'Just fine,' she said. She fished up her token and turned to leave.

'Wait a minute,' he whispered. He looked around and took hold of her wrist with fingers that were surprisingly strong. 'I got something to show you.'

'To show me?'

'Look,' he said. He slid a photograph, picture side down, through the change door. She looked at him curiously and picked it up.

At first she didn't realize what it was, it seemed like two people in a strained and unaccustomed posture, wrestlers perhaps. Then she saw it was a man and a woman, and when she discovered what they were doing to each other she felt her face redden and her hand began to shake so hard she could scarcely push the picture back through the slot. She turned to flee.

'Hey,' he called after her, and then more loudly, indignantly: 'Hey!'

She looked back for one instant.

'What's the matter?' he called. 'I thought we was friends. Ha-ha, ha-ha.' He laughed raucously, angrily, insulted and wanting to hurt her. 'Where ya going?'

She pushed her way through the turnstile, and for the first time in her life jumped aboard a subway train the instant its doors started to close. A fat man took her arm to help her as the rubber-tipped jaws snapped shut.

'What's your hurry?' he said. 'You'll get yourself killed someday. Crazy New York girls!'

New York girls, she thought, and her fright began to slip away from her. He thought she was a New York girl; did that mean she looked as if she belonged? Perhaps that terrible man in the change booth had thought she was a native New Yorker too, and hadn't realized that back home you spoke to everybody and it didn't mean a thing. She pushed her way to a seat, edging her way between two men who were dashing for it. She received a sharp elbow in the ribs, achieved the seat triumphantly, and when she saw her two competitors collide into each other she could barely keep back her smile. She was groping, but she was going to get along. Today in the office she was going to speak to that smart-looking girl in the raccoon collar, maybe they could even have lunch together someday.

At her desk, she was busy typing addresses on stickers for rejected manuscripts and looking around for Caroline when Miss Farrow came out of her office and headed for her. April was secretly fascinated by Miss Farrow; she wondered whether she had ever been married and what kind of men she saw outside the office.

'You'll have to go in and help Mr Shalimar today,' Miss Farrow said without even a good-morning. 'His secretary is out sick. It's that large office over there with the closed door. You can give the rest of those stickers to the manuscript clerk to finish.'

'Yes, ma'am,' April said, trying to conceal her delight with a mask of office dignity. She swept all the stickers together and nearly ran down the hall to the room where manuscripts were registered and handed out to readers. Mr Shalimar was the editor-in-chief of Derby Books! She had only glimpsed him through his half-opened door, a tall, older man with a grayish face and strongly hewn features, and she had never thought she would be lucky enough to meet him. Mary Agnes had told her that Mr Shalimar had known Eugene O'Neill.

'I can't help you with any more of these today,' she told the manuscript girl excitedly. 'I'm working for Mr Shalimar.'

The manuscript clerk stood there impassively in her book-lined room and snapped her chewing gum. 'We all have our troubles,' she said finally.

April looked at her, surprised, and then shrugged and hurried down the hall to the office with the closed door. She tapped on it timidly. There was no answer. She stood for a moment with her ear against the door, trying to hear if there was a conference going on inside, but she heard nothing, so she turned the knob and went in.

It was a huge, plush office, with a soft, thick carpet on the floor, a black leather sofa, and rows of bookcases lined with paperback books. In front of the wall of windows was a great wooden desk. The blinds were closed against the early-morning sunlight. In the desk chair, with his feet crossed on the blotter and his chin on his chest, was Mr Shalimar, snoring gently. She stood in the doorway, not knowing what to do. Mr Shalimar snorted in his sleep, tossed his head furiously like a dog shaking itself, and woke up.

'What? What?' he said. He lowered his feet from the desk, swiveled around in his chair, and pulled the cord of the Venetian blinds, flooding the office with light.

'I'm sorry I disturbed you,' she said timidly.

'Oh, I take a rest now and then. For a minute.' He looked at her more closely. 'Come over here.'

She stood in front of his enormous desk, feeling as if she were being interviewed all over again.

'New here, aren't you?'

She nodded.

'What's your name?'

'April Morrison.'

He interlocked his fingers on the desk in front of him. 'Do you know that for this job you have we turned away fifteen other girls?'

'No, sir.'

'What do you want to do – get married? Be an editor?'

'I . . . don't know yet.'

His brows drew together. 'What makes you think you have more of a right to be here than any of those fifteen other girls?'

She put her hands behind her back so he would not see them trembling. 'I don't know, sir,' she said. 'I haven't met them.'

'What makes you think you ought to be here instead of, say, a salesgirl in a dress shop?'

At that moment she would much rather have been a salesgirl in a dress shop, but she said bravely, 'I don't think I'd be a very good salesgirl.'

'Why not?'

'Because I'm not interested in it.'

'And you're interested in books?'

'Yes.'

He leaned back, put his hands behind his head, and laughed. For a moment she thought he was laughing at her and her eyes filled with angry tears. 'Don't mind,' he said. 'I always ask the same question of every new girl. I like to see how they think. You'd be surprised the wacky answers some of them give me.'

'Well,' April said. She was so relieved she couldn't help smiling. 'I hope I didn't give you a wacky answer.'

'Not at all,' he said. 'You're sensible as well as pretty.'

His compliment made her feel more at ease. 'Anyway, I don't think it was fair,' she said. 'After all, I'm only a typist here.'

'Is that your ambition?'

'No, I really . . . wanted to be an actress.'

'Like to read plays?'

'Very much.'

He leaned on the desk and a faraway look came over his face. 'I used to say to Eugene O'Neill . . . I knew him well, you know. In the old days, that is. Before he was famous. He was a protégé of mine.'

'You don't seem old enough.'

'But he had respect for my opinion. I used to encourage him.' He smiled at her. 'I'll tell you some stories someday. I was considered quite a boy genius as an editor, you know. That's before your time.'

'My goodness,' April said, 'I'd love to hear them.'

'Sometime when we have more time,' he said gently. 'I have a load of work to do today. How are you fixed for this afternoon? Could you stay till . . . six o'clock if we have to? My girl is sick just when I was going to do the monthly report on all our books. Could you stay?'

'I'd be glad to.'

'If it runs any later than six I'll give you money for dinner. All right?'

'All right.'

'Now, shut my door, will you, please? And turn the key. There's one thing you'll have to learn right away, and that's how to keep the pests out.'

I'm keeping the pests out of Mr Shalimar's private office, she thought, and it seemed so much more an elevated position than licking manuscript stickers that her heart began to pound with joy. A girl could do a lot worse on her second day in the working world.

What an exciting feeling to answer the telephone and recognize the name given to her as one of a famous author. She knew most of these only vaguely, as names she had heard somewhere before, but she memorized them all instantly. When Mr Shalimar went out to lunch at the Algonquin with a Hollywood writer she closed his door and read everything on his desk. Then she went downstairs to the coffee shop in the building.

The coffee shop, which doubled as a bar at night, was brightly lighted now and crowded with girls and women who all seemed to be talking at once at the top of their lungs. Six at a time would be jammed into a booth, hunched over their hamburgers and dissecting the other office personnel with venom or hilarity. Four or five harried waitresses in limp uniforms pushed their way through the crowd with plates lined along their arms from wrist to shoulder. They looked like jugglers. Every seat at the curving counter was occupied, mostly by girls, with two or three men scattered among them looking trapped behind their newspapers and greasy platters. April saw one of these men standing up to leave, and she maneuvered her way quickly to his vacant seat, feeling as if she were still on the subway. The counter in front of her, with a grease-spotted, balled-up napkin thrown into the plate, a streak of catsup where she tried to put her elbow, and some change scattered in a puddle of spilled water, made her almost lose her appetite. She turned around and saw that the girl sitting next to her was Caroline Bender.

She was wearing a black suit today and she looked like a model in a fashion magazine. Her dark hair was cut just to her ear lobes, turned under sleekly, with a fringe of bangs, and she was wearing blue eye shadow. April tried to think of something to say to her, glancing at her profile out of the corner of her eye and thinking, How sad she looks. Caroline was staring ahead at the shelf of apple and custard pies and looking right through them. Then she turned her head.

'Hi,' she said, as if she were really glad to see someone she knew, even though they didn't actually know each other. 'I know you.'

'We sit next to each other in the office, and now here,' April said. 'We should at least introduce ourselves. I'm April.'

'I'm Caroline.' Caroline held out her hand and they shook hands, each of them laughing a little for no particular reason except perhaps embarrassment and relief. 'What do you do?'

The waitress cleared away the counter in front of them, looking even more repelled than the customers. She put down two gravy-stained menus.

'I'm a typist, I guess,' April said. 'But right now I'm working for Mr Shalimar as his secretary.'

'Good for you. Do you want to be an editor eventually?'

'Why does everybody ask me that?' April said. 'I just took this job because I needed the money, and when I set foot in Mr Shalimar's office he gave me the third degree. Is it true there are all these girls battling for *my* little job?'

'That's what I was told at the employment agency. They're all college girls with good educational backgrounds and no experience and they're willing to work for practically nothing. That's why Fabian can pay so little and get away with it. And fifty dollars is good for our kind of job. Most places start their girls at forty.'

'Do *you* want to be an editor?'

Caroline smiled. 'Everyone asks me that too. I'm working for Miss Farrow temporarily and she looks at me as if I might turn around any minute and bite her jugular vein. But I think I'm beginning to understand why she does. There's something catching about ambition.'

The waitress brought their sandwiches and they ate for a minute or two in silence. 'You come from New York, don't you?' April said.

'Port Blair. That's about forty minutes away.'

'Is that like the country?'

'Well, most of the Westchester towns are. In fact, Port Blair is the only one that isn't. You have all the disadvantages of a long train ride and then when you get there you have all the disadvantages of a dirty little city.'

'Do you live with your family?'

'That's the only reason for living in a place like Port Blair.'

'I come from Colorado,' April said.

'I know.'

'You know? How do you know?'

'Mary Agnes told me.'

'Oh, she's funny. She knows everything about everybody.' April smoothed back her long tangled hair. 'I thought at first you meant you could tell because I look different. New York girls look so sophisticated.'

'Mary Agnes?' Caroline said, smiling. 'Brenda?'

'No . . . not them. But you do. You're my idea of what a New York girl should look like.'

'Well, thank you,' Caroline said. 'I take it that's a compliment?'

'Oh, it is,' April said. 'It is.'

They paid their checks and rode upstairs together in the elevator. 'Are you doing anything tomorrow after work?' Caroline asked her.

'I don't think so.'

'Well, maybe we could have supper together somewhere and go to a movie. Would you want to?'

'I'd love it!'

'Okay. We will, then. See you.'

April went into Mr Shalimar's empty office, shut the door, kicked off her shoes, and did a pirouette on the soft rug. She was very happy. She took her mirror out of her purse, and with the other hand held her hair off her neck, turning her head this way and that. How come she had never noticed before that she looked like a woolly bear? And there *was* something queer-looking about her suit. Her mother had always said that girls with blue eyes should wear pale blue, and that black was for funerals and old ladies. Well, she didn't feel a bit funereal, she felt marvelous, and tonight when Mr Shalimar gave her supper money she was going to use it to go to the beauty parlor. And on Friday when she got paid she was going to buy a black suit just like Caroline's.

Mr Shalimar wouldn't even recognize her in a couple of days. Her heart began to pound. Wasn't she lucky? She was lucky, all right. She took his ash tray out to the wastebasket in the hall and emptied it, and washed it out in the water fountain. It wasn't until she noticed Mary Agnes' shocked face that she realized she had forgotten to put on her shoes.

Dark comes quickly in January, and at five o'clock when the girls in the bullpen began to cover their typewriters and tie on their kerchiefs the sky outside was already black. Mr Shalimar was dictating the second page of the monthly report which was to be ten pages long. He had allowed April to sit on his sofa while he dictated, and she was perched there with her shoes off again and her legs curled under her, putting down his words with rapid, sure strokes. She had always hated shorthand in school, but right now she was so grateful she had learned it that she almost enjoyed it. She could see that he was pleased because he never had to pause for her to catch up. Over the sound of his voice she dimly heard the noises of departure outside, the clicking of high heels and the called goodbyes. Soon there was a different sound, the sound of utter quiet. She stood up to get a sharper pencil.

'We can stop for a minute,' he said. 'You must be tired.'

'Oh, no, I'm not tired.'

'Where are we? Halfway through?'

'Almost.'

'Are you hungry yet?'

'No, sir.'

He bent down and took a bottle of Scotch from the bottom drawer of his desk, and a nest of small metal cups. He separated two of the cups and poured Scotch into both of them. 'Like a little drink?'

She had never tasted anything stronger than a mixed drink in her life. 'I wouldn't want to waste it,' she said timidly.

He poured half of hers back into the bottle. 'Here,' he said, holding the rest out to her.

Who would ever believe it? she thought. Here she was, so tongue-tied she couldn't think of a thing to say, drinking Scotch in the office with the editor-in-chief of Derby Books. This didn't really look like an office; it looked more like the den of a luxurious home, the kind you see in the movies.

'Luck,' Mr Shalimar said briskly, and tossed off his drink in one swallow. He poured some water from his carafe and drank it, not even looking at her. Well, maybe they weren't exactly socializing, but she was present, and that was something. She tasted her Scotch gingerly and forced down a few sips, feeling the warmth travel down her throat.

Mr Shalimar poured himself another drink and looked at her for the first time. 'Want some water in it?'

'I guess so.' She let him pour water into her cup, looking down at his dark, silver-flecked hair, seeing a mole on his ear and embarrassed to be so close to him. In the moment he was weakening her drink she noticed every line and tiny mark on his face, at first with curiosity because he was a great man she knew so little about, and then with a feeling that was a kind of intimacy because she felt somehow that his wrinkles and birthmarks and imperfections belonged to his private life. But she was just indulging in hero worship, she told herself sensibly, and then she let herself indulge in it. 'Thank you,' she said, and went back to her seat on the couch.

He leaned back in his desk chair and crossed his long legs. His skin was dark with an athletic-club lunch-hour tan, and he wore a wedding ring. He looked a little like a Greek shipping magnate, or some kind of Near East tycoon, she thought. On his desk were silver-framed pictures of his family.

'You know,' he said, 'very few people realize the great future that's waiting for paperback books. Do you realize that we have a first printing of a quarter of a million copies for each and every book? How many copies do you think the average hard-cover book sells?'

'I don't know.'

'A couple of thousand copies if it's a flop. Maybe a hundred thousand copies if it's a best seller. A hundred thousand readers in the whole of America. That's not many, is it?'

'No,' she said.

'Do you realize there are towns in America where there are no libraries at all? Not even a bookstore! The only place the people in those small towns can get a book is at the drugstore. And what do they read? Our books.'

'My heavens,' she said.

'We are responsible for the changing literary taste of America,' he went on. 'People have to learn to crawl before they can walk. First they won't read anything but the most obvious kind of lurid adventure stories. Then we sneak in a good book or two. We train them. Eventually all our books will be as good or better than the best so-called literary hard-cover books. Do you think all hard-cover books are good literature just because they cost four dollars? Most of them stink.'

She smiled a little at his vehemence and took a few healthy gulps at her drink. It made her feel more confident and she finished it off.

'It's *our* books, with *our* sexy covers, and *our* low cost, and *our* mass distribution that are teaching America how to read. Let people who don't know anything say Derby Books are trash. They'll see.'

'I never thought of it that way,' she said.

He beckoned for her cup and she went to his desk and waited while he fixed her another drink. This time he tapped his cup lightly against hers before he drank. She went back to the couch, feeling suddenly very happy. No wonder everyone around here seemed so curious about her editorial ambitions. It wouldn't be a bad thing to get in on the ground floor of a – literary movement. That's what it was.

'Have you read any of our books?' he asked.

'Oh, a few, yes.'

He opened his desk drawer and took out four books and put them into an envelope. 'Here. Read these this week and let me know what you think of them. I'm interested in a young girl's opinion.'

'*Mine?*' She was incredulous.

'Use your instinct. I'm not interested in your education. Some of the people who buy our books regularly are college graduates, but most of them aren't. They either like a book or they don't. Just tell me whether you like them or not, and tell me why.'

'All right.' She realized when she stood up to get the books that she should not have gulped her second drink so quickly. Everything was rather blurry, and her face felt hot. When she took the envelope of books his hands brushed hers and she felt a great daughterly affection for him.

He looked at his watch. 'It's late. You must be starved. Tell you what. We'll go downstairs to the place in the building and grab a bite, and then we'll come back up here and finish the monthly report. Go get your coat.'

She made her way to her desk, holding on to the door as she went through. Those drinks had been stronger than she thought, and it was late. She didn't want him to notice she was high, he'd think she was a real little hick. Some food and coffee were just what she needed. As she powdered her feverish face she heard him speaking on the telephone in his office. She could not hear the words, but the tone of his voice was weary and apologetic. He was calling his wife, she was sure, to say he would not be home for dinner. She felt sorry for his wife, who had probably been looking forward all day to being with him again, and she felt rather sorry for him because he had to eat a sandwich in a greasy coffee shop and then come upstairs and dictate for two more hours to his secretary. The only one she didn't feel sorry for was herself.

'Good evening, Mr Shalimar,' the waitress said cozily, as if he were a habitué. There were little tables in the darkened bar section of the coffee shop, and the main part where April had eaten lunch was brightly lighted and closed off. Mr Shalimar led her to a table in the corner.

'Two Scotches with water on the side, and two steaks,' he said. 'Is that all right, April?'

'Yes, sir, fine.' Things weren't so blurry in the dark, and from somewhere near the ceiling soft music was playing. He was sitting next to her on the leather banquette, and he leaned forward, looking at her closely.

'You're a very beautiful girl, d'you know that?'

'Thank you,' she said, embarrassed.

'Have a lot of boy friends? What kind of man do you like?'

'I don't have any boy friends here in New York,' she admitted. 'I don't know any. Back home I had a lot of dates, I guess.'

'Anyone special?'

'Oh, no.'

'What kind of man appeals to you? What kind of man would you like to marry?'

She had discussed the question many times with her sorority sisters in the long, intimate conversations girls hold in the night, and she recited her answer surely. 'An understanding man. Someone kind and intelligent. He wouldn't have to be handsome as long as he seemed handsome to *me*. I guess if you love someone you think he's good-looking, and if you dislike someone or he's mean to you, you get to hate his looks.'

'A very good answer,' he murmured. He tapped his glass to hers. 'I hope you get him.'

'Me too,' she said. She drank her Scotch and felt like giggling.

'You have a devastating smile. When you meet that boy he won't have a chance.'

This time she *did* giggle. 'I wish I would meet him. I've never been in love – just crushes on boys, but I knew that wasn't real. I wish I were in love with someone who loved me.'

'And what about *fun?*' He was looking at her more closely. 'Wouldn't you like to meet someone you could have *fun* with, without necessarily being in love?'

'Yes . . .' she said. She wasn't quite sure what he meant. The words were innocent enough, the wise words of a father to an impatient, romantic daughter, but there was something about the way he said 'fun' that made it seem different and infinitely more mysterious than the kind of fun she'd always had with boys or anyone. 'I guess so,' she said.

He looked at her warily. 'What kind of things do the young

boys say to the young girls nowadays? What do they say when they want to . . . make love?'

'Say?' she said. 'They don't say anything. They mostly just grab.'

He laughed. 'That must be very unpleasant.'

How understanding he was! 'It is,' she said with relief. 'I just hate it.'

'How do college boys make love?'

She was a little embarrassed to be talking about kissing and petting with this man – first of all, she had never discussed sex with any man in her life, certainly not even her father, and secondly Mr Shalimar was from a world so removed from her own that she could not imagine how he could possibly be interested in her amateurish little front-seat battles. 'I'm not exactly an authority,' she said, smiling.

'Every girl is an authority about her own life,' he said.

'No wonder you're an editor. You know so much about people.'

'I know about people because I ask. I question. I'm insatiably curious about people,' he said. 'How do you think I know what every woman in America wants to read? Because I talk to women, find out what their secret dreams are, what they fear.'

She felt reassured. The waitress came with the steaks then, and April discovered she was very hungry. She began to devour hers and was halfway through before she discovered that Mr Shalimar had not taken a bite of his.

'My goodness,' she said, feeling rather concerned about his welfare. 'Don't let that go to waste.'

He took a small piece of his steak and pushed the rest around the plate with his fork, looking bemused. She supposed he was used to much fancier cooking than this; as for herself, she thought the steak was marvelous.

'You may have mine too,' he said.

'Oh, I couldn't.'

'Go ahead.' He placed his steak carefully on her plate and she smiled at him, feeling self-conscious and childlike and well cherished. 'My father used to do that,' she said.

'I imagine you were his favorite.'

'No, it's not that. It's just that my sisters were a lot older than me, and they were sort of settled in their own lives when I was only in high school. So I guess my father had more time to give to me. And also, I think parents get mellower with their youngest children.'

'Mmm-hmm,' he said. 'I imagine your father was very protective with you about boys.'

'Well, I didn't confide in him, if that's what you mean.'

He raised an eyebrow. 'Ah? You had secrets?'

'Not really.'

'Tell me, what kinds of things do the young boys do when they make love?'

'You want me to *tell* you?'

'Of course.'

She could feel her face getting hot. It wasn't that she had any interesting confessions or that she felt guilty, it was simply that one didn't discuss these things with an older man, especially an employer. It wasn't as if he were her family doctor or something, although even her family doctor never talked to her about making love. 'Oh, you know,' she said vaguely, hoping her answer would satisfy him. 'They do the same old things.'

'Sounds rather boring,' he said with a touch of amusement in his voice.

'Oh, it is!' she said, grateful to see the discussion coming to a close. 'It's *very* boring.'

He covered her hand with his for an instant and gave it a fatherly pat. 'Waitress! Check, please.'

There was only one elevator on night duty, and as they waited for it to come to take them back upstairs neither of them spoke. She was glad the steaks had sobered her; now she would be able to take good shorthand and not make mistakes. It was almost impossible to decipher what you'd written the day before if you were sloppy. They could probably finish the report in another hour, she was thinking, and she trailed him into his office glancing at the wall clock in the bullpen on the way. It seemed funny to see the office clock read ten o'clock and know it was ten o'clock at night instead of in the morning.

He had left the desk lamp on and the office was soft with shadows. What a nice living room it would be, if the desk were not there. Through the half-open slats of the Venetian blinds she could see the great, mysterious evening city. New York . . . City of excitement, of promise, gathering place of all the unknown, vibrant people she hoped someday to meet, who were at this very moment spending planned and unplanned evenings in ways that seemed so much a part of that sophisticated, gay unknown out there and so remote from everything she was used to. She leaned against the desk, moved and speechless, looking out at mecca.

'What are you thinking?' Mr Shalimar asked, behind her.

'I can't say,' she breathed. 'I wouldn't know how to say it.'

He came up to her so quickly she had more a sense of movement than any warning, and took her into his arms. His arms were like straps around her, so that she could hardly breathe, and his mouth covered hers, hot and violent and authoritative. As soon as the first instant of numb incredulity shattered she was filled with terror. She twisted her head from side to side, trying to escape the lips and teeth that were trying to devour her, and gave a choked little cry. He let her go.

'Mr *Shalimar!*' she said, and it sounded so stupid in the quiet room and so much a line from one of Fabian's own worst magazines that she started to cry.

He stood there looking at her, smiling, not particularly angry but just amused. He handed her his handkerchief, smelling of lavender. 'It's not as bad as all that,' he said, smiling.

She wiped her eyes and mouth (the mouth quickly, so he would not notice) and handed the handkerchief back. She was too embarrassed to flounce off in a huff, and she tried to think of something to say to him but her mind was completely blank with shock. An old man, at least fifty! A married man! Right in front of his wife's picture on the desk! He shook his head as one would to a child, wiped his mouth quite carefully, looked at the lipstick on his clean handkerchief, folded it, and placed it neatly in his breast pocket.

'Come on,' he said, 'I'll put you in a taxi.'

She kept a foot away from him all the way down the hall and

descending in the elevator, and when they were finally on the street. He hailed a taxi and held the door open for her. She climbed in as quickly as she could, and with her hand on the inner handle said, 'Good night.'

'Wait,' he said. He handed her two dollar bills, crumpled together. 'For the fare. I hope you don't live in the Bronx.'

She shook her head.

'Take it.' He pressed the money into her hand and she shrank from his touch. 'Your books,' he said. He had carried the envelope with the four paperback novels in it all the way down in the elevator and she had not noticed because she had deliberately been avoiding looking at him. 'Don't forget to read them,' he said pleasantly. He tipped his hat, and shut the taxi door. It took her a moment to remember her own address.

The inside of the private, dark taxi was comforting. She pushed the envelope of books to the far side of the seat as if it were a dead animal, and put her face in her hands. Funny . . . she did not feel like crying again, she did not even feel like shrinking away from the memory of the forbidden, unexpected kiss that had so frightened her. As a matter of fact, now that she was alone and safe, the feeling of the kiss returned, at first frightening and then vaguely thrilling and wonderful. *Mr Shalimar* had kissed her. Mr Shalimar . . . She should feel resentful, she knew, she should feel angered. But she felt instead the stirring of a new feeling, a kind of romantic intoxication. It warmed her, secretly and a little guiltily now that she had embraced it, all the way home.

3

Port Blair, where Caroline Bender lived with her family, is a town situated along the line of the New Haven Railroad and is distinguished by its utter lack of pleasant suburban qualities. Its major industries are a candy factory and a street of small modern bars and small old-fashioned whore houses. In the evenings its population swells with visitors from the snootier neighborhoods, mostly domestic help and chauffeurs from the homes and estates of nearby Greenwich, Scarsdale, Port Chester and Larchmont. The police roam in prowl cars picking up anyone suspicious-looking, and on Monday mornings, especially after such big weekends as July Fourth and Memorial Day, the court is overflowing. In the very center of town there is an eight-block-square oasis of large, beautiful homes, tree-lined streets and jealously guarded privacy, which fifty years ago was the original town of Port Blair. The gin mills, the honky-tonks, the cheap cafés, all came later, at first slowly, and then, as the candy factory was established, rapidly and vigorously, surrounding the old suburban area but never succeeding in choking it off.

The people who live in this eight-square-block area are the doctors, the lawyers, the large business owners and the most prosperous tradespeople of the town. They hide their homes behind tall hedges and send their children away to camp and summer resorts and college. But they always send their children to the Port Blair Public High School, because if they didn't, they would be considered snobs and it would be bad for business. Caroline's father was a physician, and he had inherited the large colonial-style house where they lived, and his practice, from his father. Caroline's mother came from a middle-class family in New York City. She and her husband had met at a college dance when he was attending medical school and she was an undergraduate. They went steady immediately, were married as soon as he was graduated, and after his internship they moved to Port Blair. At the time, the new Mrs Bender was delighted to live in what seemed to her to be the country, but she soon changed her mind. The narrow life, the small selection of close friends, the ugly little town, depressed her, and she determined that her daughter and young son would end up New Yorkers, as she was, or at least in a better part of Westchester. It was Mrs Bender who insisted that Caroline go to Radcliffe (to be near Harvard boys) and it was Mrs Bender who sat up with Caroline night after night to see that she learned her Latin verbs (Caroline's weakest subject) so that she would get a high mark on her college board exams and be accepted. Her son Mark was six years younger than Caroline, so she did not have to do anything about him at present, but she was already worrying and planning secretly to have him break out of the Port Blair High School mold and spend his senior year, at least, at Lawrenceville. It was not that she was a social climber. It was simply that she considered life in Port Blair a dead-end street to many of the things that made life rewarding and stimulating, and she did not want her children to get to like it. That would have been easy. The younger generation enjoyed life in Port Blair, they had their own friends, their parties, their groping romances. But Mrs Bender remembered something different and, to her, infinitely more desirable.

Although Mrs Bender mourned the end of her daughter's engagement to Eddie Harris, it was not for the same reasons Caroline did. She was not a sentimental woman, and because her daughter was beautiful and talented and only twenty years old she was sure that another fiancé would appear in due time. What was one Eddie Harris? One college senior looked like another to her, they were all unformed, you could only guess what their futures would be. It was true that Eddie had a great deal of charm for a boy his age, he was poised, and he knew how to talk to older people as if he really enjoyed it. His musical talent was negligible; he played the piano the way the boys in her day had played the mandolin. She could picture him better in public relations, perhaps, or in advertising. He came from a good family, he was attractive, and with his education and ambition she would have liked to see him as a husband for Caroline. When he sent Caroline that letter from Europe Mrs Bender decided immediately that he was immature, flighty and selfish. Her major regret was that Caroline had spent so much time at college with him, when she could have been meeting other desirable boys. It would not be so easy to meet 'friends' (her euphemism for 'a good catch') in Port Blair after graduation. When Caroline expressed a wish to find a job in New York, Mrs Bender was proud of her for taking the whole unhappy affair so well. She knew Caroline had no particular career ambitions, but nowadays a girl had to work even if she didn't need the money. You didn't stay home and rot, especially if you lived in a place like Port Blair – and rot was the word, Mrs Bender said, for what would happen to a girl in Port Blair.

Dr Bender was a typical small-town doctor, despite the fact that Port Blair was nothing like a typical small town. He liked people, and people liked him, coming to him with their family troubles as well as their physical ailments. He was the kind of man who is more appreciated by his friends than by his family. The women who came to him with their aches and pains, real or imaginary, went away sighing enviously for that lucky Mrs Bender the doctor's wife. He was such a gentle, giving-in sort of man, and he gave so much of himself to his patients and their silly, tedious problems that he had very little left to give to his family. He never took his son to a football game. He often fell asleep right after dinner, in front of the television set or with a medical magazine in his hands, and then like as not he would be aroused an hour later for an emergency house call. Almost the only girl in town who didn't confide in Dr Bender was his daughter Caroline. She confided exclusively in her mother, and her mother came to guard this privilege with something that was very like jealousy. It was often, 'Your father doesn't know about those things.' And Dr Bender, who loved and respected his wife very much, came to say more and more often, 'Ask Mother. She knows,' until finally there was no more reason for him to have to say it at all.

When Caroline brought home the manuscript the night of her first day at Fabian, it was her mother she told. And when she read it, and found to her amazement that she did not agree with Amanda Farrow's comments at all but found the novel to be boring in spite of its facile style, it was her mother she consulted.

'I read this book last night, Mother. Well, a manuscript really. They're probably going to publish it because Miss Farrow said it was wonderful. I read it and I thought it was downright dull. Do you think I'm in the wrong field? I thought I knew about literature, but this book really put me to sleep. Maybe there's a secret about paperback books.'

'You always had good taste,' her mother said staunchly. 'A book is just a book as far as I can see. Everybody's entitled to his own opinion. I never could stand *The Scarlet Letter* myself, and that's a classic.' This reminded Mrs Bender of an English Literature course she had taken in college, and what the professor had said to her, and she went off into one of her lengthy nostalgic anecdotes about college, which was one of her ways of escaping temporarily from life in Port Blair. Caroline had heard the story before, and many others very much like it, and she finished her breakfast coffee drifting off into her own thoughts.

They would more than likely publish the manuscript – but she thought it was so dreadful! Was it any of her business? But she'd read it . . . The manuscript was due to go next to Mr Shalimar, the editor-in-chief, and it was she who was supposed to put it on his desk. If she were to type up a comment sheet with her personal opinion of the manuscript, the worst he could do would be to throw it away and tell her to stay in her place. He wouldn't fire her; he would understand the overenthusiasm of a novice on her first job. And she might just possibly be right, or at least worth listening to. Perhaps he would let her read some other manuscripts. With her comment in such complete opposition to Miss Farrow's, she *had* to know if she was on the right track – otherwise it was all too bewildering; her editorial hopes, her beginning feelings of responsibility toward the company . . .

'I'm late,' she said, kissing her mother on the cheek. She took the envelope and headed for the door. 'Oh, I forgot. I won't be home for dinner. I'm going to eat with a girl from the office.'

'Oh? Someone interesting?'

'I hope so,' Caroline said, smiling. 'So long.'

She was ten minutes early for her train, and she stood on the outdoor platform watching her breath go off in puffs of smoke on the cold clear air. Up ahead, where the smoker would stop, were the men who commuted every day; very few, however, because most of the men who lived in Port Blair worked in Port Blair. There was Stan Rogers, hung over, leaning against one of the station pillars, his eyes heavy lidded, his face pink and shiny with razor scrape. He had been a year ahead of Caroline at the high school, which made him Eddie Harris' age, and he had married a Port Blair girl right after graduation. They now had four children, the oldest of whom was three and a half. His shoes were so worn and scuffed she could notice it from here, and she recognized his jalopy parked in the station lot as the same one that had so impressed the girls his senior year at the high. And there were the Litchfield sisters, one fat and one thin, who always dressed identically, as if they thought they were twins, or seven years old instead of thirty, and who worked as comptometer operators in an insurance company. She nodded at them and began to stroll in the other direction.

There was someone she didn't expect to see on a commuter train – Mrs Nature, a friend of her mother's and wife of the local dry-cleaning king. 'CLOTHES CLEANED THE NATURE WAY,' their signs read, and people who saw them thought it was some new mysterious and healthful process. Actually, the owner of the shops (there were four) was named Francis P. Nature. He was now one of the wealthiest men in town.

'Caroline! Yoo-hoo!' Mrs Nature was waving at her. Caroline walked over to her.

'I'm so glad to see you, Caroline. I was going to call you up tonight, but now I won't have to. I took the liberty of telling a young man to call you up.'

'Oh?'

'He used to go out with Francine; oh, not seriously, but just once in a while. She thought he was quite nice.' Since Mrs Nature had married off her only daughter she had mellowed to the extent of sending all her daughter's old beaux to the other single girls in her group. Caroline had never cared much for Francine, an extremely loud and nervous girl, and she was not particularly delighted at the prospect of one of Francine's castoffs.

'His name is Alvin Wiggs,' Mrs Nature went on. 'Now, you may hate each other – I don't know, and I never make promises. I always say to the girls: It's only one evening out of your life, and I'm not sending you a husband. Of course, if it works out, and you do find you're just crazy about each other, I'd be delighted.'

Alvin Wiggs! Caroline thought. Mrs Alvin Wiggs. God help us.

'Is he attractive?' she asked.

'You may think so. Francine thought he was very attractive. I always say looks are the same as anything else, it's a matter of taste. He's going to call you at your office. He might even call you up today, because I gave him your number last night. As I say, I never make promises, and you may hate each other. But I think he's a lovely boy.'

'Well, it was very nice of you to think of me,' Caroline said politely. It would have been nicer, she was thinking, if Mrs Nature had asked her first if she *wanted* anyone to call her up. 'What does he do?'

'He's in his family's business,' Mrs Nature said. 'He works for his father. They're in the mannequin business.'

There was the eight oh five, roaring into the station. As usual, it stopped too far ahead of the station platform and everyone had to run to board it. Caroline and Mrs Nature ran alongside each other, not really together, not really apart. 'Oh, I just hate this train,' Mrs Nature panted. 'But I have to go into New York to send some wedding gifts. I can't put it off any longer. So many of my friends' daughters have gotten married.'

'I'm going to sit in the smoking car,' Caroline said.

'Oh . . . well, I'll see you, then. I can't stand the smoker. Call me up and tell me how you like Alvin.'

They parted, waving, and Caroline crept into the last seat in the car, next to the window. She looked out through the dusty, smeared glass, and watched as the station and then the outskirts of Port Blair slipped past. Blind dates . . . She could not decide which was worse, the anticipation or the final actuality. A year ago, six months ago, she had thought she was through forever with the unholy three of the single girl: loneliness, being unprotected and blind dates. Now it had started again.

By the time she had ridden up in the elevator at Fabian, Caroline had forgotten the blind date and was caught up again in her working world feeling – half thrill, half uneasiness. As she passed through the reception room she noticed a girl about her own age sitting nervously on the edge of one of the couches, wearing a hat. She must be job-hunting, Caroline thought. The hat gave her away. Caroline and the girls she knew wore hats for only two occasions: going to a wedding or looking for a job. As soon as they were hired they put their hats back in the closet and did not wear them to the office again until (and if) they had attained the eminence of a Miss Farrow, and then they wore them all the time *in* the office.

I wonder if that girl out there will be Miss Farrow's next secretary, Caroline thought, putting a fresh comment sheet into her typewriter. Because I sure hope it won't have to be me.

She put the manuscript with Miss Farrow's and her own comments on Mr Shalimar's unoccupied desk quickly, before she lost her courage, and returned to her desk. The girls in the bullpen were engaged in their morning coffee ritual. She wondered whether any of them ever ate breakfast at home, especially the married ones, or whether even those never had time to feed their working husbands and themselves in the mornings. Brenda, who was currently buying her trousseau, had brought in the latest purchase, a white lace nightgown, and had put it on her desk in its open box so that all the other girls could see it.

'Look at that,' Mary Agnes whispered. 'She must have forty-five nightgowns by now. She buys something new every lunch hour and always puts it on her desk for everybody to ogle at. I don't know who's interested in *her* trousseau anyway.'

My goodness, Caroline thought, the frantic buying, the storing up, the preparations! She won't have any money left for after she's married, but she's probably spent her whole life building up to her wedding and never thinks about all the time that goes on afterward. She had known girls like Brenda in Port Blair, the girls who thought life stopped on their wedding day in that one moment of perfect achievement, like the figures in Keats' poem about the Greek vase. She thought for an instant of the girl Eddie had married and wondered what Helen Harris was doing right now. She forced the thought out of her mind. She wasn't going to think about Eddie and Helen, it was over for her, it was none of her business. Let them do what they wanted, wake up, go to sleep, make love, she wasn't going to sit here and say to herself, What time is it in Dallas? What are they doing now? That was a good way to make yourself morbid. She had her own life now too, she was working, she was trying to work her way up to a more interesting job. She would sit here and wait for Mr Shalimar to come in, and look at Brenda's new nightgown looking so out of place alongside her typewriter and filing cards, and amuse herself wondering what kind of man Brenda was buying all these goodies for. Some moose face, probably.

The usual procession of late-comers was straggling in through the door. Mr Rice, in that wonderful camel's-hair overcoat, with his clear-cut profile beginning to fade away a little at the edges. His eyes were slits this morning, and there was a little cut with dried blood at the corner of his mouth. He paused as usual for a long drink at the water fountain and found his way to his office like a sleepwalker.

'Psst . . . look at that!' Mary Agnes prodded her, shocked.

'Our eminent religious editor,' Caroline whispered, 'after a struggle with the devil.' She didn't know, a moment after she'd said it, why she had felt compelled to make fun of him. Actually, he fascinated her, in a way. Perhaps that was why she *had* said it.

'The devil?' Mary Agnes whispered back scornfully. 'He hangs around in those Third Avenue bars all night, drinking and reciting poetry and talking to every stranger he can lay his hands on. One of them probably hit him.'

'Doesn't he have a home?' Caroline asked. 'A wife?'

'He had a wife, but she left him. It's very sad. He lives in a real run-down hotel on the West Side. He's divorced and he has a daughter ten years old who he never sees. He writes to her all the time. I know because his secretary told me. He used to dictate these long, long letters, all about life and love and people and stuff. Sort of advice for when she grows up. That's because he thinks he'll never see her again. I can just *imagine* the kind of advice he'd give to a child.'

'Ten years old seems young for a child of his,' Caroline said.

'How old d'you think he is?'

'About forty-eight, I would guess.'

'He's *thirty*-eight. He looks that way because he lives such an unhealthy life,' Mary Agnes added disapprovingly. 'If he was married and lived with his wife and child he wouldn't look that way.'

'Marriage solves everything?' Caroline asked.

'What a funny thing to say.'

'Why is it funny?'

'Well . . .' Mary Agnes said, 'there are only two ways to live, the right way and the wrong way. If you live the right way you're happy, and if you live the wrong way you're miserable. If you get married it doesn't mean positively you're going to be happy, but if you get married and walk out on it then you *can't* be happy. You'll always know you gave up on a responsibility.'

'What if the other person walks out on you?'

'Mr Rice should have tried harder.'

'How do you know he didn't?'

'Well, that's a funny thing to think,' Mary Agnes said. 'You don't even know him.'

'I know it,' Caroline said. 'Maybe he was a beast. I'm only saying I know about being walked out on. Sometimes trying doesn't make the least bit of difference. It's almost as if there aren't two people involved at all.'

Mary Agnes looked at her, her eyes widening. 'Were *you* married?'

'No. Engaged.'

Mary Agnes glanced at Caroline's left hand. 'Oh, how terrible. How terrible.'

'Well, don't you get upset about it,' Caroline said, smiling.

'You poor thing,' Mary Agnes said. 'I'll never talk about it again, unless you bring it up. If you ever want to talk about it, you just tell me.'

And you'll tell everyone else on the thirty-fifth floor, Caroline thought, amused. Mary Agnes' air of tragedy made her begin to feel that her problems really weren't so pitiable after all. There is something to be said for someone else's exaggerated sympathy. If it happens to fall a little far afield it makes the original problem seem a bit remote and not quite worth it. Or maybe that's the first sign of health, she thought. If you get hit in the stomach it has to heal, and if you have a concussion that takes time too, but at least you can watch the progress. It's very hard to watch the imperceptible mending of a broken heart. Maybe this is the first sign of mending: the fact that Mary Agnes' pained solicitude for me this morning happens to strike me as amusing.

It was a relaxing day, because Miss Farrow disappeared directly after lunch and did not come back for the rest of the afternoon, but Caroline kept glancing nervously at Mr Shalimar's closed door, half expecting him to come roaring out of it like a bull into a ring, waving her comment sheet in fury. It was odd that she had thought of a bull, she mused, but perhaps it was because Mr Shalimar, from the few glimpses she had had of him, looked to her like an aging matador. The stiff posture, shoulders straight, the dark skin, and oddest of all that air he had of someone who has been through a great deal and still has some inner feeling urging him on but knows that he cannot answer it any longer. He struck her as a troubled man, and not just because of his responsibilities at the office, which would make anyone in charge look bemused at times. It was funny, she thought, that before she had ever had a job she had always thought of an office as a place where people came to work, but now it seemed as if it was a place where they also brought their private lives for everyone else to look at, paw over, comment on and enjoy. The typing pool in the center of the thirty-fifth floor at Fabian was like the village square, and the offices that surrounded it were like people's homes. Late in the afternoon she saw something that astonished her. Walking past one of the offices she noticed through its nearly closed door a girl leaning against the wall of the adjoining office with a water glass pressed against the wall and her ear to the other end of the water glass. On her face was a rapt and gloating expression, of an eavesdropper who is hearing what he expected he would hear. Then Caroline realized that the girl was in the office next to Mr Shalimar's. The girl evidently didn't care who noticed her, since she had not bothered to lock her door, which was probably because she intended to educate everyone in the office later in the day. Caroline wondered whether it was office politics, secrets about the work, or Mr Shalimar's private life that held her so.

At five o'clock April came out of Mr Shalimar's office and began to put her things together. 'Where do you want to eat?' she asked Caroline.

'Where do you?'

'You know, I'd like to go to Sardi's,' April said. 'I've heard a lot about it.'

Caroline looked at April. She was wearing that shiny baby-blue gabardine suit again, and tonight because she was going out she was even wearing a hat, a dreadful little white felt hat that made her look like Sunday Morning in East Cozyville. Caroline felt a pang of self-consciousness at the thought of being seen with her at a good restaurant. It was bad enough to have to go there without dates, but with April in that outfit, with that hair . . . 'Hey,' Caroline said, 'I'll bet you've never been to the Automat.'

'Wouldn't you rather go to Sardi's?' April said, sounding disappointed.

'Well, it's a little too expensive for me,' Caroline lied.

'Oh, of course.' April's face lighted up with instant sympathy. 'I know just what you mean. I shouldn't even go there myself, I have about four dollars to last me till payday. I'm so impractical, I guess I'd starve if people like you didn't look out for me.'

'You'll love the Automat,' Caroline said encouragingly.

Mr Shalimar came out of his office with his arm thrown around Mr Rice's shoulder. They were laughing together. As they passed Caroline's and April's desks they paused. 'Want to stop downstairs for a short drink, April?' Mr Shalimar said. He glanced at Caroline. 'You too.'

April immediately began to blush. 'Oh, we'd love to,' she said very softly. 'Wouldn't we, Caroline?'

'See you downstairs at the Unfriendly Irishman,' Mr Rice said. 'Step fast, girls.' The two men went off together to the elevator and April began stuffing her make-up back into her pocketbook, dropping some of it on the floor in her hurry.

'The Unfriendly Irishman,' April said. 'That's what he calls the bar in this building. Isn't he a *character*?'

It was the first time Caroline had ever been in the bar, and she peered through the gloom looking to see whom she could recognize. The room was about two thirds full, all with people she had noticed in the elevators and halls of the building. This seemed to be the unofficial Fabian Publications bar, refuge, gathering place and five-o'clock social club. Mr Shalimar and Mr Rice were seated at a corner table, with drinks in front of them, and they had pulled up two extra chairs for Caroline and April.

'What'll you have, girls?' Mr Shalimar said.

'Scotch,' said Caroline. It was the first thing she could think of.

April looked as though she was going through a mental battle. 'Me too,' she said then, very quickly and softly. She nibbled on a pretzel and began to blush again.

'Well, what do *you* do around here?' Mr Rice said to Caroline.

'I'm working for Miss Farrow this week,' she said.

He rolled his eyes in mock horror. He had a perfectly deadpan face with a light touch of cynicism on it. 'That's hell week for the sorority,' he said. 'We only save it for specially lucky girls.'

How funny! Caroline thought. That's exactly the phrase I used when I was telling Mary Agnes about it.

'So you're Caroline Bender,' said Mr Shalimar.

'Yes.' Suddenly her mouth was dry.

'I found a little report of yours on my desk,' he said.

'I know.' Why did her voice sound like a croak? She took a sip of her drink.

'I read the manuscript this afternoon,' he said. He paused and looked at her. 'You know something, Miss Bender?'

'What . . . ?'

'I happen to agree with you.'

'Oh, my goodness,' Caroline said, weak with relief.

'I don't think I'll buy that book,' he said.

'My goodness,' she said again.

His eyes narrowed. 'Make no mistake. I am the editor here, and I buy what I like and reject what I don't like, regardless of what any of my editors say. But I like having a bright, young reader who agrees with me, it makes me feel a little better.'

'I hope someday to be a reader,' Caroline said.

'All right. For the next week or two I'll give you a manuscript every night to take home and read. You give me a report on each one. After I see what you can do, maybe I'll *let* you be a reader.'

'Oh, that would be marvelous!'

Mr Rice smiled wryly. Even with the smile his face did not change much. 'The enthusiasm of youth,' he said. 'If old man Fabian had only known, he wouldn't have bothered to pay these kids for working here. He would have charged 'em.'

Mr Shalimar was looking piercingly at Caroline across the table. 'The most valuable commodity in business today, if people would only recognize it, is enthusiasm. I'm not interested in deadheads. You get the same old trite comments from the deadheads, they don't even care any more. I want editors who think that every book we put out is an important book. I don't care if it's the worst piece of crap in the world; if the author who wrote it believes in it, and the editors who help him revise it believe in it, then the people who buy it will care about it. The thing that was wrong with the manuscript you read last night was that it was phony. The author thought he was fooling his readers. Well, they never fool me. And he didn't fool you. Do you want experience?'

'Yes,' she said.

'I'll give you experience. I'll teach you. I've been forty years an editor, I've taught some of the best writers in the business. I knew Eugene O'Neill years ago, and I gave him advice.'

There was an almost inaudible sigh from April, as if at last she had achieved a moment of delight she had been waiting for for a long time. Mr Shalimar turned to include her too in his revelations. April was looking at him with her eyes shining. Mr Rice turned his glass of whisky nearly directly upside down as his throat moved rhythmically, swallowing. His eyes were closed and he did not seem to be listening to Mr Shalimar at all.

It was nine o'clock before Caroline realized that none of them had eaten anything but pretzels, and Mr Rice not even those. April seemed in a trance, leaning toward Mr Shalimar as a young plant leans toward the sun in a window, listening to every story he told with little gasps and laughs. Caroline was more interested in Mr Rice – or Mike, as she was now calling him. His attention to Mr Shalimar was obviously more loyalty than interest, and she began to suspect that Mike Rice, at least, had heard all Mr Shalimar's stories quite a few times before. He drank quietly, steadily and pleasantly, the way one plays solitaire or knits a sweater, drink after drink after drink, with no sign of getting drunk. Once in a while he would look over at her and give a faint smile and nod his head, a serious drinker giving indication that there still is communication between himself and his table partner, but without breaking his rhythm. It was Mr Shalimar who was finding the liquor hard to take.

The first indication Caroline had was a furtive bony hand touching her knee. The face and voice of Mr Shalimar, above the table, were so self-assured and so much The Boss that for a moment she had the wild thought that the hand investigating her leg belonged to someone under the table. It hardly even seemed to be connected to Mr Shalimar's arm and shoulder. Then she caught the thickening of his speech, and he leaned toward her, looking into her face.

'Mike, did you ever notice what a beautiful girl this is?' he said.

His husky voice terrified her. She moved away from his hand, upsetting her glass in the process.

'Oops,' Mike said pleasantly. He righted the glass and began to mop off Caroline's skirt with his handkerchief. There was nothing personal in his touch, for which she was grateful. 'Miss!' He beckoned to the waitress. 'Miss!'

The waitress hurried over with a handful of cloth napkins. Mr Shalimar seemed oblivious of the entire crisis; he continued to talk, more mistily now, about how lovely Caroline's face was. April began to look confused. She looked up suddenly at Mr Shalimar with a glance that carried mingled horror and delight. He must have decided to try *her* knee, Caroline thought, and instantly was taken with a fit of the giggles. She excused herself hurriedly and ran to the ladies' room.

April came in a moment after she had achieved her refuge. 'Oh, Caroline, are you all right?'

'Are *you* all right?' Caroline was doubled over, laughing until tears came into her eyes. It wasn't that anything that had happened was so funny, really, it was just that she was so glad to be able to laugh at it all when for nearly four hours she had been tense and nervous.

'I thought you were sick,' April said worriedly.

'No, I'm fine. Do you think we can get away now and eat dinner?'

'I was thinking . . . maybe they would buy us dinner? Do you think they might?'

'You want to *eat* with them?'

'Well, neither of us has any money to speak of. It would certainly help for the rest of the week if they bought our dinner tonight.'

'We could go back and say we're hungry, and see what develops.'

'Would you mind?' April asked.

'No . . . I don't mind.' She powdered her nose and put on fresh lipstick. 'I can stand it if you can.'

April turned around to look at her, surprised. 'You're laughing at *him*, aren't you!'

'Well, you must admit he was funny.'

'Funny? What was funny? I think he's the most fascinating person I ever met.'

'You do?' Caroline said dubiously.

'But the life he's led . . . the people he knows! I could listen to him talk all night.'

Caroline couldn't resist saying it. 'And he'll let you, too, as long as your leg holds out.'

April's face turned a deep pink. 'Oh, my heavens . . .' she said. She covered her face with her hands.

Caroline put her arm around April. 'He's a little plastered, that's all. Just you never mention it and he'll never mention it.'

April smiled, a bit ruefully. 'I was hoping you and I could have dinner alone together. There are so many things I'd like to talk to you about. I was hoping we could get to know each other better.'

'We will.'

'Do you have to go back to the country tonight? Maybe you could stay over at my house.'

With the Scotch she had drunk Caroline felt warm and happy and fond of the whole world. 'I think that would be fun,' she said. She had never seen the apartment of a working girl who lived alone in New York, but from the fashion magazines she had read she had her own ideas of it, and already the image arose of herself and April chatting cozily until four in the morning in a small, austere but romantically chic apartment, the kind she would like to have someday soon.

'It's kind of a dump,' April said, 'but I love it.'

'I'd love to see it. Come on, out to the wolves.' They left the ladies' room and found their way back to their corner table. Mike Rice was sitting there alone.

'Mr Shalimar had to go home,' he said.

'Oh, what a shame,' said April. 'We didn't even get a chance to thank him.'

Caroline glanced at Mike and for an instant their eyes met. She expected to find a look of amusement there, or at the least his habitual cynicism, but instead to her surprise she found a look of caution.

'You can tell him tomorrow,' he said.

'Of course,' April murmured. She sat down at her place at the table again and began to toy with her gloves, not quite sure if they were expected to leave now or stay.

Mike beckoned to the waitress and pointed at their glasses. Caroline sat down too. For a minute none of them could think of anything to say. 'You have to understand Mr Shalimar,' Mike said finally.

There was something about Mike Rice that Caroline liked; she felt she could say anything to him and he would never be shocked or think she was getting out of her place. 'Maybe I'm way out of line,' she said, 'but I had the feeling he's had a comedown and he's ashamed of it. The way he talks about the past all the time and about what he was.'

'You might as well know it,' Mike said. 'I suspect you're going to be around a long time. It isn't as if he's had a comedown from anything. He's never been anywhere.'

'But all the people he's known . . .' Caroline said. 'The stories he tells . . . Why, he never stops talking about Eugene O'Neill.'

There was not a trace of a smile on Mike's face, only a look of great pity. It was odd, Caroline thought, that a man in the shape he was in should feel sorry for someone like Mr Shalimar. 'You know how it is when people talk all the time about some celebrity,' he said. 'Mr Shalimar knows Eugene O'Neill, but Eugene O'Neill doesn't know him.'

'My gosh!' April said, biting her thumb.

'Be nice girls,' Mike said. 'Forget I ever opened my mouth. But treat Mr Shalimar with all the respect you have at your command. He's a very bitter man, but he has cause. It's a dreadful thing to know you're fifty-five years old and you have to worry all the time about losing a job that isn't even good enough for you.'

'Why should he lose his job?' Caroline asked.

'Bright young people. People like you, for instance. Kids with ambition, who write brilliant reports out of sheer instinct. A man who has to live in a past that never really was is afraid of a lot of things.'

'But not of me?' Caroline said incredulously.

'Not you now, no. Right now you're nothing to him. But you in another two years – ah, that's a different story. Listen to him. Pay attention and respect him when he teaches you anything about the business you're in. Don't think you're smart. Just listen, and remember.'

He had begun to slur his words, and Caroline realized that he was, finally, very drunk. He pulled a handful of crumpled bills out of his pocket and dropped them on to the table. 'This'll pay for the drinks and probably a sandwich for you two kids,' he said. He put his hands flat on the table and assisted himself to his feet. 'See you tomorrow.'

'Oh, thank you very much, Mr Rice,' April said.

'Yes, thank you,' Caroline murmured. She was troubled, and thinking. She didn't want to be a success if that meant watching out for people with dark lives who were afraid of you for no reason you could fathom. This morning she had been afraid even to speak to Mr Shalimar, this evening he was fondling her leg and she was being told that someday he would be afraid of her. She was thinking that she didn't like the working world at all, and yet, underneath, she was exhilarated. It was all like a dream in which you could have anything you wanted, if you were very very careful.

Mike Rice leaned over and touched her eyebrows where they were drawn together. His fingers were very gentle. 'Did I say, "Don't think you're smart"?' he said. 'I'll tell you something: I'll amend it. Don't let anyone *know* you think you're smart. Because you know something? You're *damn* smart.' He patted her cheek and walked off swiftly, making an obvious effort to walk straight, his camel's-hair coat tossed askew over one shoulder like a cape.

'What's he talking about?' April asked, looking after him.

'I don't know . . .' Caroline said. 'Yet.'

They ate at the same bar, and then Caroline telephoned her mother and bought a toothbrush and went with April to April's apartment. There was a baby carriage in the downstairs hallway, and two garbage cans, and a row of mailboxes on one wall. As they climbed the stairs Caroline heard the sound of a television set from one apartment and shrieks from another where a party was going on. The door was ajar at the party apartment. 'Look.' April nudged Caroline. 'Everyone's so friendly in this house. You could walk right in. It's so smoky in there they probably wouldn't know the difference.'

April's apartment was dark. She switched on the light and ran to the window. 'Look at my garden, Caroline!'

Caroline was looking at the room. It was tiny, and April's clothes were scattered here and there. There was a coffee cup with some cold coffee in it standing on the bridge table next to a pile of all the latest fashion magazines. There were two doors, one of which might have led off to another room, since there was no bed in sight. In fact, there was almost no furniture, and no rug. It was seedy, you had to admit that, but Caroline felt her heart begin to pound. It could be fixed up so easily, and it could be enchanting. How wonderful to have an apartment of one's own – one's own things around, one's own taste everywhere.

'The bed is in the wall,' April said. 'I'll sleep on the box-spring and you can have the mattress. Here's my bathroom, and this is the closet. This closet is the kitchen. Come see my garden, Caroline!'

Caroline looked out the window, down three floors, and saw dimly the outline of trees. They were spindly city trees, it was true, and it was hardly 'April's garden' except to look at, but as soon as she saw it Caroline was sold.

'I love your apartment. You're so lucky.'

'Do you *think* so?' April's face lighted up with delight. 'I was afraid you'd think it was a dirty old tenement.'

'I didn't expect you to live in a penthouse on fifty dollars a week.'

'Oh, I know. It's just terrible not to have enough money. I can't even go to the movies at night after I get finished paying for my rent and phone and food. I have to sit here every night and read magazines. I met a girl who lives in this house and works at Fabian. Her name is Barbara Lemont. She's secretary to the beauty editor of *America's Woman* and she's going to give me all the fashion magazines when she gets through reading them. They get all the magazines free over there. I've started to read some already.' April smiled self-consciously, like a child. 'You know what? I'm getting an education. Do you want some cocoa?'

'Love some.'

April began to putter around in her closet kitchen, making cocoa. 'I would never have met Barbara at Fabian because she works on a different floor. It's like a different world down there. My heavens, they have a regular kitchen on the thirty-first floor where they make all the recipes they take pictures of. Most of the food they can't even eat afterward because they put coloring on it to photograph better. Isn't that a terrible waste? But sometimes they let the girls take home something wonderful, like a roast turkey. I think I ought to ask for a transfer. If I sound like I'm drooling, it's because I am. I'm *always* hungry lately. I'm not used to eating just a box of fig newtons for supper. Back home we used to have enormous meals.' She put the two cups of cocoa on the bridge table, swept a pile of clothes off one of the bridge chairs, kicked off her shoes and sat down. Caroline took the other chair.

'I wish,' April went on, 'that I would meet a boy who would take me out to dinner and be good to me. Who am I kidding? I wouldn't care if he never took me out to dinner, just as long as we liked each other a lot. Do you know that Barbara Lemont is only twenty years old – our age – and she's already been married and divorced and has a baby one year old? Did you see that baby carriage downstairs? That's hers. She's trying to sell it. She doesn't have any money either. *Nobody* I know has any money.'

'That's kind of sad about the baby carriage,' Caroline said. 'Most people save baby carriages for the next baby. It's a little as if she doesn't expect to get married again.'

'It is, isn't it,' April said. 'But I guess she doesn't have room for it. None of the apartments in this house are very big. She lives with her mother and the baby – her father's dead. I bet she has a hard time on dates. Being married before, you know?'

'I know,' Caroline said. She was curled up cozily in the chair with her arms around her knees, and she hadn't had cocoa since she was a little girl. She was beginning to have that feeling that comes after midnight, of one's thoughts opening out, flowering, groping out loud for some new discovery, some new truth that is really as old as all the hundreds of years girls have been confiding to one another in the relaxing intimacy of the night. 'Boys are funny. They seem to think that girls who have been married before can't live without sex. I wonder if it's true. Do you think so?'

'I wonder too . . .' April said. She turned her cocoa cup around in her hand, looking at the roses that were painted on it as if they were very fascinating. 'Are you a virgin?'

'I must admit I am. Are you?'

'Oh, sure. What do you mean, "admit"? None of the girls back home will admit they aren't – if they aren't, which I don't know.'

'I'm not so proud of it,' Caroline said. 'It's just something I can't quite bring myself to give up. If my mother heard me talking about this in such a casual way she'd have a fit. She taught me only two major rules for life: don't let boys touch you, and join the Radcliffe Club.'

April smiled. 'Mine never taught me anything like that because we just don't talk about sex at our house. You just assume that every girl who isn't married is a virgin, unless there's somebody who there's a scandal about. My mother would no more tell me not to sleep with a boy than she would tell me not to go out and steal a car. She knows I wouldn't think of it.'

'But you do think of it?'

'I think *about* it. All the time. That's a little different, though.'

'When I'm twenty-six, if I'm not married by then, I'm going to take a lover,' Caroline said.

'Really?' April sounded a little shocked. Then she thought about it. 'I think you're right. If you're that old, you have a right to live.'

'I wanted to sleep with Eddie,' Caroline said. 'He was my fiancé in college. I really wanted to, but at the last minute I was always afraid. I think it was a combination of being afraid I'd lose him and being scared that going all the way wasn't going to be as wonderful as everything I'd always imagined. I guess people build it up in their minds as being something marvelous, and then they wait and wait, and then it gets to be too important. Like the first kiss, or the first anything. It ought to be an accident, not something you plan too carefully, or else you're apt to be disappointed.'

'I guess this sounds awfully naïve,' April said. 'But when I try to picture going to bed with somebody I can never figure out where the sheet and blankets go. Do you do it underneath the blanket, or do you take the blanket off?'

Caroline couldn't help laughing. 'Didn't you ever neck on a bed with somebody?'

'My heavens, no. Not on a bed.'

'Well, when the time comes, whoever he is, *he'll* know what to do about the blanket.'

They were silent then for a few moments, each with her own thoughts. 'If you were to take a lover next week,' April said, 'just pretend – who would you want it to be? What kind of man would you want for your first?'

'Someone I loved,' Caroline said. 'And, above all, someone considerate, who had enough experience to know what he was doing.'

'Someone older,' April said. 'I think it should be an older man.'

'Not too old.'

'Oh, no. But not twenty-one either. Just pretend that you could have anybody and you had made up your mind to have a love affair. Who would you want? It could be a movie star, or someone in the office, or anyone.'

'All right,' Caroline said.

'Do you know?'

'Mmm-hmm.' All of a sudden she did know, and the choice seemed as natural as if she had always known it, and as exciting as if it were crazily, improbably possible. 'This is just pretend, mind you.'

'Of course.'

'Mike Rice,' said Caroline.

4

Girls like Caroline, who have just finished fifteen uninterrupted years of educational routine, find themselves still dividing the year into seasons in the way they are used to, rather than by the calendar. January the first is not the birth of the new year; September is. Spring is not a time of hope and blossoming; it is a time of leave-taking and faint pangs of unhappiness. The year breaks in half at the end of January, which is the time of exams, panic, dirty clothes, sleepless nights and frantic last-minute studying. It was therefore very strange to Caroline to find herself at the end of January in New York with nothing to stir her up emotionally.

She had been taking home a manuscript every evening to read and report on, and although at first she had to write the comments over and over like a composition in order to make them short and to the point, she soon had the knack of it and could type her feelings directly on to the official comment sheet. The first few books she reported on, she felt as though she would never be able to be an editor, but at the end of three weeks she had learned something startling and encouraging: that a thing which seems mysterious can finally become almost automatic. In fact, at the end of January, she began to feel a slight touch of resentment that Mr Shalimar kept gobbling up her extra-hours production without ever giving her any sign of encouragement that she would be allowed to become an official reader.

She had fallen into the habit of taking the seven-o'clock express to Port Blair about three nights a week. Those evenings she would first stop at the Fabian bar to have a drink with Mr Shalimar, Mike,

April, and one or two or three of the other office girls whom Mr Shalimar managed to take in tow. She was pretty sure that Mr Shalimar liked her, because she and April were the only regulars. She did not like him particularly. She could not quite get over her fear of him, a fear which kept her from falling into a trance when he started telling his same old stories for the benefit of each new girl. The two things which kept her accepting his invitations were her desire to become anything like a member of the inner circle, and her companionable feeling for Mike Rice. She always managed to seat herself across the table from Mr Shalimar, not next to him, so some other girl than herself would have to be the unwilling recipient of the affectionate hand. That meant she would find herself elbow to elbow with Mike. She often looked at him on the sly and had the same feeling about him as she had about April's apartment the first time she saw it: that so much could be done to improve the run-down façade. Mike had the kind of aristocratic, well-formed face and athletic if wiry body that it is very difficult to destroy. He seemed to be doing his best to try, though.

Despite her midnight conversation with April that one night, Caroline never really thought of Mike as a romantic possibility. She wasn't quite sure how she considered him. She hoped he could someday be her friend. She knew that she trusted him, and that he represented a kind of life and a kind of world that were a mystery to her, and an interesting one. She never compared him to Eddie, nor brought up thoughts of Eddie as a defense against him. Eddie was a wound that had not yet healed, as if some important part of herself had been torn away. If she had gone out regularly with another boy, she would have been compelled to compare him with Eddie, but she did not have to compare Mike Rice with anyone. In fact, there was no one in her limited sphere whom she could have sensibly compared with Mike anyway.

Preoccupied as she was with her own feelings about a situation that was still new to her, Caroline could not help noticing the slow change that was coming over April. The first indication was the morning after their first payday, when April appeared triumphantly in the bullpen with her gold hair shorn, snail-curled and lacquered.

The effect – or rather, the contrast – was somewhat frightening, like seeing a picture of one of those ancient Egyptian princesses quite bald without her headdress. At five o'clock that day April cornered Caroline. 'It's wrong, isn't it,' April said timidly. 'There's still something not quite right.'

'It's a bit stiff,' Caroline said kindly.

'I wanted to look like you,' April said. 'Tell me where you have yours done.'

The next day April returned looking like a stranger, fluffy short hair, new penciled eyebrows that gave her a gamin look and some kind of pale powder base that hid the farm-girl freckles. Caroline had forgotten what a really beautiful face April had, but now it was completely apparent. April was wearing a very simple black jersey dress that she had seen in one of her secondhand fashion magazines.

'Well, look at the movie star!' Mr Shalimar said.

April still could blush, even under the Elizabeth Arden icing. 'I bought two more dresses and shoes and a handbag and a coat and charged the whole thing,' she confided to Caroline. 'I'll be paying it off for the next year.'

'It was worth it,' Caroline said. 'You look lovely, really lovely.'

When April smiled her new eyebrows made her look reckless, or perhaps it was the line of the hair curving around her face. 'Did you hear what he said?'

'Who? Pale hands I love by the Shalimar?'

'Oh, honestly, you're terrible,' April breathed, laughing, and hurried into Mr Shalimar's office holding her shorthand pad in one hand, and smoothing her skirt with the other.

Miss Farrow had a temporary secretary, the girl Caroline had seen sitting nervously in the reception room some weeks before. 'They might as well hire a temporary girl,' Mike had told Caroline. 'None of them stay with her longer than a few months anyway.' The girl was named Gregg Adams, and she was an actress. Caroline realized there must be thousands of actresses she had never even heard of, who make perhaps two hundred dollars a year doing walkons in television and bits in off-Broadway productions, and who spend the rest of their time making rounds and waiting fitfully in unavoidable temporary office work. This girl, Gregg, was of medium height, and slender, with the face of a fourteen-year-old. She had long straight blonde hair, not the stringy kind, but the sort that swayed all in one piece when she moved quickly. She wore all the necessary make-up but lipstick, which added to the teen-age look. Caroline was astonished to learn that she was twenty-three years old. Gregg had the sort of mouth that made smoking a cigarette look somehow sinful.

Miss Farrow treated her new secretary as one might treat a horse or a dog until the ASPCA caught up. She had a contempt for temporary office help, holding that by the time you taught them anything they were gone anyway, so it was a waste of time. 'You know what Miss Farrow did last Friday?' Mary Agnes told Caroline breathlessly. 'She gave a cocktail party and invited Gregg to come, and then she made Gregg spend the whole evening carrying hors d'oeuvres to the guests and emptying ash trays and making drinks. Just like a maid! Did you ever hear such a nerve?'

'What did Gregg do about it?'

'Nothing,' Mary Agnes said.

'You're crazy,' Caroline told Gregg later in the ladies' room. 'If you let her push you around like that she'll do worse next time.'

'It's all right,' Gregg said sweetly. She had a very tender, little-girl voice. 'Afterward, before I went home, I stole two bottles of Scotch.'

Caroline liked Gregg, and they began to have lunch together nearly every day, often with April. Gregg came from Dallas, from an upper-middle-class family, and Caroline couldn't resist asking her immediately if she knew Helen Lowe. She didn't, but she had heard of the family, of course. Gregg was the youngest of three sisters, and she had spent most of her time in boarding schools, always alone because her nearest sister was five years older and was in college when Gregg was starting high school. The parents had each been divorced and remarried several times. 'If I ever get married,' Gregg told Caroline, 'I'm going to *stay* married. I've been saying goodbye to people all my life and I'm sick of it.' The middle sister, in Texas, was twenty-eight and starting her third marriage. The oldest was divorced also. 'We're not a very faithful family,' Gregg said. 'Except me. I've got all the glue they forgot to hand out to the rest of the family, if I only had somebody to use it on!'

Neither Caroline, Gregg nor April seemed to be able to meet many boys in New York. Caroline managed a date every two weeks, mostly blind dates who were too dreadful to see again or pass on to her friends, and Gregg knew several boys from her dramatic class who had as little money as she did. Gregg's mother sent her money, enough for rent on a tiny apartment, food and some clothes, but not for the acting classes or the ballet lessons she was taking at night, which was why she had to put up with Miss Farrow at Fabian.

'Look,' Gregg said to Caroline, 'if you want to live in New York, why don't we share an apartment? I have two studio couches in my apartment, and we could share the rent, which is a hundred dollars a month. You could never find a decent apartment yourself for fifty.'

'When I get to be a reader and I get my raise, I will,' Caroline said.

'Hooray! No more cleaning La Farrow's latrines! A year away from that bitch is like five minutes away from anybody else.'

Gregg lived in a second-floor walk-up over a Chinese laundry in a respectable and safe, if run-down, neighborhood. The proprietor of the laundry had a yearning for fresh air and kept the door to his establishment wide open all day, winter and summer. Walking past it to enter the house you could hear the whoosh of the pressing machine, and on cold days the clouds of steam rising into the air gave anyone entering Gregg's apartment the feeling that he was boarding a train. Caroline didn't mind it at all, and she liked the apartment, which, being in a converted brownstone, had enormous windows from floor to ceiling with domed tops like the windows in a church. There was a tiny balcony outside each window, just large enough for several inches of grit and soot and Gregg's striped alley cat, who used the balconies for his daily promenade.

There was now more reason than ever to want the promotion, and Caroline began to worry about it. Mr Shalimar's secretary had long since returned, so April was back in the typing pool and could not tell Caroline whether or not he was considering doing anything about her reports. Every afternoon he would stop briefly at Caroline's desk and say, 'Thank you for your comments. They're very useful.' Once in a while he would say, 'I read your comment with interest, and I hope to God you're wrong.' She didn't want to push him or appear anxious, but she began to have the fear that he was using her to do two jobs at once for the salary of the lesser one and she didn't quite know what to do about it.

Meanwhile she typed up any odd work that there was no one else to do, helped the other girls, and walked past Mr Shalimar's office whenever she could think of a good excuse to do so, not because it would do her any good but because it made her feel better. She began to find an influx of work from Miss Farrow's office piled on her desk. She did it without question for a few days and then one day she asked Gregg, 'Is this all from you? Not that I mind, but I have so much of my own.'

'Miss Farrow puts it there herself,' Gregg said. 'Half the time I don't have enough to do. Either she really thinks I'm a moron or else she's just partial to your brand of typing.'

'Partial?' said Caroline. 'Now I wonder.'

With her regular work and Miss Farrow's additions Caroline was rushed all day and exhausted at the end of the day, so that the manuscripts she read at night were no longer pleasure but almost a nuisance. She would have put Miss Farrow's work off as a matter of course but every pile carried a handwritten note: 'Rush,' or 'Today, please,' or 'To be done immediately.' Caroline knew she wasn't any better a secretary than any of the other girls in the pool and she began to wonder why she was the only one singled out for these extra jobs. One day at a quarter of five she was finishing up when Miss Farrow came out of her office and dropped a sheaf of letters on her desk.

'These have been corrected. Will you type them please, Miss Bender, and put them on my desk before you go home?'

'I don't think I'll be able to finish them today, Miss Farrow.'

Miss Farrow's eyes narrowed. She took a deep breath. 'Listen, you little bitch,' she said. 'You think you're a reader, but you're not. You're just another typist here and don't you forget it. You are *not* an editor.' She turned and walked quickly back to her office.

'What did she say?' Mary Agnes said. 'What did she *say*? You look like she hit you in the face.'

For a moment Caroline was so shocked that she didn't feel anything, then she felt like crying; and a moment later when she figured it out she felt like laughing. 'I guess,' she said to Mary Agnes, 'she said I'm going to get to be a reader after all.'

It was odd, she thought, how quickly one could become attuned to the undercurrents of office feeling: the fears, the jealousies, the connivings and the secret panics. It was not safe to think that anyone was unafraid; certainly if Mr Shalimar was mistrustful of young ambition then Miss Farrow must be. The girls like Mary Agnes who had no ambition except to do their work satisfactorily, disappear at five o'clock on the dot, and line up at the bank on payday, were the backbone of the office, and the office could not run without them. But the company would not make money if every worker in it was like Mary Agnes, and everyone knew it from Mr Fabian right down to Mary Agnes herself. It was the eager newcomer, the fomenter, who set the panic wheels turning, and the people like Miss Farrow were so watchful that they knew who she was before the newcomer knew it herself. It was naïve of me, Caroline thought, to think that I could become an editor without stepping on someone's toes – or perhaps even on his shoulders – and here I am without the least desire to or idea of how to begin.

'Gee, that's great!' Mary Agnes was saying. 'And you here such a short time, too. You know, if you're going to be a reader you don't have to do all Miss Farrow's extra work like that. You won't even have time to read for Mr Shalimar if she keeps piling it up on you. You ought to go and tell him. I wouldn't let her get away with it.'

Did I say I don't have the least idea of how to begin? Caroline thought. Mary Agnes knows how to get along better than I. 'You're right,' she said. 'Thanks, Mary Agnes.'

She was planning what she would say to him the next day as she went down in the elevator, carrying the evening's manuscript. She would have liked to stop to talk to him right then, but his door was closed and she was in a hurry to meet Mrs Nature's blind date, who had finally called. She vaguely resented this boy, Alvin Wiggs, whoever he was, because his presence and his plans for her stood like a barrier between her and something which had gradually become very important in her life. The hesitant voice on the telephone that afternoon had not warmed her, nor had it promised anything, but the manuscript she hugged under her arm promised a great deal.

'Now you mustn't do work every night,' her mother had told her several times. 'You have to go out on dates too. All work and no play, you know . . .'

'I'd go out all right if anyone called me,' she had answered. Well, now someone had called her, and he was waiting for her in front of her office building. She recognized him instantly even though she had never seen him before. He was the one person in the crowd who looked as if he didn't know where he was going, walking nervously in and out of the revolving door, looking anxiously at every girl who came out. He was about thirty, of medium height and half bald.

'Caroline Bender?' he said in a loud voice as soon as she stopped. 'Are you Caroline?'

Several Fabian girls turned to look at him and Caroline curiously at the sound of her name. Caroline wanted to shrink into her skin. 'Yes,' she said quietly. She took his arm and began to lead him down the street to a safe distance.

He was looking at her from head to toe. He had moist, anxious eyes and he seemed terrified. She let go of his arm. 'You must be Alvin Wiggs,' she said pleasantly.

'That's me.'

'Well,' she said.

Now he was walking, leading her uptown. 'We'll have dinner at Schrafft's,' he said.

Schrafft's? she thought. Where I have lunch with April and

Gregg every day? A tomato surprise and a strawberry soda with all those ladies and Alvin Wiggs? 'Oh, is that one of your favorite restaurants?' she said.

He seemed flustered. 'I've . . . never been there. But my mother goes there all the time. Don't you want to go?'

'Well, I'd rather go somewhere a little more – well, darker, with music. If you don't mind.'

'I thought girls liked Schrafft's,' he said hesitantly. 'You know . . . small portions . . . We'll go anyplace you like.'

Maybe he has no money, she thought. No, Mrs Nature said he was in his father's business. They walked east toward Madison Avenue and after passing several restaurants Caroline liked they finally stopped. They were in front of a small, dark restaurant Caroline had heard of, which was supposed to be inexpensive and have good food. 'How about this?' she said.

'All right.' They went in, walked past the tiny bar, and were ushered to a table. They were the only people in the dining room.

'Cocktail?' the waitress said.

'Oh, no,' said Alvin. 'Not for me. You don't want one, do you?'

'It's only a quarter past five,' Caroline said. 'I'd like to have one first, unless you're hungry.'

She ordered a Scotch and water and Alvin Wiggs ordered nothing. She felt a little self-conscious drinking alone, but she knew that if she didn't she would never be able to get through an hour with him. She looked at him and smiled brightly. 'I should have brought you some of our latest books,' she said. 'Are you reading anything good lately?'

'I don't like books,' he said. 'It takes me about seven months to get through a novel. I like financial magazines.'

She tried again. 'It's a shame you haven't found any books you liked. What was the last one you read?'

'I don't remember.'

What interesting ice cubes those were in her glass. They had tiny bubbles in them. She had never seen ice cubes that drew her attention so.

'Mrs Nature is a nice woman, isn't she,' he said.

'Yes she is.'

'She's very nice. I like her.'

'Have you met Francine's husband?'

'No,' he said. 'I hear he's very nice. I like Francine.'

'Yes,' she said.

'Francine's nice,' he said.

Oh, we forgot *Mr* Nature! Caroline thought. She wanted to laugh. It was all of five-thirty. 'May I have another Scotch, please?'

'Are those good?'

'Yes, they're very good.'

'Maybe I'll try one. I don't drink much.'

'You'd better not.'

'Well, I'll try one,' he said.

Maybe he's just shy, she thought hopefully as Alvin downed his drink as quickly as if it were buttermilk and made a wry face.

'Do you live in Port Blair?' she asked him.

'Yes. I live with my parents.'

'Do you like that?' she asked.

'Oh, I don't mind. My parents are very good. They don't even ask me any more what time I get home at night,' he said proudly.

'How old are you? I don't think Mrs Nature told me.'

'Thirty.'

She had to have another Scotch on that one, just one, and he joined her. Then they ordered dinner. The Scotch had made her brave enough to feel she could play Sarah Bernhardt, and she decided to have a terrible headache right after dinner.

'I met a famous author when I was in Europe,' he said brightly, as if it had just occurred to him.

You see, she thought, I was wrong. I should have given him a chance. He's probably got some gay, Continental life behind him that I never even suspected. 'Oh? Who?'

'Ah . . . ah, what's his name? Oh, Ernest Hemingway. I was sitting in a little café in Spain with some friends and he was sitting at another table.' He colored slightly. 'I . . . asked him for his autograph.'

'And what happened?'

70

'He gave it to me.'

She looked at him expectantly, but it seemed that was the end of his story about the meeting with the author. Good grief, she thought, even Mr Shalimar can do better than that.

The restaurant where they were was, unfortunately, an efficient one that specialized in getting diners out in time for the theater. Besides that, they had been the first ones in the dining room. When they were drinking their coffee Caroline looked at her watch expecting it to be at least nine o'clock (of the following week) and found to her horror that it was only six-thirty. The Scotch had worn off and she didn't quite have the courage to act sick. Could she say, Oh, I'm just in time for the seven-o'clock express?

'I guess anyone who had you working for him would be very lucky,' Alvin was saying, with moist admiration in his eyes. She felt too sorry for him to dislike him, or at least, to hurt his feelings. All she wanted was to go home, go home, go home – home seemed like a refuge, a beautiful place where she hadn't been for such a long time – and to go home was such a simple thing, but impossible for her right now.

'I'd like an after-dinner brandy,' she said.

'Oh?' He seemed startled. Then he rallied. 'Two brandies, Miss.'

They served the brandy in large, lovely double brandy glasses. 'Tell me about the mannequin business,' she said. 'I've talked enough about publishing.'

You would have thought she had asked him to stand up and give an address before a crowd of hostile hundreds. He seemed to be searching his mind frantically. 'Well, it's just the family business,' he said at last. 'It's a . . . family business. Just the family.'

'But what do you *do*?' Spy? Put microfilm in their necks? she thought.

'We make mannequins for store windows. It must seem very dull to you.'

'Oh, no.'

'Well, you have . . . such an exciting life and everything. All those authors.'

'Whatever you really like is exciting,' she said.

'Do you want to do that always, or do you want to get married?'

'Can't I do both?'

He looked nonplused. 'I guess so. I never thought of it that way.'

'I'd like another brandy,' she said. 'And then I have to go home because there's a manuscript I *must* read for the office tomorrow.'

'It's so early,' he protested.

'It's a very large manuscript.'

'One brandy, please, Miss. And the check.'

If there's anything I hate, she thought, it's drinking alone while someone looks at me the way he's doing now. If there's anything duller than drinking with someone you don't like it's drinking alone and being watched by someone you don't like. 'Aren't you going to join me? Please?'

'Oh . . . all right.'

He downed the entire glass of brandy in three gulps, with that same medicine-taking look on his face, and then suddenly the wry look smoothed out and he blinked several times. 'The second one's not so bad,' he said. 'You get used to the taste.' He raised his arm and with an astonishing show of bravado snapped his fingers for the waitress.

I hate people who do that, she thought, relieved to have something definite to hold against him that really was his fault and not just an accident of personality and upbringing. 'I have to go now to catch my train,' she said.

'I've never met such a nice girl as you,' he said. 'You're the nicest girl I've ever met.' The waitress had appeared out of nowhere with two more brandies, and he drank his.

'I don't want any,' she said, pulling on her gloves.

'We'll go,' he said. 'We'll go.' He took her brandy and drank it too, looking a little self-conscious. '. . . Waste it,' he murmured, and then, unaccountably, giggled.

She stood. 'Can we go?'

He fumbled with the change and then followed her closely to the door, almost treading on her heels, like an inebriated Saint Bernard. 'Don't trip,' he breathed, clutching her arm. She had never had less intention of tripping but was not sure she could say the same for him. Just as they reached the front room she realized to her acute embarrassment that Mike Rice was sitting at the bar, alone and gazing solemnly into the mirror. She looked down into her collar hoping he would not see her with Alvin Wiggs – the only boy Mike had ever seen her with, and what an example! It was too late. He had caught sight of her in the mirror and was swiveling around slowly on the bar stool, his eyebrows raised.

'Hi,' he said. He nodded at her and at Alvin, and completed the turn to the business end of the bar. But she could see that he was still watching her in the mirror, his face as deadpan as ever, just a touch of amusement in his eyes.

'. . . That?' said Alvin.

'Shh.'

'Who?'

'He's a writer.'

'Oh, introduce me! I want to meet one of your writer friends.' He was pulling her back now, to the bar.

'Alvin, please!'

'Can I buy you kids a drink?' Mike said. His pleasant tone and the reference to herself and Alvin as 'kids' seemed to take away some of the onerousness of being here with a neurotic balding man ten years her senior who had gotten drunk on four double brandies and was determined to act ten years old.

Alvin was holding out his hand. 'I want to meet a famous author. I'm Alvin Wiggs.'

Mike allowed his hand to be used as a hitching post and looked quizzically at Caroline. She took a deep breath. 'And this is Mr F. Scott Fitzgerald,' she said.

'F. Scott Fitzgerald?' said Alvin. Slowly his face lighted up. 'Oh, we studied you in college. You wrote about . . . the twenties and things. I'm very glad to meet you.'

'I'm glad to meet you too,' Mike said. He looked from Alvin to Caroline.

'Y'know,' Alvin said, 'I thought you were dead. Isn't that awful?'

'Disgraceful,' Mike said solemnly. 'You should be ashamed to tell me such a thing. I'm hurt.'

'Oh, I'm *sorry!*' Alvin said. 'Here, let me buy you a drink. I'm so glad to meet you.'

Mike gestured to the bartender for a round of drinks. Caroline could see that he was a well-known customer here. She wondered when he would start the round of Third Avenue saloons Mary Agnes had talked about; after midnight, probably.

'Are you two old friends?' Mike asked.

'We just met tonight,' Caroline said. 'On a blind date.' She looked at him significantly.

'Wasn't that lucky?' Alvin said happily. He swallowed his drink, said thickly, ''Scuse me,' with a beatific smile, and lurched off in the direction of the men's room, bumping into a couple on the way.

'Oh, I can't stand it,' Caroline said, 'I can't stand it.' Despite her embarrassment she was so relieved to see Mike, he seemed like such a sane and welcome face, that she began to laugh.

'What are these blind dates?' he asked curiously.

'An old American institution of mismating. Haven't you ever been on one?'

'No,' he said with relief. 'I married when I was eighteen. Besides, no one I knew cared whether I had a social life or not. This barbaric custom of yours must be typically Port Blair.'

'It isn't at all.'

'How are you going to get away from him? Will you be all right?'

'It's all my fault,' she said. 'I made him take that first step on the lonesome road with Demon Rum. How was I supposed to know he was Doctor Jekyll and Mr Hyde? I really feel responsible for him now. I think I should get him safely on the train.'

'He's supposed to take care of *you*. If he can't, then ditch him.'

'That's kind of inconsiderate.'

'Oh? And was it considerate of him to take you out and act the way he's doing?'

'I guess he can't help it. He has such an inferiority complex and I think I scared him.'

He smiled at her, this time a smile that reached the rest of his face. It made him seem like someone she did not know. 'You always make excuses for everyone, don't you?' he said.

She wasn't sure whether he meant it as a compliment or just the opposite. 'That's not such a bad thing, is it?' she asked.

'It's bad for you.'

'Why?'

'If you insist on liking the wrong person, don't tell yourself fairy tales that he's this or he's that. That he's pathetic, that he needs your help, that you put him on his worst behavior . . . Just admit you like the wrong person, but don't give yourself the wrong reasons.'

She looked up and saw Alvin's white face in the distance as he made his way toward them through the darkened room. She realized that she had already forgotten what he looked like. 'I like that,' she said. 'But it certainly doesn't apply to me and Alvin. He's just someone who came into my life by accident and he's going right out again after tonight.'

'I don't necessarily mean it for you and him,' Mike said. 'I mean it for you and anyone. It might be someone you'd *get* to care about. Someone a lot closer to home.'

He was looking at her intently as he said it, and suddenly she felt, for an instant, a cold shiver pass through her. It wasn't the chill of foreboding, but rather of excitement, of the unknown, of that same unreality-coming-true feeling she'd had when he had told her Mr Shalimar was afraid of her.

'Who?' she said. 'Who?'

'It's a good thing I'm not as drunk as Alvin,' Mike said, 'or I might tell you and make a fool of myself.'

She sat there looking at him in surprise for a moment until Alvin came and jovially wedged himself in between them. But she had something to take to herself and think about, and it was enough. She felt astonished and warmed by her own feelings. Really, what had he said? Nothing. And yet, it could be a great deal.

All the way home on the train, sitting next to Alvin and pretending to look out the window, she found herself thinking about Mike. She let the thought of him enter her mind and stay there, uncautiously. He was nearly twice her age, he was used and bitter. As with any dissipated person there were many things in his past life that she was sure would arouse her sympathy – a disappointment, a heart-break, a failure – events and misfortunes that might not deserve that sympathy but which would be sure to receive it from a girl like herself to whom they would all be new and shocking and therefore poignant. That was what he was trying to warn her against, she was sure. And because he cared enough to warn her against him she found herself totally disarmed. He must care about her in some way that was more than friendship, she was thinking, or he would never have said anything. The possibility of a romance between herself and Mike was the strangest thing that had ever happened to her, and yet it was beginning to seem the most natural thing in the world.

She could not help but compare Mike and his sophisticated understanding of her secret thoughts with the succession of dreary boys she had been out with since she had been graduated from college. With each of those boys it seemed as if there was a barrier, hurled up because she was a woman and he was a man and each wanted something from the other. It was a kind of juvenile competition. With Mike, it was as if *because* he was a man and she was a woman each had something to give to the other. She wasn't afraid of him. To her, something dangerous meant being hurt. She didn't believe there could be any other kind of danger in becoming involved with him. The hazards of a changing outlook, of a mind that could become as old as his, seemed very far away.

5

Gregg Adams, in the shower, looked a great deal better than she sang; nevertheless she was happy (for her, which is to say tonight she had a general absence of depression) and so she sang and splashed, hurriedly so that she could wash all the soap off before the day's supply of hot water disappeared. A tune was going through her head, some old thing from her mother's flapper days. 'Life is Just a Bowl of Cherries'. 'Life is just a boll of weevils,' she sang to that tune. 'Da dee da da da . . . Life is just a boll of weevils, da dee da dum.' She had managed to get twelve lines in a morning soap opera for next week, with promise of more in the future. As usual she was playing a teen-ager, baby-voiced and excruciatingly sweet. That slight Western accent she hadn't been able to get rid of didn't hurt either. She had noticed that all the nauseatingly sweet little children who did commercials – 'Gee, Mom, this tastes like more!' – seemed to have a Western accent. Perhaps some executive power thought it made them sound more childlike.

She was going to a party tonight with Tony, who was in her acting class and was one of her semi-platonic friends. They lent each other money and took each other to parties where free food and liquor could be had for a minimum of charm. He was younger than she and had long hair that fell into his eyes when he shook his head, and he mumbled when he spoke. If you asked him a question he would wriggle and scratch himself and look at the floor as if he were feeling out the line, and finally he would grunt some extraordinarily emotional result like: 'Yeah, let's go to the movies.' She knew it was an act, that when he was very excited or overwrought he lapsed into the most beautifully modulated Shakespearean diction she had ever heard. All the boys in her acting class were like that, the ones who took her out and the ones who were married and even poorer and the fairies. She was bored with them all.

In her messy, overcrowded closet she found a red dress she had liked and had forgotten she owned. It was a meeting-people dress for parties; a blonde girl in a red dress always seemed to be able to manage without introductions. It wasn't as if she hoped to meet anyone non-boring at this party, actually she was only going there because there would be food and good Scotch and it would be a way not to be alone. When she was alone in her apartment she could feel the stifling sensation she had learned to fear creep up on her; one minute things were all right and then all of a sudden a ten-pound weight would establish itself on her chest and she would hardly be able to breathe, let alone swallow. Jazz music on the phonograph and cheap vermouth helped a little, telephone conversations with her friends by the hour helped even more, but all of these were merely sedatives to dull the panic and lift the weight, they could not remove it. Around the circle of light by her bed there were shadows waiting to envelop her as soon as she put down the telephone receiver and broke away from the reassuring voice at the other end.

Sometimes her cat would slip up to her and rub his furry head against her ankle, and, looking down at him, she would feel an immense, overwhelming affection for him. My little cat. Pencil-line ribs to move with breathing as he slept, signs of life to remind her that there were other worlds inside of other people's skulls, even inside a cat's little skull. It made her feel less alone, less stifled, less afraid of something she could not really name. You could die in New York behind the locked door of your apartment and no one would ever know until some neighbor complained of the smell. Yes, your friends would say then, I remember I hadn't heard from her for some time, but I thought she was just sulking. Or I thought she had a new job and was busy. Busy? Ha, Gregg thought, busy being unemployed.

Tony was an hour late, which was like him. When he finally

arrived she was so lonely she was even glad to see him. 'Hey,' he said, 'I remember that dress.' He leaned down and kissed her on the cheek.

She remembered then with embarrassment that she had worn the dress on the evening of the first and only night she had gone to bed with him. No doubt he thought of the dress with sentiment. No wonder she had forced it to the far end of her untidy closet. It was a night and a dress she wanted to forget. There were some lovers you could have once, and only once, and then you never wanted to have them again. Not that they weren't skillful and considerate, because they usually were. But they had held each other out of loneliness and fear and curiosity and lust and hope that this time they would find something beautiful. And in the morning they would find sheets that looked like a geographical terrain, and perhaps an overturned ash tray on the rug beside the bed, and no trace whatever of the face of love.

'Come on,' she said, taking his hand. 'They'll eat everything before we even get there.'

The party was at the apartment of a middle-aged actress whom Tony knew. The room was dark and already filled with smoke and people, as if they were leftover observers from a fire. Gregg coughed and moved with the clockwise motion of the crowd to the window end of the room, hoping she would find the bar there. With an icy glass in her hand she felt better. Tony put a lighted cigarette into her other hand; now she had the props and the play could begin. A play called *Isn't This Fun?*

'See those three men over there,' he whispered. 'See the tall young one? You know who he is?' Tony must have been excited, he had said three complete sentences one right after the other.

'Who?'

'David Wilder Savage.'

David Wilder Savage had been one of the first people she had heard of when she had come to New York. It was an eccentric name, and he suited it. Most people thought it was a pseudonym, taken so that he would be remembered. For whatever reason, it had worked. Nobody ever referred to him as Savage, they went through the whole routine. He had been one of the boy wonders of Broadway, producing his first play at twenty-five, a hit which had run for nearly two years. Every play he produced after that was a success, until the one he had done at the beginning of this season, which had closed in four weeks. The magic name David Wilder Savage had been the only thing to hold it on Broadway that long.

The play itself had little theatrical excitement. Thoughtful, fragile and of limited appeal, it had been written by a man who was one of the few people David Wilder Savage had ever been close to. Like many men who cut a heartless swath through the worlds of business and of bedrooms, David Wilder Savage had one friend whom he cared for deeply and whom he protected. They had been roommates in college, the author and the producer, and in the fourteen years since their graduation the author had been working on this one play while holding various jobs to make a living. That fact alone would have warned away nearly any would-be producer. It would have warned away David Wilder Savage before anyone else, because if anyone had an instinct for success and failure it was he. But this closest friend had been killed in an automobile crash in the spring, and in the fall David Wilder Savage, against the advice of anyone who dared to give it to him, put the play on Broadway. It was not because he was confused by his bereavement. He knew exactly what he was doing. It was one of the rare gestures of sentimentality – and even more, of love – from a man who was known for his ruthlessness. It was ironic that his one act from the heart should turn out to be a debacle, but not unusual, since David Wilder Savage himself would be the first to say that if a con man ever tried to save a child from drowning in a moment of pure goodness he would be sure to be eaten by a shark.

'Do you know him?' Gregg whispered back.

'I read for him once. He probably doesn't remember me.'

'Do I dare go over and talk to him?'

'Why not? It's a party,' Tony said without much enthusiasm. 'Come with me.'

He kissed her lightly on the temple, his cheek bulging out with an hors d'oeuvre he had just gobbled. 'What for? Pretty girls have much better luck alone.'

She was relieved that he didn't want to accompany her, but when she had worked her way through the crowd to where David Wilder Savage now stood by himself she was taken with panic. What could she say to him? Hello, I'm an actress. She might as well hold her hand out and ask for a dime for a cup of coffee. It would be greeted by the same enthusiasm.

What an attractive man he was! Satanic, that was the word for him. Thirty-five years old and on top of the world, with that knowing, civilized face looking down at all the ambitious people like herself who were sidling up trying to think of clever things to say to him. She looked down at her glass, wishing she could find a place to get rid of it.

'Who the hell are you?' he said pleasantly.

She looked up at him, surprised. 'Gregg Adams.'

'I'm David Wilder Savage. And as they always say at cocktail parties, what do you do?'

'I'm a dental assistant.'

He smiled. 'That's a surprise. You look like a parolee from boarding school.'

'I was once. And very sophisticated, too. Black lipstick and all.'

'Have you read a book called *Many Faces*?'

She had heard of it, the author was a Portuguese. 'I read the reviews.'

'That's not much help.'

'You'd be surprised,' she said, 'how well I can discuss a book from the reviews.'

'And a movie from the cast listing on the marquee?'

'That's right.' There was an American couple talking French at her elbow. She nodded toward them. 'And with people like that, I can say, I really understand your French perfectly, but I can't speak it back to you because my *accent* is unintelligible.'

'I'm sorry you haven't read *Many Faces*,' he said. 'I would have liked to know if it did something to you too, and what. I'm a producer, and I think there may be a good play in it.'

He had a way about him, something in the intimate lowering of his voice, that made her feel as if she and her opinions were very important to him. Actually, why should he care what she – a working girl he'd met at a party – thought of a book? Because he thought she was the average public, of course, a girl who came to Manhattan every day on the subway from Queens with her tunafish sandwich in a brown paper bag, who lived with her parents, and washed her hair every Thursday night and went to the movies with her boy friend every Saturday night. And yet, he had that way about him . . .

'I'll read it tomorrow,' she said. 'It'll be too late to tell you what I think, but now I want to read it anyway.'

'You'll love it.'

Anyone else, she was thinking, could say 'You'll love it' and it would be small talk, a mere figure of speech. With David Wilder Savage the sentence was like handing someone a gift. It was as if he wanted to give her the bit of pleasure of discovering a new idea, a magical story. Charm, she thought. Charm was just a word before, but now I know what it is. It's anything this man says.

He touched her arm. 'See that couple over there? They've come to the wrong party. There's another one in the apartment downstairs, and that's where they were supposed to go. Now he wants to leave and she says she's having a good time and wants to stay. They're having a fight.'

They were a young couple, a pouting bosomy girl in a white dress and a weak-looking man. 'Look at the gestures and angry faces,' Gregg said, laughing. 'They look like a TV set with the sound turned off.'

'Did you ever do that? Turn the sound off? Especially on a commercial? It's like an old silent movie.'

'I know. I've been doing it for years.'

'Look,' he said, amused. 'He's leaving and she's going to stay.'

'And without even so much as a glass in her hand.'

Gregg had expected to be afraid of David Wilder Savage and was surprised that she was not at all. She felt instead as if he and she standing here together laughing and observing the others were something special, the 'in group,' and everyone outside of the two of them were the 'out group.'

'Where did you get that diction?' he asked her.

'In speech class.'

'You want to be an actress.'

'I am an actress. One might say.'

'Not a dental assistant.'

She laughed. 'No, I'm really an actress. I just didn't want to waltz up and tell you because it would have sounded so damned clubby.'

'Like someone coming up to you at a cocktail party and saying, We have something in common – as if that's supposed to make you like him.'

'Exactly,' she said. 'Exactly!'

'Are you here with someone?'

Tony would understand, she thought, he'd do the same thing himself if he could. 'No,' she said. 'No, I'm not.'

'Not the dentist?'

'No one.'

'This is a very boring party, don't you think?'

She looked up at him. 'Not right in this corner.'

He took her arm. 'Let's take the corner with us.'

'I'll get my coat.' She slipped off to the hostess' bedroom to retrieve her coat, looking for Tony out of the corner of her eye but hoping that she would not be able to find him. She paused for an instant at the mirror, looking at her face. How dark her eyes were, and how much they revealed, even to herself. She had noticed another quality to David Wilder Savage, something just under the surface – a kind of hidden cruelty. It was as if he were basically a ruthless person but had a tender side that he would show only to the one person he cared about. His charm told her that the person could be her, and her sense told her it was a lie, a trap, one that few girls could be cautious enough to resist putting to a test. She pulled her coat on and lifted her long hair out of the collar. She was a near stranger to him and he to her, but she had seen the challenging combination of cruelty and tenderness. She saw it all in an instant, as a drowning person sees his life pass before his eyes, and then she plunged out of the safe room to where he was waiting for her in the hall.

It was odd – ordinarily she would have been impressed and delighted by the wave of recognition that went around the room when he took her into the restaurant for dinner. She liked walking into a room with someone who was known, it gave her confidence. And at the back of her mind was always the hope that she would be introduced to or discovered by someone who could help her in her career. But with David she found herself resenting the table hoppers who took his time, the greeters who demanded his attention. Everything he said to her seemed important, and every time he turned away to speak to someone else, she felt as if she had left the safe 'in group' for a moment and she remembered who she was and how alone she would be again in an hour or two.

When they had finished dinner it was after midnight. The diners had left the restaurant and the drinkers had appeared. 'Come uptown to my house,' he said.

Knowing herself, she tried to think of any inane remark to play for time. 'Why?'

He looked at her perfectly calmly, as if it were not an inane remark at all, and said, 'Because I want to make love to you.'

'I . . . don't want to,' she stammered.

'All right,' he said. He helped her with her coat and they went out to the street, where he hailed a taxi. 'Where do you live?'

She told him, and shrank into her corner of the taxi in a state of growing depression as the streets slipped by. He was taking her home and she didn't want to go home. Like a child, she was afraid of the dark and loneliness, and, like a child, she reached out and tugged at his sleeve. He took her hand. She knew she would never see him again and she couldn't bear it. He was something strange and exciting that had come into her life, only for one evening – really just a few hours. And what was she to him? Someone he'd had fun with, whom he might remember if her name were ever mentioned to him again. 'I don't want to go home,' she said.

'Where do you want to go, then?'

'I don't care. I just can't stand to give you up.'

He didn't seem to think it was a frantic or silly thing to say; he simply leaned forward and gave the driver his address, and then moved back and put his arm around Gregg, comfortingly, with none of the appurtenances of passion. She felt suddenly as if what she had just said to him was somehow romantic and important.

She had never seen an apartment like his before. She had always felt that you could tell more from one look at a person's apartment than you could from an hour of talk with him. There were the people who didn't care about their homes at all, and there were those who cared but had nothing to add to them. David's apartment must have contained over a thousand books. Books were in the tall bookshelves that lined an entire wall of the living room, and they spilled over to every chair in the room. On the round dining table were at least a dozen playscripts. On the floor beside the table was a large straw basket filled with magazines. He took off her coat, and with the coat still in his hand walked to the phonograph and turned it on. She noticed his records then – long-playing records, four feet of them from end to end.

At the far end of the room, between the bookshelves, was an old-fashioned fireplace with a carved black marble mantelpiece. It was a much used fireplace, with a fire screen and blackened fire tools, and logs waiting to be burned among the coals. He put her coat into his closet and knelt down to light the fire. In front of the fireplace was a long black sofa. She could imagine him sitting there in the dark staring into the flames, and it made him seem more satanic-looking than ever.

'Would you like brandy?'

'Yes, please.'

He brought a bottle of brandy and two glasses to the low coffee table in front of the sofa, and sat beside her. The music on the phonograph was a classical piece that she had never heard before, and he had it turned up loud, as if he really enjoyed hearing it, not as if it were background music to a seduction.

'Have you really read all those books?' she asked, gesturing.

'Yes.'

'And those magazines? And those scripts?'

'Yes. I'm always looking for something.'

On one of the side tables beside an armchair there were no books at all. Instead there was a large silver-framed photograph of two men on a sailboat in summer, smiling and squinting into the sun, wearing white trousers and white sweatshirts and standing with their arms loosely flung around each other. She stood and wandered over to it. One of the men was David, many years younger, with a softer, vaguer face, and the other was a rather handsome, sensitive-looking young man with the build of a large tennis player.

'Who's that?'

'Gordon McKay.'

'Oh . . .' she said. 'The one whose play you just put on.'

'That's right.' His voice seemed to have tightened, as if he were very conscious of the way it sounded in the room.

She didn't know what to say. She couldn't say, 'I'm sorry about your friend's death,' or 'I'm sorry about your friend's flop' either; somehow she felt that if she said anything like that it would destroy instantly the intimacy she and David were feeling together at this moment.

'I'm sorry I never got to see the play,' she said finally.

'More brandy?' he asked, and filled her glass without waiting for a reply.

She remembered something Tony had told her once about David Wilder Savage and Gordon McKay, some spiteful thing, the sort of thing unsuccessful people often say about successful ones, a kind of name-dropping gone one step further to become insult-dropping. What was it he'd said? Oh, yes – 'No one knows for *sure* whether they were in love with each other. But now we'll see if he can ever put on another hit or if the light has gone out for him.' That was the worst thing she had ever heard said about David Wilder Savage; most of the kids at the class discussed instead his theatrical genius and his reputation as a wolf. Why did people have to say that two men were in love with each other when they merely loved each other? Couldn't people realize what a rare and miraculous thing closeness could be, without trying to dirty it? She felt suddenly that the world was full of cruel and silly people like Tony and her family and a long, long string of girls she had gone to school with and boys who had pawed her – all of them separate and lonely and spiteful and afraid to love each other.

Like a sleepwalker she went to the sofa where David was sitting motionless. The room was dark and the redness of the flames shone on the fabric of the couch and made it look black and red both, and on the glass of brandy on the table, making it shine like a garnet. She touched his face.

He did not pull her down to the couch but stood up in one swift gesture, put his arms around her and took her to the couch with him. She felt a touch of surprise at his first kiss, as she always did with anyone's, because the shape of the mouth never seemed to be related to the feeling of the kiss it gave. With his she felt astonishment that a cruel mouth could be capable of such warmth and gentleness.

'You have the softest mouth in the history of the world,' he murmured.

'And you too.'

He was taking off her dress and slip and stockings without ever removing his lips from her mouth and face, as if his hands were an efficient, unobtrusive part of him and his love-making. She had an instant flash of her old caution at this, thinking, Oh, how practiced! He must have made love to hundreds of women . . . And then his hands were no longer disembodied and she was glad for the experience they had, as if it had all been waiting for her. The one fear hit her then, of pregnancy and disgrace, and she hated her own passion-thickened, fearful little-girl's voice which had to ask that damned question that hurtled her out of the clouds.

'Do you have something?'

'Don't you?'

'I didn't know . . .'

'All right . . .' For the moment that he was gone from her she closed her eyes, shaken with dizziness, and then he returned and took her into his arms. She felt the coolness of his skin and the warmth of the firelight as if it were all in a dream filled with pleasure that was like pain and the old, old words of demand and obscenity that seemed like words of love in his mouth. He spoke them to her and she spoke them back to him, both of them urgently, both of them with their eyes open searching each other's faces, trembling, until the last moment when passion separated them.

He did not draw away when he was finished, or let her go, but kept his arms around her, looking again into her face. The music on the phonograph had long since played out and the room was silent except for the clicking of the needle against the last groove, forgotten and alone. She held him in her arms as if he were the child this time and she a woman, and stroked his hair, wishing they could stay that way forever. Finally he drew away.

'This damned thing,' he said, amused and annoyed. 'I haven't used one of these things since I was sixteen years old.'

'You're speaking of the sixteenth of an inch between me and the Home for Unwed Mothers.'

'Well, next time you contribute.'

'Well, what did you expect? Do you think I go to every cocktail party prepared for something like this?'

'Are we having our first fight?'

From the shadows behind them the telephone rang, softly. She looked at her watch. 'My gosh! They call at two o'clock in the morning?'

He stood up. 'Drink your brandy,' he said affectionately, ruffling her hair, and went to answer the phone.

Left by herself, she smiled into the fire, feeling the hot bitterness of the brandy in her throat and the faint scratchiness of the couch fabric against her bare legs. She could hear David laughing at something the person on the telephone was saying, and his occasional exclamations of amusement. She finished her brandy and stood up languidly, groggy with the aftermath of love and the kind darkness of the heated room, and went to the phonograph. She lifted the needle and turned the record over, tuning it down very softly so it would not disturb David on the telephone. There was an overflowing ash tray on the window sill and she picked it up and took it to the kitchen to empty it. She could still hear his voice on the telephone, masculine and laughing and independent, and she remembered the way it had sounded speaking to her in the words of love-making. The sound of his voice then had been for her and her alone. She could not remember ever having felt so content.

She wondered whether the window in his kitchen was uncurtained because he did not own a curtain or because it was at the laundry. He probably didn't own one; a bachelor as busy as he wouldn't even know about those things. Wouldn't it surprise him if she made curtains for him! She could pick out some fabric tomorrow . . .

Back in the living room she watched the fire slowly dying and the brandy level going down in the bottle as David talked on and on to whomever it was on the other end of the telephone. She could tell it was a business call from the conversation, and she was not surprised because people in the theater had a way of staying up until all hours. Her wristwatch said twenty-five past two. It gave her a kind of glow to know that she was here with him, in intimacy, waiting for him in the shadows.

'All right, boy,' he said. 'Goodbye. Thanks for calling. Everything's going to be all right.' He replaced the receiver and returned to stand beside where Gregg was sitting on the couch. She looked up at him.

'I think I love you,' she said.

He smiled at her tenderly and bent down to kiss her forehead.

'I *do* love you,' she said.

He took her into his arms again.

6

Barbara Lemont, leaving the Fabian offices at five o'clock, paused for a minute in the dark outside the revolving door and let the shrill crowd of girls pour past her into the night, going to their buses and subways and trains. It was an evening late in February, and surprisingly the air was soft with false spring. The store windows around Rockefeller Plaza were very bright, and Barbara walked slowly past them, dallying, looking in, imagining that some rich man was going to give her any of their contents she might choose as a gift. Here it was February, and this afternoon she had been typing copy for the June issue of *America's Woman*, the bridal issue. All the brides in the photographs looked so young, so airy, you found yourself wondering what their lives had been like and whom they were in love with and going to marry, forgetting that they were only models. The blonde one on the cover with daisies in her hair and a look in her eyes like a child on Christmas morning had just been separated from her husband and had upset the shooting schedule the week before the picture was taken because she was in bed recovering from the results of an abortion. Perhaps that look she wore on her face for the bridal cover was a facsimile of the one she had worn on her own wedding day, and even though things had turned sour for her she remembered when they were different. Like me, Barbara thought.

She had awakened very slowly this morning, with a sense of something she didn't want to remember, and had burrowed underneath the covers like an animal in its cozy lair, until her crib-trapped daughter's screams forced her out of bed. Then she had remembered, and in the remembering had realized that it was not such a dreadful thing after all. Today would have been her wedding anniversary.

Three years – a record, really, for someone as young as she was. Most of the girls she knew at work hadn't ever been married, much less married three years. The married girls were the ones she didn't see often any more, friends of her high-school days. She and those old friends called each other on the phone now and then since her divorce, and sometimes the wives would say, 'When you have a date why don't you bring him over one evening,' and she would thank them and never do it. You couldn't take a boy to spend an evening with a young married couple, she had discovered; it would frighten him away. He would feel the trap closing in, even though it was an imaginary one, and he would think she wanted to demonstrate to him the contentment of marriage. She fitted into the married-couple conversation so well, she was so used to it, that sometimes in the midst of a discussion of recipes or household problems (I *know*, men are *terrible* about holes in socks) she would look up and catch her date looking at her with an expression that could range anywhere from boredom to panic.

She stopped at a bakery on Sixth Avenue to buy some honey buns for her mother. On the spur of the moment she bought some animal-shaped cookies for the baby. She would try to teach Hillary how to say *rabbit* when she ate the cooky, it would probably leave a more lasting impression on her than a picture of a rabbit in a book. She had been thinking for a while now of changing the baby's name, perhaps to a nickname that the baby could eventually use as her Christian name when she went to school. Barbara had named her Hillary after her husband's mother, who was dead, and at the time it had seemed a gesture of love. She had never seen his mother, and now she almost never saw him, and the name Hillary had turned into an encumbrance that she wasn't particularly fond of, reminding her of people and a time that had lost their meaning. She was only glad that the baby hadn't been a boy because she would have named him after his father, and *that* would have turned into a nuisance.

It was funny, she was thinking, how something that had seemed sentimental and important, and even more – almost sacred – could turn into nothing at all. If it had ever occurred to her in the beginning that all her love for this one man and everything they had together that was meaningful was going to disappear and be forgotten the thought would have broken her heart. Today she was grateful for the flexibility that had allowed her to forget. Mac had been her first date in high school – her first real date, that is, aside from her classmates who invited her to parties. She was sixteen and he was twenty. She was a little thrilled at his old age, but when they had spent one evening together she felt as if she had known him forever. It was love, like in the juke-box songs and the magazine stories and the pajama-party gab fests, with birds twittering and pink clouds and no sense at all. She wasn't a very pretty girl, her features were ordinary, but she was appealing-looking, and when she was in love she felt as if there must be something special about her looks to have won her such a prize as Mac. He was the best-looking boy she had ever seen, and the difference in their ages made her give him credit for more intelligence than he really had. He had just returned from the Army in Germany, and next to her classmates he seemed an experienced world traveler. On their third date he proposed, and although they kept it a secret from their parents they considered themselves engaged from that night on.

Being engaged, especially secretly engaged, was a strange, exciting state with little touch on reality. Barbara went about her daily routine, study, gym class, homework, sodas with the girls, feeling as if she were in a dream. She was Engaged to Be Married, she was In Love. She was floating thirty feet above the ground and she never stopped to find out what she really felt about things. As soon as she graduated from high school she and Mac announced their engagement, and in February they were married and left New York for Ohio State University, where he was finishing college on the GI Bill. She kept house for him there, or kept their room, rather, because it was a dingy little one-room apartment with a convertible sofa and a rickety bridge table that almost always had books and papers and the remains of the previous meal on it. They had only one closet, and the clothes popped out like a jack-in-the-box every time someone opened the door. She was taking courses at a nearby women's college and trying to keep up with her school-work and keep a home together all at the same time. When she began to be nauseated in the mornings, and often in the afternoons as well, she thought it was because she was still such an inexperi-enced cook. Mac himself had heartburn most of the time those first three months. Then she discovered that her problem wasn't indigestion at all but something she should have suspected right away.

At first she couldn't believe it. It was not that there was anything organically wrong with her, but she simply couldn't believe that she, Barbara Lemont, was capable of doing something as compli-cated and adult as conceiving a baby. She was going to produce another human being, someone who would eventually go to college and fall in love and get married just as she had done. It was unbelievable. She who had never even owned a dog was going to be responsible for a human being for at least the next fifteen years. Her disbelief turned to belief and then to fright.

She began to look fat and ungainly. She was a plain girl, but her charm was in her neatness and warmth and in a kind of piquancy. How could anyone who looked like a fat spider look piquant? She was ashamed to go to classes, feeling somehow that a girl of eight-een ought to look like those other sweatered and skirted freshmen and not like a bloated, heavy-footed matron.

The required reading for her courses, which she did faithfully, seemed both an escape and a reminder. She would be lost in the world of a novel by Thomas Mann and then look up at the sound of a group of college boys and girls laughing and tramping past her window. The apartment was on the first floor, across the street from the campus of Mac's college. The voices outside her window were discussing the class they had just attended, in heated argu-ment that bore just the faintest undercurrent of flirtation and courtship. 'Let's have a cup of coffee,' she would hear one of the boys say. 'Do you have time?' And a girl's voice would answer, 'That would be wonderful.' Her mood broken, Barbara would look around the room and notice the dust under the sofa bed, the dishes still to be washed, Mac's clothes tossed on the floor to be sent to the laundry or put away. She would get up, heavily and feeling sickish again, and put away her book. As soon as she finished cleaning the apartment she would have to mess it up again preparing dinner – it was funny how a one-room apartment looked so dirty if you displaced one or two little things in it. It would be dark outside her window then, and waiting for Mac to come home, she would realize that she missed him terribly, because he was all she had.

Neither of them quite knew what was happening to them and to their marriage, or how to prevent it. Mac believed in live and let live, and although it must have occurred to him many times to try to find out why Barbara was melancholy, he never asked. On weekends he took her to beer parties at the rooms of his college friends, and sometimes during the week he would take her to the campus beer house where the students raced up and down the aisles greeting their friends and crowded six at a time into narrow booths meant for four. The smell of the spilled beer and the half-put-out cigarettes made her feel ill. The girls who were out on dates with Mac's friends all looked so slim and carefree they made her feel twice as self-conscious as before. If she could have had one good thing: a ride in the country on a fresh day, a cleaning woman to clean up their tiny room once and for all, a new dress that was becoming, a close girl friend to confide in, everything would have been all right. Neither her mother nor Mac's father had enough money to send anything more than rent, and even that was not easy for them. Barbara had been putting off writing her mother about the baby.

After a while when Barbara said she didn't feel like going to the beer house Mac started going there alone. It was seldom enough that he had a chance to get out, what with studying and then the part-time job he had found as a busboy in the college cafeteria during the summer school. The job was to save money for the hospital bills and the expenses that would come afterward. They needed a larger apartment. As for Barbara, she didn't feel any more as if she were carrying a baby, she felt as if it were a tremendous growth, a tumor, and she wanted nothing so much as to go to the hospital at the end of the nine months and have it leave her body. Even love-making was no longer fun, or even an escape. You had to care about your own body to want to give it to someone you loved, and when you felt that you were an ugly stranger how could the giving of such a body be anything but embarrassing?

Then Barbara went to the hospital to have the baby, and overnight everything changed. One night she was in pain, screaming and wishing she were home with her mother again, and in the morning she felt for the first time that she was an adult. The first thing she saw when she awoke was her own flat stomach, her sense of identity restored. She was Barbara, of course, how could she have forgotten? The next thing she saw was her baby's round fuzzy head and its tiny body, so delicate to the touch, a sack of soft white clothing with little limbs wrapped inside.

She hadn't had the faintest idea how much she would love her baby until she touched her with her own hands. *This* was worth it, *this* was worth everything. How could she have been so childish, so ignorant, not to have realized how much love she had stored up in her own heart? Love came pouring out like an aura in the room, bringing tears to her eyes. She loved the baby, she loved Mac; how much she loved him! She had been ignoring him all these months, poor angel, and he hadn't complained or argued with her, ever. She would make it all up to him, she would make him happy. They would have a real home.

She came back from the hospital into a two-room apartment Mac had found. Barbara worked as hard as she had ever worked in her life, thoughts of further education forgotten. She cleaned the house and made the baby's formula and took all Mac's clothes to the cleaner's. She polished her nails and went on a diet and read the women's magazines to find new recipes that didn't cost much that Mac might like. At Christmas they went home for the first time, bringing Hillary. They stayed with Mac's father, and Barbara and Mac and the baby slept in Mac's old room among the framed pictures of his high-school graduating class, his track medals and his old forgotten albums of stamps. Perhaps it was the strangeness of the three of them brought together in this room that was so filled with memories of the past, or perhaps Barbara had changed her attitude too late; or perhaps it was simply that their life and their responsibilities were too much for them to understand, and love was too fragile to make up the difference . . .

'Look, Barb,' Mac said, running his tongue along his lower lip, snapping the blade of his jackknife in and out of its holder. He had found the old knife in his night-table drawer the day before. 'Look, Barb, I don't know how to say it.'

'Say what, angel?'

'Don't call me angel! It makes me feel worse.'

'Why?'

He stood up and began to pace the room, angrily, putting his feet down with every step as if he were trying to destroy something painful that had been written on sand. 'I'm not going back to Ohio.'

'Well, all right, darling. I don't care. We can leave Hillary with my mother and go back there to get all our clothes and the wedding presents. Most of the rest is junk, so we can sell it to somebody.'

'I don't mean that.'

'Well, what, then?'

He was flicking the knife blade against his thumb and it frightened her. She was afraid he might cut himself. His mouth twitched a little and he took a deep breath. 'I mean I'm not . . .' He hesitated and then plunged on, enunciating very clearly. 'I don't want to go back to Ohio and I don't want to stay here with you either. I don't think you and I should see each other for a while.'

'What? But we're *married!*'

'I don't want to be married.' Suddenly he was shouting, his face contorted with fear and guilt. 'I don't want to be married! We should never have gotten married in the first place! I'm sorry, I'm sorry . . .'

They both stared at each other in silence, realizing at last that the words had been said, and that they had been true for a long long time before they had ever been spoken.

'I'm sorry,' he said again, softly.

'Please don't leave me,' Barbara said.

'I'm doing you a favor.'

She hadn't meant to cry, but she was crying hysterically, the tears rolling down her face, her hands stiffly at her sides, not uplifted to hide her emotion. 'Don't leave me,' she wept. 'Don't leave me! I love you.' And all the time she was sobbing and crying out to him, at the back of her mind she knew she would be relieved when he was gone.

'Oh, baby.' He put his arms around her, he patted her hair.

'I love you,' she said again.

'Oh, God.'

'It's just that we both hate Ohio and that apartment,' she said, the words coming out calmer now. 'We'll come back to New York, you can find a good job, we'll have money. You can finish your credits at NYU.'

'Don't you understand?' he said.

'No, I don't. We're married. We have a child. Even if you don't love *me* any more . . .'

He was standing with his back to her now, counting out money and putting it on the table. His voice when he spoke was emotionless. 'I do love you, Barb. I don't know what's wrong with me. Maybe I should see a psychiatrist. Maybe I should never have married anyone in the first place. Maybe you shouldn't have. Or maybe we should never have married each other.'

He walked past her quickly, avoiding her hand that she stretched out to touch him. 'I'll send you money,' he said, and was gone.

The next day Barbara and Hillary moved downtown to her mother's house. She didn't know where to reach Mac, and the waiting was a nightmare for two weeks or so. Then it broke, like a fever. She felt strangely relieved and began to wonder what would happen to her now.

The next time she saw him was with the lawyer when they got the divorce, and Mac could hardly look at her. Once he looked up, as if he were seeing her for the first time, and said, 'You look beautiful. I never saw that dress.'

'Thank you,' she said politely, as if he were a stranger.

'Beautiful,' he said.

Those were the last words they spoke to each other as husband and wife. She was remembering them now, as she often did, as she walked down the last street toward the apartment she shared with her mother and the baby. Yes, she was thinking, I should change the baby's name. Perhaps Barbara would be nice, or I could even name her after my own mother. Who am I kidding? she thought, and unexpectedly her throat closed with pain. I'll never change the baby's name, or anything about her. She's the only thing I have left of him. It's too late . . . All the time I was thinking of myself and feeling confused and weighted down, it never occurred to me that Mac might be feeling the same way. Neither of us understood ourselves or the other person. How could we ever have gotten married? It's like holding hands and jumping off the top of a building; did we think it was going to be any easier because we were holding hands? And now it's too late . . .

Neither of them had remarried yet, but neither wanted to see the other again. They met once a month when Mac came to see Hillary. They would talk about the baby until they could think of nothing else to say about her, and then they would make small talk, and then he would leave. Whenever he had just left Barbara would miss him, and yet she knew it was not Mac himself that she felt the loss of. It was something else, something intangible. A different life, a happiness they had had only for such a short time, a second chance neither of them wanted to take, a childhood that had turned abruptly into womanhood without the time in between, a time-in-between that had been restored to her now that she was too changed and serious.

As she walked up the stairs to her apartment Barbara began to feel trapped. She called her apartment 'The House of Women' because it so conspicuously lacked a man's touch anywhere. Her mother, a widow. Herself, divorced. Hillary, well, it *would* be a little girl, just to round out the sewing circle. And as for the neighbors, well . . . there were the two middle-aged men who lived together in a one-and-a-half down the hall and looked more like nice old ladies than men. In fact, one of her dates had said once that they probably live in the one-and-a-half because it made it easier for them to chase each other. And there was the strange, studious young man who lived next door with his crippled mother. Once Barbara had been alone with him in the elevator and he had stared at her with such animosity that it frightened her. And then there was April Morrison. At least April was normal, and what a relief it was to hear her reassuring Colorado twang and her amusing little *faux pas* that threw her into confusion when she realized what she had said or done. And as for herself, she was on her way to another evening in front of the television set waiting for it to be late enough to go to bed. And she had thought marriage was boring!

The blare of the television set greeted her through the thin front door of her apartment. Barbara let herself in with her key and put her packages on the dinette table. Her mother was sitting in front of the television set in an armchair, dressed in a long quilted bathrobe. She watched television all day long, often not leaving the house at all, and seldom bothered to dress.

'Hi, Mom.'

'Look at this, this is a good movie,' her mother said by way of greeting. '*Lifeboat*. We missed it when it was playing around the neighborhood.'

'I brought honey buns,' Barbara said.

'That's my sweet girl.'

'We can have them for dessert. What's for dinner?'

'Oh,' her mother said, 'I didn't go to the store today. I didn't feel so well.'

'What's the matter?'

'I don't know. I had pains in my stomach. It was nothing.'

'Did you call the doctor?'

'It wasn't anything.'

'What did you do all day?' Barbara asked, already knowing the answer.

Her mother shrugged. 'What do I always do?'

'You sat in that chair and watched television. When I left for the office this morning you were glued to the "Breakfast Club." Then you saw all your soap operas and the afternoon quiz show and the

'"Twilight Movie." You probably even watched "Kukla, Fran and Ollie's" and "Lucky Pup" and any other kiddie shows they're offering today. And you complain you have pains in your stomach. Do you want to know *why* you have pains in your stomach?'

'Why?'

'Sitting down all day, that's why. Why didn't you go out for a walk or something?'

'Walk? Where should I walk?'

'Call up one of your friends.'

'Mrs Oliphant was here today for a while. She watched TV with me. Then she took the baby out for a walk. She's crazy about Hillary.'

'I'll go see her.' Barbara went into the bedroom that used to be hers before she was married and which she now shared with her child, a crib, another dresser, a bathinette and an assortment of stuffed animals, blocks and dolls. Hillary was in her crib, wearing her blue sleeper. She stood up at the sight of her mother and tried to climb over the bars. Barbara lifted her out and kissed her.

'Hello, sweetie. How's my baby? How's my angel?'

She leaned down to hold Hillary's hand, and they walked together into the living room. Her mother was avidly watching a commercial. Barbara continued into the kitchen and swung the baby up on to the drainboard, talking to her.

'Now you watch me while I fix dinner, all right? And I'll tell you what I did today. We were working on the bride's issue today, for June, you remember? Oh, it was funny, they had to take pictures of the models on the roof in filmy white nightgowns and peignoirs – against the skyline, very romantic – and the photographer had to use a filter so you wouldn't see the gooseflesh.'

The baby sat solemnly on the edge of the drainboard, her fat legs sticking straight out, chewing on a piece of bread and lulled by her mother's pleasant voice.

'Well, I guess we'll have to have canned ravioli again tonight. There's nothing else since Nana didn't go to the store. You like ravioli, don't you, angel? You know, I think I'm going to get another raise in June. I put in for one. My boss said I'm the only girl in the office who has the nerve to ask for her summer raise a month after she got her New Year's one, but she was smiling when she said it so I know she thinks the one I got last month was too small. It was a *joke*, you know that. Five dollars a month! Did you ever figure out what that is a week?'

The baby, comforted by the security of the voice she knew so well and the words she did not understand, curled up on the drainboard and fell asleep, her thumb in her mouth. Her piece of bread, damp and chewed, fell to the floor. Barbara looked at her and shrugged, smiling lovingly. She picked up the child in her arms and carried her to the crib. In the living room her mother, wreathed in cigarette smoke, was still watching television.

Barbara went back to the kitchen and began to open cans, listening to the muted sounds of voices from the other room, voices that couldn't answer, speaking to a woman who had for some reason given up caring whether she had anyone to speak to or not. Barbara heard the sound of the kitchen clock ticking, the click of a spoon on the edge of a pot. She heard a voice inside her head speaking and knew it was her own voice speaking to herself. 'Talk to me,' it said. 'Talk to me?'

'I'd love to,' she said aloud.

'Nobody in this house ever talks to me,' the voice said.

'I know,' Barbara answered. 'Me neither.'

'I bet mother had a fine talk with Mrs Oliphant this afternoon,' the voice said. 'Mrs Oliphant probably said, "It's a shame Barbara hasn't remarried. Such a nice girl." "Oh," Mother answered, "it's not for lack of being asked. She just isn't interested right now. She'll choose when she's in the mood for it." "Oh, I'm sure," Mrs Oliphant said. "I'm sure."' 'Dozens of suitors,' Barbara said. 'All of them proposing. In a pig's eye, they are.'

'And then Mrs Oliphant went away and met one of her friends,' the voice went on. 'And the friend said, "How's Barbara?" And Mrs Oliphant said, "I don't think she's so happy. I'll bet she's sorry now that she tossed away that nice Mac Lemont. I'll bet she'd like to have him back."'

'I can just hear her,' Barbara said.

'And would you?' asked the voice. 'Would you like to have him back?'

'Stop bothering me,' Barbara said.

'Would you?'

'No. I just want . . . someone to talk to. Someone to talk to me. Someone to care about. And I'll find him, so you butt out and you shut up. I'll find him, you'll see. It'll be sooner than you think.'

'To borrow your own gentle phrasing,' the voice said, 'in a pig's eye you will!'

7

In June there was an early heat spell, with waves of hot air rising from the sticky pavements and restaurant patrons complaining loudly: Hey, when're you going to get that air conditioning on? In the mechanically cooled, wide-windowed cubicles of Fabian Publications life went on as usual. Mike Rice and Caroline had fallen into the habit of meeting at five o'clock by the water cooler, nodding at each other, separating and meeting later in a small bar on Third Avenue. It was hard to keep anything private at the office. Everyone in the place knew that Miss Farrow was having an affair with one of the vice-presidents, everyone except Mary Agnes, who knew it but refused to believe it. Even though Mary Agnes managed to be first with the most in the gossip department, she could never bring herself to believe that people were actually 'doing it.' She would grin, look shocked and whisper, but at the back of her mind was always a reservation, probably because the sexual actions of the others were so removed from anything she herself would ever contemplate. Brenda had gotten married, and a week before the wedding there had been an office party, with all the girls chipping in a dollar apiece for the gift and getting slightly tipsy on one whisky sour downstairs in the bar. After the honeymoon Brenda had brought a huge white leather photograph album to the office, titled 'Our Wedding,' and had insisted that every girl in the bullpen look at it and give appropriate compliments. I was right, Caroline couldn't help thinking, he *is* a moose face.

Through Mr Shalimar's intervention Caroline had received a ten-dollar-a-week raise and the title of 'Reader,' and she had moved in with Gregg. She had the apartment to herself most of the time because Gregg was out with David Wilder Savage, an arrangement which Caroline found quite convenient. Gregg usually returned about three o'clock in the morning because David had one rule: no girl was ever allowed to spend the entire night in his apartment.

'What's the matter?' Caroline asked Gregg. 'Is he afraid for his maid?'

'He just likes to be alone at times,' Gregg said. 'He's a lone wolf.'

Wolf is right, Caroline thought, but said nothing. She wasn't quite easy in her mind about this affair. Not that she was a prude, despite her stringent upbringing and the virtuous lies she and her college friends had all told one another about their private lives. But she felt with a certainty that David Wilder Savage did not love Gregg, despite what Gregg wanted to believe. In the first place, he had never said he loved her. Then, too, there was his reputation. Why should a man like him, who had everything he wanted except a heart, turn mushy over a girl like Gregg? He never called for her or took her home, but made her meet him at his office or at a restaurant. At three o'clock in the morning he took her down to the street in front of his apartment and put her into a cab. Was this devotion? But he called Gregg every day and he saw her nearly every night, so that at least was devotion of a sort.

'Some people are made to be hurt,' Caroline told Mike one night. 'It doesn't even take much trying. Gregg is that type, and look who she's tied up with!'

'Don't you think she chose him for that purpose?' Mike asked.

'To get hurt? Not Gregg.'

'Don't you think she would have avoided him?'

'Not David Wilder Savage. I could hardly have avoided him myself.'

'You met him?'

'Twice. Gregg and I were having a drink in a restaurant before he came to meet her. He talks to you like you're the only person in the world.'

'Would you like to sleep with him?' Mike asked calmly and curiously.

'Mike! I don't think about men I meet *that* way.'

'Why not?'

'Well, girls don't.'

'Of course they do,' Mike said, finishing what was his eighth or ninth drink. 'Women have exactly the same feelings as men do, if they'd only admit it to themselves. A man sees a beautiful girl walking down the street, or he meets her somewhere, and he says to himself matter-of-factly, with no intention of doing anything about it, I'd like to sleep with that girl. That doesn't mean he'd even try to start a conversation. But he accepts his own feelings.'

'Why do you drink so much?' Caroline asked.

'Are you changing the subject?'

'Maybe it isn't such a different subject. I can't believe that anyone would drink as much as you do simply because he likes the taste.'

'You're right,' he said cheerfully.

'I sit here and watch you night after night. You drink and talk with no sign whatever that you're getting high, and then all of a sudden you get up and walk out as if you're going to fall on your face.'

'I like whisky,' he said. 'I prefer it to people.'

'Why?'

'It's simple. No problems, no responsibilities, no reproaches. Take you and me, for instance. I woke up this morning and as usual I was thinking about you. And all of a sudden I knew I was in love with you.'

He said it so matter-of-factly, with that same expressionless look on his face, that it took Caroline an instant to realize what he had just told her. She caught her breath. He was sitting there sipping his fresh drink, not expecting a reply, not asking her if she loved him in return, simply making a comment that could or could not be important to both of them. She was touched, and she realized how much she trusted him. He would take care of everything, everything would be all right.

'What did you do then?' she whispered.

'I got out of bed and found a towel, and then I went back to bed and thought about you some more.'

'Oh, Mike, you're terrible, terrible! What a way to talk!' And yet, she was still touched, despite her embarrassment.

'I'd like to have an affair with you,' he said. 'But I think if you had an affair with me it would ruin your life.' He had put down his drink now and was leaning across the table looking at her intently. He did not touch her. 'Let's have a strange affair, a private love affair all our own. A vicarious, mental affair.'

'What's that? I don't quite understand.'

'We'll tell each other everything we're thinking. We'll be absolutely honest with each other. I'll tell you everything I want to do to you, and you tell me everything you want to do to me. We'll have a real affair *of the heart*, do you understand now?'

'But why?' Caroline asked.

'Because I have my mind and my bottle, and you have your youth and your future. That's no trade, Caroline, the harm is all to you and the gain is all to me.'

'I think about you most of the time,' Caroline said softly. 'I think about all the things I want to tell you, and I remember what you've said to me. I care very much about what happens to you.'

'I warned you about that a long time ago,' he said. 'Do you remember?'

'Oh, yes.' She laughed. 'That night with that terrible blind date – what was his name? Alvin Wiggs.'

He smiled. 'Whatever happened to him?'

'He got married to a nice girl. They do, you know.'

Slowly, slowly their hands moved across the table and met. He held her hand gently, caressing the tips of her fingers with his thumb. 'Don't marry a fool,' he said. 'Don't get trapped by some "nice boy" your family parades out for you. You have brains, a future. Marry only someone you adore, someone you can't stay away from. But most of all, marry only someone you respect. If you marry a man you don't have enough respect for it will kill you.'

She thought of Eddie then and her heart turned over, but she did not remove her hand from Mike's. His hand was comforting and she wanted him to stay near her. 'I knew someone like that once,' she said. 'He's married now. I don't know if I'll ever find someone who affects me that same way . . .'

'Wait for it,' Mike said. 'There's no hurry. You have a long, long time. I wish I could have married you myself.'

'You?'

'Oh, twenty years ago, when I was your age. But you were just born then. What a marriage we could have had! And now I'm a different person, and there's a whole life between you and me. We keep making decisions, every day, half without thinking, half against our will. If we don't fight back, if we allow ourselves to change, to be changed, then once it's done we have to do other things, and on and on until the person we wanted to be is so far away in the past that we only remember him, longingly, as if he were a beloved stranger.'

'How dreadful,' Caroline said. 'I don't want that ever to happen to me.'

He didn't say anything for a minute and then lifted her hand and kissed it very gently. 'I'm afraid for you,' he said. 'You're too smart, too pretty, you want too much. You know, there's a wall in Italy covered with bits of feathers and blood because thousands and thousands of sparrows hurl themselves against it every year and are killed. Why do they do it? Who knows. You know who are the lucky ones? The Mary Agneses of this world. Mary Agnes has her whole life figured out: get married next June, save her money, plod along in her job, never look to life to give her anything more. She's the poor little product of training and ignorance and habit, and she's smarter than any of you.'

'I had plans like that once,' Caroline said.

'Well, maybe we all get one chance to be a Mary Agnes. You lose it, and that's it, you're on the way. But you see, if you were a *real* Mary Agnes, you'd find a second chance, even if it wasn't as good as the first.'

'That's just what you told me not to do,' Caroline said.

'I'm drunk,' said Mike. He stood up. 'Let's go, I'll take you home.'

He took her to her house and stood for a moment at the foot of the stairs outside. 'Think about our affair,' he said.

'All right.'

He looked at his wristwatch. 'It's eleven o'clock. I'll be home in my hotel and in bed by eleven-thirty. I'll think about you then. Will you think about me?'

'Yes,' she said.

'Think about me from eleven-thirty to twelve,' he said. 'And tomorrow when I see you, you can tell me what you thought and what you did.'

'What *should* I do?' she asked curiously.

'Whatever you want to,' he said very solemnly, and then he touched his lips in a little salute and walked quickly away into the darkness.

Upstairs in her living room Caroline put on her pajamas and drank a glass of milk. She kept her wristwatch on and looked at it every now and then as she sat on the edge of her studio-couch bed. He must be home now, she thought, in that dismal hotel where Mary Agnes said he lived. Perhaps he was stopping for a last drink at the bar. She was not in the least sleepy and she thought she might wait up for Gregg, read a magazine, listen to the radio or take a bath. She was supposed to think about Mike, but what could she think? She was not accustomed to being told to think about someone at a specific time, and all of a sudden it seemed a difficult thing to do. It was easier to think about herself.

Did she love him? No, not the way she had loved Eddie, or the way she had loved anyone in her life. He fascinated her, and she thought she might be happy if she could fall in love with him, despite his warning. She did not know any other men who understood what she was thinking. Mike seemed to be able to look deep into her heart and see not only what was puzzling her but give her the answers as well. In her mind she could hear his voice again as he said, 'I knew I was in love with you.' She said the words over and over to herself and found them both exciting and comforting. If she could love Mike, it would be the only exciting thing in her present life, she knew, and knowing it she was half in love with him already.

With any other man she would not have dared to think of falling in love, much less *try* to fall in love with him, but she felt utterly lulled and cared for. Mike was older, he was perceptive, he would never desert her as Eddie had done. He would never marry her either, but she was so young, only twenty, and she had a long time yet before she had to think seriously of marriage to anyone. It was a relief to put it off, to think of emotions and new feelings without worrying about any permanent attachment.

She never really thought of Mike in a physical sense, she could not even imagine him kissing her on the mouth. What she thought of was the challenge of him as a person, as a companion, as her dearest friend and as a lover on a plane she was only beginning to know existed. She could not tell Gregg or even April about any of this. They would never understand. And Caroline was not so sure that she herself really understood.

It was midnight. She didn't want to wait up for Gregg now, she wanted to go to sleep as quickly as possible so that she could keep all her thoughts to herself. The idea of having to talk about trivialities with anyone at this moment, even a close friend like Gregg, seemed a heavy imposition. Caroline turned off the light and curled up in her lumpy bed; and found herself dreaming of Mike, not quite sure if she were awake or really asleep.

From then on it became easier to fall into their game, or their affair, as he continued to call it. Soon the idea of calling his image to mind at a specified time did not seem bizarre at all. On any night when he forgot to tell her to think about him Caroline felt somehow deserted. She would tell herself that he had merely forgotten, and then she would wonder why. She felt as though he had left her waiting for an appointment. As for Mike, she knew that he had a more pronounced physical reaction to these thoughts of her than she did to her thoughts of him. When he told her what he did about it she was appalled.

'Why?' he asked.

'But that's so . . . that's for children. Little boys. Adolescents . . .'

'Caroline, when will you learn that nothing two people do when they love each other is wrong?'

'That's just it; it isn't two people, it's you by yourself. It's dreadful. It's so isolated.'

'It isn't isolated because it brings me closer to you.'

'How can it, when it embarrasses me even to think of your doing it?'

'If we're having a love affair,' he said, 'you mustn't be embarrassed by anything. You'll have to accept your feelings and mine too.'

'Sometimes I think it would be better if we *really* had an affair,' she said.

'Rely on me,' he said ruefully. 'It wouldn't. This way nothing can touch you, nothing can hurt you. That's all I'm concerned about – not hurting you.'

For the moment Caroline could not protest, she could only be grateful.

He never took her to his room, nor would he come to her apartment. They sat in bars: Third Avenue saloons with sawdust floors, the Fabian bar in the darkest corner, sometimes some of the cocktail lounges in Radio City. They often ran into people who worked at Fabian whom Mike knew, and after a while Caroline realized that the office gossip probably assumed that she and Mike were having an affair with each other. It was ironic, she thought, because they so obviously were *not*, and yet there was an intimacy growing between them that could never be called merely a friendship.

'You know,' she told him one night, 'if it's possible to say that one mind is sleeping with another mind, then that's what we're doing.'

'Anything is possible,' Mike said. 'Tell me what you want me to do to you.'

'You know I hate to talk that way.'

'Tell me. How else will I know?'

'It embarrasses me.'

'Do you want me to kiss you?'

'Yes,' she said.

'Then say so.'

'I want you to kiss me. *And you never do, you know!* Just good night, like an old uncle.'

He leaned across the table in the blue-lighted dark and kissed her lightly on the corner of her lips. 'There.'

'There you go again.' She couldn't help smiling.

'If I started to kiss you – really kiss you – I couldn't stop there.'

'You make me feel like such a child.'

'Come on,' he said. 'What do you want me to do to you?'

'Kiss me.'

'You said that.'

She looked down at her hands, clasped on the table top, very white against the darkness of the cocktail lounge. It was dim light, meant to be seductive, and there was nostalgic, unrecognizable music playing somewhere near by. Mike looked so much younger in this vague dimness, he looked almost thirty. And what was so wrong about being thirty-eight? He was still in his thirties, and you couldn't say that someone in his thirties was so terribly old for a girl of twenty . . .

'What else?'

'You know.'

'Do you want me to touch you?'

'Yes.'

'Where?'

At times like this Caroline was so annoyed at him she was sure that she did not love him, and yet she was powerless to stand up and walk away. His voice and his words held her captive because they were the words of love spoken in the tone of love, and they had become important to her because they came from him. Perhaps she did love him. Certainly she could think about no one else, and whenever she found herself out on a date with one of the boys she had met since her broken engagement she found herself comparing him unfavorably with Mike. They all seemed so dull, they could not stir her as he did simply by touching her hand. Because now, at last, she was thinking of Mike in a physical way, and she wished that he would simply neck and pet with her, as Eddie had, without all this solemn talk of affairs and ruining lives.

'You have to hold my hand while I'm telling you,' she said.

He reached out for her hand and grasped it very gently, and the tremor she felt from his touch reached all the way up her arm to her breast.

'You're ruining my vocabulary,' she said, smiling. 'I'm beginning to shock people without realizing it.'

'Who? That flighty roommate of yours?'

'No, not Gregg. My mother and father. I went home to Port Blair last weekend and we were having a simple conversation at dinner – or not so simple, really, because everything my mother and I talk about lately has overtones – and I looked up and saw her face looking aghast. She's not quite sure what I'm doing here in New York. She keeps saying, I hope you're meeting nice boys. She says, I hope you're having lots of fun. All with a little rise in inflection at the end of the sentence because it's really a question, not a comment. And then I said something you'd told me, I can't even remember what it was. It was something that seemed so natural when you and I were speaking together. And my mother raised her eyebrows and drew in her breath and said, "Caroline! Where do you get those ideas?"'

'I suppose your mother wants you to get married as soon as possible,' he said pleasantly. 'Then she thinks you'll be safe at last.'

'Yes, but only to someone whom she would consider "a good catch." My mother doesn't want me to marry just anyone for the sake of getting married.'

'What about love?'

'Oh, that too. But my mother thinks a sensible girl will fall in love with the right person.'

'It's so easy, isn't it?' he said. 'To tell someone else what is the *right* thing for him to do. There's no emotion involved and you see right and wrong clearly.'

'Like Mary Agnes,' Caroline said.

'Do you know how I see you?' he asked. 'I see a little girl sitting on a rock in a glade near a forest. The Pied Piper comes along playing his music, and all the other little girls leave the security of their homes and dance along after him, far, far away to another land. That's the land of marriage and respectability and who knows? Maybe disappointment for some. All of them, or nearly all, follow the Pied Piper; but you don't. Then along comes Pan, grizzled and hairy, with a leer on his human face and the sweet music of the pipes of Pan in his mouth. He goes off into the forest, and a few little girls like your friend Gregg follow him. They're the ones who have the courage to break with tradition, to live as freely as they like. You watch them disappear into the forest, but you don't follow Pan either. You want to think the way you like and live freely, but on the other hand you want to be married and conventional and have a family. So you just sit there on your rock, and you say, What will become of me?'

'What will?' Caroline asked. 'What *will* become of me?'

'Do you think I'm a prophet?' he asked with a little smile.

'Sometimes I nearly do.'

'I think you'll be very successful,' he said thoughtfully. 'I think you could love some man very much. I wish he could have been me.'

'Maybe he will be you,' Caroline said. 'Would that frighten you?'

'Only for a minute. Then I'm afraid I'd be selfish enough to be delighted.'

Spontaneously she leaned down in the darkness and kissed his hand.

'Caroline, I love you. I wish it were nineteen thirty-two.'

'Then I wouldn't be here,' she said, smiling.

'You see? We're lost.'

'Why couldn't we love each other anyway? I know a widow in Port Blair who married a man twenty years older than she is and they're very happy together.'

'And when she's sixty and he's eighty she'll be holding him up getting into taxicabs and warming his glass of milk at night and telling him the same story over and over because he forgets it as soon as she tells it.'

'Eighty!' Caroline said. 'The way *you* live, you'll *never* live to be eighty.'

'I hope not,' he said cheerfully, and swallowed his drink and what was left of hers.

'You know,' she said, 'I *have* changed. I can notice it in little reactions I have to things, a kind of acceptance of ideas that are different from mine, and of people who used to awe me. And all that in the six months we've been friends.'

'Five of those six months we would have been married to each other,' he said, 'if we had been luckier . . .'

It was the first time he had actually spoken of marriage, and Caroline was startled. He loved me long before I loved him, she thought in surprise. Longer than I ever suspected. She wondered what it might have been like to be married to Mike Rice. She could do things for him, make him drink less, give him a real home . . . Look, she thought to herself, here I am again, being the little girl on the rock, dreaming of domesticating this renegade. And yet, he appeals to me so because he knows so much of life. I can just see him in my living room at Port Blair; Sunday dinner with the in-laws.

'What are you laughing at?' Mike asked.

'Myself, I guess,' she admitted. 'For daydreaming.'

The last weekend in June all the employees at Fabian from the vice-presidents down to the shipping clerks were driven out to the country in chartered buses for the summer office party. It had been a tradition of old Clyde Fabian's to have the party at his golf club on the Hudson, and even though he was ill and incapacitated he insisted that the tradition be continued. The party was held on a Friday, starting at ten in the morning – the last workday of the week so they all could have their hang-overs on their own time the next day. There was softball, swimming, golf, a huge outdoor buffet lunch, liquor, dancing and a return trip to the city at six o'clock in the evening. Caroline went with Gregg, April and Mary Agnes.

'You know,' Mary Agnes said, 'at my girl friend's office they have the nicest thing. They invite all the husbands and wives and children to the office party, so they can all be together.'

'What?' said Gregg. 'And cramp everyone's style?'

The girls laughed, except for Mary Agnes. 'I think it would be more fun,' she protested. 'Last year when I was wearing my bathing suit Mr Shalimar kept making remarks about what nice legs I had, until I thought I would die of embarrassment. This year I almost didn't *bring* a bathing suit.'

'Just think,' April said. 'This is my first office party.'

'All of ours,' Caroline said.

'I'm dying to see a real Eastern country club,' said April.

'Are the drinks free or do we have to pay?' Gregg asked.

'Free,' said Mary Agnes. 'And everybody gets so drunk it's terrible.'

'I can't wait,' said Gregg. 'This party is my swan song. I'm going to take the three days' vacation I have coming to me and then quit.'

'Quit!'

'David is getting me a job in summer stock. I'll be the ingénue in at least four plays. Not only is it real, genuine, United States money, but I'll only be in Connecticut so I'll be able to see him.'

'That's wonderful,' Mary Agnes said.

'I never would have asked him for a favor,' Gregg said. 'But he suggested it. Isn't he a darling?'

'Imagine David Wilder Savage opening doors for you that way,' April breathed. 'You're so lucky. It's marvelous.' There was not a trace of envy in her tone, but only awe and pleasure at Gregg's good fortune. If there was any girl who was completely without jealousy or rancor, Caroline thought, it was April.

As the bus drew up in the wide white gravel driveway of the club there were varied ecstatic exclamations from the occupants. Caroline and Gregg were sitting at the back of the bus and so were the last to leave. Directly ahead of them April and Mary Agnes hurried off to join the throng. Gregg looked at Caroline.

'I don't know why we ever came,' Gregg said.

'I know. I hate a brawl. All these strangers, and Shalimar will doubtless want to act out one of the sex scenes from our latest manuscript.'

'Do you think he *can*?' Gregg asked.

'I wish they'd just give us the money instead of spending it on a party,' Caroline said.

'Me too.'

They walked slowly over to a long table which was set under a group of leafy trees and foliage, and which was obviously the bar because it was clustered four deep with Fabian employees, like ants on a wedge of cheese.

At the edge of the crowd Caroline saw Mike standing with a glass in his hand, talking with two editors from other magazines whom she had never met. He looked so adult and businesslike that for a moment she had the odd thought that she did not know him at all. Three men, probably talking business or telling the kind of jokes they did not like women to listen to. She felt very young and self-conscious, and she took hold of Gregg's arm.

'Maybe your friend has pull,' Gregg said, nodding toward Mike. 'The only place I'll get a drink in this mob is down the front of my dress.'

'I don't really want one.'

'Of course you do,' Gregg said. 'How are you going to play touch football with the mailroom boys if you don't fortify yourself first?'

Caroline laughed, but her hands were cold. It was a hot summer day with a touch of breeze that brought the smell of freshly cut grass, perfume, cigarette smoke and hickory smoke from the outdoor barbecue pit which had just been lighted. The breeze made her shiver and she didn't know why. She looked toward the periphery of the crowd of merrymakers and saw Mike looking at her, his face both solemn and a trifle amused, as if he had wandered into the wrong party. His gaze seemed to join him with her; she felt as if it were a bridge that she could climb across until she was safely by his side. She moved around the crowd, hardly feeling a heel dug into her instep and a fat arm grazing her breast, and moved breathlessly into his circle under the tree.

He introduced her and Gregg to the others. One of the men gave Gregg the drink he was holding in his hand and she beamed with delight. 'Are you having fun?' Mike asked Caroline. He took her arm and turned her deftly away from the group.

'I'm *so* glad to see you.'

'I don't know why I come to these things,' he said. 'It's harmless, I suppose . . . a little fresh air . . .' He breathed deeply.

'You like the country, don't you?' Caroline said.

'I love it. I grew up on a farm.'

'My heavens! One would never know.'

'Why? Is there a way to look if you come from a farm?'

She shrugged. 'That's just me being provincial again, I guess.'

'You should have seen the farm,' he said. 'It was for boys from four to fourteen who didn't have a home or were too ornery for their relatives to keep them. The old bastard who ran it used to beat us each with a strap on Saturday night so we'd have something to cry about in church on Sunday.'

'My God!'

'One time when I was ten years old I jumped out of the hayloft hoping I would break my neck and die, but unfortunately all I did was sprain my ankle. It didn't even incapacitate me enough to get me out of the extra chores I had to do for being so careless.'

'Why didn't you write to your family?' Caroline cried.

'Kids are funny,' he said. 'My father was dead and my mother had four younger kids at home to take care of. I was the oldest so I was the one who got sent away to that nice healthful farm in the country. I guess I felt that she didn't give a damn about me or else she would have let me stay home.'

'I think that's terrible,' Caroline said.

They were walking away by themselves now and had left the others far behind. Mike sat down cross-legged on the grass and pushed a little space in the earth for his whisky glass. Caroline sat down beside him and tucked her skirt around her legs.

'I guess it's ironic,' he said, 'that now I'm the editor of a religious magazine. The main thing I remember about my Sundays in church is that every morning before I would go there I would have elaborate fantasies about running down the aisle in the middle of the service and pulling off my clothes to show the whole congregation the welts that bastard had put there the night before. In my fantasies the minister was always saving me, he was being very fatherly and saying, This boy need never go back to the farm again. But, of course, I never had the courage to do anything of the sort.'

'I think that's just terrible,' Caroline said. 'How did you ever get out?'

'When I was fourteen I was graduated,' he said cheerfully. 'I went to work as water boy on a newspaper and that was it. Would you believe it – some of the graduates actually stayed on the farm, working as dishwashers or field hands, bullying the younger kids. It's amazing how kids can be brutalized into a mold in which they give it right back to the weaker ones and never think of escaping from the whole filthy mess.'

'I wish you hadn't told me,' Caroline said softly. 'I can just see you as a little boy and it makes me want to cry. I hate and despise people who are mean to children.'

'So do I. I never slapped my little girl, I never even raised my voice to her. I didn't even want to. That was one of the things my wife and I used to battle about; she wanted to crack the baby a lick or two and I wouldn't let her. So now she has full custody and *I'm* the unfit drunken father.' There was no bitterness in his tone and no self-pity, only that same perceptive matter-of-factness he had when he spoke of any of the things that were so important to himself or to Caroline.

The calmness in his voice moved Caroline more than any emotion could have. She was filled with feelings toward him: pity, love, tenderness, remorse. For the first time she felt the loneliness in this man and, even more, the softness. He had always been gentle, but he had been gentle and strong, the leader and instructor. Suddenly there was only one thing she wanted to say to him.

'I'll get you a drink,' he said. 'Don't you want one? In any case, I do.' He rose to his knees, starting to stand up, and Caroline was instantly on her knees in front of him, facing him with her hands touching his shoulders.

'Please, please sleep with me,' she said.

He covered her hands with his own and tenderly took them down from where they were holding his shoulders. 'No, darling.'

'*I'm* asking *you*, you're not asking me.'

'You're a virgin. Stay that way.'

'I always wanted my first love affair to happen spontaneously,' Caroline said. 'If you're going to argue with me, then it won't be spontaneous and you'll ruin it.'

He looked at her for a long time without speaking. 'If someone has to be the first,' he said finally, 'then at least it will be someone who loves you. Come on.' He took her hand and lifted her to her feet.

They ran down the hill toward the clubhouse, holding hands, not speaking but looking at each other every now and then and smiling. He squeezed her hand reassuringly and she could feel the blood pounding in her ears. 'I'll call a cab from the clubhouse,' he said. 'I don't have a car, do you?'

'No.'

They skirted a group of softball players, and Caroline recognized Brenda in a too-tight white jersey and a baseball player's cap tilted over one eye. She was playing second base and she looked very tough. The boy who delivered Caroline's mail in the morning was up at bat. In the group that was gathered around to cheer, Caroline saw Mary Agnes and April's friend, Barbara Lemont. The happy cries and noises of the watchers and the players seemed very far away, like voices heard through a glass window. She felt completely out of it, a part of her own little world and this thing that was about to happen to her, and for once she was glad to be separated from the people she knew and the things that mattered to them, things which at this moment did not seem to matter at all.

Mike went to the telephone booth behind the bar in the clubhouse, and Caroline waited for him in the cool, darkened room. Chairs were pushed against the tables and a clock ticked loudly. The club was almost deserted by its members today because of the onslaught of Fabian employees. In the gloom at the far end of the room Caroline heard the murmur of voices and saw a tall shape dressed in white and a smaller shape behind it. She recognized April, with a young man Caroline had never seen before. It seemed very important that April not turn around and notice her. Caroline tapped on the glass of the telephone booth and Mike opened the door.

She squeezed into the booth beside him. He replaced the receiver. 'He'll be here in five minutes,' he said, and kissed her on the temple. 'We'll go to your apartment. If you change your mind along the way I'll take you to a bar.'

She put her arms around his neck and he kissed her, this time really, for the first time. He stroked her shoulder blades and back and kissed her again. She loved him for saying that to her, for giving her the last-minute power of choice, and because he had she knew she would not change her mind.

On their way back to New York in the taxi neither of them spoke. They held hands and looked at each other, each in his own thoughts and finding no need for words. Now that she had decided, Caroline felt very close to him. She had a sense of unreality, and the countryside going past the taxi seemed a mass of green streaks. She was scarcely aware of the breeze blowing on her face from the open windows or of the bumps and jolts. When they reached her house she stood for a moment at the foot of the stairs while Mike paid the cab driver. Her house looked different to her, perhaps because she had never been outside it on a weekday noon. The Chinese laundry was closed for a two-week summer vacation and it was very quiet without the steam and the noise. There were two women sitting on the bottom step with baby carriages drawn up in front of them. She glanced at them and for an instant she felt a pang of unhappiness, for no reason she could mention. Then Mike walked quickly up behind her and took her arm and they climbed the stairs.

The apartment was dark and cool, with the shades drawn against the sun. He did not grab for her or kiss her immediately, for which she was grateful, but instead looked around the apartment, which he had never seen before.

'It's a nice apartment,' he said.

'Would you like a drink?'

'I'll make you one.' He went to the little metal bar in the corner and poured whisky into two glasses, and carried them into the kitchen. She could hear him taking ice cubes out of the ice tray in the refrigerator.

He came out of the kitchen and they sat together on the edge of one of the studio couches sipping at their drinks. 'Is this one your bed?' he asked.

'Yes.'

'I've tried to picture it many times.'

'Now you know.'

'A little, narrow single bed.' He smiled. 'It's just as I imagined it.'

'I ought to change the sheets. I hadn't planned on this . . .'

'Don't. Do you think I'd mind the sheets you've slept in?'

They finished their drinks and put the glasses on the floor beside the studio couch. She was suddenly taken with fright, a last-minute resistance to the giving of self, a desire for one moment of privacy and self-communication. 'I'm going to the ladies' room,' she murmured, standing.

She went into the bathroom and shut the door but did not lock it, afraid that he would hear the click of the lock and know that she was frightened. She sat on the edge of the bathtub and put her forehead against the cool white porcelain of the sink. Would he be disappointed when he saw her naked, would he think she was flat chested, would he think she was too thin? Her hands and her thighs were trembling, and yet she had never felt less in her life like making love. She felt as though she had made a bargain, and there was no backing out, not because he would not forgive her but because she would not forgive herself.

Oh, my God, she thought. I wish I had married Eddie. Why am I here instead of married to Eddie? It's unfair. And then she thought, You fool. You love Mike and you want him. Grow up.

She stood up and opened the door and went slowly into the living room where Mike was waiting for her. He had taken off the bedspread and folded it neatly at the foot of the other studio couch. When she saw the white sheets she felt more natural about the whole thing. He had taken off his jacket and tie but was otherwise fully dressed. He was standing with his back to the window, silhouetted against the dimness, and her heart was beating so violently she could scarcely see him.

'Do you have a suntan yet, darling?' he said in a pleasant, conversational tone.

She nodded.

'Show me your suntan.'

Slightly deployed, she slipped the straps of her dress off her shoulders. He put his arms around her and kissed the white marks where the straps had been, and then his lips moved to her throat and then to her lips. She stood for a moment rigidly in his arms, and then passion moved her and she felt warmed and pliable and full of feeling. She wound her arms around his neck like some sinuous plant and opened her mouth for his kisses, feeling as though she would like to be welded to him forever.

He moved away from her then and she heard the faint rustle of cloth as he dropped his clothes on the floor. She was afraid to open her eyes for a second and then she did and she was not disappointed. She closed her eyes again, as if that would somehow make her invisible, and slipped out of her dress and crinoline and underpants and kicked off her shoes, standing there in front of him with nothing on at all and clenching her fists so that she would not do something stupid like hold her hands in front of herself.

'How beautiful you are,' he said.

She opened her eyes. 'You don't think I'm flat chested?'

'You have just enough.'

He took her hand and led her to the bed and they lay there together with their arms around each other, still kissing. She realized with a start of pleasure that she had forgotten what a man's skin felt like, and yet, Mike's was different than Eddie's, he had more hair on his chest. What a marvelous feeling this slight roughness was, better than silk, better than clean sheets, better than anything she could think of.

He began to kiss her body then and she allowed him to do anything he wanted to, not moving, not touching him except to keep her fingers gently on the back of his neck as long as she could.

'Hold me,' he said.

She did.

'Now,' he said. It was not a question or a command but simply a statement that it was time for the mystery to be ended and the deeper, newer mystery to be revealed. She closed her eyes and waited, feeling her whole body waiting, at the edge of passion.

She had not believed anything could hurt so much. It was as if he were trying to drive a spike through a solid wall of flesh. Involuntarily she gave a cry.

'I'm hurting you. I'll stop.'

'No.'

She gasped with the pain and she knew that he heard her but she could not help it. Suddenly there was nothing there to hurt her, nothing, and he was holding her in his arms with his face buried against her neck.

'I'm sorry,' he said.

'It's all right, it's all right,' she whispered over and over again. 'I'm glad you stopped.' But she wasn't glad he had stopped and she knew that he knew it.

'It'll be all right in a minute or two,' she said, and reached out for him. Then she knew it would not.

'I couldn't bear to hurt you,' he said.

She kissed him on the corner of his mouth very softly, the way he used to kiss her. 'Men are complicated, aren't they?' she said.

He laughed a little, a laugh with not much humor in it. 'Yes.'

He got up then and went into the bathroom and Caroline pushed the pillow to the head of the bed and leaned against it, hugging her knees. She looked at her knee and then she put her tongue out and licked it, tasting it. It tasted slightly salty, the taste of flesh, of a body. She felt very sensual, and strange.

Was she a virgin or wasn't she? He had been inside her, she didn't know how far, and so she wasn't a virgin. But he had only done it for a moment, and had not completed the act, so perhaps she still was. She could never ask him; it would kill him. But was she?

And what had happened to her? This great act, this crossing of a threshold into womanhood – it was nothing, nothing. Was *that* all there was to it? And yet, she felt different. She was a woman, she knew she was a woman now because she knew the answer to the mystery that had seemed so complicated and yet was so very simple. She would never wonder again, and so she was a woman. She had left the continent of girls for another world. She might look for better lovers, she might look for ecstasy, but she would be searching for it as a woman searches. Now that the mystery was solved she knew it would never be so difficult to go to bed with a man again. How strange – she felt ten years older.

Mike came out of the bathroom and began to put on his clothes. 'Come on,' he said, 'I know a nice place where we can have lunch. You must be starved, it's two o'clock.'

She dressed, and they did not look at each other. When they went downstairs into the hot, quiet street she took hold of his hand, but it was as a friend, and without desire. She wondered if she would ever desire him again.

He whistled for a taxi and helped her in, and they rolled down the windows and joked and laughed together and he lighted a cigarette for himself and one for her. How strange, she thought, that this virile, sophisticated man could change so much, in just the kind of situation one would think would be his forte. She knew then that the old wives' tales are sometimes true, that absolute innocence is its own protection – but only with certain people.

8

Change in a person's character structure is slow and almost imperceptible, and although many people look back and say, *This* was the day that changed my life, they are never wholly right. The day you choose one college instead of another, or decide not to go to college at all, the day you take one job instead of another because you cannot wait, the day you meet someone you later love – all are days that lead to change, but none of them are decisive because the choice itself is the unconscious product of days that have gone before. So when April Morrison, looking back, said, 'The day of the Fabian office party in 1952 was the day that changed my life,' she was wrong. The day she cut her hair because she wanted to look like Caroline Bender, the day she decided to give up her career on the stage and work at Fabian, the day she saw her first movie and dreamed of New York – all were days that changed her life, and if it had not been for all of them she would never have become involved with Dexter Key.

The Hudson View Country Club was like nothing April had ever seen before. As soon as the rest of the employees were safely involved in softball games and rapid drinking April wandered off by herself and began to look around. There was the swimming pool, the largest she had ever seen, and the water was actually turquoise. She lifted a handful of it to see if it were really that color or if turquoise was the color of the bottom of the pool itself, but no, it was turquoise water, it really was. Around the pool were little tables with brightly striped umbrellas over them, and white jacketed waiters were setting out a buffet lunch on the longest table she had seen since her sister's wedding. There were the dressing rooms where the Fabian employees would later put on their bathing suits, and over there on that hill was the clubhouse. The Fabian people were not invited to go into the clubhouse, but they had not been warned to stay out either, and April decided to give herself the unguided tour.

The front entrance awed her, it looked so formidable, as though some snooty butler might pop out at any moment and ask her name. There was a pale blue Mercedes Benz car at one side of the entrance (she saw the name on the dealer's tag) and on the other side a white Jaguar convertible. My heavens, she thought, it looks like a movie set. I'll bet they could make movies here if they wanted to. She went around to the side entrance where there was a patio leading to a sort of cocktail bar, and walked in.

The place was deserted, there wasn't even a bartender at this hour of the morning. The heat and excitement had made her very thirsty, and when she saw a case of ginger ale on the bar she thought she might as well help herself. They surely wouldn't miss one little bottle of ginger ale, probably anyone who belonged to this club could afford to take a bath in ginger ale if he wanted to. She had put ice in a glass and was searching for a bottle opener when a boy came into the room.

'I'll steal one too,' he said.

'Do you think they'll kill us?' April asked. She looked up and he smiled at her. He was tall and dark and very handsome, and the planes of his face were rounded instead of angular, which made him look about twenty-one. He was wearing white shorts and a heavy white tennis sweater with a V neck, and his legs were so deeply tanned that standing there in the darkness behind the bar he didn't seem to have any legs at all.

'Kill us?' he said. 'Ginger ale?'

'Not *it*,' she said. '*Them. They.*'

He looked at her, amused. 'Are you drunk?'

'Of course not!'

He put his tennis racket on top of the bar and opened two bottles of ginger ale and poured them into glasses with ice. He held up his glass in a mock salute and drank the contents thirstily.

'I've never seen you before,' April said. 'You must be in Advertising.'

'That's a *non sequitur*.'

'What?'

He laughed. 'You *are* drunk.'

What a shame, she thought, that such a handsome boy was turning out to be so stupid. He must be in the mailroom, but she had thought she knew all the mailroom boys. Perhaps he was new.

'You were smart to bring your tennis racket,' she said, gesturing.

'It does make it more convenient,' he said, raising his eyebrows as if it were he and not she that was talking to the idiot.

'Are you a good player?'

'Fair. I try to play every day after work.'

'Oh?' April said. 'Where? In the park?'

'Why, am I that bad?'

'What?'

He patted her head. 'Be a good girl and stay out of that sun.'

'I know,' she said. 'I get terrible freckles.' She had discovered a glassful of swizzle sticks with the name Hudson View Club printed on them in tiny gold letters. 'Do you think anyone would mind if I took one of these?'

'That's what they're there for.'

'Isn't that nice of them!'

'Oh, it's very nice,' he said. 'They're thoughtful that way.'

She tucked two of the swizzle sticks into her purse and felt better about the whole world. 'Are you new here?' she asked kindly.

'No,' he said. 'But you must be. I've never seen you before.'

'I've never seen you either.'

He held out his hand. 'I'm Dexter Key.'

'I'm April Morrison. I work on the thirty-fifth floor.'

'And what do you *do* on the thirty-fifth floor?' he asked, looking as if he were trying to keep a straight face.

'I'm in the typing pool. Where do you work?'

'Merrill Lynch, Pierce, Fenner and Beane.'

'Oh, my gosh!' April said.

'What?'

'I thought you were . . . I thought you worked at Fabian. You must be a member.'

He began to laugh, holding on to the edge of the bar for support and shaking his head, laughing until tears came into his eyes.

'You're so pretty,' he said weakly. 'You're so pretty.'

She was biting her thumb, the way she always did when she was embarrassed or startled, and when he said she was pretty she nearly bit right into it.

'I kept thinking, this poor pretty girl, she must have hit her head on the bottom of the swimming pool,' he said, still chuckling. 'Let's break open another bottle of ginger ale to drink to your regained health.'

'I'm so embarrassed,' April said.

'Don't be. I'm glad we met.'

'So am I . . .' she said.

'Tell me, do you hate office parties as much as I do?'

'I don't know. I've never been to one before.'

'Well then, let me advise you. You'll hate it. I have a better idea. Why don't you have lunch with me?'

'In the clubhouse?'

'Well, in the dining room. They have a wonderful view of the water.'

'I'd adore it!'

He held out his arm and she took it, feeling rather stunned and very happy. What a nice name, Dexter Key; it sounded so social. And what a marvelous tan he had. He was just as handsome from the side as he was full face. For a moment she almost asked him what was Merrill Lynch, Pierce, Fenner and Beane, and then she restrained herself. The way he'd reeled it off you could tell everyone else around here knew what it was, and she didn't want him to think she was any more of a hick than she could help. Here he was, just the kind of boy she'd dreamed of meeting in New York – it was as if she'd wake up any minute and find out she was still in her roasting hot little room with the sheet tangled around her legs.

'Isn't that a nice view?' he asked.

'Oh, it *is!*'

'Do you drink before lunch?'

'I don't know.'

He smiled at her, shaking his head. 'How's a Martini, lunatic?'

'All right.'

He held up two fingers to the waiter, who hurried off to the bar. Dexter was looking at her, with his chin on his fist. 'Do you like – now, check them off – tennis, the stock market, sailing, skiing, the theater, Louis Armstrong, not getting dressed up, taking a walk somewhere you've never been?'

'Yes, I don't know, I don't know, I don't know, *yes*, and you've lost me after that.'

'Louis Armstrong.'

'Yes.'

'Not getting dressed up.'

'I love it.'

'Taking a walk somewhere you've never been?'

'I do it all the time. This is my first six months in New York. Sometimes on Sundays I walk for miles, just looking at things – and I get lost.'

'I'll bet you do,' he said, but so kindly and with such an obvious liking for her that she couldn't feel offended.

She was not quite sure afterward what she had said or what she had eaten during that long, exciting lunch. She remembered very well everything he had said, and the line of his jaw and the movements of his mouth as he spoke. She remembered his hands, very suntanned, with a callous on the thumb of the right from holding a tennis racket, and a gold seal ring on the little finger of his left. The ring bore a family crest cut deeply into the gold. Dexter's voice had a variety of tones: kind, personable and sometimes rather petulant, like a little boy. The petulance only made her feel more affectionate toward him, because it was a part of his personality. She wouldn't have stood it in anyone else, she was sure, but she would probably have forgiven him anything. She would have expected anyone with his background to be spoiled, what with going to Yale and some exclusive prep school before that, and owning his own sailboat. But he told her that he had worked in a steel mill one summer during his vacation from college, and she was amazed.

'I wrote up my experiences and tried to sell them to a magazine,' he went on. 'But they wouldn't bite. Actually, I can't write, that's the thing. But it was great experience, and I made more money than I'm making working in a brokerage house.'

'I think that's marvelous.'

'It all started as kind of a gag, that's the funny part.'

It was four o'clock when they finished lunch. It was so cool in the air-conditioned dining room and the view below was so sparkling and changeable that they lingered on and on, Dexter smoking one cigarette after another and April watching the movements of his hands as he lighted the cigarettes with an initialed gold cigarette lighter which he kept tucked casually in the pocket of his tennis sweater. She had almost forgotten that this was the day of the Fabian office party, and that she had never been to one before, and that she was missing the whole thing.

'How did you get here anyway?' he asked. 'Car, or what?'

'They have some buses,' April said.

'Are you doing anything special after this?'

'No.'

'Well, I could drive you back to New York and then you wouldn't have to go on the bus. I could change my clothes and we could have cocktails someplace. Do you feel like that?'

'That would be so nice of you . . .' April said.

He stood up. 'I have to go to New York anyway. I live there.'

'We're neighbors . . .' April breathed.

'Isn't that convenient?'

When he led her to the white Jaguar convertible parked outside the clubhouse April's heart almost stopped beating. He put the top down and then held the door open for her and helped her into the low little car. She looked back for an instant as the engine started with a roar, and she felt like waving a great white chiffon scarf, if she'd had one. She wished there had been someone she knew standing outside on the lawn to see her departing in this dreamy car with this unbelievable boy. He was still wearing his shorts and tennis sweater – imagine, April thought, being brave enough to go into New York City dressed like that. But it was obvious that Dexter Key could wear anything he wanted and get away with it.

He turned on the car radio and the music and the wind sang past her ears. 'It's so scary,' she said. 'I feel like we're going so fast.'

'That's just because you're near the ground,' he said. 'I'm only going seventy.'

'Seventy!'

'Look at that blue sky,' he said.

She put her head back against the leather of the seat and looked at the wide blue cloudless sky that always stayed the same while they traveled so fast. The radio was playing a love song and she sang along with it, flinging her arms out and feeling the wind push against them. She was so happy, so happy, so happy . . . And how blue the Hudson was below them, sparkling with white and gold from the late afternoon sun. This was the best view of New York in the whole world, she thought, coming into the city when the buildings were tipped with gold, like the whole city was on fire, all the windows brilliant, fiery golden holes. How could she have thought the Plaza at twilight was New York? *This* was New York, beside her, Dexter Key; and the marvelous secret things people did inside those tall buildings at the cocktail hour were the things he did every evening, and tonight it was all going to happen to her.

When he parked the car on the quiet tree-lined street in front of his house it was as though they were in a different world. It was a side street of brownstone houses that were former mansions. The street was empty of people, shady and cool under the spindly little trees. There were a few other sports cars parked along the curb, a bright red one, a dull green one. April had the idea that everyone who lived on this particular street was young and rich and rather special. Dexter took his tennis racket out of the car and helped her to climb out.

'Would you like to come up, or wait down here?'

Ordinarily she would have made some excuse to stay in the

street instead of going alone into a man's apartment, but because he was gentlemanly enough to anticipate the possibility of refusal she felt safe. 'I'll come up,' she said softly.

His apartment consisted of one large room with a tiny kitchen and a large dressing room and bathroom. There was a garden in back of the house and his living-room windows opened out to it. He lived on the second floor. The garden had been fixed up with a white marble statue and grass and gravel, and there was a little gray cat playing on the walk.

'Oh, whose darling cat is that?'

'Two faggots who live downstairs,' he said.

'Two what?'

He looked at her. 'Fairies.' He grinned. 'I have fairies at the bottom of my garden, as the song goes.' He fixed a drink for her and set it on the white marble coffee table in front of the fireplace and went into the dressing room. 'Make yourself at home,' he called.

She looked around. He had modern furniture, all very new and clean and comfortable looking, and obviously expensive. The brightly colored painting above the fireplace, which she couldn't make out at all, was obviously an original and not a print. There was a chest of drawers against one wall with a small bronze statue on top of it of a nude girl. There was a striped tie draped around the neck of the statue as if he had thrown it there in the morning when he put on his tennis clothes, and the incongruity of it made her smile when ordinarily she would have been a little embarrassed to be alone in a boy's apartment with a nude statue staring her in the face. The kitchen looked as if he never used it. She peeked into his icebox and all there was inside were two sealed bottles of wine lying on their sides, some frozen orange juice and a half a loaf of bread that was as hard as a rock. She sat down on the couch and sipped at her gin and tonic, listening to the faraway sound of his shower. Despite herself she couldn't help picturing him in the shower with no clothes on, and she was both thrilled and frightened. Here she was, sitting on the bed (well, sofa really, but it could convert to a bed in an instant) of a boy she hardly knew, and no more than ten feet away he was stark naked and singing as if it were the most natural situation in the world. She wondered if he wore his seal ring in the shower.

The sound of the shower stopped and she heard him padding around and slamming drawers. She picked up a magazine from the coffee table and pretended to read it so that when he came in he wouldn't suspect that she had been thinking about him.

'April?' he called. 'Hey, April, did I leave my blue tie in there?'

She looked up. 'One with red and white stripes on it?'

'That's the one.'

'It's here,' she called. She looked at the nude statue and bit her lip.

'Toss it in, will you please, honey?'

Honey! she thought. She stood up and walked to the chest, and picked the tie off the statue. Through the partly opened door she could see a mirror, and in the mirror she saw the flash of a white shirt. She opened the door and held the tie out to him.

He was wearing a clean white shirt and a pair of neatly creased dark-gray flannel pants. His hair was wet from the shower and she could see the marks his comb had left in it. 'Thanks,' he said. He flipped the tie around his neck and peered into the mirror, tying the knot.

April thought of retreating to her place on the couch but she was rooted to the spot, fascinated. She had never watched a boy get dressed before, and here she was with Dexter Key, the most fabulous boy she had ever met in her life, watching him in this situation that was somehow so intimate and yet not frightening. He looked at her.

'Nice?'

'Mmm-hmm.'

He strode over to her and put his arms around her, and before she knew what was happening he was kissing her. This wasn't like the last kiss she had received, from that dirty Mr Shalimar, and it wasn't like any kiss she remembered from the boys at home. It was magic, a pounding of the heart and a touch of something that was like silk and warmth; a kiss she couldn't remember a moment afterward because it was so emotional for her. She knew that she was kissing him in return, and that he was kissing her again, and then the movements of his hands on her body brought her back to reality.

'No!' she said, pushing him away.

'What?' he said. His eyes were still half closed, he looked as if he were asleep.

'That's enough,' she said tremulously. She retreated two steps and tried to smile.

He was looking at her then with an expression she tried to interpret. Was he annoyed? He would never want to see her again, he was insulted, he would think she was a little prude. He probably went out with sophisticated girls who went all the way and laughed afterward. But she couldn't . . . she couldn't. He would know she wasn't sophisticated, he would think she was just easy. She wanted to keep him, she had to, now that she had found him; she couldn't bear to have him think she was 'that kind of girl' and throw her away afterward. Oh, my God, April thought, what is he thinking? Say something, Dexter, please speak to me.

He walked to the mirror and looked at his reflection, and wiped her lipstick carefully off his mouth with a paper tissue. Then he combed his hair again. He seemed more interested in his appearance than in her rejection of his embraces, and April didn't know whether to be offended or relieved. He doesn't like me any more, she thought in a panic.

'Are you mad at me?' she asked softly.

'Mad? Why?'

She shrugged, feeling herself blush.

'What, mad?' he said. 'What?'

'I . . .'

'Come on, April,' he said petulantly. 'Grow up. Why should I be mad at you? I don't force anyone to do anything. I don't have to.'

'I'm sure you don't,' she said.

He was mollified and trying not to show it. She could feel her heart pounding with joy. 'It's not that I don't like you,' she said, wringing her hands together. 'I do like you. A lot.'

'Well, I like you too,' he said. He took his suit jacket out of the closet and put it on, carefully arranging a printed silk handkerchief in the pocket. He took a last glance into the mirror. 'Are you ready?' he asked pleasantly.

'Yes.' She preceded him out of the apartment and waited while he locked the door behind them. It was a little as if he were writing *The End* on a chapter, and yet she knew with a certainty that it was only the end of a chapter and not of the whole story. How handsome he was, and how nice he smelled! It was funny how when Dexter had first kissed her she had thought of Mr Shalimar as 'that dirty old man.' Already everything that had happened to her before this day seemed far away and unimportant. How could she ever have thought Mr Shalimar was glamorous? She was glad she had never let him do anything to her and that she had kept away from him whenever he was alone. Everything important was the present and the future, with Dexter Key, as if her life were really beginning on this day.

'Would you like to eat dinner outdoors?' he asked. 'I know just the place.'

He took her arm and they walked down the street, where he hailed a taxi. He wasn't annoyed, he liked her. He didn't mind that she was a bit of a prude, he liked her. In the end it would do her good. Maybe he would even fall in love with her. She was ninety-eight percent in love with him already. It was a real New York success story, she was thinking, and now she knew what she had come to New York to find. Not business success, but love. Success in love was every bit as important as success in a career – even more so for a woman. If there was anything in the world more important than love, April thought, glancing secretly at Dexter, she really couldn't imagine what it could be.

9

Summer is the worst time of year in New York. The hot breeze blows soot and sticky blackness in through opened windows, offices are running on half staff for staggered summer vacations, sidewalks grow soft and tempers short, and along the streets leading to the highways out of the city people lean on their tenement window sills and dully watch the long stream of cars nudging each other bumper to bumper at five o'clock, the hour of release.

Times Square at lunch hour looks like a carnival or a listless Mardi Gras. Winter coats hide many secrets: flaws in figure, flaws in taste; but the heat of summer reveals everything. Just by watching the people at the crossings you can never tell when the lights have changed because the crowds keep moving on regardless, the boys in their short-sleeved sports shirts, the girls in their summer dresses, bare armed, bare legged, some bare backed, skin winter white, waiting for their two weeks in the sun. Non-air-conditioned offices are a torment in the summer, ten degrees hotter as you rise from the ground in the elevator, with electric fans to stir the choking air and blow the papers off the desks to the floor. In the cool modern Radio City buildings where offices like Fabian Publications are located, the girls wear sweaters all day in the office and are often absent with brief summer colds.

In the reconverted brownstones and old apartment houses where the tenants are not allowed air conditioning or cannot afford it, summer nights are a time to go to still another air-conditioned movie, to linger for hours in a cold restaurant, or to sit out on a balcony or a fire escape and rub irritated eyelids waiting for sleep, waiting for air, waiting for day which will bring more burning sun and no relief. In those hot sleepless nights of the summer of 1952, five girls, at least, stayed awake thinking of love and careers and worrying, each in her own and different way.

Mary Agnes Russo, in the Bronx, was thinking about her wedding, which was now less than a year away. She was wondering where they would rent an apartment and whether they could afford three rooms. It would be nice to have her own living room, and a bedroom and kitchen. A bedroom – a shiver went up her back in the hot dark room as she thought of the things she had been trying not to think about all these months. She was a little bit afraid, but she knew everything would be all right once she and Bill were alone together. Someone had told her an awful story: that after the excitement of the wedding and all the bride always got the curse on her wedding night. What a horrible thing that would be, after waiting almost two years! But then, there would be all those other nights afterward, all through the years, and there would be children and a home with furniture in it, and meals to cook, and things to do as a couple, and it would all be worth the waiting. If you were going to be married forever, all the rest of your life and all through eternity, you could wait two years – couldn't you? She clenched her hands together and moved about on her rumpled sheet, trying to find a cool spot where she had not been lying before. Lately she couldn't sleep, she was getting to be a wreck. In the morning she had dark circles under her eyes. A girl should be married; it was boring being single, and it was lonely. She hated saying good night at the door and running back for one last kiss and then having to pry his hands off where they shouldn't be. 'I know,' he would agree, and put his hands in his pockets. Then, walking up the stairs to her bedroom, tiptoeing so as not to wake her father whom she could hear snoring in his bedroom, she would want nothing more than to run back down the stairs and call out to Bill before he could get away. But she would grit her teeth and continue into her room, and by the time she got there she would realize that she was so tired there was nothing to do but go to bed. And then, in bed, she couldn't sleep . . .

It's all right, Mary Agnes thought, we'll be married by this time next summer. And if it's hot and we can't sleep, we'll sit up by the window and talk, and drink a glass of milk, or maybe he'll have a cold beer. And we'll have a white French Provincial bedroom suite, with a double bed and a double dresser to match, or maybe a dresser for me and a chifforobe for him. It would seem strange to have a double bed. When she went to visit some of her girl friends from high school who were married now, and she saw a double bed in the bedroom, it would embarrass her a little. It was almost like saying, Now you know what *we* do. Never mind, Mary Agnes thought, when you're married you get used to those things. I'll bet after a while it gets to be just as ordinary as going to sleep at night. After all, that isn't the most important thing in marriage, it's the very least. The important thing is being a couple, being a wife, being married, being able to say, My husband. My husband says . . .

If I can't sleep tonight again, Mary Agnes thought, I don't know what I'll do.

In the room she shared with her one-and-a-half-year-old daughter, Barbara Lemont was awake staring at the ceiling. Every once in a while a car would go by, and its headlights would sweep across her ceiling. She wondered who was in the car and where it was going. A boy and a girl perhaps, on a date. She hadn't dated enough, she had never had a chance, and now dating was different. If only I could meet someone *interesting*, she thought. I'm so tired of sitting in a cocktail lounge where the dim light makes me want to sleep, with my jaws hurting from trying not to yawn, listening to some fool telling me dirty jokes because he thinks that's going to get me all excited. Some dumb boy dragging sex into the conversation, thinking all he has to do is talk about people going to bed together and I'll start to pant. What do these boys think anyway, that a girl who's been married is a sex machine? Those bedroom athletes probably have more of a sex life as bachelors than *I* ever had. Don't they know that when you're not getting along with your husband, making love is the last thing in the world you want to do? And don't they realize that if they bore me to death at the dinner table

I'm certainly not going to want to be bored afterward in their beds? Bored afterward, she thought, *that's* a Freudian slip.

Barbara smiled. At least I can laugh. And when you can still laugh at them you've got them all beat, no matter what happens. Don't we, Hillary baby? She got out of bed and tiptoed to her daughter's crib and bent low to look at the peaceful little face, listen to the regular breathing. I've got you to get settled too, now, she thought. God, what a responsibility! Soon you'll be old enough to talk and ask me questions about love, and about boys, and about why there aren't any daddies in this house. And I'll have to tell you that love is wonderful, and that good little girls get married and live happily ever after, and that Nana and I just weren't lucky. I wonder if you'll believe me, or if you'll be cagey enough to figure out that I don't even believe it myself.

Love, Barbara thought, is a four-letter word, but most of the boys I meet seem to have it confused with another four-letter word that people don't mention in polite company. If only, if *only* I could meet somebody interesting!

Caroline Bender, in a white nylon peignoir, was sitting on her balcony; or, rather, since there was no room on the tiny balcony for a chair, she was sitting on the window sill, with her feet on the balcony floor and Gregg's cat asleep in her lap. She stroked the cat's ear with her finger, listening to the summer night noises below. The sound of cars, the weird skitter of a bus's brakes that sounded a little like tree frogs, the screams and laughter of a group of teen-aged boys crossing the street. It was one o'clock in the morning and she was not tired enough to sleep and too sleepy to do something constructive like read another manuscript. Manuscripts were piled on her dresser among the perfume bottles, reminding her of her old college room. There was always work to do, not because Fabian made their editors take work home but because she wanted to. She remembered the first weeks after she had been graduated from college, how in the fall evenings she would be watching television and feel a sense of guilt creeping up on her, and finally realize it was because she had been so trained to do homework after dinner that being absolutely free was a sensation she would have to become used to. Fifteen years of school, fifteen years of routine and in-taking and growing and being taught to seek, and finding. All of a sudden graduation, and the discovery that the limitless walls of books are really a cloister.

Things had been different between her and Mike after that afternoon when they had left the office party – not a great difference, but both of them were aware of it. It was as if there was a slow, gradual drawing away of each from the other, very gently because each was afraid to hurt the other and each was afraid that the separation might hurt himself. They did not go out together as often, and they managed to surround themselves with people from the office, people whom they had once thought were absurd bores and whom they were now rather glad to see. She still felt an affection for Mike, but it was a changed love, without desire. When she took his hand out of fondness she was now always a little surprised because it aroused him as much as before. To her he was no longer a lover. It was not that he had failed her; actually he had given her something and she was grateful to him. She was glad it had been Mike and no one else. And yet Caroline could not help feeling, guiltily, that he *had* failed her, that they had failed each other. He had molded her mind and expected her body to follow. How could it? Everything had been a sham, their mental affair, their love and their eventual moment of passion. He had changed her, he had left her trembling, curious, half satisfied, with a mind that was demanding, perceptive, almost cynical. He would say that he had done her a favor, and she could agree. But he had closed out the field for her, and although he would say that was a favor too, Caroline wondered what would happen to her now.

There was one thing she was sure of. She was going to become an editor. She knew Mr Shalimar was relying on her reports more and more, that he regarded her opinion more highly than he regarded Miss Farrow's. If perseverence and extra work could do the trick, then Caroline would have her career. But there were difficulties. There was the time Miss Farrow had sent in the list of promotions to *Publisher's Weekly*, the Bible of the publishing business, and had omitted Caroline's name. Caroline had never heard of *Publisher's Weekly*, but she was hurt that Miss Farrow had left her out of it. Rather than make an issue of it, she just sent in a polite little note explaining the 'mistake,' and the next week she had an item all her own. After that Caroline began to realize that the older woman was wary of her; she took only two hours for lunch instead of three and fell into the habit of leafing through the manuscripts on Caroline's desk to make sure Caroline did not have anything important in her possession. At the end of August Caroline had been given her own office, the tiniest cubicle of all at the end of the row, and she began to think of Miss Farrow's daily walk there as Farrow's Prowl.

It was good to be able to care so much about work. It must be something like the way men feel, Caroline thought, except that men have to worry so much about the money. For her the thrill was in the competition and in the achievement. But she was beginning to think about money too. What kind of money was sixty dollars a week? A private secretary started at sixty-five. Mr Shalimar's secretary was making eighty-five. If Caroline was a reader, and she bought books that made money for the company, then shouldn't she be paid more? The fifty dollars that had seemed a fortune in January now seemed like a child's allowance. After withholding taxes and Social Security, what was left? And rent, and food, and a bottle of liquor now and then, and cosmetics and stockings and shoes and underwear that didn't last forever, and having her hair cut, and going out to lunch every day – she could hardly even afford to go to Port Blair for weekends. Her mother would slip her the money for the return fare when she came to visit, and Caroline would have only a momentary qualm about taking it. That was better than taking it from a man, as April was doing.

Oh, April always intended to pay it back. Dexter Key would lend her ten dollars when the corner grocery refused to let her charge any more, he had lent her fifty as an appeasement gesture when the department stores sent her the last strongest letter beginning: 'We know you don't want the embarrassment of having a bill collector come . . .' Dexter was so rich he could afford these little donations any time he cared to make them, and April felt as if every one of them was a further avowal of permanence. April had been brought up to believe that a man never takes on a woman's debts unless she is a relative, his wife or his mistress. Since April was none of these things to Dexter she was left to her own imagination, and April's imagination was one of the most romantic in the world.

Caroline stirred on the window sill trying to find a comfortable position, and the cat awoke and sprang out of her lap. It wasn't the heat that was keeping her awake like this, because if you stayed perfectly still your body heat was lowered and you could almost feel comfortable. But she had so much to worry about: what she would do first in the office tomorrow morning, that letter Mr Shalimar had said she could write to an author suggesting revisions for his book (the first time she had ever had such a responsibility and she was frightened) and all those damn Westerns she had been putting off reading that were gathering dust on the corner of her desk. If she could discover something worth while from the unsolicited pile, that would be a great step ahead, because then the author would be hers exclusively to develop and if he turned out to be able to write other good books she would be well on her way to being an editor. Perhaps at this time next year she would even have an expense account – a small one, to be sure – but one which would enable her to take her own authors out to lunch. Can you imagine *me* signing a check for a man? Caroline asked herself, and smiled thinking about it. It wasn't such an unthinkable idea, any more than any of the other things that had happened to her in the past eight months. The future, she thought, depends on luck and on other people. Your imagination, if you're coming out of a sheltered life, can't even encompass all the things that *really* happen to you.

April Morrison, for the first time, resented and loathed the protruding spring in her in-the-wall bed. The night was hot enough without having to curl yourself like a shrimp to avoid being stabbed. She picked the sheet off the bed and spread it on the floor, put down her pillow, and stretched out. There, that was better. Wasn't it funny – Dexter Key's girl having to sleep on the floor! What would the society columns say? He had told her that he was sometimes in Winchell's column, and she read it all the time now, but she never saw his name. Dexter Key, stockbroker *boulevardier*, and April Morrison, Fabian Publications' Girl Friday, an item. Wouldn't she love to see that! April closed her eyes and brought to herself an image of Dexter's face. In this daydream he was leaning close to her, holding her hand, and saying, 'I love you more and more all the time. Let's get married.' Was that what they said when they proposed? She'd never had a proposal, and she hoped it would be a romantic one when she did. Who am I kidding? April thought. If Dexter even said, 'I've got nothing to do today, let's get married,' I'd be delighted.

They could have three children, first a boy named after his father of course, and then a girl named Christina. Christina Key – that was a little hard-sounding, with the C and the K. She'd have to think of something else. Bonita was pretty, Bonnie for short . . . The daydream of Dexter's face began to move, to turn into a dream. He was whispering, he was interlacing his fingers with hers. April fell asleep, lost in a dream of her own choosing, and very content.

Gregg Adams was awake, leaning on one elbow over the sleeping body of David Wilder Savage, listening to him breathe, watching his face. How could he sleep in this heat? She was so excited and tired from doing her performance at the Playhouse and then driving two hours in the stage manager's borrowed car to get to the city to see David that she couldn't even think of sleeping. Tomorrow she would probably be exhausted, and there was that horrible drive back. Coming in to the city was always a short trip, but returning seemed four hours long. David couldn't come to see her as often as she'd hoped; poor thing, he was casting a new play. Altogether they saw each other only three times a week, and it was hell without him. She thought about him all the time, going over their conversations in her mind, trying to see if she had said the right thing, or if he had let go of something significant. What a man for hiding his feelings! How easy those first weeks seemed when they had just met, compared to now, which was so full of emotion and wondering it almost gave her a headache. She hadn't known love could be like this, a time of self-doubt and clinging, finding alternate comfort and loneliness according to the moods of the man.

He was so sweet after he had made love to her, kissing her forehead or her eyes, not rolling over as if he had finished with her as some men had done. He would hold her hand for a few minutes until the need for sleep made them both crave privacy, and then when each of them finally curled into his private world it was not as if they were saying goodbye at all. Although he had never said, 'I love you,' even at those moments when she thought passion and her insistent question would surely make him lie to her, she was sure he did love her. No one could be so tender, so affectionate, without love.

It's hell to be a woman, Gregg thought; to want so much love, to feel like only half a person, to need so much. What was it Plato had said? A man and a woman are each only half a person until they unite. Why hadn't he made that clearer to the men?

10

Autumn is rebirth in New York. The new plays open on Broadway, the stores show their changing fashions, the round of apartment hunting and moving and cocktail parties begins. Telephones ring, letters are mailed, people welcome one another back from perhaps ten blocks away geographically, but ten thousand miles away in summer lethargy. How was your vacation? everyone asks, until it becomes a tiresome question and one becomes bored with producing the expected superlatives. Caroline Bender had spent her three days in Port Blair, at the nearby beach, and was hoping to lose her tan in time to wear the new dark fall clothes. Gregg Adams had spent her three days in David Wilder Savage's apartment, a concession he had allowed her as a farewell present before she departed for summer stock. April Morrison had spent her three days alternately running up enormous bills at Bonwit Teller and Lord and Taylor on a beach and lawn wardrobe, and sailing and playing tennis with Dexter Key. Barbara Lemont had left Hillary with her mother and had spent her vacation – she had a whole week – at a resort hotel where she met several young men, all of them eligible and all of them as interested in supporting her and her child as they might be in a trip to the moon without oxygen masks. Mary Agnes, who had two whole weeks because of seniority, tried in vain to have them deferred to the following summer in order to have a four-week honeymoon, and finally settled on two weeks at home looking for dishes and silver and linens and taking occasional trips to Jones Beach with her fiancé, Bill. Mr Shalimar went to the Cape with his wife and children. Mike Rice had planned to go to Florida to visit his ex-wife and daughter but changed his mind at the last minute for some reason even Caroline could not find out, and went instead to stay with friends who had a farm in Connecticut. Altogether, everyone was glad to be back, and glad that the allotted have-fun period was over and done with for another year.

In early October, when the little scraps of sidewalk trees showed their turning leaves, and walking to work was a pleasure under the clear blue sky, Caroline was invited to a cocktail party given by a girl who had gone to Port Blair High School with her, who was now married and living in New York with her husband, a medical student. Caroline always had a kind of reluctance at the beginning of a cocktail party; she hated walking into a room of strangers alone, and she would have preferred to bring a date, anyone, but her hostess said there would be dozens of bachelors and they would need all the extra girls they could find. Although The Bachelor is always mentioned as the prime requisite for a successful party (in all the etiquette articles) an attractive single girl in her early twenties with an interesting job is just as valuable, and in this age of early marriages almost as rare.

The apartment where the party was held was in one of those large older apartment buildings inhabited mostly by families who have lived there for years. Because these apartments are rent controlled their tenants are very slow to leave, and space is hard to get. Kippie Millikin and her husband had managed to rent a three-room apartment in the back, facing a court. There were curved metal strips guarding the windows, left there by the previous tenant, who had young children, and the Millikins had not bothered to remove them. With those, the unwashed windows, and the dark court outside, Caroline felt as if she were in a trap. The apartment had been temporarily furnished with hand-me-downs from both the young couple's parents: a dark-green convertible sofa bed with a hole in one arm, a glass and rattan coffee table that had formerly stood on a porch, and an assortment of modern and Colonial lamps. Kippie, who was five months pregnant, had given up her secretarial job, and the two sets of in-laws were helping to pay the rent while her husband went to school. It was as though the two families themselves were married to each other, Caroline thought, and their children were playing house. But it was all an investment in the future, Caroline's mother had told her, adding that confidentially she hoped Caroline would fall in love with a man who was already established.

Kippie met Caroline at the door and kissed her lightly on the cheek. 'I'm so glad you came early,' Kippie said. 'We have lots of bachelors.'

Caroline took off her coat and hung it in the hall closet, looking at her friend. Kippie wore a vast accordion-pleated maternity blouse, which made her look larger than she actually was, with a low-cut neckline that was supposed to make her alluring. She'd had her hair cut short because it was easier to take care of, and she wore it straight, with even bangs. Her arms looked very thin and white, and she wore a gold-plated bracelet with part of the gold already worn off, showing the greenish metal beneath. She wore no nail polish, and her nails were clipped and rounded like a little boy's. I suppose she has to do a lot of housework, Caroline thought, and preparing for this party wasn't easy either.

'We got a new bedspread for our anniversary,' Kippie said. 'Come and see it and then I'll get you a drink.'

Caroline could think of at least a dozen things she would rather see than a new bedspread, but she followed Kippie obediently into the bedroom, glancing on the way at the small groups of people standing self-consciously in the darkened living room.

'What I *really* wanted to tell you is, there's a boy here I'm anxious for you to meet,' Kippie said confidingly. 'His name is Paul Landis. He's a lawyer, and he's very nice.'

'From New York or Port Blair?'

'New York. His sister-in-law is a friend of mine, I met her at the natural-childbirth classes. Then she had us over for cocktails last month and I met Paul. As soon as I saw him I said to myself, I'd like to fix him up with a nice girl.'

'You'd like to fix *everyone* up with a nice girl,' Caroline said, smiling.

Kippie looked blank. Then she smiled. 'Well, I like to see my friends settled. You know, it's lots of fun for you to have a job now, but in a few years you'll be tired of it. And I think a girl should have her children when she's young, too, because then she can enjoy herself when she's older and her husband has started to make real money.'

'I don't see why a girl has to quit her job just because she gets married,' Caroline said. 'I'd like to keep mine. It's really more of a career to me than a job – I like it.'

'Maybe you'll marry Paul,' Kippie said comfortably.

'I haven't even laid eyes on him yet!'

'You'll like him. He's sweet. He always kisses me goodbye, he kids me and says I'm his girl friend. It's a standing joke.'

'Oh, God.'

'No, he's funny,' Kippie said. 'He's so cute; wait and you'll see.'

Caroline was looking in the mirror, combing her hair. She glanced down at the assortment of perfume and cologne bottles on the dresser tray. 'Oh, you still wear that. I remember it from high school. You were the first girl to wear perfume instead of cologne. I remember how sophisticated and rich I thought you were.'

'My goodness, I don't remember that.'

'Oh, sure.' Caroline sniffed at the stopper. It brought back memories, one after another, like an image reflected and re-reflected in a series of mirrors. 'And I remember our freshman year when you first started to shave your legs. I was kind of shocked, for some reason.'

Kippie lifted her foot and looked ruefully at her calf. 'I hardly even have time to do that any more.'

'Why?'

'Oh, there are millions of things to do around a house. I didn't believe it either until I was married. And my natural-childbirth classes, and cooking school, and entertaining the in-laws every Sunday or going over to their house, and shopping for the baby. Maybe it doesn't sound like much, but I *make* it much because I like it.'

'As long as you're happy,' Caroline said. 'That's the main thing.'

'I am happy. I always hated my job and when I found out I was pregnant I was so delighted because then I could quit.' She took Caroline's hand. 'Come on. I want you to meet Paul.'

Caroline glanced back at the bedroom as they left. The new bedspread with its dust ruffle looked out of place next to the uncarpeted worn wooden floor. The two chairs in the bedroom did not match, and there were shades at the windows instead of venetian blinds. Caroline remembered very well the home Kippie had lived in in Port Blair, a comfortable, attractive home, much like her own. Kippie had left all her pretty bedroom furniture for her younger sister, who still went to the high school. The king-size bed here was new, and so was the dresser, but the rest would have to wait for the future. A new baby was expensive, medical school was expensive, and so were rent and food. Eventually Kippie and her husband hoped to have a house in the suburbs, where her husband could have his practice. Maybe she's right and I'm wrong, Caroline thought, but I couldn't stand to live the way she does now. It depresses me just to be here for an hour. And she hardly even sees her husband; he's always at the hospital or studying.

Could I have done it for Eddie? She remembered Eddie again, as a part of her past, the past that came back whenever she saw anyone she had known before these nine important months at Fabian. And the past still hurt a little. Of course I could have done it for Eddie, Caroline thought; I'd probably be just as boring and domestic as Kippie is. No . . . not quite as boring. I'd do all this with imagination. And Eddie was different from everyone else because he had imagination too, and humor, and life.

'I'd like you to meet Paul Landis,' Kippie said. 'This is my friend Caroline Bender from high school, you remember how many times I've told you about her.'

'Indeed I do,' Paul Landis said.

He held out his hand and Caroline shook hands with him, thinking how rather formal it was for anyone to take time out to shake hands at a cocktail party. He was a bit over six feet tall, with dark straight hair and a generous straight nose and brown horn-rimmed glasses. He reminded Caroline of a large, earnest bird. He wore a gray flannel suit that was almost black, a white shirt with a tight little round collar and a collar pin in it and a narrow black knitted tie. The suit was obviously expensive, and the collar pin looked like real gold.

'Can I get you a drink?' Paul asked.

'Yes, please, a Martini,' Caroline said.

'Oh, we don't have Martinis,' Kippie said. 'But Paul can make you one!'

'I'd be delighted,' said Paul. 'Do you have a water glass handy?'

'We even have a Martini pitcher,' said Kippie. 'A wedding present. I'll get it, you stay here.'

'You're the editor,' said Paul. 'That must be very interesting.'

'When I get a good book to read, it is,' Caroline said. 'Then I think to myself, Is this what I'm actually getting paid for?'

Paul laughed. 'Have you put out any books I might have read?'

'I don't know. Have you read *Beautiful Bodies*? Or *Tobacco Hill*?'

'They sound vaguely like steals. That, or trash.'

Caroline would ordinarily have been the first to admit that Derby Books liked to find titles that sounded either like the title of someone else's successful book or else seemed to promise carnal literary adventures, but Paul's uplifted eyebrows made her feel rather hostile toward him. 'That's the point,' she said.

'You mean, that's what people want.'

'Several million people,' she said.

'Well, I wish you'd send me some,' Paul said. 'I'd like to read them. You'd better mail them in plain wrapper, I think.'

'Why don't you buy some?'

'All right, I will. Where do I get them?'

'Any drugstore.'

'All right,' said Paul.

'Here's Kippie with the Martini pitcher,' Kippie said brightly, edging in beside them. 'Now Paul can impress you.'

If making a cocktail is supposed to impress me, Caroline thought, then I should be in love with every bartender in town. But I won't let Kippie's pushing throw me – it's childish to dislike him just because someone else is so obviously trying to make a match between us. I'm going to *try* to like him, he isn't bad, really, he's just a little stuffy.

'Let me analyze you,' Paul Landis said, stirring the Martini briskly. 'Now, none of this is from Kippie, I'm getting it from looking at you. You went to either Radcliffe or Wellesley.'

'Radcliffe,' said Caroline. 'And there's a great difference.'

'All you Radcliffe girls say that. You live on the East Side between Fiftieth and Eightieth.'

'A safe guess,' Caroline said.

'Am I right?'

'Yes, but I happen to live far enough east so it's no longer chic. Only inexpensive.'

'You have a roommate.'

Somehow it annoyed her that he was categorizing her so neatly, even though he happened to be correct. It's as if he's not really looking at *me*, Caroline thought, but just at what he wants me to look like. 'Right again,' she said. 'Gregg Adams.'

'Gregg?' He lifted his eyebrows, not really because he thought Gregg was a man's name – he wouldn't believe that in a million years – but because he couldn't let the chance for the feeble joke pass untaken.

'Gregg with two G's,' Caroline said. 'She's an actress.'

'You get along together very well because she's hardly ever there,' he went on.

'Also because we like each other.'

'I assumed that.'

'You're cross-examining me,' Caroline said. 'I can tell *you're* a lawyer.'

'Does it bother you?'

'Not particularly. But I'd like another Martini.'

'A girl after my own heart! I'll have one with you.' He bent over the Martini pitcher, measuring out the gin and vermouth, and Caroline looked around the room. There was Kippie's husband Don, round, bouncing, cheerfully putting his arm around his friends' necks. Everyone in Port Blair thought he was a genius, they said what a great future he would have. Perhaps so, Caroline thought, and I'll bet he has an endearing bedside manner. For the patients, that is. I can't imagine him and Kippie sleeping together, even though they obviously have. He looks to me like a shaved Teddy bear.

'What do you like to do?' asked Paul, handing her the drink. 'Go to the theater? The ballet? Watch out, that glass is dripping.' He quickly handed her a cocktail napkin, took the glass from her hand and wiped off the bottom of it with another napkin, and handed it gingerly back. 'Be careful. I miscalculated.'

'It's all right now.'

'I hope you didn't get any on your dress.'

'No, it's fine.'

'That's a beautiful dress, by the way,' Paul said. 'I like girls who wear black. To me, there isn't any other color.'

There wouldn't be, Caroline couldn't help thinking. But he was nice, he cared about her welfare, and he noticed things. If her ideas and feelings couldn't be pigeonholed quite so neatly as he expected them to, perhaps it wasn't his fault, perhaps it was hers.

'I guess every winter dress I own is either black or gray,' she said.

'That's good fabric, too. I notice fabrics because my dad is in the textile business. I couldn't help picking up little bits of information.'

'Well, I'm glad to know an authority approves,' Caroline said, smiling.

'Oh, I'm not an authority. He wanted me to go into business with him when I was graduated from Columbia, but I put my foot down. I went on to law school instead.'

'Are you going to do courtroom work?'

'No. Contracts and corporations. There's a lot of money in that.'

'Somehow I always thought of the lawyer being clever in a courtroom as a very romantic figure,' Caroline said. 'Too many movies, I guess. But I'm a little disappointed you aren't one of those. I've always wanted to meet one.'

'I've been lucky enough to get into one of the best firms,' Paul said. 'There's a future in it, and I love the work. If you're interested in books, you should be interested in hearing about some of our cases. They'd make a novel, or at least a short story.'

'I'd like to hear one,' Caroline said, hoping he wouldn't tell it. For some reason she was tired, very tired. It had been a rough day today: Miss Farrow breathing down her neck, Mr Shalimar deciding that the yen he'd had for her all these months was too beautiful to be denied and trying to kiss her behind his filing cabinet, the manuscript clerk losing one of their most important manuscripts and general hysteria throughout the office until it had been found again.

'How about dinner later?' Paul asked. 'I feel like having a steak. How about you?'

'That's very nice of you. But I'm so tired I thought I'd just go right home to bed.'

'You have to have dinner! You're not going to go to bed without dinner? The bad little child sent to bed without any supper?'

Caroline held her hands out in a gesture of helplessness. 'I'm just not up to going out and being entertaining. I'd only make you feel sleepy too. Those things are contagious, you know.'

'You don't have to talk to me. I'll talk to you. I'll feed you a steak and another Martini and then I'll take you right home.'

He *was* nice, what could she say to him? To tell the truth, she was hungry, and she hadn't had steak since she couldn't remember when. He liked to talk, and she could listen to him, which would make him happy evidently. Perhaps he had no one to keep him company, perhaps he was lonely. Perhaps despite her coldness toward him he really thought he liked her. Perhaps she had been unfair to him, and if she got to know him better she would be glad she'd taken the time.

'Well, I'd love to, if you really mean it about taking me home early.'

'That's a promise.'

She smiled at him. 'I'm ready to go whenever you are.'

He downed his Martini and they went together to say goodbye to their host and hostess. Paul put his arm around Kippie and kissed her soundly on the cheek. 'My girl friend,' he said. Kippie grinned.

'You're going out to dinner, you two?' she asked.

'We're going to the Steak Bit,' Paul said. He put his arm around Caroline.

'Oh . . . I love the Steak Bit!' Kippie sighed. 'Don and I used to go there before we were married. Remember, honey?'

'If you're going to kiss my wife goodbye, then I want to kiss Caroline goodbye,' Don said. He advanced upon Caroline, his Teddy-bear arms outstretched. Caroline turned her head but not quickly enough; unexpectedly Don was kissing her on the mouth. She could feel his teeth behind his lips, then his tongue was trying to probe further. She pulled away from him and smiled in a friendly way for Kippie's benefit.

'Thank you for the lovely party,' Caroline said.

'Thank you for coming,' said Kippie. 'Have a good time with my boy friend.' She put her arm around her husband's waist and beamed at Paul and Caroline.

'Come back soon,' Don said.

'Yes,' said Kippie. 'The four of us can play bridge together some night. Wouldn't that be fun? I'll call you *soon*, Caroline.' She nodded significantly.

'Good night.'

'Good night.'

In the cool air of the street Caroline felt more awake. She moved away from Paul's encircling arm and transferred her purse to the hand that was nearer him so he could not hold her hand. She could see into the lighted rooms of some of the apartments on lower floors across the street, and in one of them she saw people moving about as if they too were at a cocktail party. She wondered whether there was a girl there being introduced to a boy she might marry, or a husband who was clandestinely kissing his wife's school friend in a meaningless moment of extracurricular yearning. She felt lonely and, for some unknown reason, rather sad.

The restaurant where Paul took her was one of those substantial, plain-looking places where the high price is always a surprise. The steaks were served charcoal black on the outside, red inside, and must have weighed two pounds apiece. The Martini before the food had made Caroline feel pleasantly fuzzy. She knew that the depression which had hit her in the street was waiting somewhere outside this temporary euphoria, but if she concentrated she could manage to keep it away, at least for a while. She smiled at him when she leaned forward for him to light her cigarette.

'You don't eat much,' he said. 'No wonder you're so thin. I like girls who have a little more . . . um . . .'

'Shape?'

'No, you have a good shape. I just think you could use a little more of it.'

'You sound like an old-fashioned man.'

'Maybe I am,' Paul said. 'I like gracious living, three-hour dinners, a home that always has fresh flowers in it, and a girl with comfortable curves. I guess I should have been born at the turn of the century.'

'So that you could eat fourteen-course meals and have a wife who weighs two hundred pounds.'

'Ugh,' he said. 'Not a fourteen-course meal. Just a leisurely one, with brandy afterward and lots of time to talk. Speaking of brandy, what kind would you prefer?'

'I'm ashamed to say I don't know the difference.' But she wasn't ashamed, she really didn't care.

He ordered two ponies of brandy for them and leaned back, lighting his cigarette. 'I asked you and you didn't answer me; do you like the theater?'

'I love it.'

'I'll get tickets for next Saturday night if you'll go with me.'

Did she want to go? Why not? He was kind to her and she liked the theater, so she would be a fool not to accept – and yet, something warned her. She didn't have the faintest idea what it was, it was simply a premonition, and she quickly pushed it out of her mind.

'I think that would be fun,' Caroline said.

'Good. Supper afterward instead of before, we won't have to rush that way.'

How planned everything was with him, how efficient! He was Gracious Living with capital letters. She remembered how the official watchword at Radcliffe had been Gracious Living, and how most of the girls had turned it into a kind of joke. Gracious Living meant you had to wear a dress to dinner instead of slacks, it meant demitasse in the living room afterward, and to Caroline and her friends it had seemed like a silly struggle to retain the superficial when the deeper things were collapsing all around them. Demitasse and forced conversation when you were failing in three subjects, demitasse and conversation when the boy you loved hadn't phoned for ten days, demitasse and conversation when your period was late and you were starting to feel mysteriously sick in the mornings? Here she was with Paul Landis in an expensive restaurant, drinking the best brandy, talking of ways to make life pleasant, and she wanted to cry out to him, Reach me! Say something that *means* something to me, anything, I don't even know what myself. Look into my face the way Mike used to do, the way Eddie used to do, and say something to show you're here with *me*, Caroline Bender, not just a thin girl in a chic black dress who also likes the theater.

It was too much to ask on a first date, and yet her instinct told her that he would never look deeper. I'll have a good time, she thought; he's a perfect escort. He's kind. What am I looking for, a neurotic like Mike, like Eddie? Here's a nice solid young man who evidently likes me. Period.

'Would you like to take a walk for a few blocks?' Paul asked.

'Yes. I need to recover from that huge dinner.'

'I'm going to send you a box of candy tomorrow. And you eat it. You need it.'

She laughed.

While he was recovering his hat from the checkroom Caroline looked at him critically. It was typical of him that he should wear a hat, but it had a small brim and a jaunty look to it, so it was not, at least, the kind her father would wear. His large nose was a little shiny from the heat in the restaurant, but he had a clear, ruddy complexion with health radiating from it. She was sure he went to bed before twelve on week nights and never drank too much. The fit of his suit was impeccable. There was nothing effeminate about him, and yet he had the kind of build that made his body seem simply not to exist. He was an expensive suit reaching from a pair of the proper-size shoulders down to a pair of English shoes. He was tall, he weighed perhaps a hundred and seventy-five pounds, but these were statistics she had to bring to mind consciously. It was like trying to categorize something in order to make it exist. Perhaps that's how he feels about me, Caroline thought, he has to categorize me to make me exist for him.

In the street again she was acutely conscious of the sounds and colors around her: the neon lights above the other restaurants, the traffic noises, the laughter and conversation of people who passed by in an instant, never to be seen again, or if they should be seen, never to be recognized. The world was suddenly very interesting to her, and she clung to every facet of it, everything she could see and smell and hear. She hardly noticed that Paul had finally launched on a lengthy account of one of his legal cases 'that would make a good story.'

'You must be fascinated with your work,' Caroline said. 'That's wonderful.'

'I am. The same way I guess you are. Although, I can't understand why you waste your time with trash. You seem to be an intelligent girl, with a good educational background. Couldn't you have found something better?'

'Not at the time. The employment agency offered me this job and it seemed like a good thing. I just wanted to be busy, I didn't care at what. There was something I was trying hard to forget.'

'You don't seem like a girl who has anything she doesn't want to remember.'

'Every girl has,' Caroline said. 'Life isn't that perfect. Haven't you?'

He thought for a moment. 'No . . . offhand I can't think of anything. I've been lucky. I've always had enough money, I got into the schools of my choice, I like all my friends. I get along with my family, I've never had any illnesses other than measles and chicken pox, and I'm enthusiastic about my work. I broke both my legs once when I was learning to ski, but it wasn't so bad after all because I had a chance to lie in bed and read things I'd never have had time to otherwise.'

'What a wonderful, even life you've had,' Caroline said, sighing. 'No ups and downs, just straight all along.'

'What are you talking about?' Paul said. 'So have you. Don't tell me anything has happened to you that a year from now you will be able to look back at and honestly say was a crisis.'

'How smug you are! I might have been in reform school, I might be an orphan. How do you know? Just because I have good manners and live in a certain thirty-block area?'

'I don't know,' Paul said seriously. 'Maybe you have been in reform school, since you mention it. But if you have, I don't want to know about it. I like you the way you are, to me, tonight.'

'But if it happened to me,' Caroline said, 'then it's part of me. It *is* me. And the things I think – they're what made all the things that did or didn't happen to me important.'

'Well, have you been in reform school?' he asked, his eyes twinkling.

'Of course not.'

'I didn't think so.'

'You don't understand,' Caroline said. 'You don't understand at all.'

Paul hailed a taxi and helped her into it. 'You see?' he said. 'I'm getting you home early, just as I promised.'

'I'd forgotten all about that.'

'Good,' he said. He put his arm around the back of the seat, his fingers just touching her shoulder. He took off his hat and placed it on the seat between him and the window. 'I like the way you argue, Caroline.'

'Thank you.'

His hand was holding her shoulder now, lightly, and he moved closer to her. He took her hand from her lap and held it in his gloved hand. She could feel his breath on her cheek as he spoke. 'It's a pleasure to meet a girl who thinks,' he said.

But you don't know how I think, she wanted to say. She smiled at him a little nervously. She knew he was preparing to kiss her, and she didn't want to offend him, but she didn't want to kiss him either. Suddenly the image of Mike's face came up between them, looking knowing and a little mournful. If Paul Landis knew about me and Mike, Caroline thought, he would die. It seemed a little like a weapon in her hand; Mike, her affair with Mike, her communication with Mike and his understanding of her which this confident, content, ordinary boy would never be able to grasp.

'You're very nice,' Caroline said. 'You're a nice person.' She turned away and rolled down the window, half leaning out of it. 'Look how pretty the park is at night. It's a shame people can't walk in the park without being hit on the head. I wish I could go to the zoo sometime at night; it would be sort of crazy, don't you think? All the animals would be asleep and it would be too dark to see anything anyway.' She was aware that she was talking gibberish.

'Come here,' he said.

He took her face in one hand and drew her to him with the other. He had removed his gloves and his palm was slightly moist. He's as nervous as I am, she thought, and closed her eyes, submitting. He kissed her once, a long kiss, but only one. Then he kissed her lightly on the cheek and released her. Caroline could barely suppress a sigh of relief. Paul settled his arm more comfortably around her shoulders and leaned his head against the back of the taxi seat, closing his eyes.

'I'll take you to the zoo sometime at night,' he murmured. 'If you really want to go.'

When he delivered her to her front door Paul held her hand for a moment but did not ask if he might come in. 'Thank you for a wonderful evening,' he said.

'Thank *you*.'

He made a fist and tapped her playfully on the chin. 'Next Saturday – remember. I'll speak to you before that.'

He was gone then, and Caroline shut the door and locked it. She went into the bathroom and looked at herself in the mirror. She looked prettier than she had looked in a long time, hair curly from the damp of a fall night, mouth rather voluptuous-looking from her smeared lipstick, eyes large and very blue in her tanned face. Why was it always like this, that one looked so much prettier when one was out with a boy who meant nothing? It was unfair, somehow. But no wonder he had liked her; she did look nice. She looked – appealing. That was it. Or did she feel appealing because Paul so obviously admired her? It was pleasant to be liked by someone who was not a complete cluck, you had to admit that. He made her feel contented. But she also felt contented because she had locked the door of her own apartment and Paul Landis was somewhere on the outside of it while she was safe inside. It was as if she had completed a tiring mission and now could rest and recover alone.

Caroline wandered about the room, undressing, putting on her pajamas and turning down her bed. She washed off her make-up and brushed her teeth and drank a glass of water. Then, with her hand on the lamp to turn it out, a wave of melancholy hit her as strongly as if it had been a wave of nausea. She sat down on the bed, giving herself to the sensation, feeling as if a hand had tightened around her throat. Someone . . . she needed someone to talk to . . . why didn't Gregg come home? It was too early for Gregg, that was why. She knew whom she needed to talk to, whom she wanted to see more than anyone else in the world at this moment. But she didn't want to call him, for what good would it do? What could he do for her? Go to sleep, she thought, and forget it; tomorrow you'll feel fine. But she knew if she lay down on the bed she would never be able to sleep.

Picking up the phone book was a comforting act in itself. Caroline leafed through it, feeling her heart pounding. She found the name of Mike's hotel and dialed it, realizing only at that moment that it was too early for Mike to be home either. I hope he's out somewhere, she thought and then an instant later: Please be home, please!

'Mike Rice, please.'

How bored the switchboard operator sounded, as if she hated everybody, and at this moment Mike Rice in particular. There was a long wait. I know he isn't there, Caroline thought, but now that she was sure he was away she was glad she had called just to find out.

'Hello,' Mike Rice said.

'Oh, Mike!'

'Caroline?'

'Yes.'

'Where are you? Caroline . . .'

'At home,' she said lightly. 'Where else should I be?'

'Oh.' He sounded disappointed.

'Well, where did you think I was?'

'I thought you might be hung up at a dull party, that was all.' His voice was as casual as her own.

'No. I was at a cocktail party and then I went to dinner with a boy I met there. He's a lawyer named Paul Landis.'

'Did you like him?' Casual, very casual, with just an undertone of anxiety that he could not quite hide.

'He's nice . . . you know what I mean? What somebody else might call Mister Nice, only I don't feel the same way about that kind of person.'

'Of course not,' Mike said sympathetically.

His agreement made her feel that they were both being unfair to Paul. 'But he *is* nice.'

'How old is he?'

'About twenty-five, I think. It's hard to tell. He's almost no age. But he looks twenty-five.'

'Did he try to sleep with you?'

'Heavens, no. You seem to think everyone wants to make out with me.'

'He'll try.'

'Not Paul,' Caroline said. 'I know he won't. He's marriage and two children and a two-car garage.'

'That's what you want eventually,' Mike said.

'I know. But not with him. Or at least, I'm almost positive not with him.'

'Well, I'm glad you had a good evening, anyway.'

'Yes.'

'Are you going to go to bed now?'

'Yes.'

His voice was hesitant. 'Are you tired?'

'I am now,' she whispered. 'I couldn't sleep, but it's made me feel a lot better just to talk to you.'

'I'm glad.'

'Well . . .'

'Caroline?'

'Yes?'

'Good night . . . sleep well.'

'Good night, darling,' Caroline said softly. 'I love you.'

'I love you too.' He paused. 'I love you too.'

When she had replaced the receiver Caroline felt very tired, a good kind of tiredness that meant relaxation and sleep. She pulled the covers up to her chin and turned the light out, and felt the way she had as a child when her mother had told her a story that the whole room was full of angels guarding over her rest.

The next afternoon when she returned from the office there was a box of red roses leaning against her door. 'You need the candy,' the card read, 'but flowers are more romantic. Paul.'

She put the flowers into a vase of water and tucked the card next to the base of the vase. Not because she cared, but because Paul would notice it when he came to call for her on Saturday, and it might please him to know that she had saved his card all through the week.

II

'I'm glad your parents liked me,' April Morrison said. 'I was afraid.'

April and Dexter Key were sitting on the low stone wall on the clubhouse terrace at the Hudson View Country Club. It was three-thirty Sunday morning, one of a series of clear nights and days in November. Above them were the tiny high stars, and ahead of them were the lighted windows of the clubhouse ballroom, through which April could see the last of the dancers gathered in groups to say goodbye, and the bass player putting the case around his fiddle. She was wearing Dexter's dinner jacket over her bare shoulders, and all she could see of Dexter here in the quiet shadows was the white of his shirt and the red glow of the tip of his cigarette. When he smiled she saw his white teeth. 'Why shouldn't they like you?' he said. 'They like all my girls. I have good taste.'

'Well . . . I thought they might be a little more critical of me. Because we're going steady and all. And I'm not . . . society or anything.'

'Society?' said Dexter. 'Who *is* society any more?'

'Lots of people. And you know it.'

There were leaves all around their feet, which made a dry, sad sound when you kicked them. April moved her silver slippers around in the leaves, thinking how it was at home with great piles of leaves lying along the street outside her house. 'These are the last leaves for the season,' she said softly. 'This is the last really fall weekend. I've never had such a good time in my life.'

'You always have a good time with me, don't you?' he asked, nuzzling her neck.

'Yes.'

'We'll drive into town and I'll make breakfast for you,' he murmured. 'I've never done that, have I?'

'No . . . I'd love it. You know what? Let's stay up all night and then go to church.'

'Church?'

'I haven't gone once since I met you,' April said. 'I promised my father I'd go every Sunday when I came to New York, but every Sunday morning I'm sound asleep.'

'And how many times did you go before you met me?'

'Twice,' she said softly, embarrassed. 'The first two Sundays I was here. It was mostly because I was lonely, I guess.'

'Then don't blame me,' Dexter said, a little defensively.

'I'm not blaming you, honey. I just thought it would be nice if we went to church together today.'

'I never told you what to do,' Dexter said. 'I've never made you do anything you didn't want to do – have I?'

'No . . .'

'Then stop nagging me.'

Tears came into April's eyes. 'Dexter, you get so surly some-times! I don't know why, either.' She wished she might actually cry, it would serve him right, it would show him how much he hurt her by these casual comments he flung out.

'What did I say?'

'You said I'm nagging you.'

'Well, you are.' He stood up. 'Let's go,' he said, not unkindly. 'They'll lock the doors and we'll have to sleep on the terrace.'

She followed him, a step behind him, as they walked across the polished ballroom floor to the checkroom. How handsome he looked in his formal clothes! She was so proud of him. She could see that his mother was proud of him too, the way her eyes never left him. She'd hardly looked at April. But then, at the last, she had shaken April's hand warmly and said, 'You must come to lunch with me someday soon.' My goodness, April thought, what would I ever say to her? I'd probably drop the lettuce right in my lap. But imagine – Dexter's mother wanted to have lunch with her. It was obvious she knew that April meant more to Dexter than all those other girls he used to take out and even sleep with.

Dexter put the top up on his Jaguar, and inside it was cozy and warm. April put her hands into her coat pockets and smiled at him. 'I'm going to go to church anyway today. By myself, if you won't go.'

Dexter shrugged. 'What's all this revivalism all of a sudden?'

'It's just that I've been so lucky lately. Being in New York, my job, knowing you, all the things you do for me. I feel as though I ought to do something in return.'

'Well, do something for me, then,' Dexter said.

'I'd do anything for you! Tell me what.'

He was looking straight ahead through the windshield, and he smiled, shaking his head a little. 'Stop rejecting me.'

'Oh, Dexter! I'm not rejecting you. I love you.'

'You have a fine way of showing it.'

'You know I do show it,' April said, lowering her head as she felt herself begin to blush. Some of the things they did when they were necking; she preferred not to think about them at other times.

'You have such a strange little morality,' Dexter said. 'Do you think it's going to make me think more of you if you keep pushing me away?'

'I can't help it.'

'That's the weakest logic I've ever heard. *Everyone* can help *everything* he does, or he should do his damnedest to be able to. If he's that namby-pamby he's not worth knowing.'

'Please don't fight with me,' April said. 'I was having such a wonderful time.'

'I'm not fighting,' he said coolly. 'It's just that I know you're going to give in eventually so I don't see why you have to make us both suffer by dragging it out.'

'I'm sorry.'

'You're obviously *not* sorry.'

Neither of them spoke for a long time.

'Dexter?' April said. 'Would you ever marry a girl who wasn't a virgin?'

'Of course.'

'I don't mean a girl who'd had a lot of lovers. I mean – for instance – a girl who was a virgin until she started going with you.'

'I wouldn't even care if she'd had a lot of lovers,' Dexter said. 'If I loved her, and if I wanted to be with her for the rest of my life, then I'd marry her. Period.'

April was moistening her lips and avidly watching her hand where it was picking at the bits of wool on her coat. 'You'd know if you were the first that it was because you meant a very great deal to the girl . . . wouldn't you? That it was a real struggle for her . . .'

'That's why I hate going to bed with a virgin,' Dexter said firmly. 'They think they're giving you the greatest thing they have to give in their whole lives. What are they giving you? It hurts them, they don't know one thing about how to conduct themselves in the sack . . . the whole procedure is a pain in the ass for the guy. If I know a girl's a virgin I won't even make a pass at her.'

'Well, I'm a virgin,' April said indignantly.

He reached over and took her hand. 'That's different,' he said, half in humor. 'I love you, so I'm willing to put up with the inconvenience.'

'Oh, Dexter! Nothing's sacred to you, is it?'

'Not that.'

'Well, what is?'

'Love,' Dexter said. 'What two people have together when they're talking and when they're being quiet together. The ability to feel, to care. If I love a girl I want a whole relationship, not a part of one. I want to be with her all the time, every minute, in every way, not have a sophomoric wrestling match every time I say good night.'

'We don't wrestle,' April said, hanging her head.

'Maybe you call it saving your honor. I call it goddam boring.'

'I just don't know what to do,' April said.

His tone was indifferent, a little hurt. 'Do what you want.'

'I'm afraid to do what I want,' April said softly.

'Don't ask me to lead you down the garden path,' said Dexter. 'I don't want you blaming me afterward for ruining your life.'

'But you *wouldn't* ruin my life!'

'Well, thank you for that, at least.'

'Oh, Dexter.'

There was another long silence between them. April could see the lights of the city in the distance, and for some reason they made her feel depressed. It was the first time that the sight of New York, the realization again that she was coming into the city of her dreams, had failed to thrill her. She was too wound up to feel sleepy, but all the same she was tired. How complicated life had become! There were so many people here, doing so many different things, each living his own life which was so different from the life and wants of his neighbor – it made you have to stop and turn around once in a while to find your own identity. If she had any identity at all, April thought, looking at Dexter's profile (sullen, set against any further argument, and so handsome) it was through love. Being loved made a girl feel secure and strong, it made her feel totally different from the way she had when she'd first come here from home. Then she had been wide eyed, a tourist, a little wraith, skipping along the surface of the fortress city. Now she belonged, to New York, to herself, but most of all to Dexter.

'Do we have to stop at the all-night delicatessen?' she asked. 'Do you need anything?'

'I think we could use some bread,' he said.

How wonderful it was to be talking of these mundane household things: groceries, meals, things that people did together when they lived together and were used to each other. You'd almost think she and Dexter were living together, you'd think they were married. They would be married someday, April was sure of it. Because with all the time he spent with her, when did he ever get a chance to meet any other girl? She moved closer to him and put her head on his shoulder, and after an instant he took one hand off the wheel and put his arm around her, holding her to him, safe and warm.

12

About two weeks before Christmas the tree arrived for the reception room at Fabian Publications and the secretaries began decorating the offices. Wreaths and little colored glass balls were taped to the cubicle doors, and some of the larger offices even sported their own miniature Christmas trees. A week before Christmas five of the girls in the thirty-fifth-floor typing pool spent their entire afternoon putting up a display on one of the manuscript tables which had been filched for the occasion: artificial snow, tiny trees, houses and reindeer, and even a scrap of mirror to simulate a skating pond. They dusted the whole paraphernalia with tinsel, and their bosses, who had stacks of last-minute work to be done before the long weekend, waited for them to be finished with smiles of false jolly cheer on their faces and hot annoyance boiling up in their hearts.

Since Christmas fell on a Thursday that year, and Christmas Eve was a time that everyone wanted to spend with his family, the annual office party was to be held on Tuesday, two days before Christmas. The grand ballroom at the President Hoover Hotel had been hired for dinner and dancing afterward. Because of the expense, which was rumored to be fifteen dollars a head, no wives, husbands or friends of employees were to be permitted. 'This way they encourage incest,' Gregg said to Caroline with an uplifted eyebrow when Caroline reported the plans to her.

'I don't know who I'm going to have incest with this year,' Caroline said. 'Mike and I are kind of . . . just friends, and most of the other men I've seen around the office give me the creeps.'

She was rather surprised to hear herself talking this way, even as a joke. But she felt nervous and unfulfilled, and making light of it in her conversations with Gregg was an outlet, the only outlet she had. Paul Landis had been taking her out once a week since they had met, and although there was a certain pleasure in going out with an attentive escort she liked, someone whose every reaction she could gauge in advance, she just could not feel any warmer toward him than she had the first time they met. He sent her flowers, he took her to night clubs, they had seen all the good shows, and she was eating better than she had in months. In return he asked only for goodnight kisses (three or four now instead of one) and an appreciative companion. He treated her like a glass doll. Necking with Paul was the most harmless, sexless sex Caroline had ever known, and when he stood close to her and she realized it meant more than that to him she was somehow rather shocked. It was as if one were to kiss one's favorite uncle and suddenly find him panting.

'Besides,' Gregg was saying, 'they're nearly all married, aren't they? Married or Queersville or so young and poor they'd hardly be able to take you to the Automat.'

'It seems like a waste of money,' Caroline said, 'to have such a nice party for a lot of people who really don't like one another very much. I don't have to get dressed up to go to the President Hoover to drink eggnog with Mary Agnes.'

'And that expensive orchestra so you can dance with Mr Shalimar,' said Gregg. 'I'm glad I don't work there any more.'

'Paul wants me to meet him after the party,' Caroline said. 'I suppose I might as well.'

'The other day I was sitting around with nothing to do and I thought of a marvelous name for Paul,' Gregg said. 'Bermuda Schwartz.'

'Oh, God,' Caroline said, laughing.

'Isn't that perfect?'

'It is, but we're so mean to laugh at him this way. He's a lot happier now than either of us.'

'Happy like that I wouldn't want to be,' Gregg said.

'Sometimes I think I would, but I can't. Being married to Paul

I'd have a diamond ring, a mink coat in twenty years, he'd never forget an anniversary, and I'd be running to the beauty parlor twice a week to forget that I really didn't love him.'

'Has he proposed to you?' Gregg asked, her eyes lighting up.

'He hints. You know, the usual comparison of interests leading into the topic of the domestic ones.'

'Some nice girl is probably pining over him right now,' Gregg said wryly.

'I know. I'm a fool. But somehow I can't believe that I am.'

'You stick to love.'

'Do you suppose,' Caroline said, 'that every girl has a Bermuda Schwartz, and every Bermuda Schwartz has someone else who is a Bermuda Schwartz to *him*?'

'I'll bet they do.'

'My mother says that everyone wants to better himself; including the men,' said Caroline.

'Especially the men,' said Gregg, 'the bastards.'

Nevertheless, the day of the Christmas party Caroline found that she was really looking forward to it. She hadn't, after all, seen much of the Fabian summer party, and this would be totally new. There might be someone interesting there from another department, she was thinking. There might even be a vice-president who would throw the caste system aside after a few Scotches. If the rumors were true it hadn't done Miss Farrow any harm to take up with a vice-president. She herself could never become someone's mistress in order to advance her career, but there were other kinds of personal relationships which were not wrong, and which would still help to make her stand out in the crowd of ambitious young Fabian secretaries and readers.

It seemed strange to be putting on all her make-up and jewelry and perfume at eight o'clock in the morning. After trying on and discarding a few dresses as too dressed up Caroline finally decided on a plain, expensive, black wool dress that she sometimes wore for dinner dates after work. Gregg, under the bedcovers, watched with one sleepy eye.

'Have a good time,' Gregg said. 'Get drunk for me.'

'I'm going to stay un-drunk, for *me*,' Caroline said. But she had a feeling that if she were a little high she would do a lot better.

When she arrived in the office at nine-fifteen April was waiting for her, sitting behind Caroline's desk and bright-eyed with repressed giggles. 'You have to walk around with me and get the fashion show,' April said.

April was wearing a tight, sleek beige wool dress, and there was a matching cashmere coat hanging on Caroline's coat rack. They were part of the winter wardrobe she had charged at the department stores before she had even paid for her summer one. The tawny colors of the dress and coat blended with April's gold hair and made her look startlingly beautiful. Caroline remembered the girl with the shiny baby-blue gabardine suit and long tangled curls who had come into this office a year before and she could hardly believe it was the same person. She remembered very well how that other April had looked, but it was as if she were remembering a girl they both had known who had gone away, never to be seen again, to be thought of once in a while with affectionate, pitying smiles.

'This is not to be missed,' April said, taking Caroline's hand and leading her out into the bullpen.

There was Brenda at her desk, resplendent in gold lamé, very tight, with a bow right under where she sat. She wore spike-heeled bronze kid pumps and a great many strings of fake beads. She was drinking her morning coffee out of a paper container, leaving a semicircle of lipstick on the rim, and there was a stack of letters at her elbow, although no one would do much filing today.

'Call girl after a hard night,' Caroline whispered.

'Do you think she wore that on the *subway* this morning?' April whispered back, gulping in her laughter.

'Never mind,' Caroline said, 'her husband thinks she's gorgeous.'

Mary Agnes waved at them. She was wearing a pale aqua dress of some soft, fuzzy material that looked like angora or rabbit's fur, and it had a little white angora collar around the high neck. She looked thin, flat chested and about sixteen years old.

'Gee,' Mary Agnes said, 'aren't you two going to get dressed up for the Christmas party?'

'We *are* dressed up,' Caroline said.

Mary Agnes looked blank and then shrugged.

Some of the other girls in the pool were more conservatively dressed, in black velvet skirts and white beaded sweaters, or plain taffeta with swishing crinolines. The teletype operator was married and thought the whole Christmas party would be a waste of time without her husband, so she had compromised by wearing an ordinary tweed office dress with a spray of tinseled Christmas baubles pinned to the shoulder.

'Where's Miss Farrow today?' Caroline asked. 'It seems warm in here without those cold chills running down my back.'

'Oh, she never comes in on the day of the office party,' Mary Agnes said. 'She considers the whole thing a waste of time. She just takes the day off on the grounds that she deserves it.'

'Well, I'm glad she did,' said April, 'because I know I deserve it. You'd think she would have told me, though.' Since Gregg had left, April had been filling in as Miss Farrow's secretary until a permanent replacement could be found. Actually, it was not such an unpleasant job during the Christmas season, because April spent most of her days in the department stores purchasing Miss Farrow's Christmas list. There were presents for Miss Farrow's whole family: her mother, her father, her sister, and two brothers and their children back home in Racine, Wisconsin. There were also several expensive presents for men. Since Miss Farrow made April bring these to the office so she could deliver them to the recipients herself, April was sure they were not for any relatives. April and Caroline had decided that no one would buy both a smoking jacket and a silk bathrobe for the same man at the same time, and so there must be two.

'Mr Bossart must have a rival,' Caroline had said.

'Do you think one's for him?' April had hugged herself with glee.

'If they're lovers, then I should think she'd give him a Christmas present. Even if – knowing Miss Farrow – it was only to be sure to get something in return.'

'Don't you think she's capable of love?'

'Maybe she loves him. Mr Bossart is quite handsome, in an older-man sort of way.'

'Maybe she loves the other one,' April had breathed. 'The rival.'

Now, standing in the office with April and Mary Agnes, Caroline remembered that conversation, and her thoughts moved quickly. There were so many things that one could do if one were truly bitchy, but Caroline knew she was not the kind of girl who could do any of them. An office flirtation could probably be quite useful, but an office affair could not help but be dangerous. Despite all the rumors about Miss Farrow and Mr Bossart, Caroline still felt that a girl got ahead in spite of an office affair, not because of one. After all, Mr Bossart was married, he had children, and a reputation in his suburban community which he could not afford to ruin. Perhaps it was true, as everyone said, that no matter what she did or did not do in the office, no one could fire Miss Farrow because she was sleeping with Mr Bossart. But Caroline could not help wondering whether perhaps, despite sex, Mr Bossart might not be relieved if Miss Farrow were to disappear gracefully out of his sight. He must have heard the rumors by now; even though he was a vice-president he was not *that* far away from it all.

She remembered other office rumors she had heard. Mr Bossart had a tape recorder in his office, hooked up under his desk, so he could take recordings of everything you said when you were with him. Old man Fabian had all the phones tapped so he would know who was disloyal to the company. One of the Norwegian cleaning women was really a company spy. Caroline was sure that none of these was true – and yet, how could you be absolutely sure? A great many employees believed other things that were the product of ignorance, fear and a wish to make a humdrum life more exciting. Certainly it was more interesting to make a routine boring phone call to the printing plant when you suspected that Mr Fabian himself was listening in on the line.

At half past three the girls in the bullpen began going out to the washroom in groups, to recomb their hair, apply perfume and chatter excitedly. One of the men from Advertising, full of

Christmas spirits, came downstairs to see Mr Shalimar on business, stopped dead in his tracks at the sight of Brenda in her gold lamé, and gave her an embrace and a hearty kiss, which sent the rest of the girls in the typing pool off into uncontrollable titters. At four-thirty the trek to the President Hoover Hotel began, with people gathering together to share the rush-hour taxicabs.

Mike came out of his office and met Caroline at the water cooler. 'Want to share my cab?' he asked.

'That would be wonderful. We have to take April too, I promised her I'd go with her.'

Caroline, April and Mike Rice had a taxi exclusively for the three of them, agilely flagged down by Mike. Caroline had always liked a man who could take over, find a taxi during the rush, maneuver her through a jam of people, manage to attract a waiter's attention in a crowded restaurant, act as though he had enough self-respect to demand his rights. Since she had known Mike she had been noticing this lack in many of the younger men who took her out; they were either too demanding, or petulant, or inaudible with self-consciousness. She had never noticed these little things so much before, and she was glad she did now because they made life easier, and sorry too, because, of course, when you are more demanding life is never easier.

In front of the grand ballroom at the President Hoover Hotel there was a mirrored gallery with a bar in it and several little round tables. The Fabian employees checked their coats on the mezzanine and then went to the gallery for pre-dinner cocktails. At the right of the ballroom was a small salon where a five-piece band played for dancing. The ballroom itself was filled with larger round tables with white cloths and floral centerpieces, and red-jacketed waiters glided about placing trays of dead-looking hard rolls and pitchers of ice water on the tables and trying to squeeze in an extra place setting here and there. Caroline walked into the gallery between Mike and April. She knew many of the people who were already there, and she felt confident and at home. It was a far cry from the shy girl who had come reluctantly to the summer office party wishing she had stayed in the city instead.

Mike maneuvered his way through the crowd surrounding the bar and came back with drinks for the three of them. Caroline could not help remembering the feelings she had had about him at the other party, which now seemed so long ago, and as his eyes met hers she realized he was thinking about it too. For an instant the spark arose between them again, and her heart began to pound. She was filled with a sweetness mixed with sadness.

Mike leaned down and kissed her very lightly on the lips. 'Merry Christmas,' he said softly.

She could barely whisper, 'Merry Christmas.'

'April, too. Merry Christmas, April.' He kissed April. Waiters were moving through the crowd with trays of highballs, and everyone was drinking as if he were about to be set adrift on a raft. Mike finished his drink in a minute and went to the bar for more. Caroline looked around. There was Mr Bossart, with thick silver-flecked brown hair that reminded her of a nutria coat her mother used to wear, and a square face that must have had a chorus-boy prettiness when he was in his twenties but now had become handsome in his fifties with the illusion of strength that age sometimes gives. He was wearing gray flannel trousers and a brown tweed jacket with tiny lapels and two vents in the back that made him look rather like a gander. He wore a red wool tie with little white sports cars printed on it. Caroline tried to keep track of him as he worked his way through the mob greeting everyone he knew, but he soon vanished. She saw some of the secretaries hovering together in bunches, looking like wallflowers in their party dresses, and talking to one another as animatedly as if they had just met instead of having been working at adjoining desks all day. And there were some of the unlikeliest sights – Mr Shalimar with Barbara Lemont, Kingsley the confessed office fairy, from *Unveiled*, with Brenda, and the sweet-looking gray-haired lady who was Mr Bossart's secretary hooking her hand around a glassful of straight whisky and gulping it down as if she were Tugboat Annie herself.

Mike returned with three glasses of Scotch and soda and a new joke someone had told him while he was waiting in line. Caroline was beginning to feel a pleasant glow. It was very light whisky, obviously the least expensive the hotel had to offer, and it went down painlessly. April was beginning to look as if she could not see too well, as she always did after her second drink. 'Caroline,' she murmured, 'come to the ladies' room with me.'

'Why do girls always have to go to the ladies' room in pairs?' Mike asked, amused.

'To talk about boys, of course,' Caroline said. 'We'll be right back, please save our places.'

It was too early for the ladies' room to be crowded. April sat on a bench in the dressing-room section and peered fuzzily into the mirror. There was a box of public cosmetics on the shelf in front of her – cheap cologne, smeary-looking lipsticks and a box of face powder with a community puff. April picked up one of the bottles of cologne and sniffed at it as if she really did not smell it at all and put it back. 'Tell me,' she said in a soft, small voice, 'do you think a girl looks different if she's having an affair? Can people tell?'

'I hope not,' Caroline said.

'I just wondered.'

'What a strange idea. What brought that up all of a sudden?'

'Oh, Caroline,' April said. 'I've been wanting to tell you ever since it happened, but how can you just tell somebody?'

'You and Dexter?' said Caroline.

April blushed. 'We've been sleeping together for two whole weeks.'

Caroline tried not to smile. 'The way you say that sounds like "two whole years."'

'Are you shocked?'

'Of course not.'

'I remember how you and I used to talk about it,' April said. 'Remember?'

'I certainly do.'

'And remember how we were trying to figure out whether you did it under the sheets or on top of them?'

'Yes.'

April looked at her nails and shrugged, smiling to herself. 'Well

'. . . the first time . . . right in the middle of it, I suddenly thought to myself, Now I know. And I remembered how you and I were wondering, and I thought, I must tell Caroline.'

'*That's* what you thought about?'

'I guess people think funny things the first time,' April said. 'It seems so . . . incongruous, doesn't it? All of a sudden the world seems to be made of all different layers of feelings, happy, scared, romantic and very very ordinary, and you feel them all at once. I've been feeling like that for the past two weeks.'

'Don't worry,' Caroline said, 'I've been feeling that way all my life.'

'You're my best friend,' April said. 'I'd never tell anyone else.'

'I'm glad you did tell me.'

'It's not just an affair,' April said dreamily. 'We're going to get married. I know we are. You know, you can sense those things.'

'Do you want to marry him?'

'Of course!' April's eyes widened with shock. Then she smiled and bit her lip. 'I guess I sound awfully innocent, but I could *never* sleep with Dexter if he weren't the only man in the world for me. I'm dying to marry him.'

'I hope you do, and soon,' Caroline said warmly.

'Caroline, he's so good to me,' April said, sighing. 'He's so sweet; he really loves me, I'm sure. He's going to come to Springs for Christmas to meet my family.'

'That's wonderful!'

'It's not exactly definite that he can come with me. He's going to try to get out of some family parties of his own. His mother always has a big deal with Christmas dinner and the whole family from his ninety-year-old grandfather down to the great-grand-children who have to eat pablum. But he's going to try – and if he likes my family and they like him, well . . .'

'Otherwise perhaps you could go to his family dinner,' Caroline said. 'Besides, I don't know where in the world you're going to get the money for your train fare.'

'He *gave* it to me,' April said. 'He gave me a darling little red felt stocking with a round-trip plane ticket tucked inside it. He said he knew I was homesick, and we are getting four days off for Christmas.'

'He *is* good to you!'

'The awful part of it is,' April confessed, 'I'm not a bit homesick. I'll be more homesick for him those four days if he stays here than I've been my entire year alone in New York. But I didn't have the heart to tell him after he'd been so generous about the tickets. Frankly, I was kind of hoping that I would be able to go to his family's Christmas party, because I've never met any of them but his mother and father, and I've never really gotten to know them well at all. I had thought that when I got my two weeks off next summer I would go home then and really have a nice long stay. I'd be home for my birthday and everything.' She brightened. 'But now that I have the tickets and I know I'm really going home, I'm so excited I can hardly wait.'

'Your family won't recognize you.'

'I know,' April said. 'I was up all night thinking of ways to stun them when I get off the plane. I thought I'd buy a pair of white French poodles and carry one under each arm, and wear my new coat, and have Claude do my hair . . .'

'Let's not go crazy, now,' Caroline said. 'If I know mothers, the first thing yours will say is "How thin you've gotten!" and not even notice the rest.'

'I feel as if I've been away for years and years. I wish Dexter could come with me.'

'He probably will,' Caroline said reassuringly.

'Well, I'm not going to think that he can't until it actually happens,' said April. 'That way I'd suffer twice. If I pretend he *will* be with me and then he disappoints me, I'll only suffer once.'

And that, Caroline thought with the first faint stirrings of uneasiness, is April's whole philosophy of life in a nutshell. 'Let's go back to the party,' she said gently. 'Mike won't be able to save our places any longer and he'll think we deserted him.'

She walked out of the ladies' room after April, looking at the straight back, the burnished fluffy hair, and the model's profile as April turned her head, and she thought, It's almost a crime that she's so pretty and chic. People always think that a girl who looks like her is strong and particular and lucky with men. What a lot of nonsense! It's like wearing armor made of Christmas wrapping.

When they came into the gallery it had already half emptied out, and the tables in the ballroom were beginning to be filled. People were pairing off, looking around for their friends, waving at one another. Caroline looked at their table in the bar for Mike but he had gone. Then she saw him standing in front of a table in the center of the ballroom, trying to catch her attention.

'Isn't he wonderful the way he takes care of us?' she said to April. They managed to edge their way through the closely packed rows of chairs and tables and milling employees to where Mike was waiting for them. In the corner the band, which had moved from the salon, was playing something with a great many stringed instruments, bright and jazzy and barely audible above the conversation and laughter.

'We're sitting with Mr Bossart!' April whispered.

The table was really only large enough for six to sit in comfort but a seventh chair and place setting had been forced in with the others. There were Mr Shalimar and Barbara Lemont, already seated, Mr Bossart, who stood up when the two girls approached, two empty chairs and Mike Rice standing with his arm protectively around Mary Agnes. Mary Agnes looked awed and rather frightened, as if she wasn't quite sure what she was doing in this distinguished company.

'Do you know everyone here?' Mike asked. 'You know Mr Bossart, don't you? Caroline Bender and April Morrison.'

Mr Bossart held out his hand and Caroline took it. It was a very hard, square hand with a silky palm, a hand she somehow did not like. It was like shaking a block of wood. But he smiled ingratiatingly at her, showing white, chorus-boy teeth, and she smiled back and sat down next to him.

'May I sit here?'

'Please do,' Mr Bossart said.

April sat in the other empty chair between Caroline and Mike. There was a bottle of whisky on the table, a bucket of ice cubes, a pitcher of water and two bottles of soda. Mike poured drinks for Caroline and April.

'She's my little reader,' Mr Shalimar said, pointing at Caroline and leaning forward over the table. 'D'you know that, Arthur? She's my little reader.' His voice was slightly thickened and aggressive, and Caroline realized Mr Shalimar must be the one responsible for the halfway mark on their whisky bottle.

'Oh, yes,' Arthur Bossart said silkily. He glanced at Caroline with somewhat heightened interest. 'Cigarette?'

'Thank you.'

'She's been here only a year and she's a reader,' Mr Shalimar persisted. 'Only a year ago . . . She's very ambitious. Very ambitious.'

'And talented too, I presume,' Mr Bossart said.

'What's talent?' Mr Shalimar said. His tone had become more aggressive. 'Training, that's what you need. Experience and training. Little college girls walk in here and think they're going to tell everybody what to do. Think they can eat the world in three bites. They don't know how long it takes to become an editor.'

'I'm sure Miss Bender will get the best of training from you,' Mr Bossart said pleasantly.

'Talent,' Mr Shalimar said. '*She* thinks she can get there with *talent*.'

Caroline clenched her hands together under the table and took a deep breath, smiling at Mr Shalimar in what she hoped was an innocent and winsome way. 'I guess the thing that first made me feel I could ever hope to be an editor was something you said to me when I first came here, Mr Shalimar,' she began, looking at him and then at Mr Bossart. 'I remember that we were all down in the bar – Mike was there, remember?' She turned to Mike and then back to Mr Shalimar and Mr Bossart. 'You told me that an instinct for the work was the most important thing an editor could have. That and enthusiasm. It seems to me that proper instinct is a form of talent, wouldn't you say so?'

'Seems that way to me,' Mr Bossart said, nodding. Mr Shalimar was silent, beginning to scowl.

'Here's the soup,' Mike said. 'Look out, girls, it's hot.' He moved aside as the waiter put down the plates of steaming soup, and when

Caroline glanced at him he winked at her almost imperceptibly.

He remembers, Caroline thought. And he knows that it wasn't Shalimar who said instinct was all-important but Mike himself. But it was what Mr Shalimar had been thinking. How Mr Shalimar must dislike me, and I never really realized it!

Mr Bossart was stirring his soup so it would cool. Mr Shalimar's attention was momentarily distracted by a fresh highball which he was consuming instead of the soup, and Barbara Lemont was looking at him with a mixture of curiosity and amusement. Cornered between Mr Shalimar and Mike, Mary Agnes was mechanically spooning up her soup because it was in front of her. The room was very noisy with the cacophony of voices and the clink of spoons against heavy china.

'Where did you go to college, Miss Bender?' Mr Bossart asked. Somehow he had a way of making even a simple question like that sound intimate.

'Please call me Caroline.'

'Caroline.'

'I went to Radcliffe.'

'Oh, really?' His youngest daughter was trying to get into Radcliffe this year, Caroline knew, but she was sure he wouldn't mention that or the daughter. He didn't. 'I hear they're still wearing raccoon coats to football games up there,' he said. 'Is that true?'

'Some of the girls do. They buy old ratty ones for five or ten dollars, left over from the twenties.'

Mr Bossart laughed. 'With built-in hip flask pockets and built-in fleas.'

'Gee, I hope not fleas.'

'Did you go to the Harvard–Yale game this year?'

'No.'

'Watched it on television, I hope.'

'I'm afraid not.'

'What kind of alumnus are you?'

'Nose-in-the-book type, I guess,' Caroline said, smiling.

'I don't believe that. You're too pretty.'

'Thank you.'

Across the table Mr Shalimar was talking to Barbara, looking at her intently. Without being able to read lips, Caroline was quite sure he was telling her about his former glories. Barbara had never heard his stories before and she was listening with respectful interest but not with the kind of fascination that April had shown. She had, instead, the unguarded look people have when they are in one-way conversation with a garrulous drunk; and she looked as if she were trying to figure out what sort of man he was when he was sober.

'Do you live here in the city?' Mr Bossart asked.

'I do now. My family lives in Port Blair.'

'Oh, really? You go up weekends, I suppose.'

'Not always,' Caroline said.

'Too much social life here, eh?'

She smiled prettily.

The waiter had taken away the soup bowls and replaced them with plates of chicken and peas and tiny potatoes. Mr Bossart took out of his pocket something that looked like a fourteen-carat-gold Boy Scout knife and began to cut his chicken with it. 'Christmas present,' he said to Caroline, not the slightest bit abashed.

'It's beautiful.'

He wiped the blade he had used on his napkin. 'See, it has three blades of different sizes, and a bottle opener, and a nail file and a chisel. You've never seen a pocketknife with a chisel in it before, have you?'

'I never saw a gold one either.'

'I have seventy-two knives at home,' Mr Bossart said. 'Been collecting them for years.'

'My heavens, you could start a revolution.'

'And I have thirty-five antique guns. I have a pair of authentic seventeenth-century dueling pistols, and one of the first single-action revolvers ever made. But you probably don't know what I'm talking about.'

'It's very interesting.'

'Collecting guns and knives is purely a man's interest, women are bored to death when we talk about it. You're a sweet girl to pretend you care.' He smiled at her in a chummy sort of way, with just a touch of condescension.

What sort of bird have we here? Caroline thought. 'I'll admit it's a bit above my head,' she said.

'I've been thinking for a long time of starting a man's magazine,' Mr Bossart said. 'I discussed it with Clyde Fabian before he had his stroke, and he was interested too. You know, there are a slew of magazines in the field, but they're mostly girlie magazines – sexy pictures, lewd jokes, photos of girls in negligees. Even the ones with good fiction and articles go very heavy on the sex angle. What I want to do is something new. A *real* man's magazine, with nothing about women in it. Just hunting, fishing, sports cars, mountain climbing, bullfighting and derring-do.'

'Do you think most men would like that?' Caroline asked dubiously.

'Why not? There would be nothing in this magazine for college boys, or for the armchair athletes. Oh, we'd have entertainment features. Theater, books of interest to men, and of course a section on the bar.'

'How about food?' Caroline asked.

'None of these fancy color photographs of apothecary jars filled with uncooked macaroni,' Mr Bossart said scornfully. 'We'd have a piece on how to dress and cook wild ducks after you've shot 'em, on how to barbecue venison and antelope, and so forth.'

And in December you can bind the Christmas issue in fur, Caroline thought. 'It sounds different,' she said.

'It *is* different.'

The waiter removed the main course and brought ice cream with chocolate sauce. Caroline turned around for a moment and April nodded at her with a little half-smile, as if to say, Well, *you're* doing all right. She smiled back.

'We won't have any women on the staff,' Mr Bossart went on. 'You know half these magazines for men are dominated by harpies. Women don't know what men want.' He winked at her. 'Well, at least, they don't know what men want in a magazine. We'll keep the women in the kitchen and in the typing pool, where they belong.'

'How about at Derby Books?' Caroline asked.

He looked a little flustered, but only for an instant. 'Derby Books is a good place to have a woman or two because many of their readers are women. A woman should not try to think like a man, because she can't even if she tries. A woman's weapon is in her femininity.'

That's not where Miss Farrow's weapon is, Caroline thought. 'You're absolutely right,' she said.

'It's fun talking to you,' he said. 'More coffee?'

'No, thanks.'

'Well, why don't we dance?'

'I'd love to.'

He stood up, pulled out her chair, and nodded to the others at the table. Then he led her across the ballroom to the tiny space that had been left clear for dancing. Caroline walked into his arms. It was like embracing a slab of burr-covered wood. The hard mechanical palm he had extended to her in his handshake had not been a unique phenomenon, it had simply been an uncovered part of the entire unyielding whole. I can't imagine him and Amanda Farrow as lovers, Caroline thought. I can hardly think of two less loving people in this world.

They danced without speaking. Caroline glanced surreptitiously around the room and saw Brenda look at her with round eyes and then nudge the girl next to her. Caroline could already imagine what they would say to her on Monday. I saw *you* dancing with Mr Bossart! The waiters, who were anxious to clear the tables and get home, were removing coffeepots and plates of *petits fours* before they had been emptied and snatching partly filled whisky bottles off the tables. Caroline caught sight of Mike Rice with a bottle under each arm heading for the salon, followed by April.

'There's more room in the salon,' Mr Bossart said. 'Do you want to go in there or shall we head for the bar?'

'Maybe there's a bar in the salon. Let's look.' Caroline liked being seen with him, but she didn't want to be seen going off with him alone. It would be too easy to start office gossip and what would be the good of having Miss Farrow's reputation without any of Miss Farrow's privileges?

It was after nine, and some of the girls who had dates or husbands to go to were leaving. Caroline saw Mary Agnes heading toward the elevators. It was an orderly party, much more so than any of the intimate pre-holiday get-togethers in the office were, perhaps because the formal atmosphere of a large hotel subdued the people who would ordinarily have been clowning drunkenly and letting loose with all the frustrations that bound them during the year. Mr Bossart found an empty table in the corner of the sparsely occupied salon and pulled out a chair for her.

'There is a bar,' he said. 'We're in luck. What would you like?'

'Scotch, please.'

He brought drinks and moved his chair closer to hers, and put his arm around her tightly. 'Can I give you a ride home when we leave?'

'Well, I have to meet someone in the Fifties at ten-thirty. If that would be on your way I'd love it, but I'm sure it isn't if you're going to the highway.'

'Your boy friend?'

'He's a boy and a friend, yes.'

Mr Bossart smiled. 'If it were a girl I might make the trip. It's a shame you can't see my little sports car. You'd like it.'

'I'm sure I would, too.'

'Well. Another time.'

'Another time.' She smiled ruefully at him, but she was sure there would be no other time, at least not for her. Even trying to please him, smiling and trying hard to find the right thing to say, was fun because he was Mr Bossart, the figurehead, the inscrutable, the celebrity. But as a person he bored her. She was surprised at herself for feeling this way. When she had first sat next to him at the table it had seemed the start of an adventure. She could have imagined herself rejected by him but never bored. And yet they were completely incompatible because neither of them was the kind of person the other wanted to know better. He wanted a conquest from her, perhaps. Perhaps his offer of a lift home was only harmless chivalry, but she suspected she could easily make it something more personal. And she wanted a conquest from him too, in a way. She wanted his notice. And that was the only compatibility between them, the mutual desire for conquest – not even a very passionate desire at that – and she could remember few times when she had been more uncomfortable. When she noticed Mr Shalimar and Barbara coming toward their table she was almost glad to see them.

'Have you met Miss Lemont?' Mr Shalimar asked. His speech was considerably thicker than it had been at the dinner table and Caroline was surprised. She had never seen him this way before although she knew that didn't mean it was unusual with him.

'Yes, we have,' Mr Bossart said pleasantly.

Mr Shalimar held Barbara's chair for her, sat down beside her, and put his hand under the table. 'I've never met Miss Lemont before,' he said. 'I've just met her tonight. She's a lovely-looking girl, don't you think?'

'Yes, indeed,' Mr Bossart said. Barbara looked odd, either embarrassed or trying not to laugh. She stirred a little in her chair, evidently trying to dislodge the Shalimar tentacles from investigating any farther up her knee.

'She looks like a Mona Lisa,' Mr Shalimar said. 'Look at that smile.'

Barbara did look a little like a Mona Lisa, Caroline was thinking. She had straight, medium-brown hair tucked behind her ears, and regular features. There was an air of plainness about her face that was somehow also attractive, and she seemed to be trying hard not to reveal any of her feelings. Only that slight curve of an upturned mouth gave her away. She's probably the kind of person, Caroline thought, who looks prettiest when she's happy, and least pretty when she's asleep.

'Little Mona Lisa,' Mr Shalimar said. Barbara winced, smiled at him sweetly, and moved away a little farther.

'I'd love a ginger ale,' Barbara said, somewhat desperately.

'We'll get a waiter.'

'There aren't any,' she said, a little more desperately. 'I guess we'll have to get up and get our own.'

'I'll get some,' Mr Bossart said comfortably. 'I'm about ready for a refill anyway.' He went over to the bar and came back with drinks for them all.

'It's a nice party,' Caroline said, at a loss for conversation. 'Isn't it?'

'Very nice,' Mr Bossart agreed.

'I'm glad I met this girl,' said Mr Shalimar. His eyes were half closed, but instead of looking sleepy he looked like an animal that is about to pounce. 'She's an intelligent girl. And pretty too. Y'know, she supports her child and her mother on what she makes here. How d'you like that, Art?'

'Is that a compliment to your large earning powers or your resourcefulness?' Mr Bossart asked.

'My resourcefulness,' Barbara said.

'Let's see, you work on *America's Woman*, don't you,' Mr Bossart said.

'Yes. I'm Assistant Beauty Editor. I used to be a secretary, but I was promoted this Christmas.'

'Oh, yes . . . I remember now. Barbara Lemont. They're very pleased with you up there.'

'I'm glad,' Barbara said.

'She's got a good future,' Mr Shalimar murmured. He leaned over and brushed Barbara's cheek with a kiss. She glanced at him from underneath her eyelashes as if she would like to wipe her cheek with her hand, but she was still smiling that inscrutable little smile.

'How old are you, if you don't mind my asking?' Mr Bossart asked.

'Twenty-one.'

'My! And how old is your child?'

'She's two.' For the first time Barbara's smile became truly warm. 'She was two last week.'

'Isn't she a lovely thing, Art?' Mr Shalimar said. He put his hand behind Barbara's head. 'Give us a Christmas kiss.'

Caroline imagined she saw Barbara shudder imperceptibly.

There was a long embarrassing moment while Mr Shalimar swooped upon Barbara and held her in a kiss, he moving his head from side to side, she with her neck and shoulders held so stiffly they looked as if they might snap. Caroline looked at Mr Bossart, wondering what he might do, but he did not seem to be particularly surprised or displeased. He's probably watched this kind of display year after year, Caroline thought, disgusted. Let the executives kick up their heels a little bit, it's Christmas.

When Mr Shalimar finally drew lingeringly away from her Barbara turned to her glass of ginger ale as if nothing had happened. She sipped at it, her eyes lowered. But the skin around her mouth was white. Mr Shalimar lifted his highball glass and drank the entire contents. Caroline realized for the first time how much she disliked him. It was partly because he had revealed that he disliked her, and that was going to make working with him more difficult. His mere distrust of her ambition and ability would not have made her feel this way about him, for under other circumstances it could have been stimulating. But all the weakening respect she had had for him was rapidly vanishing, and without it he looked like nothing more than a foolish old lecher.

'Another drink,' said Mr Shalimar. 'Another drink.' He rose to his feet slowly and walked to the bar. I hope he passes out, Caroline thought. She glanced at her watch, but it was only nine-thirty, too early to meet Paul, and she wasn't anxious to wait alone in a hotel bar.

'He's certainly full of Christmas spirit,' Mr Bossart said. His tone was pleasant and cheerful, but there was an undertone of apology in it.

'Yes,' Barbara said.

'I guess you'll be having Christmas with your family.'

Barbara nodded. 'I'm going to put up the tree tonight when I get home. It's mostly for my daughter, I think she's old enough now to appreciate it. And old enough to know not to pull anything off it.' She smiled.

'Two years old?' Mr Bossart said. 'She must be bright.'

'You should hear how well she talks,' Barbara said.

Mr Shalimar came back with two filled glasses in his hand. He put them on the table but he did not sit down. He stood there in front of Barbara, bracing himself with his palms on the edge of the table. 'I like your looks,' he said thickly. 'You're plain but you're pretty. You have a nice bone structure in your face. I'll bet you have nice legs. I love girls' legs. They're the most important part of a girl's body. Do you have pretty legs?'

Barbara looked at him without answering.

'Then . . . I'll see for myself,' he said. Clumsily he lowered himself to the floor on all fours and crept under the table. His body was hidden by the white tablecloth, but his legs, in black trousers and impeccably shined narrow black shoes, protruded in full view of everyone in the room. Caroline stared at those legs and shoes in fascination, not knowing quite whether to laugh or bite her nails. There was a grunting sound from the depths under the table and some muffled words. Then slowly, his dark face darker from the exertion, Mr Shalimar crawled backward out from under the table and raised himself to his feet.

'You have beau-ti-ful legs,' he said.

From around the small room there arose a sound that was at first like a sigh or intake of breath, and then swiftly, as if it could not be contained, it turned into laughter. If anyone had been looking at Mr Shalimar under the table, and they evidently had, then it would have been impossible not to hear his words. Caroline saw two girls and two men at the table not two feet away from theirs choking with shocked laughter and pointing at him. When they noticed her looking at them they stopped laughing and put their glasses to their mouths to hide their smiles. Mr Shalimar was oblivious to it. He was still standing, leaning across the table to Barbara, trying to kiss her. This time Barbara ducked and turned her head and he missed her face entirely, kissing at the air.

Mr Shalimar wavered, his fingers clutching at the wrinkled tablecloth. He scowled. 'Bitch!' he said, and then louder, 'Bitch!'

Barbara could not stand up to leave, she was hemmed in between Mr Shalimar and Mr Bossart, who was watching her with a look of real concern on his face.

'I only wanted to kiss you,' Mr Shalimar went on, his voice rising. 'What did you think I wanted to do, rape you?' The room was as silent as a snowbound night.

'You little bitch,' Mr Shalimar cried, choking. 'You're fired. Don't you dare come into this office on Monday. Don't you dare!'

Mr Bossart stood up swiftly and took Mr Shalimar by the arm. He looked at Barbara and Caroline as if he wanted to say something, anything, but then he shook his head in helpless disgust and led Mr Shalimar from the room. Mr Shalimar was tractable, now that his instantaneous fury had flared up and exploded like a Roman candle, and he allowed himself to be removed from the shocked whispering that echoed and re-echoed all around him.

Barbara was staring straight ahead, angry tears in her eyes. 'Don't you worry,' Caroline said, putting her arm around her. 'He hasn't any authority to fire you. You're not even in his department. Besides, Mr Bossart will probably laugh in his face and give you the Purple Heart.'

Barbara turned to look at her. For the first time that evening her feelings were revealed completely on her face – resolution, fury and desperation. 'I *need* this job,' she said. 'He's not going to take it away from me if I have to go to Mr Fabian himself. You bet Shalimar's not going to have me fired. That dirty old man!'

13

Barbara Lemont continued to sit at the table where she had been humiliated, her fists clenched. What she would have liked to do when Shalimar was under the table looking at her legs was put her foot squarely in his face. It had been so close to her she had felt his hot breath on her shins. With all the alcohol that was in that blast it was a wonder he hadn't melted her nylons. What a shame that the delightful thought of kicking him had come to her only now, when it was obviously too late. Well, maybe there was truth in the adage 'Heaven Will Protect the Working Girl.' If she'd kicked him, he really might have been able to fire her.

Here was Mr Bossart coming back, alone. He reminded her of a clothing-store dummy, or one of those models who pose in the men's fashion section of a magazine. He sat down beside her and folded his hands like a deacon, looking down at his square, antiseptically manicured thumbs. He cleared his throat.

'There's always an incident or two at even the best-run office party,' Mr Bossart began. He looked at her and smiled winningly. 'You seem like a very poised, sensible girl. I know you'll take it for what it was worth, and let the office gossip die down as quickly as possible by not adding to what is said after tonight.'

'I never gossip,' Barbara said coldly. Despite her control, tears came into her eyes. There was nothing like being called a bitch to make a girl fall to pieces. It had always been that way with her, and 'little bitch' was somehow even worse.

'I'm sure tomorrow Mr Shalimar won't even remember any of this,' Mr Bossart said. 'If and when he does remember, it will upset him very much.'

And we mustn't let it do *that*, Barbara thought. She said nothing.

Mr Bossart smiled again. 'You'll forgive him, won't you?'

'Why are you sticking up for him?' she asked curiously.

'I like him.'

'Oh.'

'Now, don't say "Oh" like that, Barbara. I think you're a lovely, refined girl. I like you too. I wouldn't be going to all this trouble apologizing for him, trying to make amends, if I thought you were just like some of the other little typists who think an incident like this is worth a week or two of coffee-break jokes.'

'Excuse me,' Caroline Bender said. She stood up. 'I have to meet someone. Good night.'

'Good night,' Mr Bossart said.

Caroline picked up her purse and mouthed a kiss at Barbara. Then she made a fist over the back of Mr Bossart's head and made a face of mock fury which turned into a grin. Barbara couldn't help grinning back as Caroline slipped away.

'Good,' Mr Bossart said, noticing her expression. 'You're forgetting about it already.'

Barbara didn't answer.

'We'll go somewhere and have a drink and forget about it.'

So he was asking her out. Evidently he had asked Caroline first, because he had been with her all evening, and she had said no because she had another appointment. Now, in the guise of atonement, he was making her second fiddle. Did she want to go with him? Why not? Mr Bossart was too much of a stuffed shirt to try to pull a Shalimar, even a minor variation, and she certainly didn't want to stay here any longer. People at the other tables were still looking at her, waiting to see what would happen next.

'All right,' Barbara said pleasantly.

While Mr Bossart was getting her coat Barbara leaned tiredly against the checkroom counter. What a disappointment this party had been. She hadn't met a soul, and Mr Shalimar, whose reputation and reminiscences had intrigued her, had turned out to be a garter-snapper of the worst order. A mental picture of him, running along a line of girls and snapping their garters as fast as his fingers could move, like one of those trick camera stills of recorded motion, arose in her mind and she laughed to herself.

'Now! You look like a different girl.' Mr Bossart was holding her coat for her to put on. She slipped her arms into the sleeves. He wasn't so bad, he was trying hard. After all, he would sacrifice an assistant for an editor-in-chief any day, but he didn't want to sacrifice either. She had a good job, she'd gotten her promotion and the raise that went with it, so she'd be a good sport. Mr Bossart would remember this the next time she asked for a raise, which would be soon . . .

He took her to a small, dim, fairly expensive bar on a side street off Madison Avenue. Barbara recognized it instantly as the type of bar she and her friends referred to as a 'married-man's bar,' which meant no one who knew him or his wife would be apt to know about it, and if they did come there, it was too dark to see anyone else anyway.

'I often come here when I stay late in town,' Mr Bossart said. 'It's very pleasant.'

'Yes,' Barbara said. She leaned back against the leather banquette and sipped her drink. There were three Hawaiian musicians roaming the room, stopping at each table to play Hawaiian songs on their strange instruments that always sounded to her like the tropical surf at midnight. If there were music coming off the moon, she thought, it would sound like that.

'Hey! Sidney!' Mr Bossart called softly, leaning forward. Barbara looked up. The man who had passed their table to go to the bar stopped and looked back.

'Hey, Art!' He smiled, the most arresting smile Barbara had ever seen. It was the kind of smile that made you forget completely what the rest of his face was like, it had in it so much sweetness and genuine pleasure and deviltry all combined. Not that the rest of his features were bad. They were quite likable in fact, and very young for a man whose hair was completely silver gray. He did not look older than forty.

'All alone?' said Mr Bossart.

'Yes. Thought I'd stop in for one or two before I made the train.'
He looked at Barbara and started to go back to the bar.

'Sit down with us,' Mr Bossart said, already moving aside.

'All right.' He sat down next to Barbara and gave her a modified version of that smile, which was still enough to make her sit up straight.

'Barbara Lemont, Sidney Carter,' Mr Bossart said.

'I'm very glad to meet you.'

'How do you do,' Barbara said softly.

'We've just been at the annual Fabian blowout,' Mr Bossart said, as if he wanted to reassure Sidney Carter that Barbara wasn't one of his regular dates.

'Oh? How was it?'

'Very fine,' Mr Bossart said. 'Very fine.'

'Lovely,' Barbara said, without much enthusiasm.

'We aren't having a party this year,' said Sidney Carter. 'I discovered that everyone on my staff was looking forward to it with the same dread that I was, so I gave them all bigger bonuses instead and called it a day. We're lucky in that we all get along with one another very well, but in some companies I don't see how they get through the merry Yule without a fist fight or two.'

Barbara laughed.

'What do you do at Fabian?' Sidney Carter asked her.

'Besides have fist fights?'

'Yes.'

'I'm Assistant Beauty Editor on *America's Woman*. As of yesterday, actually.'

'Now you can tell her about Wonderful,' Mr Bossart said.

'Wonderful perfume? Do you make it?'

'Oh, no. We try to sell it,' Sidney Carter said. 'It's one of our accounts.'

'The Sidney Carter Agency,' Barbara said. 'Of course. I remember now.'

Sidney pretended to sniff at her neck. 'You don't wear it.'

'I have a surprise for *you*,' Barbara said. She opened her purse, and there, as she had remembered it was, was the flacon of

Wonderful she carried when she went on dates. There were only a few drops left at the bottom. 'Look, I have some right with me.'

'Well, would you believe it?' Sidney cried. 'You're almost out, too. I'll send you a two-ounce bottle next week.'

'Thank you.'

'It's a good thing,' Sidney said, 'that I didn't mention our golf-club account. She'd probably have a set of those hidden in her coat sleeve.'

The strolling Hawaiians stopped in front of their table and began to play 'The Hawaiian War Chant' loudly and with enthusiasm. For some reason it put Barbara in a very good mood again, she found herself humming along with it and tapping on the table edge with her fingers. Sidney looked at her and slipped the leader a folded bill.

'Play the beer commercial,' he said.

The leader grinned. The Hawaiians glanced at one another with unconcealed delight and began the funniest song Barbara had ever heard. It was 'Piels is the beer for me, boys, Piels is the beer for me,' played in a jazzed-up Hawaiian rhythm and accompanied by the Hawaiians singing the words at the top of their voices in Hawaiian.

'Play it again,' she said when they had finished, 'Please!'

Sidney nodded at the musicians. 'Well, just once more,' the leader said reluctantly, and then they went through the whole thing again.

'I could listen to that all night,' Barbara said when they had finished and gone to the next table.

'Well, I couldn't,' said Mr Bossart, shuddering in mock horror. He stood up and went off to the men's room.

Left alone with Sidney Carter, Barbara couldn't think of anything to say. She bit her lip. All the things she would ordinarily say to a date or a boy her age she couldn't say to this man, because he obviously was married and an executive and probably should have caught a commuter train that left two hours ago. Anything polite and forced she would ordinarily say to a business acquaintance she couldn't say either because Sidney Carter had a glint in his eye and a contagious smile and he had changed her evening in ten minutes from a thing of hopelessness to something delightful.

'I might run an ad for Wonderful in *America's Woman*,' he said. 'Do you think that would be a good idea?'

'Of course.'

'No, seriously. Don't just say yes because you work there and you're out with one of the vice-presidents. I want to know what you think as an editor and a woman.'

She was so self-conscious she knew she was saying the wrong thing but she couldn't seem to stop herself. 'I'm not "out with" Mr Bossart the way you think I am. And I'm not an editor, I'm just an assistant editor, and I'm not really even a woman; I'm twenty-one.'

'Then answer me according to all those things.'

She paused. 'Frankly, I think Wonderful is too expensive for our readers. They're mostly young housewives who don't get a chance to shop in big department stores. They buy everything at the super-market or the shopping center and they have to drag their babies along when they do shop because they only have part-time help if at all. They buy cologne in the drugstore, and for special occasions, like Christmas or a birthday, their husbands sometimes buy perfume for them but more often a big appliance like a washing machine, which they need a lot more.'

Sidney Carter nodded. 'But you use Wonderful. Then tell me what you're like.'

She paused again. How much could she tell him? Obviously he wanted to know how much she was typical, not atypical. 'I'm a working girl,' Barbara said finally. 'This is my first job. I went to college for a while and never finished, and then I took a secretarial course, and I found my job through an employment agency. I don't make very much money but how I look is important to me, partly because of vanity and morale and partly because of the kind of work I'm in. I'd spend practically my last cent on cosmetics and perfume if nobody gave them to me for presents. I don't see any point in buying cheap perfume because *I* have to smell it too.'

'Did you get that little bottle of Wonderful for a present?'

'No. I bought it for myself.' She smiled. 'That's why it's so little.'

He put his elbow on the table, leaned his chin on his fist, and looked at her for a while. 'What kinds of presents do you get from the boys who take you out?'

'I get *them*,' Barbara said. She didn't realize how bitter her tone sounded until the words were already out and it was too late.

Sidney smiled. But this time it wasn't that devastating smile, it was totally different – full of understanding and a little sad. 'Haven't you met anybody you liked?' he asked gently.

Suddenly she wanted to pour everything out to him, a stranger.

She turned her head away. There was Mr Bossart standing at the very end of the bar, she noticed with desperation, with his arm around a big beefy man. He looked as if he were settled for the next half hour. Oh, I hate this Sidney Carter, she thought. Why is he so kind? He's making me feel sorry for myself.

'Not yet,' she answered lightly.

'You ought to be married,' he said. 'I can tell.'

'I was married.'

'Divorced?' There was so much compassion in his tone that in that instant the entire last scene with Mac came back as if it had happened that very evening. And not only that evening but every single evening, relentlessly, since he had left her.

'Yes,' she said.

'And you live alone?'

'I have a daughter,' she said.

'Oh . . .' She could see it on his face then, what he was thinking: this poor girl, so young, no wonder she never has enough money, how lonely she must be, and how frightened of the future.

'Doesn't anyone take care of you? Your parents?'

'I take care of my mother and she takes care of the baby. My father died when I was nine. My ex-husband sends us a little money, of course.'

'You'll find someone who'll take care of you,' he said.

From anyone else she would have mistrusted that statement, it would have aroused all her protective instincts, real and imaginary, and she would have thought, Why, the old sugar daddy! But Sidney's tone was so obviously impersonal, and yet so obviously concerned with her needs, that she knew he was envisioning a nice young bachelor, and the contrast between his opinion of what she deserved and what she was actually receiving broke down the last of the wall of reserve she had carefully kept around her since she had come back to New York.

'Oh, no I won't!' she said in a quiet voice that was just on the edge of tears.

'You *should* have someone to care for you,' he said. 'What's the matter with all these boys?'

'They're just getting started in their careers, the same as I am. If they have any children in the next few years they want them to be their own babies.'

He shook his head slowly, looking at her with eyes that were troubled.

'I think all the time,' Barbara said, 'What about *my* baby? She's *here*. She has a right to be happy, to have a home and a father. What am I supposed to do, forget she exists? I was at the office party tonight and there was an old bastard moving in on me, making passes. He was a very important man in the company and I knew I couldn't make a scene in front of other people.' She caught Sidney's surprised look and added quickly, 'Oh, no, it wasn't Mr Bossart. It was someone else, I won't say who. The whole time he was pawing my leg and trying to kiss me and making me sick to my stomach one thought kept running through my mind. What will happen to my daughter if I lose my job? I realize now it was panic, that I could quit tomorrow and tell my new boss exactly why, or threaten to and keep the job I have – but at the time I wasn't rational. I just kept thinking about my baby.' Her voice broke then and she knew that tears were running out of her eyes but she couldn't hold herself back any longer. And for some reason in front of Sidney she didn't feel like a fool at all.

'I'm just like a man,' Barbara went on. 'I have to work like a man, fight for my job like a man, think like a man. I don't want to be a man, I want to be a woman – and I know damn well I'm not a woman at all even at my better moments, I'm just a young girl with so many responsibilities it throws me into a state of shock.'

Sidney took his handkerchief out of his breast pocket and unfolded it for her. She wiped her eyes, trying to smile at him, and saw that her mascara had left black streaks on his handkerchief.

'I'm sorry . . .' she said.

'I'm glad it's finally being used,' he said. 'It's just a decoration up there.'

'You've been very kind. I guess you weren't expecting Niagara Falls. It doesn't really go with the Hawaiians, does it?'

'They're fun, aren't they,' he agreed.

'I'm glad I met you,' Barbara said sincerely.

'I don't see why. You've spent most of the time feeling miserable.' He smiled at her then, the having-fun smile.

'It was a relief. It must have been a crashing bore for you, though.'

'Don't be silly.'

'It's just that I've had a tough evening,' Barbara said apologetically. 'I'm not usually like this. And I'm probably a little high, too.'

'Barbara . . .'

'What?'

'Don't go off into your shell again. When I first met you this evening I couldn't quite figure you out. You look so young, but there's something withdrawn about you. Not natural shyness but a kind of bitterness. Now, of course, I realize why. But I didn't like you that way and I like you this way. You don't *have* to be like a man, as you put it.'

'I don't know what way to be any more,' Barbara said.

'So you met a few insensitive boys who couldn't realize your needs. It won't always be like that.'

'I know,' Barbara said. 'But I only know it in my head.'

'Whenever you're miserable,' Sidney said, 'it seems as though you've always been unhappy and you remember all the bad and disappointing things that ever happened to you. And when things are going wonderfully well it suddenly seems as though life had never really been so bad.'

'How do you know!'

He laughed. 'Why? Do you think the blues are the exclusive property of the young?'

She couldn't help laughing with him.

'Glad to see you two are having a good time,' Mr Bossart said, looming over them, his tweedy outline a little fuzzy in the dim room. He eased himself into his place beside Barbara. 'Did I miss anything?'

'About four thousand drinks,' said Sidney.

'Then I beat you at the bar. Y'know who I just ran into? Old George. The best poker player the New Haven Railroad ever had on board.'

'He doesn't look like he'll play much of a game tonight,' Sidney said, glancing at the beefy man drooping over the bar.

'Oh, he's staying in town tonight.' Mr Bossart looked at his watch. 'Well. Are we about ready to leave?'

'Yes,' Barbara said softly, reluctantly.

As the three of them went to the door Mr Bossart looked back and held up one hand in the direction of his friend at the bar. They nodded at each other and waved.

The air was cold when Barbara reached the street, the night black and clear, with the deceptive frosty atmosphere that makes you think you are somewhere in the country instead of breathing city fumes. A cab came cruising up the side street, its light on top looking like a Christmas ornament. Mr Bossart opened the taxi door.

'You can have the first taxi, Barbara,' he said. He patted her shoulder. 'Get home safe, now, and good night, and Merry Christmas.'

She didn't get into the cab but turned and looked at him.

'Barbara and I might as well share a cab,' Sidney said casually. 'We're both going in the same direction.'

'Aren't you going to the train?' Mr Bossart asked.

'An account of ours is having an open house. I might as well show up for a few minutes and then take the milk train, as long as it's this late already. He'll be hurt if I don't show.'

'Good night, Sid.' Mr Bossart put one arm around Sidney Carter's shoulders and with the other hand pumped his hand. 'Take care.'

'You too.'

'Good night, Mr Bossart,' Barbara said. Sidney helped her into the taxi, and it drove off. She glanced back through the rear window and saw Mr Bossart going back into the bar. She gave the driver her address in a taut voice and turned to Sidney.

'How far are you going?' she asked.

'I'm just going to drop you off and then go to the train. I couldn't let our middle-aged Boy Scout send you off by yourself at this hour of the morning.'

'There *is* no party?'

'Not that I know of.'

'You're so nice,' Barbara said. 'You know – Mr Bossart means absolutely nothing to me, you know that, and yet when I looked back just now and realized that he was just trying to get rid of me so he could go back to his poker-playing friend I felt sort of odd. I had this thought: that all over New York City right now, this minute, there are people trying to get rid of other people because they're bored with them. And somehow it depressed me.'

'But the people who have been gotten rid of are probably relieved to be free again. Haven't you thought of that aspect of it?'

Barbara thought for a moment. 'You're absolutely right. That's just how I feel.'

Sidney put his hand on the seat beside hers and then picked her hand up in his. 'May I?'

'Yes.' She hadn't expected her heart to turn over the way it did when he took hold of her hand, it was half fright and half what she suddenly realized was excitement and desire. She held her fingers stiffly in his, and when he pressed them she did not respond.

'This isn't a pass,' he said quietly. 'It's just a braille the sighted have worked out for things they've realized they can't see.'

She looked straight ahead, reading the driver's number on the little card posted in front of them, reading his name and not remembering it one instant after she had read it. All the time she was acutely aware of Sidney's hand attached to hers, even though he was holding it lightly, and she felt as if her entire arm had turned into a heavy tree trunk. Then he let go, and her arm came to life again, and her hand, alone and deserted on the leather seat, felt cold.

'Here's my house,' she said, wishing it weren't.

He paid the driver and walked to the door. He paused on the top step. 'Will you be all right?'

'Yes. Thank you.'

He looked up at the windows of her apartment house. 'Which windows are yours? Can we see them from here?'

Barbara pointed, feeling rather warmed. 'Yes, see that one with the Christmas tree?'

'The tree lights are on. That's nice to come home to.'

'My mother stays up late watching television.'

Sidney looked up at the lights for a moment longer. Then he looked down at her, very seriously. 'If I telephoned you and asked you to have dinner with me some night, would you?'

Her voice sounded strange, not her own voice at all but something without breath. 'You're married, aren't you?'

'Yes.'

She had known, of course, the minute he said he had to make the train, the minute she saw he was over thirty-five, but all the same having him tell her outright, irrevocably, came as a shock. She tried to think of something to say quickly to hide her disappointment.

'How many . . . children do you have?'

'One son, twelve years old.'

'Oh.'

He was waiting, looking at her with a guarded look on his face. Barbara looked fixedly at the knot of his necktie. 'Don't call me,' she said. 'I don't mean that nastily, I just mean, please don't.'

'That's why I asked,' Sidney said quietly.

'I like you,' she said. 'I *like* you. I've had a happier, more comfortable time tonight than I've had in . . . I can't remember how long. You know all about me. You know who I am – I'm Barbara Lemont, the girl who wants to get married again. I can't just think about myself. So . . . please don't call me.'

'All right,' he said gently.

He stood there smiling as she fitted her key into the lock and swung the door open. She paused for a moment looking at him before she went in. 'Good night.'

'Good night, Barbara.' He took a breath, as if he wanted to say something else, but then he said nothing and turned and walked down the stairs. She went quickly into her house and shut the door before she would have to hear the sound of his footsteps dying away.

When you live in a walk-up it's like living in a village, every landing and every apartment has its own sounds and smells. The elevator, which had worked sporadically, had finally been abandoned. As Barbara walked the stairs to her own apartment those signs of private lives all came to her, one by one, familiar and yet each with their own secrets. The Goldsteins, on the second floor, who had the biggest grocery order and always cooked chicken very early on Friday evening; the Keans, third floor rear, who had eight children and left their apartment door unlatched all day so that the neighborhood kids could run in and out; the newlyweds down the hall who walked their gray French poodle every evening with the same air of self-conscious pride, as if it were their first child; the two middle-aged fairies in their one-and-a-half-room apartment, their door closed against the world. Everyone had a family of sorts, even they. Everyone had someone to come home to, to be with when it was time for doors to be closed and the rest of the world had divided off. She had a family too, but it wasn't the kind she wanted. There are all kinds of love, Barbara was thinking, love for a parent, love for a child, love for a friend, but none of them is a substitute for any of the others. None of them is the same in any way as love for a man who loves you too.

She was alone, a small figure in an empty hall surrounded by closed doors that contained people who loved one another. As she walked, the stairs seemed like a treadmill. She remembered what Sidney had said, that when things have been going badly it seems as though they have always been that way. What else could she possibly have told him but not to call? He was married, he was living with his wife, he had no right to want to see another girl. She would have been a fool to tell him she would see him again. He knows my address, she thought. Maybe he'll call anyway.

Barbara paused on her own landing, hesitating before going down the hall to her apartment, waiting for one last moment alone with the emotion that made her so confused she could hardly think. He's married, she thought. He's married, and he's the one man I've met whom I could love. Could love? I think I love him already. You only live once. All these things have happened in my life and I haven't lived at all. How long can I go on like this, resentful, frightened, alone? Oh, phone me, Sidney, please *please* phone me!

He won't call. I told him not to, so he won't. He's old enough to take no for an answer. And it's a good thing for me that he won't call. How could I say no again, how could I keep away from him? Does a two-month-old baby run away from home?

He'll never call me, Barbara thought, so I can think what I want about him. It's perfectly safe to have fantasies. I love him. It's just a crush, but I *feel* it. I feel something. I feel alive. I want to talk to him and look at him, and have him hold my hand again and even . . . She knew what happened to girls who fell in love with married men. The men stayed married and the girls turned down their suitors until they had lost them all. Oh, occasionally men divorced their wives to marry younger girls, but these were caricatures, the rich, foolish businessman and the peroxided chippy. It hadn't happened to anyone Barbara had ever known. Her own boss, an attractive woman who was forty years old and looked thirty, had never married. Once when she and Barbara had had lunch together preceded by a Martini, her boss had said, for no reason, 'Don't ever fall in love with a married man.' Now Barbara knew it had been for a reason after all, it was the reason why a woman who was so well groomed and charming was still alone. What good was a love affair that ended with the last train to the country, and Christmas presents that had to be given the day before Christmas because holidays were family times, and knowing that you would still be as alone as before because you could never telephone the man you loved when you needed him? She knew about affairs with married men, she was no fool.

Sidney Carter was probably on the train now, and soon he would be walking up a path to the doorway of his house in the country. He would let himself into the house with his key. He would be home. No matter how bored he was – if he *was* bored – he would not be lonely. He would go to bed with his wife and forget Barbara. He might want Barbara, but he didn't need her. He won't ever call me, Barbara thought. But, oh, God, maybe he will; and if he does, I'm going to be a damn fool and I don't care.

14

On February 14, 1953, Valentine's Day, Caroline Bender received a dozen long-stemmed red roses from Paul Landis with a humorous card. Mary Agnes Russo received a box of chocolates in a heart-shaped red box trimmed with white paper lace from her fiancé Bill. Gregg Adams didn't know it was Valentine's Day because she had a hangover and she was trying to revive herself sufficiently to attend a general audition for the ingénue lead in a forthcoming Broadway play, a role requiring a girl with clear eyes and a winningly fresh face. Barbara Lemont stopped on her way to work to buy some heart-shaped candies for her daughter Hillary. And April Morrison fainted on the sidewalk in front of Rockefeller Plaza.

When April revived she was lying on a bench in a travel agency. She thought at first she had died and was laid out on a marble slab. The next thing she thought was that she had never been so nauseated in her life and if all those strangers didn't go away and stop staring at her she would throw up right in front of them.

'Are you all right now, honey?' a woman asked. She had a round white face with black mascara on her eyelashes that made each eyelash stand out separately. April concentrated on those spiky eyelashes – that woman looked just like Betty Boop – and finally the nausea receded and she could breathe again.

'That's right, honey, take a deep breath now. Drink some more of this water.'

April sat up. 'I have to go to my office, what time is it?'

'Only nine-twenty-five. Drink some water.'

'No . . . no. I hate water.' Why hadn't she realized before that the taste of water made her sick to her stomach? 'Thank you for looking after me. I have to go to work now.'

'You look awful pale, honey.'

So do you, April wanted to say. She felt strange: warm and secret and like laughing softly to herself. She felt completely away from everybody else, from the kind woman with the paper cup of water, from those people looking through the travel-agency window, from all the noises of Fifth Avenue traffic she could hear as she opened the door. 'Thank you,' she said. 'I'm all right now, I'm fine.'

As she rode up in the elevator to the thirty-fifth floor April automatically folded her arms across her stomach. Wasn't that silly, when she was sure that whatever was in there was the size of the head of a pin! But she had to protect it. It was hers.

At first, when she had suspected she was pregnant, she had been terrified. She had run to the ladies' room so many times to look and see if at last perhaps it wasn't true that Miss Farrow had begun to make sarcastic remarks. She had no idea what had given her the presence of mind to have lunch with Barbara and ask her (casually, very casually, in the guise of interest) who was the baby doctor who took care of Hillary now. For some reason she had thought a pediatrician was as good as a gynecologist in cases like this, but when she had gotten to the office the pediatrician had sent her to another doctor. She didn't dare say her name was Mrs Key. Someone might have heard of Dexter, someone might ask questions or talk. She had tried to think of a nice, refined, married-sounding married name, and finally she had thought of Mary Agnes, the most blamelessly moral girl she knew. She had said her name was Mrs Russo. The doctor had no reason not to believe her.

'I'd say you're about six weeks pregnant, Mrs Russo.'

'Thank you,' April said. 'Would you please give me the bill now, I'll pay it while we still have the money.' She gave a self-conscious little laugh, just so the doctor wouldn't be insulted at having to talk about money.

The gynecologist had given her a careful look. 'My nurse will give you the bill,' he said pleasantly. 'Here's a prescription for your vitamins, and on your way out you can make an appointment for next month.'

How easy it seemed to him! Come back next month, Mrs Russo. And the month after that, and the month after that. She would never see him again. The next time she went to a doctor she couldn't say, I'm not Mrs Russo any more, I'm Mrs Key; so she would have to find another doctor. That wouldn't be hard. Once she was Mrs Key she could ask her in-laws.

At first she had wanted to tell Dexter the news instantly, she couldn't wait. But the night after her visit to the doctor Dexter had to go to someone's party without her, and she couldn't tell him on the telephone. She had sat alone in her apartment thinking of how best she could tell him, and a great warmth and serenity had settled over her. Who would have believed it? The terrible thing, Being Disgraced, the fear, wasn't such a monster after all. Somehow she felt rather proud of herself. She was going to have a baby, she and Dexter, Dexter's child. It was a love link, a bond and, even more, a person. Already she thought of the baby as a person, not a formless speck. She sat in her armchair, surrounding and guarding her baby, and she didn't feel like an Unwed Mother at all, she felt like a kind of Madonna. Was that sinful? Shouldn't she be afraid? But April felt a great peace and calmness. This morning when she had fainted in front of the office was her first sick day.

After work she met Dexter at his apartment. She sat on his sofa and allowed him to put a cold drink into her hand, and the entire time she was savoring the last instant of special secrecy before she would share her news. She couldn't imagine what he would say but she knew he would take care of everything. Dexter could always cope with anything.

'I want to play my new record for you,' Dexter said. 'Wait till you hear this!'

'Dexter . . .'

He turned, already kneeling over the phonograph, the record in his hand. 'What?'

'What's it called?'

'It's an old classic. Bix Beiderbecke. I had to brush two inches of dust off it in the back room of the record store before I found it.'

She would listen to the record, she had time. It was like savoring the last bittersweet moments of near-passion before you gave yourself up to it. She was dying to tell him, but she would wait, because she could only tell him once and it had to be right. She hardly heard the music. It came to her through a fog, in isolated snatches. I am going to have a baby. Dexter, I am going to have a baby.

'How did you like that?'

'Beautiful,' she murmured.

He put something else on the phonograph and came to sit beside her. He put his head on her shoulder. She put her arms around him and rested her chin on his head and stared across the room. She felt detached from him. The secret was all she could think about, the wonderful news that really should frighten her but didn't. She pulled away from him gently.

'Dexter . . .'

'What, honey?'

'Sit up, please.'

'Why?'

'Well, just sit up, that's all. I want to tell you something.'

He sat up then, looking at her with an It-Had-Better-Be-Big look on his face. For some reason that made her lose patience with him, because it *was* big, and she blurted it out. 'Dexter, I went to the doctor yesterday and he says I'm pregnant.'

He looked at her, eyes round, lips slightly parted, his hands hanging limply across his knees. He looked like a frightened little boy. 'Is he sure?'

'Of course.'

'Some of these guys just like to scare you. Did he take a test?'

'Of course.'

He didn't say anything then, he just looked at her.

'I . . . had to tell you first thing,' April said.

'It's all right,' he said, rather frantically it seemed to her. 'Don't worry.'

She wanted him to be the one to do the proposing, it was only proper. She didn't want to say, When will we get married? She waited, and Dexter sat there looking frightened and worried and not saying anything at all.

'What shall we do, Dexter?'

'It's all right,' he said. 'It's all right. I'm thinking.'

'The baby isn't due until next fall.'

He took a deep breath that was more like a sigh. 'The sooner the better then, I guess. Are you free all next weekend?'

Her heart leaped as if it were going to fly out through her throat. She felt happy tears come into her eyes. 'We'll elope, it'll be crazy!'

He was scowling at her. 'Elope?'

'We'll have to call my parents first. It'll be such a shock to them. I told them all about you when I was home for Christmas, though, and I know they'll be happy.'

'We can't get *married*,' Dexter said.

'What do you mean?'

'How would it look, to be married now and have an eight-pound baby in seven and a half months? We couldn't pass that off as premature.'

'I won't eat a thing,' April said quickly. 'I'll practically starve myself. I'll keep it a very small baby.' And already she was feeling sorry for her baby, who would be hungry before he was even born.

Dexter shook his head. 'Don't be off in your little dream world, honey, this is serious business. We'll go away on Friday.'

'Where? What for?'

He sounded so casual you'd think he was talking about a social involvement they couldn't get out of. 'To take care of it.'

She clamped her knees together and moved away from him on the couch, as if he were already about to do something terrible to her. 'You wouldn't do that!'

'Honey . . . honey . . . what else can we do?'

She bit her lip to keep the words from coming out, but she had to say them, it was self-preservation. Romance was gone, she couldn't wait for him to propose, and already April felt as if she had died. The room was very white. 'We could get married.'

'Married! How can we get married? Do you want to print a

banner and run it up on a flagpole? *Shotgun wedding.* What are you going to do, tell everyone to send the kid's birthday presents six months late for the rest of his life?'

'I want to have this baby,' April said in a small voice.

'We'll have other babies.'

'People die from abortions,' she whispered.

'Look,' Dexter said gently, 'you won't even feel sick. It's very clean, it's like a doctor's office. I'll go with you.'

'How do *you* know so much about an . . . abortionist's . . . *den?* Do you send all your girls there?' She was angry and hurt, lashing out at him.

'No. No.'

'Then how do you know?'

'I know about these things,' he said, slowly and clearly, trying to pacify her but visibly insulted.

'Have you ever taken a girl to an abortionist before?'

'No.'

'Really?'

'Really.'

'Did you ever . . . make a girl pregnant before?'

'Not that I know of.'

'Not that you know of!' April's voice rose in her shock. 'Do you mean some girl became pregnant and didn't tell you?'

'Some girls don't,' he said quietly.

'But *how* can they not tell you?'

'Maybe they're not sure I'd believe it was mine.'

'You know that this one is yours!' April said. 'Don't you?'

'Yes.'

April covered her face with her hands. 'Oh, Dexter, let's not talk this way, it makes me sick. It sounds like we're talking about a lot of hard, awful strangers. It isn't us. We're different.'

'It's going to be all right, honey,' he said. 'You sit back and rest. I'll make you a drink.'

'Do you think I should have a drink? It's not good for the baby.'

Dexter stared at her as if she were demented and he had just realized it. 'Well, I don't see as how that makes a hell of a lot of difference now, do you?' he said. He crossed the room to the bar and made her a drink and handed it to her. 'Here, drink it. You'll feel better.'

April held out her hand like someone hypnotized and accepted the glass. It felt hard and smooth and cold in her palm. She looked at it as if it might be poison and slowly lifted it to her mouth and sipped at the contents. It was only Scotch and soda. But she wished it were poison. She wished it were hemlock so she might die and never have to face another day.

In all her fantasies about unwed motherhood April had never imagined the efficiency or the speed with which alien forces would mobilize to help her. With one half of her mind she realized she should be grateful – there were total strangers with hearts in this city. Speed, they said, was important. It was almost as if they were all talking about a diseased appendix. Cut it out, cut it out fast. Time is of the essence. And with the other half of her mind April felt abused, about to be ravished, about to have something stolen from her which she knew logically she had no right to keep and which she knew emotionally she had to keep or something else within her, something more important, would die with it.

Because she knew that there was no chance she would be allowed to have this baby (unless she should run away, and where could she go?) every moment became very valuable to her. She felt as if she were spending the last days with someone she loved whom she would never see again. She would never see this baby at all, she would never know if it was a boy or a girl. Perhaps it could have been a talented person, someone who would have done something for the world. But all these were emotional thoughts, and the other side of her mind kept saying, You don't appreciate how lucky you are. What else could you do? It will all be over soon. You'll forget, and you'll be grateful that Dexter took care of everything.

It was strange that now, even though there was no more reason to fear pregnancy because it had already happened, she could not bear to have Dexter touch her. You're such a fool, the logical half of her mind told her, they say this is the best time for sex. It's the one time you'll really enjoy it because you won't be the slightest bit afraid of the consequences. You'll be sorry later you didn't take advantage of these last days. But the part of her mind that ruled her heart and her life said, Keep away from me, Dexter, you destroyer.

Dexter was gentle and almost seemed a little afraid to try to make love to her now. He would only make a tentative advance, which was unlike him, and then when she demurred he would give up. They did not discuss the baby or their appointment for the weekend, except for a few terse announcements about the time and place. Otherwise he tried to be light and pleasant, he tried to pretend that nothing had changed. He was going to pick her up Friday evening at her apartment and take her to a doctor in New Jersey. Or at least she hoped it would be a doctor. In her mind she had a picture of a dried-up little man in a doctor's white jacket, with long dirty fingernails. Assisting him would be a gross woman who smelled of bacon fat, with a round, bloated face. They would both hate her. They would both be thinking that she was going to do something dangerous and inconvenient for them, like die, and for that they despised her. They would both think she was a fool for not knowing any better than to get herself in this predicament. April didn't even dare think about her parents. Whenever she thought of her mother, and how her mother would feel if she mysteriously died, her heart almost stopped beating then and there.

She wanted to go home, to her mother's arms, and confess everything and be cared for, but she knew that was impossible. Her mother would never be able to comprehend this terrible thing, it would be something that would hang over them for the rest of their lives. There was no reason to ruin the futures of an entire family – she had gotten into this trouble alone with Dexter and she would get over it with Dexter. At least he hadn't run away. You had to say that for him, he hadn't left her side for a minute since she had told him.

The only person April had told besides Dexter was Caroline.

She had never expected the feeling of warmth she could get from a friend's honest concern, and Caroline's devotion was the only thing in this whole situation that comforted her. There was no panic in Caroline. 'What can I do?' Caroline asked. And when April told her that Dexter had arranged for the abortion Caroline had seemed to sense immediately how April felt about all men at this moment.

'Have him drive you up to my house in Port Blair for the weekend,' Caroline said. 'You mustn't be alone in your apartment after an operation. You can stay with me and we'll take care of you. You'll rest and eat well and I'll keep you company. Dexter can stay too, or he can pick you up on Sunday night if you prefer.'

'Do you think he'll be insulted if I tell him I want to stay with you alone?' April asked.

'Insulted?' Caroline's voice shook with emotion. 'Insulted? What right has *he* to be insulted about anything?'

'It's funny,' April said, 'I love him but I just can't face being with him afterward. I know I'll say the wrong thing, or he will. I feel so strange.'

'I know it sounds stupid to tell you everything will be all right, knowing the way you feel,' Caroline said, 'but, believe me, it *will* be all right. All your friends love you. I love you. We all care very much what happens to you. If there's anything friends can do for you now, we'll do it.'

'I know,' April said softly. 'Thank you.' For the first time in her life she felt as if she had crossed over a bridge which had no way to return. She was twenty-one years old but she was no longer a young girl in any way and she could not turn to her family or any friends of the family for help, but only to her own contemporaries. Without her friends she would be alone. And her friends understood how she felt and were not shocked, only indignant that she had to suffer pain and near-disaster instead of having the husband and child she wanted more than anything in the world. Instinctively April knew that if she were to tell Barbara, Barbara would feel the same way as Caroline did.

'I'll come back with you after work on Friday and stay with you until Dexter comes,' Caroline said. 'We'll have a drink or two and I'll help you pack for the country.'

'I'll feel scared facing your family,' April said. 'Your father's a doctor. Do you think he'll be able to tell from looking at me that something just happened?'

Caroline laughed. 'Do you think doctors have X-ray eyes? My father will take one look at your young fresh face and leave us scrupulously alone so we can giggle together about our boy friends.'

'Yes . . .' April said. 'So would mine . . . Thank God. My poor father . . .'

On Friday April was almost unable to do any work. She tried harder than ever to concentrate on her typing, but all the time she was thinking how silly it was to be so careful not to make mistakes because Monday morning Miss Farrow would probably have to ask for a new secretary. These letters, this work she was doing in the office, suddenly took on a great importance, as if she had already died and was looking at them from a poignant, untouchable distance, like Emily in *Our Town* after she had died. She wanted to make a mark somewhere, leave something; and on an impulse she took her initialed handkerchief out of her purse and tucked it under the edge of her blotter. They could find it on Monday. But when five o'clock came and it was time to make the mad rush out of the office for the elevators April reached the door of the bullpen and then came back and took the handkerchief out of the blotter and put it back into her purse. She didn't want anything of her own to remain alone and unprotected if she was not there to own it, not even a handkerchief with her name on it.

It was only a short walk from the office to April's apartment, but Caroline insisted on taking her there in a taxi and paying for it. Upstairs April sat on her chair and looked at the furniture in her room, hardly seeing it. Caroline was briskly removing underthings and a nightgown from the bureau drawer and looking for April's suitcase. She had brought a pint bottle of gin.

'You'll never get high enough on Scotch,' Caroline said. 'Where do you keep the orange juice, or haven't you any?'

'I don't know.'

'I'll go downstairs and get some. You stay here. Don't move.'

'Where would I go?' April asked hopelessly.

Caroline returned in a few minutes with a paper container of orange juice from the grocery store. 'This is the special Harvard Weekend punch,' she said cheerfully, mixing it in a pot she had found on the stove. 'You don't even taste the gin, and then – boom!'

April smiled weakly.

'More innocent girls have been seduced as a result of this punch than you could imagine,' Caroline went on. 'You won't even want an anesthetic.'

'They're not going to give me one!'

'Well, I'm giving you one. Old Caroline is here. Drink this, my dear innocent girl.'

April sipped at the drink, forcing the sweetness past the obstruction that seemed to have lodged in her throat. Even at that moment, knowing everything was settled and almost finished, the thought came to her that orange juice was good for pregnant women. She wondered whether someone who was about to be put into the electric chair and was being given his last dinner would refrain from eating dessert because he was on a diet. I would, she thought. But then, I'm a fool.

The doorbell rang and April jumped. Caroline walked to the door and opened it. 'Hello, Dexter,' she said sweetly, as if he had come to pick up April to take her to the movies.

How proper Dexter was, how polite. He smiled and asked Caroline how she was feeling. April wondered whether he was resenting the fact that Caroline was there. Caroline was telling him how to get to Port Blair from the Merritt Parkway and he was nodding studiously.

'We may be a little late,' he said. 'I know it will be long after dinner.'

The cocktail party, April thought bitterly, may last longer than we expect. Her palms were moist and her heart was pounding in terror. Perhaps, she thought, I'll lose the baby right here and save us all that trouble.

He helped April on with her coat and lifted her suitcase. When April started down the stairs it was Caroline, not Dexter, who held her arm. It was the closest April had come in the entire time to bursting into tears.

They came out into the early darkness of a winter evening. The street was lighted with street lamps and there was a small crowd of neighborhood children gathered around the curb. At the curb, in front of April's apartment house, there was a long black shiny Cadillac limousine, the kind with two rows of seats in the back instead of one, and a closed-off front seat compartment for the chauffeur. The chauffeur got out of the car when they approached and opened the door to the back. He was a small, wiry man dressed in a grayish uniform with leather boots that made him look a little like a Western Union messenger. Dexter handed April's suitcase to him and reached inside the car, bringing out a huge bouquet of pink roses wrapped in green florist's paper.

'For you,' he said, laying the bouquet in April's arms.

'Whose car is that?' April whispered.

'I rented it. Shall we go?' He held out his hand to Caroline. 'Goodbye, Caroline. I'd drop you off at the station but we have an appointment and we mustn't be late. We'll see you later this evening.'

'All right,' Caroline said. She kissed April on the cheek. 'I'll see you soon. You look like a star after opening night with those flowers.'

Don't leave me, April wanted to say, but instead she smiled. 'Goodbye.' She allowed Dexter to help her into the limousine while the chauffeur held the door open. She had never been inside a car like this and despite her nervousness about what was going to happen to her she began to feel almost cheerful again. The gin and orange juice that Caroline had made her drink made her feel rather light-headed and the roses in her arms were cool and silky to the touch and smelled beautiful. Dexter settled beside her and lighted a cigarette.

'All right, Fred,' he said.

There was a remote-control panel in the armrest of the back

seat that could turn the radio on. Dexter tuned it in to play soft music. As the limousine crept through the traffic April could see people turning around to look at them, and when they stopped for a light the people in the cars waiting next to theirs turned their heads to see who was inside such a distinguished-looking car. Perhaps they thought she really was a star, with those roses, and the chauffeur, and Dexter looking so handsome and sophisticated next to her in his black chesterfield overcoat and the white cigarette in the corner of his mouth. If she tried she could pretend that they were going to a house party in the country.

'Do you like it?' Dexter asked, grinning.

'I'm overwhelmed.'

'I have something else,' he said. In the pocket of his overcoat he had a silver flask. He unscrewed the cover, and the cover became a little silver cup. 'Bonded bourbon.'

'I just had gin.'

'That's all right. It's not the combination that makes people sick, it's the quantity. Drink up.'

She took the little cup from him and swallowed the contents in one gulp, as if it were medicine, swallowing again to keep it down. She shuddered and felt better. They were on the broad highway now, heading for New Jersey, the car rocking from side to side as they sped along. Through the open windows came the sulphur smell of the factories along the New Jersey flatlands, making April feel like retching. She leaned out of the window and all of a sudden the mile-long limousine with the two of them in it and the liveried chauffeur and the armful of roses and the soft music and the hip flask of bourbon wasn't glamorous any more, it was ridiculous; they were two frantic, stupid people speeding through an ugly-smelling countryside to attend the murder of love. It was limousines like this that people rented to go to weddings and to funerals. Had anyone ever rented one before to go to an abortion? She should by all rights be going to her wedding now, and instead she was possibly going to her funeral. April glanced at Dexter. She wondered whether he had ever really loved her at all.

Dexter was quietly drinking bourbon from his flask, directly from the neck of it. Perhaps he needed it as much as she did to calm his nerves. Perhaps it still wasn't too late after all. 'Dexter . . .'

'What?'

'We could get married secretly in New Jersey and then tell people that we were secretly married six weeks ago. They would never know the difference.' But at the back of her mind April knew it was a lame excuse, more a chance for Dexter to prove he really did love her. 'Dexter?'

'That's crazy,' Dexter said. 'You know it is. No one would believe it for a minute. They would laugh.'

'Not once we were married. When you're really married people don't laugh.'

'We're not going to discuss it any more, honey, it's all arranged.'

April wrung her hands together, feeling her nails cutting into the skin and really not feeling the pain at all. Everything was falling away, everything, until she could hardly even believe in his promises for the future. He had betrayed her now, so might he not desert her again later? 'You said we could have other babies later, when we're married . . .' she said. 'Sometimes people who have abortions can't ever have any more children.' But that too, she knew, was only an excuse, a feeler to see if there were any promises left that she could believe in, or if marriage, love and security were things that belonged to a past that had somehow eluded her.

'Everything will be all right,' Dexter said with a hint of petulance in his voice, 'I *told* you.' He screwed the top back on the flask and put the flask into his coat pocket. April watched his hands, hardly knowing them. They were the hands of a stranger. Then he looked at her with his face surprisingly clear and guileless.

'We can get married this spring if you like,' he said.

Her heart turned over. Warmth came back slowly, bringing the frozen dead to life. 'I'd like that,' she said, and then with real feeling, 'Oh, I'd like that very much!' She hugged his arm with both her arms and Dexter looked down and kissed her. The lights of the town sped toward them, shimmering, haloed, and not so terrible after all.

The place where Dexter Key took April was not a doctor's office in the conventional sense of the word, but what at first glance seemed to be simply a door set among a row of stores in the commercial section of town. If you were not particularly looking for it you would be sure to miss it. There was a small brass name plate on the wall beside the door, brownish with age and not very legible, reading, Dr Thomas, Surgeon. Behind the door was a flight of narrow stairs leading almost straight upward like a ladder. The stairs and the walls were painted a light pea green. At the top of the stairs was a corridor leading to a locked door. Dexter rang the bell.

A buzzer rang and clicked from within, and Dexter pushed the door open. He led April inside. There was a small square waiting room with some silent people in it. April had not expected other people, she had thought she and Dexter would be alone, and she was so startled at the sight of them that she almost turned to flee. There was an elderly woman, very thin and obviously much too old to be here for anything to do with childbirth, sitting quietly with her hands folded on her lap. She had a great growth on the side of her neck. There was a plump and frowzy-looking girl about nineteen years old with reddish nostrils and pink-rimmed eyes, twisting the handle of her plastic pocketbook around her forefinger and sitting next to a boy who looked not much older than she, uncomfortably dressed up in a cheap-looking brown suit. She looked to April exactly like someone who needed an abortion. The three of them looked up when they heard April and Dexter enter, looked at them, and down again. April put her ringless hands into her coat pockets.

The room was filled with overstuffed and shabby-looking furniture, done in colors that reminded April of the words *dun* and *puce*. There were lace antimacassars on the arms of the sofa and chairs, although the upholstery was too far gone for them to do much good. But the room seemed to be very clean. On a spindly table next to the sofa was a pile of ragged old magazines. April was afraid to touch them for fear she would catch some disease. She sat down next to Dexter on the sofa and unbuttoned the top button of her coat.

'Do you want to take your coat off?' he murmured politely.

'No thank you.'

Directly in front of her on the wall there was a framed print of a water color depicting a shaggy collie dog being hugged around the neck by a little boy. Underneath the print in small red letters set into a white banner were the words *Man's Best Friend*. Somehow that struck April as amusing, she smiled and fixed her eyes upon it, reading it over and over again for comfort. If the doctor could put up a picture like that he couldn't be such an ogre.

A nurse came out of the back room wearing a clean, starched white uniform and a hair net. She wore heavy white shoes and had a cold, lined face. April stared at her from head to toe as she crossed the room with a small blue watering can in her hand and sprinkled a plant that was standing on a table in front of the window. The window looked down on the commercial street, but the pane had not been washed for a long time and there was a cross-hatching of what looked like chicken wire set into the glass, so you could hardly make out the view. The nurse finished watering the plant and went back into the rear room. It seemed to April like a callous gesture, when the patients trembling out here obviously needed the nurse's attention more than the potted plant did. She looked at her watch. It was six-thirty. She realized with a start of embarrassment, because it seemed so out of place, that she was hungry.

She tried to think of some casual conversation to make with Dexter. He was reading a magazine. *He was reading a magazine!* She could see his eyes moving from side to side as he read the lines. How could he be so calm? The nurse emerged again and nodded briskly at April. 'You can come in now,' she said.

April touched Dexter's arm. He looked up from his magazine and smiled at her. 'Go ahead,' he whispered. 'If you want to leave your coat here I'll watch it for you.'

She shed her coat and left it lying in a heap on the sofa. The other patients who were waiting glanced up at her for an instant as she walked, terrified, across the room. From the expressions on their faces she could tell that their only feeling was mild jealousy that she, the latest arrival, had been allowed to see the doctor first, while they had to wait and miss their dinners.

It was strange that afterward April could hardly remember what had happened in the doctor's office. On the way home she wanted to describe it to Dexter, but all she could say was that, yes, it had hurt, but she really couldn't remember about the hurting. It was more a fact than a feeling. The doctor had looked exactly as she had imagined him, except that his fingernails had not been long and dirty at all but clipped and very clean. The nurse had given her a sedative pill and a paper cup of water. With that and the bourbon and gin she had drunk, and her numbing fright, and her eyes tightly closed the entire time of the operation, the whole experience seemed like a half-remembered dream. When she was dressed to leave the doctor gave her six different envelopes of colored pills. They were to pep her up and calm her down, stop the bleeding and make her sleep, and as soon as he had explained to her what each was for she immediately forgot it. He had written on the outside of each envelope how many she was to take each day, and that was all she knew.

She hardly even noticed the trip in the limousine to Port Blair for her overwhelming sense of relief. She loved the doctor, he was kind, and she wished she had given some of her roses to the nurse. Her tongue felt fuzzy. She couldn't believe anything had happened, she only had the slightest sense of discomfort, and she had to tell herself she didn't have her baby any more. Perhaps they had made a mistake and not taken the baby at all. She had read about that once in one of her confession magazines. She hoped the doctor had taken the baby. She couldn't bear it if he had only hurt it, and left it to grow up deformed. When she had left the doctor had said, 'Everything will be just as it was before.' She knew what that meant. It meant, *forget*. All this never happened. Tomorrow you will forget it. Tomorrow you will be well.

When they drove up to Caroline's driveway the lights were on above the front door. Caroline came out of the house when she heard the car. She peered anxiously at April's face in the darkness and glanced at Dexter questioningly. 'She'd better go to bed,' Dexter said.

'I sent my parents to the movies,' Caroline said.

April opened her mouth to say something but no words came out. She felt drugged. How funny it would be, how it would startle them, if she were to ask as if nothing had happened, 'Oh, what movie did they see?' But she couldn't speak, she felt too tired. She felt a swinging sensation as Dexter lifted her into his arms. There was a raising and lowering as he climbed the stairs. She closed her eyes and heard footsteps and murmuring voices and felt the coolness of a pillowcase. Oh . . . she tried to say, what movie did they see? But the thought of the words swung around her in a great arc and swallowed her up.

April slept soundly until eight o'clock in the morning, turned over luxuriously in the guest-room bed, and drifted off into a dream. There was a little boy about three years old, dressed in a light-blue cotton suit, with Dexter's face and eyes and her fair hair. He was half running along the edge of the little lake in Central Park, the one where children sail their toy boats in fine weather. He was following his boat, skipping and running, and April saw herself standing nearby next to a park bench. She knew in the dream that he was her child, and she was smiling with love for him. Suddenly something catapulted her forward and she was pushing the child into the lake, feeling the resiliency of his small body against her hands. He did not even protest, he only looked at her with astonishment and the beginning of the realization of betrayal. It was she who was protesting, crying and screaming with the tears running down her face, and hurling him into the lake regardless, powerless to stop. He sank to the bottom as cleanly as an angel flies. There was no struggle, he was simply dead. She knew from looking at him through the layers of murky blue and black water that he had died. It was she who felt the choking of drowning lungs, it was she who struggled for breath, feeling against her hands even at that moment the outline of the innocent body.

She woke up crying, and lay there crying for a long time afterward, not quite sure why. I killed him, I killed him, I killed him, I hate Dexter, she murmured to herself, long after she knew it had been only a dream. Was it a kind of mystic dream? Was that what her child would have looked like, had he lived?

She slept fitfully until after noon, when Caroline came to open the blinds and give her a glass of orange juice. In those few hours dreams came and went, all of them horrible, all of them wakening her with tears and fright. In every dream the child was a boy, and he was always three or four years old, never a tiny baby. April became sure that the dreams contained something of the supernatural, that she was seeing the only glimpse she would ever have of the baby who was vanished forever.

'Did you sleep well?' Caroline asked.

'I kept dreaming.'

'I don't wonder,' Caroline said. 'You had a hard day yesterday. You'll rest up this weekend. Which pills do you have to take?' She was pouring out the pills onto April's palm, counting them, arranging for everything like a nurse. 'Do you think you can make it downstairs to lunch?'

'I have to wash my face.'

'I unpacked for you last night. Your clothes are in the closet and your toothbrush and things are on the sink. The white towels are yours.'

April got out of bed and walked gingerly to the mirror. Her face was white, her eyes had dark shadows under them. She looked anemic. Perhaps she had lost a lot of blood. She didn't really care.

'If you start to feel faint or anything give a yell. I'll be lurking in the hall.'

'Thank you,' April said.

When April had washed and dressed and combed her hair she felt utterly drained. Her movements were automatic. She felt as though something very sad and useless and unavoidable had happened to her, but she could not quite figure out what it was. It was as though she had put a great guilty secret out of her mind but its imprint remained, hovering, waiting to grow again into the dreaded original. I won't think about it any more today, she told herself firmly.

Caroline's mother was standing in the dining room, arranging leaves in a bowl of fruit that stood on the center of the table. She had met April once before, in New York. 'Hello, April,' she said warmly.

'Hello, Mrs Bender. How are you?'

'Oh, fine.'

There were four at the table, Caroline and April and Caroline's parents. Caroline's younger brother was visiting friends of his. The colored maid brought out cups of bouillon. Dr Bender ate silently, watching the women with a look of amusement on his face. It was as if he knew he was outnumbered and would have to spend the entire meal listening to gossip, and had determined to make the best of it and even like it. April could hardly meet his eyes. She wondered whether he would think she was pale.

'I saw Kitty today,' Mrs Bender said to Caroline. 'She certainly has her troubles.'

'Why?' asked Caroline, buttering a roll.

'You know that nice son of hers, the oldest one who was just graduated from Princeton?' Mrs Bender turned apologetically to April. 'Forgive us for talking about people you don't know, but I hardly ever see my daughter any more since she's working and has her own apartment, so when she favors us with a visit I have to catch up.'

'I don't mind at all,' April said.

'Excuse me,' said Caroline, and turned to the maid. 'April takes milk.'

'I wish *you'd* drink milk,' said Mrs Bender, 'instead of all those Martinis.'

'Oh, Mother!' Caroline said, laughing.

'That's why April has such beautiful teeth,' Mrs Bender said.

I never drink milk, April thought, glancing at Caroline. It's just now when I'm sick. If she only knew.

'All right,' said Caroline, 'all right. I'll have some milk too.'

'Good for you,' said her mother. She helped herself to some cold roast beef from a platter the maid was passing around. 'Anyway, poor Kitty. You know her son was going to go to medical school.

He was accepted in three of them. And during the summer he got mixed up with a girl – I won't say exactly what kind of girl, but she's the type who won't stop at anything to get what she wants. She's a model in a department store, but she's not pretty. I don't know why she was hired, except she has a well-proportioned figure. Now here's a boy with more money than he can spend, a wonderful future, handsome and popular as can be. You should see the girl, hard as nails. She was obviously after his money, because for her birthday he bought her a mink stole. Can you imagine? Everybody knew something funny was going on.'

April cut her roast beef into tiny pieces and tried to eat one but it stopped at her throat.

'Well, Kitty just kept hoping, closing her eyes to what was going on. How can you tell a twenty-one-year-old boy what to do? Believe me, Kitty cried her eyes out in secret. The next thing we knew, that girl got herself pregnant and *now* he's going to marry her!'

Dr Bender looked up with a twinkle in his eye. 'If she "got herself" pregnant all by herself, as you seem to imply, I'd like to meet her. She'd make a fascinating medical history for an article I could write.'

'You know what I mean,' Mrs Bender said. 'Those girls know how to hook a man. Don't tell me they don't know how to be careful.' She glanced around the table. 'April, dear, you aren't eating a thing. Would you like some mustard for your roast beef?'

'No, thank you,' April said.

'It's very good roast beef. We had it last night. I'm sorry you came too late for dinner.'

'So am I,' April said. Her voice was hardly audible.

'Well, anyway,' Mrs Bender continued cheerfully, 'this girl is two months gone and— '

'Mother,' Caroline interrupted with a touch of acerbity, 'we have a wonderful new book coming out that I know you'd love to read. I'll try to steal one of the first copies and bring it home for you next time I come.'

'That'll be nice,' Mrs Bender said. 'You'll probably be coming up in about ten days to go to that wedding. You can see the gloating bride and the poor foolish boy.' She shook her head. 'You know, you read about these things happening all the time, but if it ever really happens to someone you know it's such a shock. It's just a shame, a nice young boy like that with his future ahead of him. Now he'll have a stigma over him for the rest of his life.'

'Don't be dramatic, Mother,' Caroline said dryly. She turned to April. 'My mother's just peeved because she had her eye on him as a prospect for me.'

'Oh, Caroline!' her mother said.

April could see the room moving in waves of color. She looked down at her plate. The roast beef looked so bloody where she had cut it that it turned her stomach. She could taste something like the beginning of tears in the back of her throat.

'Well,' Mrs Bender said lightly, 'we won't talk about such gruesome things. We'll just be glad we don't hear about more people like that, or at least no one *we* know.' She smiled at April. 'You don't eat a thing, April, no wonder you're so thin. You and Caroline. You must be trying to starve yourselves to death.'

It wouldn't be such a bad idea, April was thinking. She smiled weakly at Mrs Bender and concentrated on her plate, trying to eat, trying to block out the sound of that cheerful, insensitive voice and the words it was saying, the moral pronunciamentos, the shared hypocritical grief, the shocked glee. She wondered whether things like that would affect her now, this way, for the rest of her life.

15

The tag end of winter is a dull time for actors in New York; the plays have opened for the season and those few that remain to open have already been cast, it is too early for summer stock, and all that is left is television and radio. Gregg Adams was among the fairly lucky ones. She found enough work to keep alive, and although none of it brought her to the attention of the public it still kept her from having to get a job as a waitress or a filing clerk, as many of her friends had to do. She played one of a group of teenagers in a filmed television commercial, and every time it was put on the air she received a check. She had two small parts in an early-morning radio serial. These paid for her rent and her large monthly telephone bill, and since she had never particularly cared about eating and David Wilder Savage took her to dinner four or five times a week, she managed to get along quite well. During the day she made the rounds or slept, and on the evenings when she was forced to be alone she would go to Downey's in the theater district or to Maxie's Bar near the Winter Garden and look for people she knew so that she could sit with them, drink coffee, and spend the rest of the early-morning hours peering around looking for David Wilder Savage.

Occasionally she would see him come into the place with other people and she would sense a strange, sickening tingling of her nerve ends and would hardly be able to breathe. The conversation of the young actors in her booth would fade away as if she were falling asleep and she would get up and walk past the booth where David Wilder Savage was sitting so that he would notice her. Then he would look pleased and surprised and ask her to join him. It never seemed to occur to him how planned these chance encounters had been, or if he knew, he gave no indication.

She had known him for such a long time now, and yet she could not quite figure him out. She was convinced that he loved her. And still, they had reached a plateau on which she suffered and he seemed quite content. What could she do to break through? She remembered a Chinese proverb she had read: 'It takes six years to make a friend and six minutes to lose one.' Perhaps this was too cynical. But why hadn't anyone, even the Chinese in their ancient wisdom, made up a proverb to tell how to turn a friendly lover into one who couldn't live without you? Every month when she discovered she was not caught she would give up a little prayer of thanksgiving, and then, because she knew she was quite safe again, she would allow herself to feel the pang of disappointment that was at the back of her mind. Perhaps something drastic would make David take action, something demanding immediate decision, something which would make him take stock of how valuable she was to him. But she knew that a girl had to take care of herself, so she kept on taking precautions not to conceive, not to change the status quo, not to change the even nature of their relationship when all the while she was alternately boiling and shivering inside with the force of her emotions.

She was making curtains for David Wilder Savage's kitchen, at last. Although she hardly knew how to sew, and certainly had never cared about putting up a stepped-in hem when a tiny safety pin could do, Gregg was painstakingly hemming curtains in an expensive fabric that could have sent her on her rounds in taxis for a week. Whoever made their own kitchen curtains nowadays? But there was something symbolic about the act, something that broke through the veneer of Broadway and cocktail parties and bright quips and might even break through the veneer of the man she was desperate to marry. It was so old-fashioned, so out of place with them and their friends. She had the curtains finished on a day in March, just before his play was due to open out of town. She decided to wait and save them for a surprise after he had the suspense of the opening and the reviews and the possible revisions out of the way. When he invited her to go with him to Boston for the opening, after warning her that he would hardly be able to pay any attention to her if she did come with him, she packed her best cocktail dress for the festivities, a pair of slacks for lounging in the front row of the theater during last-minute rehearsals, and put the kitchen curtains in the bottom of her suitcase. It made her feel good just to look at them, as if she really were married to him and had to do domestic things. It was a laugh, really, to look at her own unkempt apartment and then think of all the wifely chores she was anxious to do for his, but Gregg didn't care about her apartment. It was a place to sleep and change her clothes and take phone calls, that was all.

They arrived in Boston in cold, sleety weather. There was ice packed hard on the paths in the Common, and the sky was as gray as twilight even at noon. Gregg had never been in Boston before, and the city came to her in a series of impressions: the view of a statue from the window of her hotel room, the inside of the theater (just like the inside of any theater), the spires of a subway kiosk, a pair of extraordinarily ugly green suède shoes in a store window which she passed every day on her way from the hotel to the theater. But most of all Boston was a time of painful shock, of picking up the morning papers and reading reviews that made her suddenly feel as if she were not in any land she knew but had been dropped down in the country of the Hottentots.

The reviews were condescending. There was not praise for the leading lady but pity that she had to suffer so. It was so incredible that were it not for the name of the play and the names of the members of the cast and the producer, Gregg would have thought it was a review of some other play entirely. And yet at the back of her mind she had to admit that she had never really liked the script but had thought that if David Wilder Savage had chosen it to produce it must have some theatrical merit that was way above her head. Except for Gordon McKay's play it was his first failure. Gregg hated her friends in New York already for what they might say, what they might imply. If Tony dared to smirk in front of her and repeat what he had told her months ago she would slap him in the face. It was simply that everyone had a right to make a mistake, and in David Wilder Savage's case the wonder was that the mistake had been so long overdue.

The play closed 'temporarily' in Boston. There was no reason to try it in New York. The morning the reviews had come out David had put on his coat, left the hotel, and not returned for eight hours. Gregg did not know what to do. She had visions of his tall form striding through the gray mists of Boston like an avenging ghost, she pictured him getting drunk in a bar and falling under the wheels of a trolley and being killed; she did not know whether to stay in her hotel room next to the phone or wander from bar to bar in search of him. Every minute seemed like ten, an hour was unspeakable. She finally left a note in the room and a message at the desk and went out into the freezing day. The sleet had turned to drizzle. It was vaguely refreshing against her face, and the cold that hurt her fingertips gave her something to think about. She must have walked for miles, peering into the early gloom, not knowing where to go but not being able to bear staying still. She pictured him walking toward her, and herself falling into his arms with an hysterical cry of relief. It was not so much that she was afraid of what would happen to him, because she knew he was moody but not reckless, but the terror that overtook her without him. She hated Boston as she had hated no other city before.

Finally she went to the empty theater and entered through the stage door. It seemed to be her destiny that she would find him there and she wondered why she had not thought of it before. He would be sitting alone in the very center of the orchestra, lost in thought, his long legs doubled up against the back of the seat in front of him, his neck resting on the back of his. But the theater was totally empty, dark and silent and smelling of dry old upholstery. She knew then at last, because she had been so sure he would be there and he was not, that it was useless to try to estimate his thoughts. He was too separate from her, his life was a world of his own. And at that moment every importance her own life and privacy had had for her vanished completely.

When she came back to the hotel, exhausted, he was there, in the brightly lighted drugstore talking to the director, looking not appreciably changed. She ran over to him, squeezed herself into the booth beside him and gasped, '*Where were you?*'

He looked down at her with a slight appearance of annoyance. 'Do you want some coffee?' he asked kindly, although he was interrupting a sentence to ask it.

'Where were you? Where were you?'

'Ivan and I have been sitting here talking for the last hour. You'll have to be quiet and listen if you're going to stay.'

Gregg wiped bits of ice off her hair with her hands and leaned forward to peer at him to see if his eyes were bloodshot or if he had changed in any way at all.

'She's all wet,' Ivan said. 'She looks like Little Nell.' He was a large, ruddy-faced man with a high voice for someone of his size.

'You'd better have some coffee,' David said, warming her hands in his own. He glanced at her curiously because she seemed so obviously frantic and bedraggled but he did not ask her what the matter was and he gestured to the waitress to bring more hot coffee.

'We're discussing whether or not we can salvage our poor murdered play,' Ivan said. He had several sheets of paper in front of him on the table, covered with tiny handwriting.

Gregg looked at him. He was friendly, he was kind, and she wanted him to leave so desperately that she almost thought the force of the wish alone would spirit him away. She turned to David, clutching his warm hands in her cold ones. 'Are you all right?'

'Yes.'

'I didn't know what happened to you. Why didn't you tell me where you were going?'

'Drink your coffee,' he said pleasantly. He brought over the shaker of sugar from the edge of the table and set it next to her cup. 'We can talk later, after this business.'

Gregg drank her coffee, listening to the voices of the two men and hardly hearing them. He *knew* how much he meant to her, he had invited her to come all the way to Boston with him, and then when he needed her he had run away. Why hadn't he turned to her for comfort, why hadn't he said something? And here he was, face calm again, trying to save a play that was obviously not worth saving, and leaving her out of it completely. He had asked her for neither comfort nor encouragement, he had simply ignored her. Why had he asked her to come with him if he intended to ignore her? She wasn't his friend only when things were going well. In fact, she would be thankful for a chance to show him how stalwart she could be when things were going badly. Perhaps that would be the chance she had been waiting for, to comfort him when he was in need and no longer the strong one.

Ivan was standing up now, smiling at her. 'So long,' he said. 'See you on the train.'

'Goodbye.' She was so glad to see him go that she could even be cordial. As soon as he had left she turned to David.

'Are you going to try the play again?'

'Weren't you listening?' he asked, rather surprised.

'Of course,' she lied. She looked down at her hands. They were warm now and looked red. 'You know I would do anything for you. That's what I'm here for. You don't seem to realize that.'

He smoothed her hair gently. 'I know.'

'I want to *help* you,' she said.

'You do.'

'I wonder.'

He stood up and put some money on the table. 'We have to go and pack now, we're leaving on the five-o'clock train. I have to see someone first and then I'll meet you upstairs.'

'Please let me go with you,' Gregg said.

'I'll only be gone for half an hour. Will you do me a favor and pack for me?'

'Please let me go with you. I missed you when you were gone.'

'There's no reason for you to tag along,' he said, still pleasantly and gently, as if he were talking to a five-year-old child. 'I'll be right back.'

'Who are you going to see?'

He suddenly looked very tired, as if the toll of staying up all night had finally caught up with him. 'All right,' he said quietly.

'I'm not going to see anyone. I'm just going to walk around the block. You know what last night and this morning meant to me. I want to walk around the block and think about what I'm going to do.'

Gregg took his hand. 'I'll walk with you and I won't say a word.'

He loosened his hand from her grasp. 'You said you wanted to help me.'

'I do!'

'Then let me be by myself for a while. Sometimes the greatest favor you can do for someone is to let him be alone.'

'Come right back,' Gregg said, her voice shaking a little, trying to sound cheerful.

He ruffled her hair, the way he had when he had first made love to her and had left her to talk on the telephone, and walked out of the drugstore. The affectionate gesture melted her completely, she knew he could not possibly be angry at her, and she knew also that she could not bear to sit alone in the hotel room even for half an hour, remembering that gesture and feeling the strange walls closing in about her. She snatched her purse and hurried out of the drugstore after him, not even bothering to button up her coat.

She saw him at the end of the block, walking quickly, his hands in his coat pockets, his collar turned up. She scurried down the street, hiding behind a parked car when he turned the corner so he would not see her. He did not seem to have any definite direction, he was simply walking. The odd, crazy thought hit her then that perhaps, after all, he was going to meet someone, and he was a little early. Oh, God, Gregg thought, oh, God. Just the sight of David ahead of her reassured her, she felt that as long as she could keep him before her eyes everything would be all right. She was being careful that he would not notice her following him but she half hoped that he would turn around and see her and let her walk with him at last.

He went into the Common and began to walk more slowly, strolling down the ice-bordered path. The park was deserted, it was a very cold afternoon. The trees looked like thin black lines against the gray sky and the brownish buildings beyond, rows of trees, rows of houses, all strange to her and of no importance, as if they hardly existed. The only thing in the world was this man she was following secretly, keeping him always in sight because he meant warmth and life and cheerfulness even in this bleak, empty landscape of the park. She followed him not for half an hour but an hour. She was getting numb with the cold and she was afraid they would miss their train. Finally David headed back for their hotel, and a moment after he entered the lobby Gregg darted in after him. She waited until the elevator he was in had gone upstairs and then she went to it and rang the bell.

He was in his room, which adjoined hers, packing his suitcase. 'Hi,' Gregg said. He didn't answer, he was folding his dressing gown and doing it badly.

She went to him and took the dressing gown out of his hands. 'Let me do that.'

'We missed the train,' he said. 'We'll take the six o'clock.'

'I know. What took you so long?'

He turned and looked at her. She had never seen his face so withdrawn. 'I was waiting for you to get tired of following me and give up.'

What could she say? Bravado was the only answer. 'How did you know?' Gregg asked with a nervous little smile.

'I turned around at least twice and saw you. You don't make a very good detective.' The words were pleasant enough but the tone was distant and strained.

'I didn't bother you,' she said.

'You bothered the hell out of me.'

'Why? Why?'

'Look . . .' he said. He sighed. 'If I want to be alone, *alone*, and I ask you to let me be alone, can't you respect my wishes? I would let you be alone instantly if you requested it.'

'But I'd never request it. I hate to be alone.'

'Does everyone have to be exactly like you?' he asked quietly.

'Of course not. But I just want to be with you.'

'You're always with me. You'll be with me for five hours on the train. Do you think you can make it into your room all by yourself to gather up your things or do I have to come in and hold your hand?'

'I'm sorry,' she said. 'I didn't know I would upset you.'

'You do know,' he said, 'because I tell you. But you don't seem to care. If you were playing a part in a play do you think I would stand in the wings during the whole performance blowing kisses and whispering and throwing folded-up notes at you?'

'Don't be sarcastic.'

'I will explain it to you just once more,' he said, speaking very slowly, as if he were really too tired to make the effort. 'There are times when a person wants to be alone, to think, or just not to think at all. Perhaps I'm worse than other people, perhaps I need to be alone more often. But if this is the case it's the way I am, and I want you to try to understand it. If you can't, then I don't think you and I should see each other any more.'

His words were like a knife stripping off her skin, sure and cold and terrifying. 'No,' Gregg said. 'No! We have to see each other.'

He sat down on the edge of the bed, right on the tangle of unpacked clothing. 'I'm so tired,' he said.

Gregg crossed the room to him in an instant and sat down beside him, putting her arms around his neck. 'We have to see each other,' she said. 'We have to! I'll leave you alone, I promise.'

He did not push her away or draw away at all, he simply sat there, allowing her to cling to him, his eyes shut. Finally he spoke, quietly, in a nearly expressionless voice. 'Start now,' he said.

On the train all the way from Boston to New York David Wilder Savage slept, his head back against the back of his seat, his face grayish with strain and fatigue. Gregg tried to rest but couldn't. She was so tired that she felt as if any little thing would make her crack wide open like Humpty Dumpty falling off the wall, and nothing could put her together again, not even twelve hours of sleep with a sleeping pill. How long ago the beginning of their relationship seemed, as if it had happened to two other people! Every day now things were more unbearable; it was a marriage after the honeymoon was over but with nothing to replace the lost romance. In the beginning newness had made her casual and wary so that she had kept her sense of humor and had managed to amuse him even when she was more concerned than he ever suspected. But now every little word, every look or movement, cut into the festering wound of panic that she kept inside her heart. Even her actions of the summer, her casual and loving goodbyes when she drove back to the country for summer stock, seemed to be the motions of a happy stranger. The worst of it was that there was neither a going back nor a reformation possible. She was what she was, and she had made of their relationship the tense and teetering thing it was. She knew it, and she was powerless to do anything about it, so everything she said was wrong and everything she did was wrong, and with every mistake her need of his forgiveness grew, until Gregg felt as if she were living in a nightmare. This was not she, nor was it David. It was a hoax, a horrible trick of fate. All she wanted was to love and be loved in return; it was cruel.

Walking up the ramp in the cold of Grand Central Station Gregg felt more reassured. They were going home and things would be better. They talked casually, they smiled at each other, and after they had deposited their suitcases at his apartment he took her to a small restaurant for dinner. It was an inexpensive cellar place, frequented mostly by Ivy League college students and their dates, with red checked tablecloths and the kind of food that gives you heartburn before you are even finished eating it. There was no liquor, only wine and beer. It was a place where no one would recognize David Wilder Savage and ask him how the play had gone or, worse, know how it had gone and try to offer sympathy, real or false. It was eleven o'clock at night and they were the only two people in the restaurant except for their gnomelike waiter, who popped in and out of the kitchen carrying their plates and chewing surreptitiously.

'I'm glad to be back in New York,' Gregg said.

'So am I.'

'We ought to send out for a bottle. Do you think they have a little courier who runs across the street and brings back something alcoholic?'

'That waiter is trying to eat his dinner and go home,' David said. 'We can have a drink at my place.'

'Let's hope he's not eating *ours*.'

David smiled. They were together again, they were two in a close little group observing and commenting on the world; not important comments or even very witty ones at this moment, but vital because they were a bond. 'If he is,' Gregg went on, 'I wish he would look a little less disgusted.'

'What time is it?'

'Five minutes to twelve.' Gregg put her napkin under her coffee cup where some coffee had spilled on to the saucer. 'I wish people could always be sure of each other, do you know what I mean? Never have to guess what the other one is thinking or going to do.'

'I hope all that midnight philosophy didn't come from your uneasiness about your spaghetti,' David said lightly. 'You must be tired.'

'I don't mean other people,' Gregg said. 'I mean us.'

'That would be boring, wouldn't it?'

'Not to me.'

'No . . .' he said thoughtfully. 'Not to you.'

'What does that mean?'

'I'm just repeating what you said.'

'The most important thing in the world is communication,' Gregg said desperately. 'That's why people can talk, so they can comfort one another and amuse one another and cry out for help.'

'And tell one another dull stories and sell one another the Brooklyn Bridge,' David said, smiling. 'You left out a lot more.'

'Well, we'll have to ignore those because I'm talking about something else.'

'All right.'

'*Why won't you ever say that you love me?*'

It was out now, the accusation, the all-consuming question. They looked at each other across the table for a moment in silence, Gregg tense and frightened and rebellious and relieved all at once, and he rather sad.

'Because it's not the answer to the question you're asking,' he said.

'What do you mean?'

'The college girl in the parked car asks, "Do you love me?" and the boy with her says yes. But what she means is "Will you respect me?" and what he means is "I want to sleep with you." The child asks his mother if she loves him and what he means is "Will you protect me? Do you approve of me?" You ask me if I love you and what you really mean is will I devour you, envelop you, obliterate life for you and, worse, will I allow you to do that to me. That's why I never answer you, because I do love you, but not in the way you want, and I never will.'

Gregg stared at him for a moment, shocked. Everything he had just said traveled downward through her mind like a paper piano roll and stopped at the line next to the end. 'You do love me,' she whispered. 'You do.'

'Did you listen to the rest?'

'You said you loved me.'

He sighed and shook his head. 'God help me, I must love you,' he said.

She stood up and ran to him and kissed him, right in the restaurant, her arms wound around his neck, tears in her eyes. 'That's the curtain line,' she said, 'and the orchestra starts to play and the audience rise to their feet as if they were pulled by strings, and it's a rouser!'

'And then they leave,' he said, 'and they go to Nedick's.' He stood up, unwound her arms from his neck, and put her coat tenderly about her shoulders.

'Oh, why are you so cynical?' Gregg asked, hugging his arm, her head on his shoulder. Her head just reached his shoulder, her blonde hair hung down over his lapel. As they walked out of the restaurant that way they passed an old-fashioned pier glass hung against the wall next to the checkroom. Gregg stopped walking. 'Look at us.'

'You look like a mermaid clutching a drowning sailor,' David Wilder Savage said.

When they entered his apartment he put a record on the phonograph immediately, as he always did, and lighted the fire in the fireplace. Gregg tossed her coat over a chair and slipped out of her shoes. In her stockinged feet she padded over to the couch and sat down, her knees drawn up to her chin, her arms clutched around her knees, her eyes moving as she watched his every move. 'I have a present for you,' she said dreamily. 'I'll give it to you later.'

'Really?' He looked amused.

'Not what you think. A real present. A thing.'

'Well, you'd better give it to me soon because I'm dead tired and I'm going to put you in a cab and go to bed.'

Her mood was shattered, she felt herself beginning to tremble. 'It's my present and I'll give it to you when I feel like it,' she said, hurt.

'I'm sorry, darling. I'd love to have it. Where is it?'

'When you get a present from somebody you don't just throw him out afterward,' she said.

'Then give it to me tomorrow when neither of us is so tired,' he said.

'Don't you want it?'

'Not if it's going to make you upset.'

'If I want to give you a present you have to take it,' she said, 'whether you want to or not.'

'Then *give* me the goddamned thing!'

'Don't you love me?' Her voice was the voice of a small girl, she heard it in the still room as if it belonged to someone else, and that made it even more frightening to have to wait for the answer, because the answer would belong to her and not to someone else.

'What the hell has a goddamned present to do with whether I love you or not?'

'It has everything to do with it.'

'Gregg,' he said, 'I am not going to humor you tonight.'

'What has loving me got to do with humoring me?'

He closed his eyes. 'I'm so tired,' he said.

'Do you love me?'

'. . . Yes.'

'Then why can't I stay all night?'

'Stay all night. Stay all night.'

'Why didn't you ever let me stay all night before?'

'I think there's a clean toothbrush in the medicine chest,' he said. 'Top shelf.'

'I know,' Gregg said.

'There's a white nightgown in the bottom drawer of the dresser,' he went on. 'But I suppose you know that too.'

'No, there isn't. I never saw . . .' She stopped when she saw the way he was looking at her. 'Well . . .'

'You can wear my pajama top if you like to wear something in bed in the wintertime,' he said.

'I don't. Oh, there are so many little things we don't know about each other. It hurts me just to think about all the little things we've missed.' She put her arms around him. 'Why didn't you ever let me stay all night before?'

'You stayed for three days this summer.'

'That wasn't like staying all night, it was like coming for a visit.'

'Oh, there's a difference, is there?'

'Why are you so sadistic?'

'You stayed other nights too, as I remember. You stayed during the summer whenever you drove down from your job.'

'I should hope so,' Gregg said angrily, 'after driving all that way.'

'Oh, my God,' he said. 'What is the difference? Stay all night, don't stay all night, just don't analyze it.'

'I have to,' she said. 'You're very strange.'

'Yes,' he said. 'I am.'

She stared at him for a moment, partly in anger and partly in fright. She remembered what Tony had said so long ago about David Wilder Savage and Gordon McKay – 'No one knows for sure whether or not they were in love with each other.' And he seemed so afraid to love her. Strange . . . strange . . . Perhaps he was strange, but not in that way. If it were true she wouldn't be afraid to face it, because she was sophisticated enough, and goodness knows she had met enough men who turned out to be different than she had thought. But she knew it wasn't true about

David Wilder Savage, not that. She would have heard rumors from other people besides Tony, because everyone seemed to know every shameful thing about a celebrity, and David Wilder Savage was a celebrity in their group of people who lived for the theater.

'Well, don't gloat about it,' she said coldly.

'I am strange,' he went on, 'to put up with what you do to me. You cling, you choke me, you demand, you don't try to understand. You never think am *I* unhappy, it's only you who are unhappy. You follow me, you go through my bureau drawers, you're jealous of my friends. You lie in wait for me in bars – oh, don't think I didn't know that too. Just because I always ask you to come and sit with me doesn't mean I don't know why you're there.'

'I have a right to be there.'

'Yes.'

'Then why are you angry?' Gregg cried. 'I thought you loved me.'

'I'm not angry,' he said quietly. 'I'm sorry for you.'

'*Why?*'

'Because you need someone who will love you for these things and be warmed by them, not someone who finds them harder and harder to forgive.'

The pain that settled in her chest was worse than any she had felt when she was alone; this was not a mere ten pounds but fifty. When she answered, she spoke through the pain, and only made the effort because not to speak would have hurt her more. 'You have to *forgive* me for loving you?'

'The love you have to give isn't the kind of love I need,' he said. He smiled and touched her cheek with his fingertips. 'We're two slightly neurotic people whose neuroses don't happen to complement each other. Come on, let's go to sleep. Things will look a lot better in the morning.'

'Sleep? Do you think I could ever sleep now?'

'I'll give you some warm milk and a sleeping pill. How's that? And I'll take one too. We'll be unconscious together.'

'We're never together,' she said. She put her hands over her face, shoulders tensed, waiting for him to come over to comfort her. He didn't. She heard him walk out of the room and looked up in a panic, but a moment later he returned, carrying a small medicine bottle which he set on the coffee table. 'What kind of love *do* you need?' Gregg asked.

He was still smiling. 'A gentle love, like in the song.'

'No, seriously.'

'I am serious.'

What in the world was a gentle love? Gregg had a mental image of a little mouse of a girl, a girl with wispy hair and no face, who would be content to spend her life on the periphery of David Wilder Savage's life, admiring him, waiting for him to notice her, the kind of girl that girls like Gregg were always sorry for. And yet she would be the luckiest girl in the world, because David Wilder Savage would cherish her, and he would care what happened to her no matter where he was. 'I'll heat the milk,' he said. He walked into the kitchen. The curtainless kitchen. Should she give him the curtains now? That would show him she was a gentle girl, the kind who sat at home night after night and hemmed those goddamned things. Gregg jumped to her feet and ran to her suitcase, spilling her clothes and shoes on to the floor in her hurry to get the curtains out from underneath.

She walked into the kitchen with the curtains held behind her back. He had put two heavy porcelain mugs on the drainboard and a pot of milk was heating on top of the stove. 'Surprise,' Gregg said.

She was holding the curtains out in front of her and he was looking at them with a pleased and slightly perplexed expression. 'Let's put them up now,' Gregg said.

'Curtains?'

'Yes.'

'Well, they're lovely, darling.'

'I made them.'

'Did you!'

And suddenly she realized that he would have been just as pleased if she had given him a new record or a bottle of wine.

The curtains had absolutely no extra symbolism to him, none at all, and they could not change her or what she meant to him any more than the fact that a monkey is taught to eat from a spoon can turn him into a baby. She folded the curtains carefully and put them on the kitchen table. 'We'll hang them up tomorrow,' she said, keeping her voice steady and giving him a stiff smile.

'It was sweet of you, darling, to go to all that trouble.'

'You don't know the half of how homey I am,' she said lightly. She fled into the living room.

The light of the fire was hot on her face, she felt it burning her eyelids. The little bottle of sleeping pills was ruddy in the firelight, its edge red. She could take them all, eat them up like aspirin, and curl up on this couch for good before he had even finished warming the milk. He would think she was asleep and he would not want to disturb her. He would put her mug of milk down quietly on the coffee table and bend to pick up the bottle of sleeping pills. Then he would notice for the first time that it was empty. He would be concerned, upset, he would shake her and call the hospital. All the way to the hospital in the ambulance he would sit beside her as she had seen bereaved relatives sitting beside the sheet-covered hump in many an ambulance that shrieked past her in the street. He would be wondering what would happen if he lost her. He would know why she wanted to kill herself. She would never have to tell him how unhappy she was again.

There was a click as he set the mugs on the coffee table. 'We can sleep all day,' he said.

It had been just a wild fantasy, the suicide. She knew she would never do it. People who really meant to kill themselves shot themselves through the head or jumped in front of trains, they did not take pills when they knew there was someone near at hand to make sure it was not too late. This pill bit was a woman's trick, a device of the lovelorn. It didn't take courage. Courage was to live. Gregg had the oddest feeling, as if someone had given her her life back again. It wasn't worth much, but it was her own life. If she wasn't going to die, at least she was going to live as she pleased, whatever that meant. She wondered whether she had ever done anything because she really wanted to, or only because she had to, like the suicide drawn irresistibly down the platform toward the train.

16

In the early spring of that year, 1953, when the first hardy horseback riders appeared in Central Park and the first earnest, shivering, undershirted runners began trotting around the reservoir in the foggy mornings, Mary Agnes Russo began preparing for her wedding. Her conversation, which had formerly centered around office gossip, now centered on herself. If Caroline asked, 'How are you today?' she would say, 'I picked out the menu for my wedding dinner. We're going to have fruit cup, soup, chicken, peas, potatoes lyonnaise, salad, little rolls, ice cream and wedding cake. And a bottle of liquor on each table.' Major items, like the fact that she had gone for a fitting of her wedding dress, needed no introduction. The only thing she kept a secret from the other girls in the office was her wedding invitations, because her friends were going to receive them, and Mary Agnes wanted them to be a surprise. Caroline couldn't help wondering what could be so different about a printed wedding invitation, but knowing Mary Agnes she was prepared for anything.

'And she used to make fun of Brenda!' April said.

'At least she doesn't bring her underwear to the office,' Caroline answered.

For an instant April's smile disappeared, and then she looked amused again. 'I suppose it seems funny to us because we're not involved,' April said. 'I'd probably be as much of a fool about *my* wedding plans.'

Saks Fifth Avenue had all their front windows full of mannequins in wedding gowns, and Caroline knew that April had gone there on her lunch hour every day that week, to try them on, gaze at herself, feel the material, and regretfully take them off. Dexter had never mentioned marriage again since that evening on the ride to the abortionist in New Jersey, and April, who always took silence for consent, at least had the presence of mind not to purchase a wedding dress, only try them on just in case. Caroline was sure that Dexter would never marry April and she could hardly trust herself to talk pleasantly to him on the few occasions they happened to meet, for fear she would lash out and tell him what she thought of him. She had never disliked anyone so much. His handsome face, which still had some of the aesthetic interest of a work of art for her, filled her with distaste because it reflected his expressions and mirrored his words. Caroline imagined she knew how April felt when she was trying on the wedding dresses; she herself had once done a silly thing like that when she was planning to marry Eddie Harris, but then she at least had a promise. The pleasure of trying on a dress you would wear on an unforgettable occasion for someone you adored was so entirely different than even buying your first formal gown for a dance that she could hardly describe it. The saleswomen looked beautiful, the dressing room was roseate, she herself had never looked better. Every dress seemed to cling to her excited hands just before she slipped it over her head, as if to say, Is this the one? Will this piece of cloth and work suddenly turn into the dress you will remember all your life? She felt so sorry for April on her solitary lunch-hour excursions that she couldn't bear to think about it.

'Dexter's taking his vacation in the fall instead of this summer,' April told her. 'He says the fall is the only time to go to Europe if you can't go in the spring. We'll go there for our honeymoon.'

'It's all set then!' Caroline cried, relieved.

'Well . . . not the date or anything. But we discussed it.'

'I'm so glad! What did you decide?'

'Well, I said I'd always wanted to go to Europe for my honeymoon and he said he had too. And he said fall was a good time, like I told you, and then he said he was going to take his vacation in the fall. And he said Europe is wonderful in the fall even if you aren't on a honeymoon. That there are lots of girls there.'

Oh, God, Caroline thought. 'But he said he'd take you there?'

'Well not just like that: 'I'll take you there. But I know he will. He can certainly afford it.'

Caroline tried to keep her face expressionless, not knowing what to say or how to say it, not wanting April to see into her eyes and know that this poor little deception was fooling no one except herself. But suddenly April's smile vanished, as it had so often these days, and her fingers were cold as she took hold of Caroline's arm. 'I *know* he wants to marry me,' April said softly and frantically. 'He said so. Remember when I told you he said so? He's never said he didn't. If you're engaged you don't get un-engaged unless one of the people actually says so. It's too important. People don't kid about marriage.'

'Some people don't,' Caroline said, hating herself for having to say it.

'It's his family,' April went on. 'They're so rich, society . . . and they're kind of social climbers, I have to admit it. I can't understand why people who have all they have need to worry about appearances. But Dexter says his parents need some time to get used to the idea of his not marrying one of the girls he grew up with.'

'A horse-faced deb with a hockey-field stride and a tweed suit with a little tweed hat to match,' Caroline said, trying to cheer April up. 'I know the type, I went to school with some of them.'

'Oh, no,' April said. 'These are pretty. We were having lunch in one of the supper clubs last Saturday – isn't that funny, lunch in a supper club? – and he introduced me to three girls he used to take out. They were terribly pretty, and two of them had fur coats.'

'You ought to try to meet some other boys,' Caroline said. 'If only to scare him a little.'

April smiled. 'I've met dozens of Dexter's friends. They always dance with me at the club dances, and one of them even asked me to go out in New York with him.'

'Then go.'

'Oh, I couldn't. I don't know how to describe it, but he sort of scared me. I mean, he was one of Dexter's *best* friends, and I know Dexter's told him all about us, and yet when he was helping me on with my coat while Dexter was getting the car he put his hand right on my . . . well, right here.' She put her palm on her breast.

'Was he drunk?'

'No. Those boys never seem to get drunk, they drink so much I guess they've gotten immune.'

'Nobody gets immune,' Caroline said, 'and that's another thing you'd better learn.'

'Well he wasn't drunk,' April said thoughtfully. 'I know that.'

The girls in the typing pool were trying to decide whether to give a shower for Mary Agnes or collect money and give her one large gift. Because Caroline and April had been friendly with her in the bullpen they were invited to contribute. There was much whispering in the thirty-fifth-floor ladies' room and it was finally decided that since Mary Agnes and Bill were both young and just starting to furnish their first home they would appreciate a gift certificate instead of a party.

'I'll appreciate it too,' Caroline said to Mike Rice. 'If I have to sit through one more "surprise" engagement luncheon where the bride-to-be just happens to arrive at the office in her best dress and everybody giggles and runs out of the office at five minutes to twelve, leaving the guest of honor sitting alone at her desk as if she had the plague and loving every minute of it, and then one of her cronies says let's have lunch together and they get to the restaurant where all the typists are pie-eyed from half a daiquiri and they all yell "Surprise!" I'll die.'

'Slow down, slow down,' Mike said, chuckling.

'Oh, and the gifts!' Caroline went on. 'Somebody gives her a toy baby bottle and somebody else thinks it's terribly funny to give her a sex book, and everybody has one more daiquiri which just about tips the boat and then they all start talking about *their* boy friends, and finally they all come reeling back to the office at three o'clock and the high finance department begins, with division of the check and tip down to the last penny and a half. The worst of it is she'll keep on working for a while after she's married and soon she'll be pregnant and we'll have to start the whole thing over again.'

'You're very young to be so cynical,' Mike teased.

'I'm not cynical, I'm practical. I'm going to start making a list of all the money I've given out for wedding and baby parties, and when I get married – if I ever do – believe me, I'm going to get it all back.'

Mike laughed. 'It's nonsense to you and to me, but it's very important to that girl out there that she have her little moment of attention. It's hard for you to see that. You know, I think Mary Agnes will be very disappointed that the girls decided not to give her a party.'

'Practical Mary Agnes, who's been engaged these two years now because she was saving her money? I think she'll be delighted to have the gift certificate instead.'

'Engaged two years . . .' Mike said thoughtfully. 'When you wait that long for anything you want the getting of it to be very special. While you're waiting, not saying anything, everyone else forgets about it, but you build it up in your mind until it becomes the most important thing in the world.'

He looked at her for an instant unguardedly, and as her eyes met his Caroline felt a start, something that was like surprise and pain. He could mean so many other things, none of them having to do with Mary Agnes. It was hard to know what Mike was thinking when he wanted you to know something that was personal and important to him; he would give you a little and then make you reach out to understand the rest.

'I should think just getting it at last would be enough,' she said, eyes lowered.

'It is, for us. But we're more imaginative. Mary Agnes needs a little confetti.' He reached into his pocket and took out his wallet, running his thumb across the bills, counting them. 'Look . . . tomorrow you ask her to have a coke with you after work. And tell the other girls. I'll buy some liquor and rent some glasses and all that stuff and we'll have a little party of our own for her. But ask her today so I can know in advance, I'd hate to have to drink up all that Scotch by myself, not that I couldn't do it.'

'Mike! You're the most softhearted man I know.'

He shrugged. 'I like Mary Agnes. Oh, and ask her to invite that fiancé of hers. I don't want to be the only man, defenseless, in that mob of girls tomorrow.'

Caroline grinned at him. 'Why don't you invite Mr Shalimar too?'

He grinned back at her – if, coming from Mike, it could be called a grin. Everyone had heard the Shalimar story almost as soon as it had happened, it had gone into the realm of office legends by now. 'What? He might decide to look at *Mary Agnes'* legs this time, and the whole wedding might be called off.'

Caroline looked at him affectionately. He was her friend, he was funny, he was wise, he was sad, and he loved her as much as she loved him. She no longer thought of him as a lover, only as an ex-lover, and that as if it had happened to two other people long ago. She remembered that afternoon occasionally with twinges of guilt, and then when she saw him the guilt disappeared and she remembered it with a vague sadness because neither of them had found the magic they had pretended they believed was in the other. 'I love you, Mike,' she said.

Her friendship for him was in her tone and he did not misinterpret it. 'I love you too,' he said lightly, smiling at her. 'And I always will.'

So in the end, Mary Agnes had her party and her present too. Her fiancé arrived near the end of the cocktail party, shy, ill at ease, in a cheap tweed overcoat. He seemed awed by all these strange women who were obviously sizing him up, and covered it with a smile of bravado, a Look-at-Me-Girls-I'm-the-Great-Lover smile which was belied by the way he followed Mary Agnes with his eyes. But it was obvious that he, not Mary Agnes, was the boss. She took on a new femininity when she was with him, which made her seem very different from the way she was in the office surrounded by her friends and co-workers.

'I guess Mary Agnes tells you all the office gossip,' Caroline said, smiling, trying to make conversation.

Mary Agnes and Bill exchanged a glance, like two high-school children caught whispering in the back row of the classroom by their teacher, and grinned at each other.

'Yeah,' he said. 'She certainly chews my ear off!'

Mike took him into the corner with a bottle of Scotch and two glasses and after a moment of self-consciousness Bill seemed much happier. Mary Agnes turned to Caroline. 'Isn't he cute?'

His dark hair was much too long and he was a little too heavy-set for Caroline's taste but he had a pleasant round face. 'Yes,' Caroline said. 'He's very cute.'

Mary Agnes looked pleased. 'This is a nice party,' she said. 'It was awfully nice of Mr Rice to throw it for me. He does some things sometimes that really surprise me. I mean, he didn't have to give this party. He hardly knows me.'

'He likes you,' Caroline said.

'Well, I like him too. I'm sorry for him and the way he lives and everything, but I like him. And now that he's been so nice to me I'm even sorrier for him.'

'Just don't get depressed at your own party,' Caroline said, smiling.

Mary Agnes picked a potato chip out of a paper bagful with one small prehensile claw. 'I wouldn't dream of it,' she said. She nibbled at the potato chip. 'You're coming to the wedding, I hope. I sent your invitation already.'

'I'd love to.'

'I sent Mr Rice one too.' She looked rakish. 'You can come to the wedding with him if he accepts. Unless, of course, you're going with someone and you'd like to take him.'

'I'm not going with anyone,' Caroline said.

'You'll find somebody,' Mary Agnes said. 'Don't you worry.'

'I'm not worried, Mother,' Caroline said.

'That's a good attitude,' said Mary Agnes, licking the salt off her fingers. 'I admire you for it. Most girls our age are scared to death if there's nobody on the horizon, and that's silly. Because if you look at the girls five years older than we are, why, I don't know one who isn't married.'

'I do.'

'Are they terribly ugly?'

'Quite the contrary. I've met some at parties who are very pretty and smart, too, with good jobs.'

Mary Agnes' eyes widened as if she were about to expound some great and mysterious bit of philosophy. 'Well,' she said, 'perhaps there's something psychologically wrong with them.'

Caroline clamped her lips together to keep from laughing and jiggled her empty glass so Mary Agnes could see it. 'I've got to get a refill,' she gasped, and fled to the desk that was serving as a bar. The whole conversation had been so ludicrous, really, with Mary Agnes smug now that she had landed her man and she herself the adventurous but rather pathetic figure of the attractive unattached girl. It made her want to laugh when she thought of Mary Agnes' comments, and yet, unaccountably, they hurt a little too. Because as always she could see and hear everything on two levels, the one that told her how silly it was and the one that allowed her to become affected and upset. She was only twenty-two, she had been out of college only two years, and she knew she was going to get married someday, just as she had known ever since she was a little girl that she was eventually going to go to college and that she was going to work for a while afterward at an interesting job. These were the things that happened to girls like herself, they were the things one did. But underneath, where lay the things she always had to admit to herself eventually, Caroline knew she had lied to Mary Agnes because one always lied to such people if one intended to survive. But she couldn't lie to herself. She *was* worried about getting married. She knew it was ridiculous, but she was worried. She wondered whether every girl felt the same way she did, or whether it was a personal foolishness.

The days preceding the day of Mary Agnes' wedding were feverish ones. Most of the time Mary Agnes arrived late at the office or left early, and the powers that governed the typing pool, ever respectful of love and romance, pretended not to notice. She and Bill were going to go to Bermuda on their honeymoon and her desk was littered with travel folders depicting pink beaches and couples in long shorts riding bicycles. Caroline could hardly imagine Mary Agnes pedaling a bicycle, and the subject came up, of course, eventually, in the bullpen, with the inevitable giggling comment from someone that Mary Agnes and Bill would return with not a trace of a sunburn and leaving behind a well-used hotel room. One day Mary Agnes returned from lunch with a paper box containing a bridal veil. It was a short white veil attached to a circlet of waxen-looking orange blossoms, and when she tried it on in front of the mirror after very little coaxing it made her look quite bridal. It's strange, Caroline thought, we've been thinking about Mary Agnes' wedding for so long it doesn't seem real any more, and now in that veil I can see it's all true. Mary Agnes had picked out her wedding ring, part of a set to match her engagement ring and the groom's ring. There was a drawing of it in a magazine advertisement that Mary Agnes had brought to the office – a narrow white-gold band set with infinitesimal diamond chips. For the first time during all these insistent preparations April drew close to Mary Agnes' desk.

'Oh . . . let me try your engagement ring on, please,' April breathed. 'If you don't have any special feeling for not taking it off, I mean.'

'I take it off at night when I go to bed,' Mary Agnes said, quite pleased at this new attention. She twisted the ring off her finger. 'I always keep it in the little velvet box, on my dresser. I'd hate to go to sleep with such an expensive ring on, it makes me feel funny somehow.'

She handed the ring to April, a narrow white-gold band with a little round diamond sparkling in the center of it set with four prongs in a sort of square frame that made the diamond look larger. April held it for an instant, looking at it, before she slipped it on her finger. Her eyes were fixed on the blue gleam and her lips moved almost imperceptibly, as if she were speaking to someone. Then she put the ring on her third finger, left hand and held her hand out, looking at it.

'Wow,' Mary Agnes said. 'I was afraid it'd be too small and then you'd never get it off. You'd have to keep it.' She laughed.

'Nah,' Brenda said from the next desk. 'We'd just cut her finger off!'

April turned and looked at Brenda with a little smile. 'I'm going to take it. You cut my finger off.' They all laughed. But Caroline didn't like the way April's mouth pulled when she smiled, a false smile, and a laugh that did not sound true. April slipped the ring off her finger and handed it to Mary Agnes on the palm of her hand. 'Thank you,' she said. 'It's beautiful, Mary Agnes.'

'I got my going-away suit,' Mary Agnes said. 'It's navy-blue butcher linen. It's really a sleeveless dress with a little jacket, so I can wear the dress alone in the evenings. Did you get the invitations yet?'

'Yes,' Caroline said. 'They're very nice.' They were just like every other wedding invitation she had ever received in her life.

'They're engraved,' Mary Agnes said. 'You can feel it with your finger, how it's raised. I hate the other kind.'

'They're lovely,' Caroline said.

'Well, you have to answer them, you can't just tell me in the office,' Mary Agnes said happily. 'I want everybody to answer them.'

'I did already,' Caroline said.

'Me too,' said April. She smiled mischievously. 'But I won't tell you whether I'm coming or not, *you'll* have to wait until my answer comes to find out.'

'We ordered the champagne,' Mary Agnes continued, captivated by her captive audience. 'Four whole cases! And we're having a photographer to take movies and stills, and a wedding cake with a bride and groom on top. And everybody's going to get some cake to take home to sleep on.'

'The man you dream about is supposed to be the man you marry, isn't it?' April said. 'I never had the nerve.'

'Neither did I,' said Caroline. 'With the crumbs dribbling from under the pillow down my neck, I was afraid I would have a nightmare.' They all laughed. Why is it, Caroline wondered, that every girl thinks her wedding plans are so fascinating to everyone else when they're exactly like every wedding that everyone else has ever been to?

And then, at last, it was the day of the wedding. Caroline woke up in the morning with the sensation that it was a special day and she couldn't quite remember why. Then she remembered. The wedding was at four o'clock, with a reception afterward and then a dinner.

'Did you ever have the feeling,' she said to Gregg, 'that you've been waiting for something for so long that on the right day you're going to wake up and find you've slept right through it and missed the whole thing?'

'You might be better off if you had,' Gregg mumbled, rolled over, and went back to sleep with the sheet over her head. She had not been invited, of course, because she hardly even remembered Mary Agnes, but she remembered her well enough to know that Mary Agnes was one of a vast group of girls she herself viewed with complete incomprehension. 'The Happy Ones,' Gregg called them, not knowing exactly why they were happy and not wanting to join them, but sometimes going so far as to say that it was a shame she couldn't end up in such a bovine and contented way. She also called them 'The Grapefruits,' because she said if you were to slice one of them in half she would be revealed to be all partitioned off into nice little predictable segments, every one the same.

Maybe I *should* have slept through the wedding, Caroline thought as she and April climbed up the steps of the church. Weddings always gave her mixed feelings: if it was the wedding of a very close friend she felt happy and excited and nostalgic and a little lonely because, without either of them wishing it, things would be different between them, and if it were a wedding of an acquaintance, like Mary Agnes, her feelings swung between boredom because weddings were always exactly the same and a kind of daydreaming because they were beautiful too. She and April paused for a moment in the vestibule, delaying, looking around. April wore a pale gray linen dress and a straw skimmer like a gondolier's hat with gray, yellow and white ribbons around it.

'How nice you look!' Caroline said.

'You too.'

'Let's go in.'

They took each other's hands and tiptoed into the church. An organ was playing softly. Two ushers swooped down upon them, extending crooked black-sleeved arms terminating in spotless white gloves. 'Bride's or Groom's?'

'Bride's,' Caroline whispered.

They were led to an empty pew near the back. The front pews were by now half filled with relatives and close friends of the bride and groom, all dressed up, and in the second row a woman was already weeping into a handkerchief. Caroline looked around. She had never been in this church before – in fact, she had never been in the Bronx. The walls on both sides were lined with tall stained-glass windows in beautiful colors. The altar was bathed in shimmering golden light that drew the eye toward it. It always made her feel religious to be in this kind of atmosphere, it made her believe in a God who watched over her and knew she existed, and yet she never went. She hadn't even gone to Sunday school after the first protesting year. None of her friends went to their families' various places of worship oftener than once a year either, not even April, who had talked a great deal about churchgoing and religion when she had first come to New York but now seemed to have dropped the subject altogether. Whenever she was inside a church for someone's wedding Caroline would have the feeling that there was a kind of peace attainable for her somewhere, at least for a while, and that she should try. I could come here whenever I was lonely, she would think, and I could meditate even if I felt self-conscious trying to pray after so long. But when she was out on the street again in the air the feeling would evaporate and she would forget about it. It was like sitting at the ballet enraptured with the beauty of it and telling yourself you would take ballet lessons at night so you could be like those soaring dancers, and then having the rest of the things in your life push the thought out of your mind.

Now, sitting in the pew, listening to the soft organ music and looking at the glow inundating the altar, she wondered whether this sort of addition to her life would be an answer. Being alone in a place like this for an hour wasn't the same as being alone in one's apartment, because you weren't really alone. There were people praying quietly, perhaps only one or two, and there were silent, robed figures moving in and out of your line of vision every now and then. There was a kind of hidden life in a church. And if you weren't really sure you believed in God in your apartment you could be more sure in a place that had been built for and dedicated to belief. Surely if God was anywhere He would be there, if only because so many people were looking for Him.

Beside her April stirred, Caroline could hear her intake of breath. She could imagine she knew what April was thinking. If anybody was thinking about going to church more often at this moment it would be April.

The music had changed, it was now suddenly the music everyone remembered. The pews had filled up with people, sitting up straight, looking to the side and to the back waiting for something to happen. An usher came down the aisle escorting a thin woman in violet lace – evidently Mary Agnes' mother. She wore a violet-strewn hat to match and she had black hair and a very white face. She was trying not to smile as she recognized certain people at the ends of each pew and she looked thrilled and happy. Where were the groom's parents? Caroline realized she must have missed them in the excitement. There were several new people sitting down front, and she supposed two of them were they. And now here were the groom and best man, nervous and practically ignored, walking fast. Then, in measured step, teetering a little on very high heels, the bridesmaids began to walk down the aisle. There were six of them of varying heights and sizes: a thin, dark girl who was Mary Agnes' younger unmarried sister, a bosomy blonde with pink cheeks who was her best friend from high school, a round-faced brunette who looked different from any of the other girls and was evidently a sister or cousin of the groom's. Mary Agnes' older sister, who was married, was six months pregnant, and so she could not be a bridesmaid, and the other three bridesmaids were other friends of Mary Agnes' childhood. Caroline had heard the list described so often she could almost tell who was who. There was one thing they all had in common and that was that they were not particularly pretty. Caroline thought back and remembered that she had never been to a wedding where the bridesmaids were prettier than the bride.

She wondered whether it was because the bride took special pains with her appearance on her wedding day or whether she always chose her attendants with this consideration in mind. Because it was June the bridesmaids were dressed in matching dresses of stiff mauve-pink organdie with skirts that belled out over petticoats. They wore little wreaths of fresh flowers and carried tiny old-fashioned bouquets with streamers on them. Mary Agnes had chosen mauve because she liked it, but it happened to be a color that made the dark girls look sallow and the blonde look like a milkmaid. Caroline remembered the three bridesmaid dresses she herself had hanging in her closet, which she had never worn again, and she had to smile.

The organ began playing the wedding march. Mary Agnes floated into sight from somewhere in the darkness of the back of the church, on the arm of her father. She was wearing the circlet of orange blossoms with its veil which Caroline had seen in the office, and somehow it reassured Caroline that this was the same girl, because everything else was different. The veil made Mary Agnes' face look obscure and misty and unusually lovely for her. Her eyes were gleaming, her lips were moist and red with new lipstick, her cheeks were flushed. She wore a floor-length white satin gown with a long train. There were circles of lace centered with pearls sewn at intervals all over the dress, and Caroline was sure it had cost over a hundred dollars. It had a high neckline and a tiny tight-fitting waist and long tight sleeves ending in points. But the surprise was Mary Agnes' curvaceous bosom, which had evidently come with the undergarments that were worn with this dress and was *de rigueur* for a bride on her public day, even though all her friends knew she had never had one.

At the altar the groom moved forward and took the bride from her father in the age-old symbolic gesture. Mary Agnes and Bill knelt before the priest. Caroline leaned forward, straining her ears to hear the words, but as usual if you were sitting in the back of the church the answers of the emotion-filled young couple were completely inaudible. She had a moment of resentment. I come all the way up here to the Bronx to see the wedding and I can't hear a word. From the back the veiled white figure and the stocky dark-coated one could be anybody. The pageantry was the same, the ceremony was the same, and Caroline's thoughts began to drift. Everyone was so still, awed, listening, watching. Half an hour of words, of promises, and you were bound for a lifetime. Or, at least, you thought at the time it was for a lifetime. Mary Agnes knew it had to be. There was something frightening in knowing you could never get out of this pact, and yet, Caroline thought, there must be security in it too. Never to have to think of anything but how to make the best of the life you had chosen. But isn't that what we all do anyway, in our own way, until something goes wrong? And if it goes wrong, and you know you made a mistake, you try to find the good things again.

She imagined herself for an instant standing at some altar marrying Paul. Bermuda Schwartz. Oh, God, she would flee, she would turn and say, I can't do it, I can't, at the last moment. When you were actually at a wedding and you realized how awesome it could be, you knew you couldn't toy with fantasies about marrying someone you didn't love, no matter how good he was to you and however much he cared for you. Because Paul Landis loved her. He had told her many times, in a veiled, half-joking way so that he would not be hurt if she showed that she did not return his feelings. And she didn't. She was very fond of him, but marriage? Marriage belonged to the person your heart reached out to like arms, to someone like Eddie Harris.

She had admitted it now, and it didn't hurt, strangely. She was suffused with remembered love for Eddie, a warm, yearning, tender love for him as he had been two years ago, and even as he must be now. That bride there, kneeling and probably faint with excitement, should be she. The groom should have been Eddie. How real all the words of the marriage ceremony would be suddenly, if they were for her and Eddie! I still love him, Caroline thought. Eddie, I will never, never stop loving you as long as I live.

The priest had stopped speaking in Latin now and was saying something in English, clearly so that she could hear him. 'These two young people,' he said, 'have entered into the bond of matrimony. They realize that their promise is a promise to God. It is not to be undertaken lightly. It is a promise that can never be broken as long as they are on this earth.'

I could promise that, Caroline thought, if I were promising it about Eddie. I wouldn't have an instant's hesitation. Eddie would be my life.

'Because they realize the seriousness of their promise to God, these two young people have given it careful thought. They know what they are doing.'

Did Eddie know what he was doing when he married Helen Lowe? Caroline thought. He was so young then, only a baby. What did he know about forever? What did he even know about love? Does he still love her, I wonder, does he still want to be with her for the rest of his life?

The priest was speaking in Latin again, and Bill was slipping the ring on Mary Agnes' finger. Unconsciously Caroline flexed her ringless fingers, imagining Eddie was putting a wide gold band on hers. She would want a wide band, with a comfortable wide feeling, large and golden so that no one could miss seeing it. When she walked into a room with Eddie everyone would know very soon that she was his wife. It was not hard to pretend that this was not Mary Agnes' wedding after all, but her own to Eddie Harris. I do, she said to herself. Forever and ever, in sickness and health (and depression and joy), to have and to hold from this day forward. I, Caroline Bender, take thee, Eddie Harris . . . No one would be able to hear her voice either if they were sitting farther back than the first three rows, and now Caroline understood why. I'd be the only bride who ever cried at her own wedding.

The organ burst out into the joyous music of 'Here Comes the Bride,' that corny old song that Caroline had never paid much attention to. But at this moment it made her want to laugh with happiness. Mary Agnes, her veil thrown back to reveal her beaming face, was half running back up the aisle hand in hand with Bill. Her friends were reaching out their hands to congratulate her, not even able to wait until the recessional was over. But no one seemed to mind. Everyone was radiant, the music seemed to be soaring up into the very vault of the room, and at the back Caroline could see the white form of Mary Agnes being embraced by one of her bridesmaids. It's *my* wedding, Caroline thought, and I'm laughing and crying all at once and I can't take my eyes off Eddie long enough to let my relatives kiss me.

People were standing up, starting to leave. It was over. Now the bride and groom would hurry to the hotel where the reception and dinner would take place. We'd better hurry too, Caroline thought reluctantly, or we'll never find the hotel by ourselves. She turned to April, who had been sitting forgotten by her side.

'What the hell is Bill's last name?' Caroline whispered. 'I never can remember.' She stopped because April didn't even seem to know she was being spoken to. April was looking straight ahead at nothing, her lipstick worn off, her handkerchief wadded into a lacy ball in one fist. Her eyes were very shiny, but not with tears. Caroline realized then that she had not been the only one to pretend that the wedding which had just taken place was really happening to two other people.

Outside the church there were two long, shiny black limousines for the bride and groom and their wedding party, and an assortment of much older automobiles belonging to some of the guests. Caroline and April managed to find a taxi, which established itself at the end of the train of cars, and so they made their way to the hotel. There was a little room with the receiving line in it, and a three-piece band playing love songs in the corner. Before she could even get on the end of the line of people waiting to congratulate Mary Agnes and Bill, Caroline found herself with a glass of champagne in her hand threatening to overflow and dribble down her wrist. She drank it to get rid of it, and it was immediately refilled by a waiter with a happy grin.

'It's going to be *that* kind of party, is it?' she whispered to April.

They crept along with the slowly moving well-wishers, Caroline gulping down her champagne and looking desperately for a place to stash the glass before she had to shake hands with all these strangers. April had removed her gondolier's hat and was holding it in front of her, hiding her glass of champagne behind it. She looked very ill at ease. But when they finally got to the groom he was holding a glass of champagne too, in two stubby fingers, looking pink cheeked and moist eyed, as if he'd already had his share. Caroline shook hands with him and then on impulse embraced Mary Agnes.

'I'm so happy for you.'

'Thank you,' Mary Agnes said. She lowered her voice conspiratorially. 'Is my hair mussed from the veil?'

'No, you look lovely.'

She was rewarded with a fixed smile as Mary Agnes turned to greet the next guests on the line, who were already crowding to get to her. 'What a beautiful bride!' a middle-aged woman cried, dabbing at her eyes with a handkerchief. 'What a beautiful wedding!'

'Beautiful wedding!'

'Adorable bride!'

'Lovely wedding!'

Caroline edged hurriedly through the crowd, holding April's wrist.

'Whew!'

'Did you catch the names of all those other relatives?' April asked.

'No. Did you?'

'Not one. Let's sit down.' But there was no place to sit, and for the next half hour they stood near the perimeter of the crowd where there was some fresh air and listened to the babble of voices and the feeble strains of the band. Waiters hurried by with round trays covered with champagne glasses filled to the brim, balancing them as expertly as jugglers as they snaked their way around the tight knots of excited, oblivious people. In their corner Caroline and April were ignored, for which Caroline was just as glad. The two glasses of champagne had made her feel warm, and it was close and hot in the room. Her feet hurt. 'Please, please,' someone said loudly, 'when you're through the receiving line go into the other room. Lots of space in the next room.' But no one seemed to pay any attention.

'Come on.' Caroline and April edged their way through the crowd again and finally found themselves in another, much larger room, which had a wooden dance floor in the center of it surrounded by round tables. At one end of the room was a raised dais, as for a banquet, with a long table set upon it. The flowers on this long table were much more ornate than those in the center of each of the round tables because it was set aside for the principals in the wedding. Caroline and April searched among the round tables until they found one with their place cards on it. There were three people already seated at their table: Brenda and her husband the moose, and a thin young man in his mid-twenties with lank reddish hair, a protruding Adam's apple and thick eyeglasses. Caroline noticed to her regret that he was sitting between her and April.

'Hi,' Brenda called, waving airily. She was wearing a very tight, low-cut dress of pink cotton brocade, and a matched set of pink rhinestone necklace, a pink rhinestone bracelet and pink rhinestone earrings. Caroline had never seen pink rhinestones before on a person, only in store windows. 'This is my husband, Lenny. April and Caroline from the office.' She pronounced it *aw-fice*.

So this is the rich husband, Caroline thought. He had a long oval face, a long oval jaw, a long upper lip, a long nose and a short forehead capped with cropped dark hair. 'How do you do,' he said, rising a little from his chair.

'Nice to meet you.'

The boy between Caroline and April turned to Caroline, holding out his place card. 'This is me,' he said. 'My first name is Donald.'

'I'm Caroline and this is April.'

He turned to April. 'April? Is that your real name?'

April looked so astonished that for a moment she couldn't answer. 'Why, sure,' she said.

'Didn't Mary Agnes look pretty!' Brenda said.

'Yes,' April and Caroline chorused, nodding. 'She certainly did.'

'Sure was a nice wedding,' Donald said.

'Yes, it was.'

'You girls are good friends of Mary Agnes'?'

'We work together,' Caroline said, smiling. 'We've known one another about a year and a half.'

'Oh, I beat you,' said Donald. 'I've known her for about fifteen years.'

'Really!'

'Yes.'

Another couple arrived then and introduced themselves as Bo-and-Dotty-something that Caroline didn't catch. Bo was over six feet tall, with pink, scrubbed-looking skin and the build of a professional athlete. Intermittently he would crack the knuckles of each finger, separately, like ten tiny firecrackers going off. Dotty wore a maternity suit and a hat with a veil and whenever she smiled her plump lower lip came up over her upper lip and her eyes disappeared in a crinkle of mascaraed eyelashes and laugh lines. She was another childhood friend of Mary Agnes'. She reminded Caroline of her friend Kippie Millikin, who had introduced her to Paul, and she remembered that she hadn't telephoned Kippie for over a month. She would have to remember to do it tomorrow. Kippie probably thought she was so busy having a romance with Paul that she didn't have time to call her old friends – knowing Kippie, that was probably exactly what she thought and she was no doubt delighted but a little annoyed because she considered herself responsible for this 'romance' and she considered it her due to be kept up to date.

'Doesn't Mary Agnes look beautiful!' Dotty said.

'Yes.'

The bride and groom were out in the center of the dance floor now, in the first dance. With everyone looking at them, they were stiff and self-conscious, but they were enjoying every minute of it. Then the dance was over and Mary Agnes' father came out on to the dance floor to claim her for a dance, and Bill was dancing with his mother. The floor began to fill with couples. A little boy about ten years old was leading a middle-aged woman around in a two step, looking very earnest and pleased with himself.

'Shall we?' Donald asked, turning to Caroline.

'All right.'

He was a pumper, she should have known from looking at him. One hand held her in a firm, splayed grasp in the center of her back and the other arm was held out stiffly, like the handle of a pump, going up and down in time to the beat of the music. His forehead was beginning to perspire. 'I'm not much on dancing,' he admitted.

'You're perfectly fine.'

'You sure are a woman full of flattery.' He laughed timidly at this bit of bold wit and pumped a little harder.

This number is almost over and then we can sit down, Caroline thought with relief. But the end of the song glided into the beginning of the next one without a break, and she was trapped in another five minutes of athletics. 'Let's see what they have to eat,' she said finally.

He dropped his hands from her waist and hand as if she were on fire and trotted obediently back to their table. Poor thing, Caroline thought regretfully, I hope he isn't insulted.

By the time they were halfway finished with their soup course Dotty was handing around snapshots of her two children, aged two and one. 'Isn't he a love?'

'Just darling. What adorable fat cheeks,' Brenda said.

'Do you have any children?'

'Not yet.' Brenda glanced at her husband, and over her face came a look that could only be described as utter coyness. 'But we're going to have one in February.'

'How nice!' Dotty said. 'You really don't look . . . but February's in *ten* months!'

'I know,' Brenda said calmly.

Donald turned to April. 'Care to try a dance?'

'All right,' April said, rising. They went out on to the dance floor, and Caroline could see his arm moving up and down, up and down, in time to the music. A middle-aged man with a large round stomach and a bottle of champagne in his hand was making his way across the dance floor to Caroline's table. He stopped on the way and put his arm around Donald's shoulder, looking into April's face like a little old elf. Caroline could see Donald introducing them, and then the man continued across the floor. He stopped in front of Caroline and beamed at her.

'I'm Mary Agnes' Uncle Fred. Who are you?'

'I'm her friend Caroline.'

He looked at the two empty chairs. 'May I sit down?'

'Of course.'

He put the bottle of champagne on the table in front of them with an unsteady hand, turned one of the chairs around and straddled it, his arms crossed on top of the back of it, his chin on his forearms. He peered at Caroline. 'Are you having a good time?'

'Very good, thank you.'

'You're a pretty little girl. Are you married?'

'No.'

He beamed at her more widely. 'You are cute.' He turned then to the table and the bottle of champagne. 'Look what I have. Shampoo. Do you like shampoo?'

'Yes . . .' Caroline said rather dubiously. Uncle Fred's cheeks were as red as Santa Claus's and he sprayed her when he spoke into her face. She figured he'd had quite a bit of shampoo already.

'Here.' He took her half-filled water glass and dumped the contents, ice cubes and all, into the centerpiece. Then he filled the water glass to the top with champagne.

'Oh, that's really too much,' Caroline said.

'I'll help you,' he said sweetly. 'It's a kind of loving cup.' He raised the glass to his lips and took several thirsty swallows. 'I love weddings, don't you?'

'Yes.'

'I'll go to your wedding. I'll drink shampoo and dance. Will you invite me to your wedding?'

'Of course,' Caroline said.

He pinched her cheek. 'You *are* cute.'

'You haven't met the rest of the people at the table,' Caroline said desperately. 'Brenda!' Brenda looked at her. 'This is Mary Agnes' Uncle Fred. Brenda and her husband, Lenny. And I guess you know Dotty and Bo.'

'Hi, Uncle Fred,' said Dotty, waggling two fingers at him.

'Hi there, Dottikins.'

Brenda and Lenny, who were across the table and seemed to know when they were safely out of it, smiled pleasantly and nodded. Uncle Fred turned back immediately to Caroline. 'I'd *like* to dance with *you*.'

'I've just been dancing,' she said. 'I'm very tired.'

'Tired! At Mary Agnes' wedding? What kind of friend are you?'

'I've . . . taken my shoes off,' she lied. 'They're somewhere under the table and I can't find them. Maybe later.'

'Well, dance without them! Now we'll really have fun!' He took hold of her arm. She sighed and let him pull her to her feet.

Uncle Fred was exactly the same height as she was. When he held her in the steps of the foxtrot the band was playing his large round stomach kept bumping into hers. It was an extremely hard stomach and there seemed to be no escape from it. 'I'm sorry I've never met you before,' Uncle Fred said.

Caroline felt her smile becoming fixed as she looked over his shoulder at the other couples. All of them looked as if they were having such a good time. Perhaps she did too. She felt Uncle Fred's breath spraying her cheek. 'You don't look at me when I'm talking to you,' he said in what was meant to be a reproachful and piteous tone. With an effort she turned her head.

'You probably don't want to look at me,' he went on, in that same sad voice. 'Because I'm just an old man. You probably think I'm just an old man. But I like to look at you because you're so young and pretty.'

She didn't know whether or not to feel sorry for him because she couldn't decide whether or not he was really sorry for himself. 'Thank you,' she said.

'Oh,' he went on, 'I'm just an old man. I have four daughters, all married. I married every one of them off in a great big wedding. Each one wanted a wedding bigger and fancier than her sister before her. Nobody cares about the old man. Just pay the bills, that's all he's good for.'

Caroline looked at him really then, startled, but he was smiling in his elfin and now half-rueful way, and she still couldn't decide if he was unhappy or just bantering.

'Oh, I don't care,' Uncle Fred said. 'I love weddings. Dance, have fun, drink, meet pretty girls. Weddings are fun. After all, it's only once in a lifetime. Then you have the housework and the babies and the work begins. A girl has to have something to remember. Y'know?' He gave Caroline's waist a squeeze.

'Yes,' she said.

'I don't mind paying the bills.'

The music had stopped playing, the dance was over. Caroline heard the silence with a gasp of relief and disengaged herself from Uncle Fred's embrace. 'I promised the next dance to Donald.'

Uncle Fred took her elbow and escorted her back to the table. Donald was sitting there with April and there was a plate of ice cream at everyone's place. 'Look sharp,' Donald said, 'the bride's going to cut the cake.'

The band broke into the strains of 'The Bride Cuts the Cake,' and on the dais Mary Agnes and Bill stood up. In front of them was a huge three-tiered wedding cake decorated with swirls of icing and bells, and topped with a tiny bride and groom under a bower. Mary Agnes held a large knife with a white bow tied on the handle. She held it aloft like a celebrity christening a ship and flash bulbs popped and blossomed from the floor below. She and Bill were looking at each other and at the cake, posing, while more pictures were taken, the guests tried to hush one another, and the band played on. Then Mary Agnes' arm rose and fell as the blade sank into the cake, and everyone applauded. Flushed with achievement, she turned the knife over to one of the waiters to finish the job. She and Bill sat down again and a young man on the dais stood up.

'I'd like to propose a toast.' He raised his glass and there was silence from everyone in the room. He bowed toward the bride and groom and began a rapid recitation of something Caroline realized was a poem. She caught only a word here and there because he was almost inaudible with embarrassment at his public appearance. The people closer to the dais heard it though, and there was laughter and applause when he sat down, his ears red. Everyone in the room raised his glass and drank. Uncle Fred, whose water-champagne glass had been removed by a waiter, lifted the champagne bottle to his lips and drank from that.

'Isn't this the height of luxury?' he asked Caroline, jiggling the bottle and chuckling happily.

Finally, after what seemed hours to Caroline, there was no more to eat and very little more to drink, the dancers had exhausted themselves, and someone noticed that Mary Agnes had slipped away to change her clothes. Uncle Fred had rediscovered April, and had placed his chair close to hers so that he could pat her cheek, squeeze her hand, and offer her the remains of his champagne, which she kept refusing politely. Caroline wondered where his wife and four married daughters were, and why they didn't come to claim him. But they were probably used to him by now; after all, he was one of the family.

'Oh, look! Here she is! Here's Mary Agnes!' came the excited voices. Mary Agnes, in her navy-blue butcher linen going-away suit, with a handbag to match and a little pink flowered hat on, was standing near the door. She was holding her bridal bouquet.

'Line up, girls!' Uncle Fred said. He nudged April and turned to prod Caroline. 'Line up to catch the bouquet.'

April and Caroline exchanged a glance. It was a silly superstition that had always embarrassed Caroline, and more so because she partly believed in it. She'd caught several bouquets when friends of hers from Port Blair or college had been married, and it had evidently done no good. She was sure other girls had too. Yet, there was always that thundering run to be nearest to the tossed bouquet, hands outstretched, and the accompaniment of squeals and laughter. She stood up reluctantly and followed April to the center of the dance floor where a dozen other single girls were already waiting. Mary Agnes waited until the room was entirely still. Then she raised her arm, took a deep breath, and the white bouquet curved into the air trailing its streamers like a bird's tail, and swooped downward. There were screams and a galloping rush. One of the girls from the front of the group emerged with the bouquet held triumphantly aloft. Everyone applauded, and the girl with the bouquet and Mary Agnes hugged each other.

'Goodbye, goodbye, goodbye!'

Bill was there beside Mary Agnes, already holding her small overnight bag. They were to spend their wedding night in a hotel and in the morning take an early plane to Bermuda. Mary Agnes' mother ran to her and kissed her on both cheeks. Then she kissed Bill. 'Goodbye, goodbye!'

'Goodbye.'

They were gone. Caroline turned to April. 'I guess we should be going now, it's pretty late.'

'Should we say goodbye to Donald?'

'You can. I'm afraid of Uncle Fred.'

'Me too,' April admitted with a little smile. They looked around for Mary Agnes' parents to thank them but they had vanished into a crowd of their good friends. 'Let's just go,' April said. 'I'm so tired. Nobody cares if we go or stay.'

'I'm tired too.' They slipped out of the room and walked down a hall to the hotel lobby and through the revolving door.

The spring night was soft and warm, filled with the sound of the wind blowing through leafy trees and the whir of auto tires over pavement. The street was brightly lighted with street lamps and the neon sign of the hotel. 'Let's walk to the corner.'

They walked in silence, listening to the faint click of their heels on the sidewalk and the sound of the band playing through the opened windows of the hotel they had just left. Caroline was not sure whether it was the band from Mary Agnes' wedding or some other party; they all had that happy, festive sound when you were on the outside listening in. At the corner they turned into the neon-bright Grand Concourse. It was a Saturday night and there was a line outside the movie theater. Teen-agers, girls in pastel summer dresses with flat-heeled shoes to match, boys with their hair falling into their eyes, couples holding hands, some with their arms around each other's waists. People were driving by in cars, older couples in their twenties and thirties, out for a night on the town while the baby-sitter stayed home with their children. In front of a store that sold popcorn and pizzas there was a group of teen-aged boys, without dates, whistling at the girls who walked by. And coming out of the early show at the movie, which was just breaking, were girls in their twenties, who didn't have dates either, and who had met each other for an early movie before they went home to watch television.

This was where Mary Agnes and Bill had been born, and where they had grown up and met and fallen in love, and where they had gotten married, and where they would live and bring up their children. Perhaps they would move away after a year or two, to Levittown or Forest Hills or even to Manhattan. It didn't matter. Wherever they lived it would be the same. Mary Agnes had been working for four years, two years longer than Caroline, but it had not made her change in any way. When she came downtown to Rockefeller Center every morning she brought her world with her, insulating and protecting her. The office was a place to work and earn money, that was all. The people she met there passed through her life at a safe and amusing distance, interesting to watch and talk about, but not really of personal concern to her. Mary Agnes knew more private gossip than any other girl in the typing pool, but she might as well have been telling the plot of a story she had read in *Unveiled* – it was sheer entertainment. Her real life, the things that mattered to her, was at home on Crescent Avenue, in her cedar hope chest.

Those teen-agers standing now in front of the movie theater holding hands might someday marry each other or perhaps some-one else who was right now standing in front of Loew's instead of RKO. Then they would join the married couples, driving in cars to a party at the home of a friend for beer and television and cards and pretzels and gossip and coffee and cake. Their children would stay home with the baby-sitter. And later the children would be old enough to go out alone on Saturday night, and they would be holding hands in front of the movie theater.

The girls would dream for years of a big wedding, as Mary Agnes had, of a day when there would be one star and many admirers, even if it was only for a few hours. Caroline was sure that the wedding had cost over two thousand dollars, with the hotel and the catering and the food and liquor and flowers – nearly what Mary Agnes made in an entire year. Perhaps it had cost much more, she didn't know about these things. Mary Agnes had been saving her money for two years, bringing her lunch to the office in paper bags, and perhaps her parents had been saving up for her wedding for the past twenty. And it was over in five hours, with nothing left but an album of photographs and a reel or two of movie film and a dress that would have to be kept in a box with moth balls, and a million confused and blurred memories. Caroline remembered an ad she had read in the newspaper one night with a picture of a bride in it and the headline: 'GIVE HER A WEDDING SHE'LL REMEMBER ALL HER LIFE.' That's what Mary Agnes had been given, display and applause and all. What a beautiful bride, a hundred people had said, how beautiful she is! No one but her husband might ever think it again, but it didn't matter. For twenty-two years Mary Agnes had been a plain, thin, flat-chested little girl, and for this one evening, the culmination of all her dreams and plans, she had been a radiant beauty. She would remember it all the rest of her life.

17

Some girls know that there is a fifth season in New York, the season of the Summer Bachelor. Wives and children are sent off to the Cape, to Southampton and Martha's Vineyard and the Maine woods, and on Friday afternoon helicopters whir and railroads attach extra cars, and airplanes are reserved full with the standing weekend reservations that last from late June until after Labor Day. Monday night through Thursday night the Summer Bachelor is alone, to dine in restaurants and seek out other lonely friends or work late at the office or perhaps to remember a girl he met last winter and never thought he would see again. Some of these men act like schoolboys on vacation from a liquorless early-to-bed prep school, and some of them are decorous and hard-working and virtuously bored, and some of them intend to be neither but simply drift into something they had hardly expected and certainly never hoped for.

On a Tuesday afternoon in late July the telephone on Barbara Lemont's desk rang. She answered it automatically without the slightest pounding of the heart. She had put Sidney Carter out of her mind, forcibly, months before.

'Hello?'

'Barbara?'

'Who is this?' But she knew, she recognized the voice, and the surprise of hearing it occupied her for a moment so that she did not have time to feel any emotion.

'It's Sidney Carter. Do you remember me?'

'Yes . . . yes.' And suddenly everything came back and she could hardly catch her breath.

'How are you?'

'I'm all right.' She gave a nervous little laugh. 'You forgot to send me that perfume, do you know that?'

'I didn't forget. I thought about it several times but I was afraid it would seem as if I were chasing you.'

'Oh.' It might have, too, she thought. She remembered how many mornings she had waited nervously for the mailroom boy to bring down her mail, hoping against all her better instincts that the perfume would be there so that she could call Sidney and thank him. 'How have *you* been?' she asked.

'All right.' He didn't sound happy, he sounded tired. It suddenly occurred to her that perhaps he was not calling her because he wanted to speak to her at all; perhaps it was on some matter of business. Already disappointment was draining her of hope.

'I . . . I'm writing a little column now,' Barbara said. 'It's a beauty column. Do you ever read it?'

'Yes,' he said. 'I read it all the time.'

'It's kind of routine. But it's a break for me. I get my name in the magazine and of course more money.'

'How's your little girl?'

'Fine,' Barbara said. 'Just fine. How's . . . your son?'

'Wonderful. He's at Nantucket. We've rented a little cottage out there, on the beach.'

'Oh. I was thinking of going there for my vacation this summer with two of the girls from the office. It's supposed to be a great place to meet boys, if you're interested in that sort of thing. Isn't that funny – you and I might have met on the beach by accident.'

'We're not where all you kids are,' Sidney said. 'We're over on the other side of the island with the old settled folk.'

'That's good. I was intending not to go at all for a moment.' Why was she trying to be nasty to him, when that wasn't what she meant to be at all? But she resented him and she wanted him and she was frightened of him, all together, and she hardly knew what she was going to say next.

'You said, "If you're interested in that sort of thing,"' he said casually, ignoring her last remark. 'Does that mean *you* are, or you aren't?'

'Interested in meeting boys?'

'Yes.'

'I'm always interested,' she said lightly. 'Do you know anybody for me?'

'No. I'll look.'

'Do.' And at the moment she was saying it she felt like biting her tongue because it wasn't what she wanted to say to him at all. Oh, Sidney, she thought, please don't pay any attention. There was a pause that seemed to Barbara to be five minutes long.

'I was wondering if you'd like to have a drink with me after work,' he said finally. He didn't add, 'I'll tell you about Nantucket,' he didn't add anything, he just waited.

Am I strong enough? she thought. Can I bear it? She had put him out of her mind, but now his remembered voice brought it all back, his face, his smile, his understanding. She wanted to run out of her office that instant to wherever he was. 'I think that would be nice,' she said casually.

'I'll pick you up outside your office at five o'clock.'

'All right.'

'I'll be looking forward to it.'

Her tone was very polite. 'So will I.'

When she replaced the receiver she realized that her hand was shaking so hard she could scarcely light her cigarette.

It was only an hour until five o'clock but it seemed endless. Barbara went into the ladies' room and washed her face and put on fresh make-up. That took only ten minutes. She went back into her office and tried to read back issues of the magazine but she couldn't. She knew she would be able to do no more work that day. She picked up the receiver and telephoned her mother.

'I'm going out for a drink after work. I don't know if I'll be back for dinner so you'd better eat without me. And would you feed Hillary, please?'

'Oh?' her mother said. 'Do you have a date?'

'Not really. It's just business.'

'Oh,' her mother said cheerfully, 'too bad. Well, have fun if you can. I'll hold the fort.'

What's wrong with me? Barbara thought. How can I do this? She felt as if she was putting her mother to a great deal of unnecessary trouble, but she knew that was only because she felt guilty. Her mother would give Hillary corn flakes and it wouldn't be any trouble at all. The trouble, she knew, would be what she would have if she let the one cocktail turn into an evening with Sidney. I'll just have one drink and go home, she thought. But she was watching the clock and her hands were cold.

When she came out of her office building at one minute after five Sidney was already waiting for her. She saw him standing near the edge of the building entrance looking a little self-conscious. His self-consciousness transmitted itself to her and she wanted to turn and run away. It was the first time she had seen him not in complete possession of himself and the situation.

'Hi,' he said, smiling, holding up his hand. He had a tan and with his gray hair and young face it made him look like some kind of a diplomat or international playboy. He was wearing a black raw silk suit and he looked thinner. He walked over to her and took hold of her arm very lightly.

'How nice you look!' he said. He led her over to a taxi at the curb.

'Thank you.'

When they were in the taxi and he had given the driver the address of a bar Barbara felt better. Sidney was sitting way over on his side of the seat, leaning against the window and looking at her in a friendly way. 'I've never seen you in the daytime,' he said.

'No.' We've hardly seen each other at all, she was thinking, we hardly know each other. All these months I was in love with a fantasy. But all the same, she hardly noticed anything outside the taxi windows and she couldn't take her eyes off Sidney's face.

'I'm glad you called,' she said finally.

'I was afraid you'd hang up.'

'No.'

'I used to think about you sometimes: whenever I heard the Hawaiians, whenever I saw a young girl with brown hair pushing a baby carriage, whenever I picked up a copy of *America's Woman*. I guess that means practically all the time.'

'Really?' she said, more sharply than she had intended. 'Is that true?'

'I wanted to call you to find out how you were, if you were any happier, if things were going well for you. But I couldn't trust myself not to ask you to see me again, and so I didn't call.'

'Until your wife went away for the summer,' Barbara said. She didn't dare even smile to pretend it was a joke because it was too important to her, but she was afraid to look at him.

He didn't answer because the taxi had pulled up to the curb, and he leaned forward and paid the driver and opened the door for Barbara. She stepped out on to the sidewalk and Sidney followed her and waited until the taxi had pulled away.

'Look,' he said evenly. 'I didn't want to talk this way in front of the cab driver, but if you like I'll get another taxi and take you home right now. I know you think I'm the lowest form of roué, and you're right to think so because I probably am. I don't know what I'm going to do an hour from now and neither do you. But all I can say is I called you because I missed you. The fact that my family is away has nothing to do with it. The only reason I go up to Nantucket at all on weekends is to see my son. If he had gone to camp as my wife and I thought he should, I doubt that she and I would have seen each other at all, except for parties where we're invited together. As you may have guessed, we see very little of each other. I'm not saying this to lead you on or to imply that we're legally separated, because we're not. I'm not taking you out to seduce you because if I wanted to seduce somebody I'd do it to someone who intended it that way as much as I did. I called you because I like you. I *like* you. That's all.'

'I said that to you once,' Barbara said softly.

'I remember.'

She stood there on the sidewalk in the bright July late-afternoon sunlight, biting her lip. 'I guess we might as well go in and have a drink.'

Inside, the bar was very dark and cool. They sat at a little square table with a black glass top. She ordered gin and tonic and poured the whole bottle of tonic into her glass because she wanted to stay sober. But she had the strange feeling that she wanted to be drunk, not to be responsible, to be able to do all the dreadful irresponsible things she really wanted to do and never feel ashamed of herself afterward. She wanted to reach out and lay her cheek on his cool hand and tell him all the crazy things she had said to him in her daydreams all these months. And at the same time she wanted to say everything new and listen to what he would say and wait to see where the moment would take them. She hardly recognized herself.

'I went to Haiti for a while in February,' Sidney said. 'It's beautiful there. Have you ever been there?'

'No.'

'I didn't do much – just hid and rested in the sun. I was exhausted.'

'I hate February,' Barbara said. 'I think whoever made the calendar was smart to make it the shortest month. Every February I always think: if I can only get through February everything will be all right.'

'What did you do this February?'

She shrugged and stirred her drink, trying to remember. *Thought about you.* 'Nothing much. Went out with a few boys whose names I can't recall any more, saw some movies and a play or two.'

'That doesn't sound bad.'

'No,' she said, 'it was fun.'

He smiled at her. 'You say that as if you were going to cry.'

'I love the way you smile.'

He didn't answer. Barbara picked up her drink and drank it all down without stopping. It did nothing to her but she felt better just for having drunk it. She was sorry she'd said that about his smile, it was too personal. She would have to be more careful.

'Would you like another drink?'

She was going to have one cocktail with him and leave. But she had finished her one drink in five minutes and now what could she do? 'Yes,' she said. A line from a song ran through her head – *Cocktails and laughter, and what comes after nobody knows.*

'You know,' he said, 'I haven't seen Art Bossart since that night we met, would you believe it?'

'I thought you two were good friends.'

'No. We're drinking friends. We both have two or three dozen of them, for what that's worth.'

'I see him in the elevator sometimes,' Barbara said. 'He says hello, like this –' She imitated him, cold, aloof, as if he hardly remembered her. 'Hello. It seems so funny to go out for a drink with someone after a party and the next day have him act as if he doesn't remember your first name.'

'That's the law of the Great American Christmas Party, isn't it?' Sidney said, looking amused. 'Think of the girls who go to bed with some executive and then have to go through that hello routine in the elevator the next day.'

'It curdles my blood.' He's talking about bed, she thought unhappily; right at the start he's talking about bed to grease the skids. They're all the same. But despite her mistrust she couldn't quite believe it about Sidney, not yet. He was looking at her closely.

'I said something, didn't I,' he said. 'What was it?'

'What?'

'Your face closed up like that – click. Is it something about someone at the office and I should have minded my own business?'

'No, of course not.'

He looked relieved. 'It's something though.'

'It's nothing.' This time she poured only half the bottle of tonic into her gin and she had finished the whole drink before she noticed what she was doing. Or was it a command from her subconscious? She felt better though, more at ease. 'It scares me a little the way you notice everything. I'll have to be careful.' She laughed lightly.

'It's no great art. It's just experience. You'll notice everything too when you're my age.'

'How old is that?'

'Forty.'

'I think I like older men. At least then if you *want* them to notice something they will. My husband never had the faintest idea what

I was thinking. I shouldn't blame him though. I didn't understand him very well either.'

'That was so long ago,' Sidney said.

'Two years and five thousand hours of hand-to-hand combat away.'

He laughed. 'That's the last word on the gentle art of dating.'

'If they only knew.'

'I'm trying to think back to when I was about twenty-five,' Sidney said. 'I can't remember ever forcing myself on a girl.'

'And you were probably more successful than these strong-arm men.'

'I guess I was.'

Now I'm talking about it, Barbara thought, and I brought it up myself. Sex, sex, why can't I think of some small talk instead of this? Is it because it's what we're both thinking about, even I, without really wanting to? I *hate* it. But she kept on talking, like someone talking in his sleep, in a pleasant, emotionless voice that was meant to be the sort of voice one uses for small talk but which concealed so much more. 'I'll tell you about the date I had last Saturday night, if you can bear it.'

'Tell me.'

'Well, I'd seen him around at parties but he'd never said more than hello to me. And then one night he called me and asked me out, so I went on Saturday. The first thing we did was go to his apartment for cocktails, and he played some dirty songs on his hi-fi set.'

'On a hi-fi set!'

'With three speakers, so you would be sure not to miss a word, God forbid. Then we went out to dinner at a terribly expensive place, and he turned out to be suave and intelligent and I was really starting to like him despite the dirty records. I figured that was probably his sense of humor and I shouldn't be a prude. Everything was fine until we got to my house and he asked if he could come in and have a drink. I didn't want to seem mean, after all, the dinner had been so expensive and it was only eleven-thirty. My mother knew I had a date and she always scuttles into her bedroom when she hears my key in the lock because she knows how difficult it is for me to have to live with her and entertain my friends at the same time she's in the living room. So there we were, he and I, and I gave him a drink and he didn't even touch it. He leaped on me. I swear, he was just one generation away from growling.'

Sidney smiled. 'Then . . . ?'

What was making her tell this dreadful story, she was embarrassed already. It was too late, he was waiting. Why didn't I keep my mouth shut, she thought, why did I have that second drink? What's the matter with me? 'Well . . . nowadays when you snap a girl's garter you're pretty far up. I kept trying to struggle away from those clutching hands and I'm sure it was perfectly obvious to him that I hated every minute of it. I didn't dare make any noise because I didn't want my mother to hear – it made me feel silly. And I was afraid to wake the baby. It was kind of a silent death struggle, and then do you know what he had the nerve to say to me? He said, as if that made everything perfectly all right, "Don't worry, I won't lay you, I just want to neck with you."'

'If I were a girl I would have taken off my shoe and hit him with it,' Sidney said. 'That raises quite a welt.'

'With the heel or the sole?'

'The heel.'

'I wish I had.'

'What *did* you do?'

'I got away from him and he was angry, of course. I never heard from him again and I never will, unless it's second hand about what a drip he thinks I am.'

Sidney shook his head. 'It sounds incredible,' he said sympathetically. 'Where do you find these oafs?'

'I'm lucky, I guess.'

'When my son grows up, I hope he won't be like that.'

'How could he be?' Barbara said.

They looked at each other for an instant and Barbara felt the meeting of their mutual glance with almost a physical impact. She forgot entirely what she was going to say next and simply looked into Sidney's face, helplessly. He looked away first. 'Do you want another drink?'

'No, thank you.'

He beckoned to the waiter and held up one finger.

'What's that song,' Barbara said, floundering, 'or is it a comedy routine . . . "I'm going to put sand in that baby's spinach because he might grow up and marry my daughter"?'

'Grow up and date my daughter sounds more likely,' Sidney said. He reached over and took hold of her wrist very lightly with two fingers. 'Look . . . I have to meet some people for dinner. Will you come with me?'

Other people; what could be safer? She was relieved, and yet, in a way, she was disappointed. She was beginning to feel warm and cozy inside, she didn't want to talk to anyone but Sidney. But this way was obviously more sensible. 'Yes,' she said, 'I'd like that very much.'

She was astonished, first of all, to find that he did not take her to a married-man's restaurant counterpart of the married-man's bar where they had met. He took her to a well-known, luxurious, brightly lighted place where people went who could afford the prices and liked gourmet food, a place that attracted both success-ful people and the oglers who follow them. They met another couple who were already waiting for them at the bar. The wife was a former movie actress who had now settled down to being a mother; Barbara had never seen her in a movie theater but she had seen her once on television in a rerun of an old motion picture. Her husband was a press agent. They seemed neither surprised nor shocked that Sidney was there with a girl, nor did they act as if they had met him dozens of times with other girls. Barbara felt at ease in a moment, even though they were much older than she was, and halfway through the meal she found herself talking to the other woman about make-up and clothes and the problems of bringing up young children. Sidney had made no excuses for Barbara when he introduced them, he had not said that she was an old friend or a business contact, and yet no one showed by extra solicitude that they considered her an oddity. It was a strange situation to her; somehow she had expected everything to be different. And that's how provincial I am, she thought.

They finished dinner at eleven o'clock. Despite the fact that she had never before known anyone who could afford to take her to this restaurant, and she had always wanted to go, Barbara could hardly eat anything. The wine she had drunk during dinner and the after-dinner brandy made her feel rather odd, as if she knew she ought to be high and yet she wasn't. She had the feeling that everything she would say would be perfectly sensible and yet she had to be careful still because it might sound different to someone else.

When the other couple were about to climb into a taxi the actress leaned over and kissed her on the cheek. 'Barbara dear, I'm glad we met. You will send me a copy of your magazine, won't you?'

'Of course.' She stood there with Sidney as their taxi drove away. 'Why do people always ask me to send them a copy of the magazine when they can buy it anywhere any time, for a quarter?' she asked him. 'Not that I mind at all.'

'It's her way of keeping up with you. She liked you.'

'I liked her too.'

'I'm glad.' He took her hand and she gave it only an instant's thought, it seemed so natural a gesture. 'Those are two of my favorite people. I hardly see them, though, maybe six times a year. I hardly have time to see anybody I want to.'

'You're working nearly all the time, aren't you?'

'Nearly. The stupid part is I don't really have to. You get in a rut, think you can stay at the office one more hour, do one more thing. Then you get tied up in something and you can't leave. Let's go someplace for a brandy.'

'All right.'

They walked down the street in the dark, hand in hand, and although Barbara had always disliked holding a boy's hand on the street because it looked so soupy and teen-agey, with Sidney it suddenly seemed as if it was the only thing to do. She didn't care who walked past and saw them. They strolled up Fifth Avenue looking into all the store windows. 'I like that,' he would say, or 'I think that's awful, don't you?' and she would find herself agreeing with everything. They stopped in front of one garish display, shaking with laughter.

'That's just what I need!'

'I want a dozen!'

It was trite, just as trite as holding hands in public, but with Sidney it was new. She remembered what he had said that night when he held her hand, that it was a braille the sighted had worked out to learn things they couldn't see. There were all sorts of signals, the first tentative relationship between a man and a woman was full of them. Even such a silly thing as midnight window-shopping was one of them. Barbara remembered all the dull first dates she had had with boys in which the entire evening was spent exchanging likes and dislikes: records, politics, books, places to dine. It had been so mechanical, so boring. And here, for no reason she could reasonably think of, every interest of Sidney's was fascinating to her. She wanted to find out everything he had ever liked and pour out to him everything that she had ever found important.

They went to the Oak Bar at the Plaza for a drink and sat at a table in the corner. 'You know,' Barbara said, 'more and more lately whenever I see people who have been married for a long time, whether happily or unhappily, I wonder, How did they meet? What makes two people decide to stay together for the rest of their lives? It seems so long ago that I got married, and all for the wrong reasons, that I guess I'm looking for a formula in somebody else.'

'Somebody else's marriage is always a little of a mystery,' Sidney said. 'Isn't it? Especially if they're happy. You wonder how they did it. You wonder what they have that you never managed to have. I think about it too.'

She looked at him in the dim light. 'Maybe this is none of my business, and tell me so if it isn't. You're unhappy, aren't you?'

'I guess so, if I stop to think about it. That's why I don't think about it.'

Something inside her moved, painfully. 'Then it *is* none of my business.'

He covered her hand, on the table, with his. 'I'll tell you anything you want to know.'

'I never ask anybody personal things. I don't know why I asked you. I'm a little high, as usual, I guess. You've never really seen me at my best.'

'If we don't ask each other personal things how will we get to know each other? We don't have much time.'

'We don't . . . do we?' It hit her then, the futility of it, the haste and the artificiality. They didn't have much time because each of them had his own life, Sidney at least had, although hers was far from full. And soon his wife and son would be coming back, although she was sure that hadn't been what he meant at all. Haste, haste, a quick romance, a few dinners, a few more drinks, a few evenings in bed. What could they offer each other that was lasting, that would not die of its own helplessness? Of course they had to hurry, because the ending would be upon them before they knew it, and the beginning was so full of doubts, and the only part that mattered was the high point in between. Whatever had moved inside her moved again, until it filled her chest, and Barbara turned her head away, looking at a mural on the wall.

'I shouldn't have said that,' Sidney said. 'It was a stupid thing to say.'

She turned to look at him. 'What?'

'We have all the time we want. You know that, don't you?'

'Yes.'

For the first time she felt relaxed, calmed, and a real warmth came over her. He was not like other men, she knew that now. And she wanted to see him. She no longer felt as if it were a battle of wits, she could really be herself. He had taken the tension out of their relationship constantly all evening by the little things he did and said, and now by this final promise. 'Tell me,' she said, leaning forward, 'how you met your wife.'

'At a party in Greenwich Village when we were both twenty-four. It doesn't sound like me now, does it? She was a ballet dancer, or at least she was taking ballet lessons three hours a day, and I was working in an advertising agency. During the day I wore a gray flannel suit and at night and on the weekends I used to hang around the Village with a group of guys I'd met when I first came to New York.'

'From where?'

'Lebanon, Pennsylvania. They were from all over the place. There was one who wrote for little magazines, and one who painted terrible pictures and never washed the paint off his arms, and one who played the guitar. There's always somebody who plays the guitar. It was two years before the war broke out in Europe and we were all very nervous and full of ideals and we used to talk each other to death. I guess all over the Village there were other groups of kids who thought they were going to be the Thomas Wolfes and Picassos of tomorrow, just like us. Anyway, I met this lovely, graceful girl and took her home from the party. She was living alone in a dreadful little cold-water flat, but it was summer and we both thought the place was beautiful. I never left. We were each of us lonely without admitting it, and we thought we were being very Bohemian. When we decided to get married we went to Cartier's in blue jeans on a Saturday afternoon to pick out the ring. I remember wondering what would happen if anyone from my office saw us.'

'It doesn't sound like you at all,' Barbara said. 'I can hardly picture it.'

'Well after a while all the guys I knew got married, one by one, and became respectable. We were becoming pretty respectable ourselves. After my wife had our baby she gave up ballet for good and we decided to move to the country. That was probably the worst idea we ever had. As a matter of fact, it was my idea, I had to talk her into it. Some of my friends, the newly respectable, were moving to Westchester. So we went too, and after a year I was all ready to move back but she liked it. We stayed, and finally we bought the house where we are now. The trouble is, it was such a long trip from the city and I had to work so late some nights that we really only saw each other on weekends. I had one set of friends in the city and she had another in the tall-grass Upper Bohemia. It took us ten years to discover that we hardly knew each other any more.'

'Why didn't you move back to the city then,' Barbara asked, 'before it was too late?'

'If I had been sure it was the country that was to blame I would have insisted on it. But I was never quite sure. That's what I keep asking myself. I wish I really knew, I'd feel better then.'

'They say people outgrow each other,' Barbara said. '*That* was a bitchy thing to say, wasn't it! If anyone had said that to my husband while I was married to him and I knew about it . . .'

'It wasn't bitchy. I know how you meant it. Look, Barbara, you can say something in malice and it means one thing, and you can say it because you're a sympathetic thinking human being and it means quite another.'

'You keep giving me credit,' she murmured.

'Why? Do you picture yourself the homewrecker? Do you think this is a very dramatic situation?' His smile took the edge off his words. He could smile at me that way, she thought, and call me anything he wanted and I think I'd take it.

'I can't say I'm not sorry you're married,' she admitted.

'There are a lot of other things wrong with me,' he said, smiling. 'Just pretend the main obstacle to our romance is that I'm too old – which is to be considered, by the way – and you'll feel better.'

'I know . . . it's silly. I go out with lots of boys I know I could never marry, but that's because I don't want them or they don't want me. But when I know that even if you and I for some utterly crazy reason decided to fall in love I couldn't have you, then it scares me.'

'Trust me. You won't fall in love with me.'

'That's a dangerous thing to say to a girl,' Barbara said lightly. 'Why?'

'I don't know. It just makes the wheels start to whir. The only thing more dangerous is to say, "*I* won't ever fall in love with *you.*"'

He didn't answer for a while. 'Then I won't say it,' he said finally. 'But not for that reason.'

'There's one thing I know,' Barbara said. 'Married men don't divorce their wives for other women. They divorce their wives because they don't want to be with the wives any more. I'm not talking about old fools or lechers or neurotics, I mean the kind of married man a girl like me might fall for. A man like you. I'm right, aren't I?'

'Yes.'

'Well. Now that we've got that settled, let's change the subject.'

He looked at her carefully. 'You are extraordinary.'

'No, you are.'

'I?'

'Because you're so honest,' Barbara said.

There was nothing more to be said for a moment and they sat together, shoulders touching, finishing their brandy. He was no longer holding her hand, and the pressure of his shoulder against hers was very light, a mere transmission of body heat, but Barbara was extremely aware of him. She should feel sad, she should feel fated for disappointment and perhaps worse, but she felt only contentment. She liked him so much, she was so fond of him, that merely sitting next to him without words made her feel as though she could face anything: the garter snappers, the boys who 'only wanted to neck' with her, the search for someone compatible whom she could love. She knew that, after their long separation, she again was dangerously close to being in love with Sidney Carter, but this time it was not a childish crush and she felt she could handle it. To fall desperately in love with him, to spoil this warmth she felt and turn it into the cold chills of an emotional problem, would be idiocy. She had been forewarned. But she knew that, despite their best intentions, people reached a point beyond which they could not return but could only hope for a safe landing.

He paid the check and they walked slowly out of the bar and through the hotel lobby. Sidney stopped at the news stand and bought a copy of each of the morning newspapers for himself and one of each for her. 'I'll never have time to read them all,' Barbara said. 'Do you, before you go to sleep?'

'Every night.'

'I'm glad I'm not an executive!'

He laughed. 'It's a train habit. You have to do something when you commute, and I don't play cards. Now that I'm not commuting for the summer I can't seem to get out of the habit so I read the papers in my room.'

'You're . . . in the city?'

'I'm staying at a hotel. It's only four nights a week, and I hate going up to that old barn alone.'

Why did it frighten her a little to learn that he was staying by himself so near by? Was it because she expected him to lure her upstairs and seduce her? Or because she wanted him to? I'm a veteran of attempted seductions, Barbara told herself, and I haven't been trapped yet. It's up to the girl. 'It's pretty late,' she said. 'I'd better go home now.'

'That's where I'm taking you.'

When the taxi arrived in front of her apartment, Sidney got out with her and walked up the steps. She opened the heavy front door with her key and kept on walking and he continued beside her. 'It's a walk-up,' she warned.

He looked amused. 'Am I invited?'

'Of course, you're always invited.'

She felt a little ashamed of the stairwells and halls of her apartment house, because they looked so dingy compared to what she was sure he was used to, because they still smelled of cooking from the evening meal. He wasn't a boy of twenty-four any more, escorting a Bohemian ballet dancer home to her romantic cold-water flat. He was forty years old and he ate at Le Pavillon, and cabbage smelled like cabbage. As for her, she wasn't living here because she thought it was a lark, she lived here because it was the only thing her family could afford. An ugly image went through her mind: the poor young magazine assistant and the rich older executive. But when she unlocked the door to her apartment there was a lamp lighted softly on the end table next to the sofa and the only thing you could smell was the faint odor of baby talcum from the room she shared with Hillary. All the windows in the living room were wide open and there was the beginning of a cool night breeze. She switched on the overhead light.

'Do you want a drink?'

'I don't think so. I'm keeping you up.' He was looking around. 'Is that where your mother scuttles when she hears your key in the lock?'

'Yes.'

He gestured toward the sofa. 'And that's the scene of the many battles.'

She couldn't help smiling. 'Yes.'

He walked over to the end table and looked at two pictures which were on it. 'Who is this?'

'My father.'

'And this is your little girl. She's pretty.'

'She's prettier now.'

He picked up his newspapers and put them under one arm. 'I'm going now. I just wanted to spy a little.' He walked to the door, and Barbara followed him. At the door he stopped and looked down at her. 'Thank you for a wonderful evening.'

'Thank *you*.'

'Could you have dinner with me on Thursday?'

'Yes,' she said softly.

They stood there looking at each other, he holding his armful of newspapers, she with one hand almost reaching the knob of the door to open it. Neither of them moved. Barbara felt as if she were paralyzed.

'Look,' Sidney said, 'this is silly.' With a swift gesture he deposited the newspapers on a chair and put his arms around her. With one hand reaching out in back of her he switched off the overhead light. She could have stepped back and he would have released her but she could no more bring herself to do it than she could have hurled herself down the stairwell. When he kissed her she had an instant of detached resistance, a second when she said to herself, *This* is more silly . . . But then she had the oddest sensation, as if for the first time she was aware of every vein and artery in her body because warmth and blood were coursing through them, and the feeling she had fought off when every boy kissed her over-powered her and was finally welcome. She put her arms around his neck and kissed him back, recognizing her own desire as if it were a stranger because it had been such a long time, and as an old friend because it made her so happy.

He was the one who drew away first. He looked down at her affectionately and grinned, with that glint in his eye she had seen the first night she had met him. 'Hell,' he said, 'don't worry. I don't want to neck with you. I just want to sleep with you.'

He picked up his newspapers, opened the door, and was gone, blowing her a kiss. 'Call you tomorrow.'

She stood there in her doorway, looking after him, touching her lips with the fingers of one hand, wondering for the first time how they had felt to someone else.

That night she fell asleep immediately and slept dreamlessly, and when her alarm went off in the morning she was not tired because she was so anxious to get to the office where Sidney might call her. The day that stretched ahead seemed pleasant, everything that was going to happen to her was going to be good. For the first time in over two years she had something to look forward to. Knowing that Sidney would call her, and that she would see him the next evening, made even the smallest most boring bits of office routine take on a new dimension. She loved her job, she loved walking to work in the early morning before the sun made the streets begin to sizzle, today she loved her reflection in the plate-glass window in front of the delicatessen near her apartment house. How jaunty that girl looked, the girl Sidney Carter liked and found interesting.

He called her at three o'clock. Barbara had closed the blinds of her office against the glaring afternoon sun, and it was dim and cool in her little cubicle, shut away from the rest of the offices and their noises, with something of the drowsy and luxurious feeling of being in bed in the middle of the afternoon. When she heard his voice on the telephone it completed the feeling and she wondered why she had never before realized that three o'clock in the afternoon would be the best time of the entire day or night for making love.

'What are you doing?' he asked her.

'Just sitting here. I'm going to try to write some copy in a few minutes. It seemed too soon after lunch to grapple with the problems of teen-age acne.'

He laughed. 'I have four people waiting outside my office to see me but I wanted to talk to you first.'

They were both busy, they both had responsibilities, and yet for this instant everything else was shut out. 'I'm glad you called,' she said.

'So am I . . .'

'What time will I see you tomorrow?'

'Five o'clock outside your office.'

She could see him there already, in her mind, and she was filled with happiness and excitement. 'I have to go now,' he said. 'I only wanted to speak to you for a minute.'

'Go and work.'

'You too . . .'

She hung up the receiver and sat for a moment motionless, remembering their conversation, not so much his words as the tone in which they had been spoken. Fondness had been in it, genuine fondness. A busy man in the middle of the working day had stopped to say a few meaningless things on the telephone because he wanted to; the day stopped for a moment and went on. It was that pause that made all the rest worthwhile. Barbara had the feeling that it had meant as much to him as it had to her. It wasn't hard now to turn around on her swivel chair and pound at her typewriter. 'A new powder base for teen-age problem skin . . .' Poor teen-agers, they wanted to be admired too, inferiority complexes and pimples and all – didn't everybody?

On Thursday afternoon there was a quick thunderstorm that vanished after fifteen minutes and left the streets wet and cooled with rain. Barbara came out of her office in a new red linen dress she had bought at the beginning of the summer and had never yet had the interest to wear. She had drenched herself in Wonderful perfume, half as a joke because it was one of Sidney's accounts and half because she really liked it. She had washed her hair the night before, the sky was dazzlingly blue, the afternoon was cool enough so that she would not wilt before they got into an air-conditioned bar, and her heart was pounding. When Sidney came up to her and took her arm to lead her to a taxi she had the feeling that all this had happened to the two of them not just once but many many times before.

'What a beautiful dress.'

'It's new.'

In the taxi he sat again facing her, but not as far away as the last time. She was so glad to see him, she felt so at ease with him. 'What are you thinking?' he asked.

'I was wishing that everybody could meet for the first time on a second date, like this, and never have the mistrust and misunder-standings people often have in the beginning – the way we almost had when we first went out for cocktails, remember? And then I was thinking that if we had started off on our second date I would have missed all the fun we had together Tuesday.'

'You should have said yes when I asked you last Christmas. We could have had months together.'

'I know,' Barbara said. 'But I was different then.'

'Different? How?'

She grinned at him. 'Smarter, maybe.'

'Busier, maybe.'

'You always turn everything into a compliment.'

He took her to a bar far over on the East Side where they sat in a little enclosed garden with a striped awning overhead and clean gray pebbles underfoot. It had white metal chairs and small round white metal tables. Everyone there looked very Madison Avenue, three men in earnest conversation, a girl with a poodle leashed to the leg of her chair, a young couple on a date looking stiff and self-conscious. The young man wore a red-and-blue-striped tie and a seersucker suit, his blond hair was cut very short and it made his neck look like raw veal. The girl looked as if she had just come from her office, because she was not very dressed up but there was something chic and businesslike about her. She was evidently trying hard to keep up a drowning conversation.

'Look there,' Barbara said. 'That used to be me.'

'Do you know him?'

'No. But I can tell you some things about him. He works on Madison Avenue or perhaps on Wall Street and he's been out with her before, but not frequently.'

'It looks to me like a blind date,' Sidney said, 'and not a very successful one.'

'No. He wouldn't take her to such an expensive place if it were a blind date. After all, he might not have liked her.'

'What a formula you have!' he said, amused. 'Tell me more, but first have a Martini.'

He ordered drinks, and Barbara looked more closely at the couple in the corner, which was not too easy as they were far away. But the tables between were still empty because it was early. 'She's doing all the talking, what little there is, but that isn't necessarily because she likes him. She looks as if she thinks it's her duty. And he evidently does too, because he isn't trying at all.'

'Sounds like misery for all concerned,' Sidney said.

'That's a nice dress but it's very inexpensive. Twelve ninety-five, I'd say. I think she's a secretary, she looks like one.'

Barbara sipped at her Martini. The glass was frosted and the drink was very cold and hot at the same time. 'Look how fast they finished their drinks,' she said. 'Two while we were waiting for our first. I know just how she feels, I've done that myself on occasion.'

'Well, why did she go out with him?'

'I bet she shares an apartment with two other girls and she wants to get away from them. She isn't wearing any stockings, they've probably borrowed them all.'

Sidney squinted. 'She has nice legs. That's probably one of the reasons he's out with her.'

'What are the others?'

'You tell me.'

'No,' Barbara said, 'you tell me. You're speaking for the men.'

'He looks so bored right now I'd say he just wants to get her in the hay.'

'Poor girl. But she'll be married to someone by next year, they always are.'

'Not to him.'

'No, sir.'

Sidney laughed. 'I feel sorry for him. You have no sympathy.'

'I know,' she said, laughing too, 'I'm a beast. And I feel so superior just now because I'm having such a good time and I remember all the times I didn't.'

'That's the price one pays for the eventual happy ending. Surely your mother must have told you that.'

'She has. But I'm still waiting.'

The couple across the room in the corner stood up. The man held the girl's chair for her as she gathered up her purse and gloves. Sidney nudged Barbara's knee under the table with his. 'Your friends are going.'

'Shh.'

They were crossing the room now, passing directly in front of the table where Barbara and Sidney were sitting. Barbara looked up at them curiously. They were so close she caught a whiff of smoke from the young man's lighted cigarette. The hand he was holding it in bore a thin gold wedding band. Barbara turned, with a little shock of surprise, to look at the girl's fingers. She, too, wore a thin gold band, so narrow it had been invisible from across the room.

'They're married!'

She looked at Sidney and he looked at her and they smiled at each other with surprise and amusement. 'But they looked so miserable!' she said.

His smile faded a little, but enough so that Barbara noticed it. 'Yes,' he said.

'I am dumb,' she said softly. 'I even forgot about how I used to look. People get so tied up in their own grudges and problems they forget about other people.'

'It was fun,' he said. He looked almost as contented as he had before, the moment of revelation had been only a flash. He *is* unhappy, she thought, I know he is. And although she hated to know that anything made him suffer, Barbara had to admit to herself with a perverse little stab of pleasure that she was rather glad. It meant he was more accessible, it meant . . . Oh, I *am* a fool, she thought. This kind of thinking is the oldest trap in the world.

At eight o'clock they left the bar and walked to a restaurant for dinner. It was sunset and the sky was streaked with deep colors. The streets were deserted and quiet because it was the dinner hour of a summer night and everyone who could go was either in the country or in an air-conditioned room. Without the crowds and traffic the streets looked unusually wide. The whole evening stretched out in front of them, like a vacation. No one knew where they were and no one cared, and they were together. I wish life could always be like this minute, Barbara thought. When Sidney held open the door of the restaurant for her a blast of artificially cold air hit them and there was the sound of music and voices. It was a brightly lighted restaurant with murals on the walls and fresh flowers on the tables and a menu a yard long written in undecipherable French handwriting. There were carts of elaborate pastries lined up along one wall, covered with tarts and cakes with swirls of whipped cream. Barbara had never felt less hungry in her life. She looked around the room. How bright it was, how gay, and how insensitive those people seemed gobbling their food and howling with laughter.

'Two, sir?' the headwaiter asked, flourishing a menu. Sidney looked down at Barbara. 'We'll have a drink at the bar first,' he said abruptly.

They sat at the bar on high slippery red leather chairs. Barbara looked into her Martini. 'You'll think I'm crazy,' she said, 'but I don't want to stay here. Do you mind?'

He was already standing. 'Let's go.'

Out on the street again in the soft purple early darkness she felt better. 'It was just that it was so . . .'

'Bright and noisy and not for us,' Sidney said. 'The minute we walked in I knew this wasn't a night for L'Oiseau's.'

'Can we walk for a while?'

He took her arm protectively and they walked down the street to nowhere in particular. 'Are you hungry?' he asked.

'No. Are you?'

He shook his head.

They walked east, toward the river. Every now and then as they passed a restaurant or a bar people would come walking out in close groups, laughing and talking and looking slightly drunk and very well fed. Of course, Barbara thought, it's Thursday, the maid's night out. Other people's customs, other people's households, seemed very far away. She felt curiously detached. She was a little high from the Martinis but not in the least drunk, her lips were not numb and she could see everything clearly. The landscape changed, from office buildings and stores and restaurants to dingy apartment houses and then finally to the large luxurious new buildings near the water, sitting side by side with tenements that were waiting to be torn down. There was a sidewalk and a railing and some benches, and beyond that the slowly moving black water and the lights of the shore on the other side. They leaned on the railing, side by side, and Sidney lighted a cigarette for himself and one for her.

'It's funny,' Barbara said. 'I live in New York and I've never been here before.'

'I haven't been here in years.'

She turned around with her back to the railing and her elbows leaning on it and looked up at the lights in the apartment buildings. Up there, on what seemed to be the twentieth floor, there was a terrace with people moving about on it. They were only black specks. She was happier with Sidney Carter than she had ever been in her life, and yet she felt nervous and dissatisfied, as if there were another person inside her skin that was trying to burst out. She wanted to run and run down the street along the river and never stop, or leap into the water and swim to the other side, or throw her arms around Sidney's neck and tell him never to let her go. But she did none of these things, she merely turned around again and tossed her cigarette into the water.

'Do you want to go to hear some jazz?' he asked.

'Do you?'

'No.'

He lighted another cigarette for her and they were silent, looking out at the river, not touching. 'I don't know what's wrong with me,' she said. 'I'm so nervous.' He tossed his cigarette into the water and she watched it arc, the tiny red glowing tip. It seemed very important to watch it, to keep track of it, to concentrate on it instead of the vague and disturbing feelings that were making her teeth begin to chatter even though it was a warm night. He moved to her then and put his arms around her, not demandingly but protectively, and Barbara put her face against his lapel. She could feel his heart beating very hard against her cheek, but he did not move or speak for a long time and neither did she.

She stirred only to put her arms around his waist. Inside she wanted to cry and laugh at once, but outside she felt incapable of speaking a word. She was aware that she was shivering.

'We can't stand here all night,' he said gently.

'No.'

But neither of them moved. 'I didn't think it would be like this,' he said at last.

'Is it "like this"?'

'Is it, for you?'

'. . . Yes.'

She looked up at him then and he lowered his head and kissed her. She had never kissed anyone the way she was kissing him, she realized, as if she wanted to draw all his breath into her body because without it she would choke. His arms were around her so tightly they hurt her ribs but she didn't mind, the discomfort was at the back of her mind, it was a pain that was a part of pleasure. He took a step to the side and they sank down on to a bench, arms still tightly wound around each other, mouths still together. She heard herself breathing, or was it he? There seemed to be no difference between breath and breath. He was kissing her neck and her throat and her ear, and then he drew away a little and looked at her. Their faces were only a few inches apart and she saw his lips move before he began to speak, as if he could hardly speak at all.

'We'll be picked up for vagrants,' he murmured.

'Oh . . .'

'Come with me.'

'Yes.'

They were running then, hand in hand, across the street and through the empty canyons between the dark buildings, like children, their footsteps echoing in the summer night. The sky was a very dark blue-black, streaked with white clouds and stabbed with stars, a display of nighttime pyrotechnics. A doorman standing on the sidewalk in front of a huge whitish building looked at them curiously as they ran past. There was a taxi cruising along First Avenue. Sidney waved at it and it stopped and they climbed in and sat very close together, each holding both the other's hands tightly as the taxi rocketed across town to his hotel. Barbara was afraid to think, she held his hands against her pounding heart and closed her eyes. When they walked through the brightly lighted lobby of his hotel she kept her head down and her eyes closed, shutting out reality, letting him lead her, and briefly aware that this carpeted lobby that was suddenly the scene of the most important and shortest and most dreamlike walk she had ever taken was the same ordinary place where she had waited many times for girls to meet her for lunch or boys to meet her for cocktails.

He opened the door of his room with a key and turned on the light. It was not a hotel room, it was an entire suite. There was a small balcony outside the living-room window and long white curtains covered it, billowing slightly. There was a huge fireplace which looked as if it had never been used, and two sofas, and a coffee table littered with papers and mail. The combination of the cold impersonality of this hotel suite and Sidney's work tossed on the table filled Barbara with a kind of poignancy. There was a bar set against one wall with some bottles and decanters on it. Sidney was moving about quickly, turning on a lamp, switching off the hall light. The room was softly lighted, bluish with shadows. Barbara put her purse on a sofa and walked to the window, looking out, feeling the breeze against her face. There were millions of lights out there, and the dark, light-dotted area of the park. From behind her she heard the click of ice cubes being dropped into a glass. She turned and shook her head.

Sidney put the bottle back on the bar, unopened, and stood there for a moment, his hand still around the neck of it, looking at her. 'Will you do something for me?' he asked very quietly.

Barbara nodded.

'Stand there and hold out your arms.'

She did. He looked at her for an instant more and then walked to her very quickly and took her into his arms. 'God,' he murmured into her hair, 'that's the most beautiful sight in the world.'

'It's the way I feel about you,' Barbara said.

There were twin beds separated by a night table. Sidney and Barbara were shedding their clothes all the way to the bedroom, leaving a trail, with that same breathless hurry that had made them run down the street to the cab. They stopped at the doorway to the bedroom, arms around each other, looking at those two ridiculous narrow beds and each of them beginning to smile at the same time. 'Decisions,' Sidney said, 'nothing but decisions.'

'Oh, I love you.'

They fell on one of the beds and this time it was Barbara who reached out and turned off the light. There was enough light streaming in through the open doorway to the living room so that she could dimly see Sidney's profile as he leaned over her breast. Why had she never realized before what a beautiful face he had? It was a pleasure just to look at it. Oh, I love him, she thought, I love him, I do. Just knowing that she loved him was enough, even if she was not allowed to. She could feel. That was worth everything; feeling, caring, no matter what happened to make it end in emptiness, because having the capacity to love was so beautiful. She knew that she had never truly loved any man before in her life.

She had never felt this physical pleasure before, to such a degree, and she realized it was love that made the difference. She had not been to bed with any man since her husband, and it had been two years, a long time, so that at first Sidney hurt her, but only for a second. Then she welcomed him. She had not known such skill existed, and yet she was not surprised because she had known that Sidney Carter would do everything well, she had never doubted it. The only thing that surprised her was her own reaction; she was suddenly a creature without shame, all made of sensations and motion without any consciousness of what was happening outside of herself and him. She heard herself screaming in her throat as at a great distance, and felt him very gently putting the corner of the pillow between her teeth. What a monster I am! she thought, and then she did not care in the least.

They were bathed in perspiration and she did not care about that either, although she had ordinarily found that an unpleasant part of love-making. Afterward he continued to hold her in his arms for a while until the breeze that came in through the window felt cold, and then he sat up and pulled up the sheet. 'What are you thinking?' he asked.

'Nothing. Except that I'm happy.'

'So am I.'

But under the clean sheet with its crisp fresh-laundry smell, reality returned, and sense, and Barbara thought of two things. 'I'll probably get pregnant,' she murmured.

'No you won't. I was careful.'

She reached out for his hand and grasped it and he returned the pressure. They were silent for a while. 'Something else,' Barbara said. 'Something worse.'

'What?'

'I told you I love you.'

'I know. Several times.'

'Several times!' She hadn't realized it was as bad as that. 'Do you mind?'

'Oh!' he said, a half-deprecating, half-angry sound that wasn't even a word. 'How could I object? I wish to hell I did.'

She was lying on her back with her arms crossed under her head. He leaned down and kissed the smooth place beneath her arm. 'How can you do that?' she asked.

'Why not?'

'I don't know.'

He shut his eyes. His voice when he spoke was in that same strained, almost angry tone. 'I guess I love you too.'

'You don't have to say that,' Barbara said gently. 'I won't ask you for anything.'

'Remember when I said you wouldn't fall in love with me and you said that was a dangerous thing to say to you?'

'Yes . . .'

'Well, what you just said is a dangerous thing to say to me.'

'Oh, darling, I meant it.'

He was leaning on one elbow looking down at her and he smoothed her hair off her forehead. 'You're Barbara Lemont, the girl who wants to get married. I remember that too.'

'All girls want to get married.'

'I want you to get married. I want you to be happy. You're such a good person.'

'I *will* get married someday,' Barbara said, trying to sound cheerful. 'You said that to me once, and I have a good memory too.'

'You make me feel like a bastard.'

'Why? I never thought I would find anyone to love, and then I found you. So it stands to reason that I'll find someone to marry eventually, because that's much less of a miracle.'

He took her into his arms and held her tightly without a word. Then he released her. His face was troubled. 'Get dressed,' he said. 'We'll go down to the bar and have a drink.'

They had two drinks in the bar, holding hands under the table. Barbara wondered whether anyone who saw them there could possibly guess that they had just gotten out of bed. She glanced at her reflection in the mirror behind them and she knew she had never looked better in her life. She felt calm and relaxed and very happy.

At twelve-thirty he took her home. He went upstairs with her and stopped just outside her apartment door. 'I won't come in,' he whispered. 'I don't want your mother to have to jump up from the *Late Show*.'

Barbara smiled. 'When will I see you?'

'Tomorrow?'

'Yes.'

He put his arms around her and stood there for a moment with his lips against her cheek. She could feel them move as he spoke to her and she could feel the whisper of his breath. 'What will become of us?' he murmured.

She couldn't answer. She didn't know.

All the next day at her office a silly line kept running through Barbara's head, like something out of one of *America's Woman's* own stories. *I love him so much I can't see straight.* She had never thought that she would ever think anything like that, and what was more, believe it. Love covered her, she felt it. What could be more idiotic, and she had never been happier. At lunchtime she had a sandwich sent in and closed the door to her office and sat there and mooned. She had never thought that she, Barbara Lemont, the girl who would jump three feet if you touched her, would turn into such a love-sick creature. She was waiting outside her office at five minutes to five. She saw Sidney crossing the street and hurrying when he noticed her waiting for him.

'Hello,' she said. She had the feeling that her smile covered her entire face and what was more that she was possibly blushing.

'How lovely you look.' He sounded disturbed as he looked at her, and took her arm quickly.

When he took her to the married-man's bar where they had first met Barbara thought it was amusing. It was very dark in there and they were alone except for the bartender polishing glasses. It was too early for the Hawaiians to appear, and evidently also too early for their lively clientele. Sidney ordered two Martinis.

'I have to leave at seven o'clock,' he said. 'I have a business meeting.'

'Oh . . . All right.' She reached for his hand. 'I'm glad I could see you at all.'

'Barbara,' he said, 'don't make it difficult for me, please. I feel like such a bastard. I just don't know what to tell you.'

She withdrew her hand and crossed her arms and grinned at him. 'I don't know how to tell you,' she said, imitating his solemn voice, 'but I'm married. I was afraid to tell you for fear you wouldn't like me any more.'

He smiled back at her and she noticed for the first time how tired he looked, like someone with a pain who is laughing anyway because the joke is funny, even though laughing makes it hurt more. 'What is it?' she asked.

He picked up his Martini and nodded at her, so she lifted hers and took a sip of it. 'I'll make you a prophecy,' he said. 'This time next year you'll be drinking one of these with someone you love.'

'Who?' But she knew without asking what he meant and she felt a stab of pain that they would have to subject themselves to such a tiresome discussion. Why did he have to spoil everything?

'I don't know yet,' he said. 'But I hope you'll tell me when you find him.'

'That's a safe promise.'

'You call me up, and say, "Sidney, I'm in love."' He smiled at her, this time his old smile, full of pleasure and charm. 'No, you'll forget to tell me. And then I'll know you really love him.'

'Do we have to talk about him, whoever he is? It's making me feel uncomfortable.'

'Were you drunk last night?' he asked abruptly.

'No. Why, did I do something silly?'

'No. Oh, God, no,' he said. 'That was just me giving myself a last little trap door to slide out from under my conscience.'

'Well, I wasn't drunk and you didn't seduce me,' Barbara said, 'and I should think you'd feel *less* conscience-stricken in that case.'

'As a matter of fact I don't.'

I have a feeling I'm going to need this Martini, she thought, and she drank it down, the entire thing, like medicine, and coughed. 'I don't understand.'

'I've been trying to figure it out in myself, because I'm actually not this sort of person. Obviously a guy who calls you up cold-bloodedly and leads you off to the sack is not going to be the same guy who cringes with conscience afterward. And yet I am.'

'Obviously,' Barbara said, 'a man who can make a speech like that *is* "that sort of person," as you put it. I haven't heard many such speeches in my long career.'

'You haven't had a long career.'

'Not of giving in, no. But I've met enough wolves to know which are the real ones.'

He said nothing, but smoked his cigarette, and when it was finished he put it out and drank his Martini and gestured to the waiter for two more, all still in silence.

'Well,' Barbara said, 'I had a funny kind of day today,' and she went on, describing things that had happened which she thought might amuse him, although it was extremely difficult to say cheerful things to someone who was obviously making an effort not to feel depressed. They had their round of drinks, and then another, making conversation which would have seemed pleasant enough to anyone else but which Barbara realized instantly and with pain was entirely strained. Small talk, but this time without the glow of two people realizing they are falling in love and learning about each other. There must be many kinds of small talk, she was thinking, and this kind is the one that says everything is dying. Why? *Why?*

Sidney looked at his watch. 'It's a quarter to seven. I'd never just get up and walk away, you know that, don't you?'

'. . . Yes.'

'I'm not going to call you any more,' he said. 'But if you ever need anything – anything – if you're in trouble or you need help from me as a friend who cares about you a great deal, then you call me.'

'What does that mean?' Barbara asked, her throat tight.

'It means,' he said, smiling, 'that I know a little bit more than a girl half my age.'

'All of a sudden you're playing Father Time,' Barbara said lightly.

'The difference in our ages means absolutely nothing to me,' he said. 'I guess it was a badly chosen phrase.'

Barbara looked at her hands. They looked so lonely; she had come in here with them and soon she would leave with them, always empty. 'A better phrase would be: It was great fun, but it was just one of those things,' she said. She tried to keep her face pleasant, with no trace of bitterness in her tone. 'Right?'

'Don't make me angry.'

Tears sprang into her eyes. 'Angry? Angry? You terrify me.'

'I'd like to kiss you right now,' he said quietly. 'I'd like to take you by the hand and bring you to my room and keep you there for a year.' He stood up. 'But I'm not even going to think about any of those things any more. Ready?'

She did not rise but sat there looking up at him. 'You should have told me all this last night,' she said bitterly. 'When we had just gotten out of bed and you were zipping up my dress. That would have been even more appropriate.' She stood then, keeping her eyes away from his face, and picked up her purse and gloves. She followed Sidney out of the bar and on to the sidewalk. The late afternoon sun hurt her eyes.

'I'll take you home,' he said.

'I don't feel like going home right now. Thank you just the same. I think I'll walk for a while. I'd go shopping, but the stores aren't open late tonight, it's Friday.' She looked at him for the first time. 'It *is* Friday. I forgot all about it. Aren't you going to Nantucket?'

'On the eight-o'clock plane,' he said.

That hurt, more than anything else. He had tried to make it easier for her by saying it was a business conference, but he was going to his family. Perhaps he loved her, perhaps he would have a harder time keeping the proper face over the dinner table than she would, but he was going to his family. It was his life, part of his routine and, even more, his obligation. She wondered what the virtue was in an obligation that meant life without love, but she said nothing.

'Barbara,' he said. 'Please.'

'You told me to call you if I need you,' she said. 'If I call you and tell you I need you to love me, what will you do?'

He didn't answer for a moment. 'I won't take you out,' he said finally. 'And then you'll know that I do.'

She stood there on the sidewalk looking at him, memorizing

his face, not able to bear leaving him and at the same time trying to pull herself together. Don't drag it out, she told herself, don't make a fool of yourself. He obviously wants to get rid of you. Be gracious, say the right thing, so that at least he will remember you well and not with distaste.

She held out her hand, immaculate in its fresh white glove. 'Goodbye,' she said. 'You'd better not miss your plane.'

He took her hand almost gingerly. 'If . . .' he began, and then stopped. There was a taxi cruising along the street and he waved at it. It pulled up to the curb. 'Goodbye,' he said, and added foolishly, 'Give my love to your little girl.'

'Give *my* love to your little boy. And read my column.'

'I will.'

He climbed into the taxi and it drove off with a grinding of gears. Barbara began to walk quickly in the opposite direction so that in case Sidney turned around for one last look he would know that she already had someplace to go.

She walked for hours, looking into shop windows and not seeing anything that was before her eyes, bumping into people and murmuring, 'Excuse me,' and wishing she could thrash out and strike one of those unfeeling bodies. There was such a pain in her heart she could hardly breathe. She had never before believed that the word heartache had any basis in anatomical fact, but now she knew it was true. She could almost believe it was also true that someone could die of a broken heart. What had she done wrong? Perhaps, Barbara thought, I should never have gone to bed with him. He had me and he's finished. There are men like that. But they don't call it quits after one night; if a girl's reasonably good in bed and they think she's easy, they come back, at least for a while. I couldn't have been that bad in bed, I know I wasn't. And I didn't ask him to marry me, I always made it plain that I was glad just to know him. What did I do wrong?

She was afraid to go home because she felt so fragile that she knew if anyone said one out-of-the-way thing to her she would fall apart. Her mother expected her to be out for the evening and would take care of Hillary. Barbara passed an art movie theater with no line in front of it and bought a ticket and went in. She sat far over on the side, with nearly a whole row of empty seats between her and the other people. It was the middle of the picture and as she looked at it she could hardly make out the forms of the actors and objects. It was just a lot of motion and whiteness and noise. She covered her face with her hands and cried.

On Monday at the office Barbara tried to immerse herself in work. They were closing an issue and fortunately everyone was frantic with last-minute hurry. It was easier not to think when she had so much to do, but every time the phone rang her heart nearly stopped and when she lifted the receiver and heard someone else's voice – not Sidney's – she could hardly summon up the cheerfulness to speak. But she knew he would never call. This other, this hope, was only a delusion she gave herself in order to go on. You could say, He'll call in a month, and then you could go on functioning until that month was over. On Wednesday afternoon her boss called her into her office.

'We have some wonderful news, Barbara.'

There are two of us, Barbara thought, looking at this woman behind the huge desk; both of us in love with married men. Now I understand you. 'Yes? What?'

'The Sidney Carter Agency called and they're going to run an ad for Wonderful perfume every other month for the next year. They said they're going to advertise because they like *your* column so much, and the way they want to advertise is to have you mention the perfume in your column. I spoke to Mr Bossart about it and he says there's no reason why not since you're such a clever writer.'

'That's crazy,' Barbara murmured. 'I can't write about the same perfume every month.'

'That's what we thought, and that's why we decided we're going to give you *two* columns to do starting with the December issue. One will be shop talk about different products, but written with a flair and style so that it seems much more personal than that. And the other will be the same beauty column you've been doing all along. I called Sidney Carter himself and asked him what he thought of it, and he said that was fine, as long as you were doing the writing. How do you like that?'

'Can I sit down?' Barbara asked weakly.

Her boss laughed. 'Sure. Sit down. And here, have a cigarette. We're all very proud of you. You're going to go far at *America's Woman*, you'll see.'

Barbara accepted a cigarette, lighted it, and promptly dropped it into her lap. She jumped up, brushing off the sparks. 'I'm so excited . . . I'd better go and have a cup of coffee downstairs. May I?'

'Go ahead,' her boss said, smiling happily. 'You'll have a secretary to *bring* you coffee in a few months.'

Barbara fled downstairs to the luncheonette. The hot coffee burned her tongue and she spilled half of it into the saucer by mistake. So Sidney had done this for her. Why? It was a present, obviously, to sweeten his goodbye, or to thank her for their two days together. He was not the sort of man to send a mink coat or a piece of jewelry; if he had been she would have thrown the gift in his face. He had given her what he had to give, what he thought she could most graciously accept. So this is the way you get ahead, Barbara thought bitterly. Now I'm learning. I may turn out to be a successful career woman after all.

It was strange, she thought as the days went by; she could not help but be excited about her new column, even though she knew why she had been given it. Doors had opened, and with them a much-needed raise and more prestige. She was busier than ever. And when, two weeks later, her period arrived on time, she felt as if this was the end of something tenuous but important that she had had with Sidney, and now there was nothing. She felt empty. Physically she was just as she had been before she and Sidney had ever met. But in every other way she knew that she had changed, and she wondered whether she would ever forget.

18

You see them on the bus in the morning: girls reading the news-paper, girls with lending-library novels and girls simply staring off into space. If it is not a rainy day and the bus is not crowded with strap-hangers pushing one another up the aisle you can see each face clearly. Each of them is a self-contained little mask, decorated with cosmetics, keeping its private thoughts secluded in a public vehicle. Some of these girls are going to their offices because each day is another step to the success they dream of, and others are going to work because they cannot live without the money, and some are going because that's where they go on weekdays and they never give it another thought. They go to their typing pool or their calculating machines as to a waiting place, a limbo for single girls who are waiting for love and marriage. Perhaps the girl sitting on the bus reading her plastic-covered lending-library novel is reading of love, or perhaps she is simply looking at the page and thinking of herself. X meets Y and there is magic. Or X meets Y and there is nothing; it might not have been that kind of year, maybe a year or two from now Y would have looked much more desirable to X. Or perhaps X meets Z and falls desperately in love, a kind of self-hypnosis, when a year or two later if X had only then met Z she might have been spared.

In the autumn of 1953 April Morrison began preparing for her wedding, in some ways as Mary Agnes had, and in others that Mary Agnes had never dreamed of. For one thing, Dexter had not presented her with a ring, nor had he agreed to set a date. His plans were so nebulous as to be almost nonexistent, but April, who had always felt that a wedding was mostly the girl's responsibility and the boy's bother, was busily writing home to her relatives in Colorado to tell them to expect the good news any time now and to find out when their church would be available.

She had seen Dexter's parents often but briefly during this second summer, to smile at across the room during Hudson View Club dances, or in passing on the club terrace, and she felt rather disappointed that she had never gotten to know them better. Although both generations went to the same parties at the Hudson View Club they always left each other strictly alone in the interests of a more relaxed time. No one would dream of saying, Hey, Mr Allison, your son passed out in the men's shower! Did he? Then it was his own responsibility, and the responsibility of one of his more sober friends to drive his date home or to wherever she was houseguesting for the weekend. At dances the younger people congregated around the bar while the older people sat at tables on the terrace, where three aging waiters brought them their drinks. You couldn't plow up to a group and say, I'd like to sit with you; the lines had been drawn years before. April finally decided that there must be another way, and she felt that since she was younger than Dexter's mother the responsibility of breaking the ice was hers.

'Your mother said once she'd like to have lunch with me,' April said to Dexter. 'That was so long ago. I feel terrible that I never did anything about it. I'm going to call her.'

'What for?' Dexter asked. He was reading the newspaper.

'To have lunch with me. Do you think that's all right?'

'Go ahead,' Dexter said, as if it had never occurred to him. 'She'd probably like that. She likes young girls.'

I could wear my dark-green suit with the little mink collar, April was thinking. It was the last thing she had bought before her charge account had been closed down for nonpayment of an eight-month-old bill. She had been terrified for a while that the stores would come to repossess her clothes, but they had not, they had simply continued to send her threatening letters and telephone her warning of law suits, and when she had gotten her summer raise and was finally able to make ends meet she had begun sending the stores part payments. She didn't want to go to jail and have Dexter's family think he was marrying a crook or a female con man or something. It was just that she was so impractical.

The next morning, not too early, she called Dexter's mother from her office, but the maid said Mrs Key was already out. April left her name and her office number. By five-thirty Dexter's mother had not called back, and since everyone had long since left the office and she was a little afraid to stay there alone, April decided to call her.

'Mrs Key?'

'Who is this?'

'April.'

There was a pause. The voice at the other end was noncommittal and a little confused. 'Oh?'

'April. Dexter's April.'

'Oh . . . oh, of course. Dexter's friend April. How silly of me. Of course.' Mrs Key began to laugh. 'You know, when you left your name this morning – "Miss Morrison" – I couldn't figure out who it was. That's why I didn't call you back.'

This is the strangest woman I ever spoke to, April thought. Dexter must have told her about me millions of times. Maybe she's drunk or sick or something. These society people drink like fish. 'How are you?' April asked politely.

'I'm fine, thank you. How are you?'

'Just fine, thanks. I guess you're wondering why I called.'

The laugh that came through the receiver was slightly flustered, but with an obvious attempt at warmth. 'Well, yes, I was.'

'I'd like to have lunch with you one day next week if you're free.'

'Why . . . that's nice. Is it anything special?'

'I just thought we should get to know each other better,' April said shyly.

'How sweet, dear . . . how very sweet. I'll have to look at my calendar.'

'I'll hold on.'

The pause was very brief. 'Let's see now,' Mrs Key said, 'I'm afraid next week is just about impossible. I have something every day.'

'How about the week after? I'm free every day.'

'Could I call you?'

'Of course,' April said, disappointed. 'You don't have to give me much notice in advance, because I'll break any appointment I have . . .'

'Well, I'll call you.'

'Do you have my number?'

'The maid took it down so it must be here someplace. I'll find it.'

'I'll give it to you now,' April said quickly. She did, slowly, so that Dexter's mother could write it down. 'I'm here every day from nine to five. It's my office. I'll be looking forward to hearing from you.'

'Thank you for calling,' Mrs Key said. 'It was very sweet of you.'

April replaced the receiver and sat for a moment with her hand still on it. Something was going through her mind, the kind of ugly thought that one had to keep out by force or risk being one of those people who always feels persecuted. *I could swear she didn't know I was someone special.* She sounded as if I made her feel uncomfortable. Made Dexter's mother feel uncomfortable! Imagine that!

When she met Dexter for dinner later April didn't know quite how to tell him. She didn't want him to think for a minute that she wanted to imply his mother wasn't polite or, worse, that she might be eccentric. 'I . . . phoned your mother,' she said finally.

'Yes . . .' he said, looking rather pleased and amused, 'she told me. I called her up tonight and she said she thought it was awfully cute of you. Hey, let's have Gibsons tonight instead of Martinis, I bought some onions.'

'Awfully cute . . .' April repeated softly.

'Do you want a lot of onions or just one?'

'Dexter! Doesn't your mother like me?'

'Well, how the hell should I know?' Dexter asked irritably. 'She hardly knows you.'

April felt a flush coming over her face. 'I want her to like me.'

Dexter smiled. 'She will. I'll take you to a party over there some-time and you'll get to know her.'

'She wasn't . . . mad or anything, was she, when you told her we were going to get married?'

'Mad? Why should she be mad?'

'Some mothers are more possessive than others – you know. I just thought she might have mentioned something.'

Dexter held the Gibson very carefully so that it would not spill over the brim and took a sip at it. He seemed much more interested in the mechanics of the glass and liquid than the situation called for. 'As a matter of fact,' he admitted casually, 'I didn't tell her.'

'Dexter!' April said, stunned. 'Why *not?*'

'I was looking forward to having a nice evening,' Dexter said. 'Do you want to start an argument, is that what you want to do?'

April had never thought she had so much courage, but shock and indignation and fright made her bold. 'I want to find out if you and I are going to get married; *that's* what I want.'

He looked at her levelly for a minute and then his brows drew together. 'Well, we're not,' he said flatly.

'Dexter, don't tease me,' April said shakily. She tried to laugh, but the sound that came out was so pathetic it sounded to her more like a cat's mew. 'I just don't have any sense of humor about things like that, I've waited for you too long.'

He was almost smiling. 'Why, was it such a bore?'

'How could it be a bore when you just nearly gave me a heart attack?' April said. She stood up and went to him and put her arms around him, with her head against his shoulder. 'I couldn't live without you, you know that.'

He was standing there so stiffly and so cautiously that she felt as if she were embracing a stranger. 'Maybe it was a mistake to go on so long,' he said. 'I don't know. But you knew what you were doing. I told you a year ago that I never force anyone to do anything. I don't want to feel that your unhappiness is due to me.'

'All my happiness has been due to you,' April said. 'The other too. But that's what happens when people are in love, they affect each other.'

'Any man could make you unhappy,' he said. 'He'd snap his fingers and you'd be unhappy.' He was mumbling, sounding a little as if he were trying to justify himself. 'You don't know about life.'

'Life?'

Dexter held his palm out, his fingers bent, and looked at it, as if life were something like an egg that you could hold and look at and feel. 'Yes, life.' His voice rose. 'Life, darling! You don't know anything about it.'

'I do so know about life,' April said. 'I know as much about it as I want to know.' She hesitated for a moment and then said it: 'I still have nightmares about my baby.'

Dexter moved away from her. 'That's not what I meant,' he said.

'You said you would marry me in the spring,' April said. 'Then you said the fall. What am I to think? Of course I thought we were going to get married soon; you promised.'

She had never seen him so stripped of poise and sophistication; he seemed almost frightened. 'When did I promise?' he said.

'Don't you want to marry me? *Ever?*'

'Why did you have to do this?' he asked. He sounded almost sorry for himself.

'Do what, Dexter?'

'Make everything so emotional.'

'*Emotional?* After a year together how can you say that?'

'You're twenty-two years old,' Dexter said. 'What kind of big deal is one year in your life?'

'Oh, Dexter! Nothing is sacred to you, is it?'

'You always say that.'

'It's true!'

'All right,' he said angrily. 'If you say it's true, it's true. Insult me. I'm a libertine. Hm?' He sat in the corner of the sofa, behind his knees, and lighted a cigarette, puffing out clouds of smoke.

'What's the matter with you?' April asked worriedly.

'Nothing.'

'Are you angry because I called your mother?'

'Why the hell should I care if you call my mother or not? You can telephone my whole family for all I care.'

April stood there looking at him, biting her thumb as she always did when she was excited or nervous, her mind in a turmoil. A year ago if he had acted this way – and he sometimes did – she would have been hysterical. But by now she was used to it and, even more, she herself had changed. Especially in the past seven months, ever since what she secretly thought of as the death of her child, she had changed. It was not that she had become harder in any way but she had realized the value of strength. With April strength was more the kind of desperation that comes with weakness, the power that gives a ninety-pound woman drowning in the water the ability to swamp a careless lifeguard. There was only one thing she knew: she had to survive, and survival meant hope and love. If Dexter said marriage, she had to believe him. If he put it off, she had to forgive him and keep her mind fixed on the future date. This was survival, this was keeping her life together, this was being a woman. But Dexter was so unpredictable and she herself was so naïve that somehow it never seemed to work out as well as she thought it should.

'Dexter,' April said slowly, 'if you don't want a big church wedding we can just go down to City Hall someday. I wanted a church wedding but I'll give it up for you.'

The gaze he gave her was blank.

'It means a lot to me,' April went on, beginning to stumble a little in the face of that insensitive gaze, 'but I want to do what *you* want. I know it's a lot of trouble for you to come all the way to Colorado . . . and really, it's kind of a silly custom anyway . . . I feel sort of like a New Yorker . . .'

'What are you talking about?'

'Our wedding,' April said.

He lighted another cigarette with the butt of the first one. 'You don't have to make plans so far in advance.'

'But it's September already.'

'I'm not getting married this fall,' Dexter said.

'Why not?'

'Why not? Why not? What do you mean, why not? Don't you think women should let the men do the proposing?'

'Yes, I do . . .' April said, her voice faltering, wringing her hands together behind her back. 'But you did propose, and now I'm just making a few plans.'

'I proposed? Do you see a ring?'

'You said, "We can get married in the spring." I remember that. That's what you said. And then later you said you were taking your vacation in the fall and Europe was a good place for a honeymoon.'

'That adds up to a proposal?'

How could he be so cruel? He was worse tonight than he had ever been, she hardly knew him. 'We . . . can . . . get . . . married . . . in . . . the . . . spring,' she repeated, fighting back the tears.

'That was an awfully long time ago,' he said coolly. 'You know, if you find a package in the bus and nobody claims it for ninety days it's dead, it's not his any more. You take a lease on a building and it has a time limit. How long do you think that chance remark has any validity?'

There had been times before that she had thought she could never suffer any more, but now she knew she had been wrong. This was the cruelest time, and what was worse, she could not understand it at all. The world was falling away, nothing made any sense, Dexter was suddenly a villain. Even his face had changed, it bore the marks of secrecy and fright. But even at this moment, terrified and hurt and angry at his strange behavior, April could not help noticing how handsome that face was and how she loved it, and she wanted to kiss him and tell him to smile at her and stop this dreadful scene.

Dexter stood up, walked to his kitchenette, and tossed the remains of his Gibson into the sink. 'Do you want to go out for dinner,' he said, 'or do you want to argue all night?'

'We're not arguing. We're discussing our whole future, yours and mine. I'm . . . I'm not the kind of girl who can live with a man and just . . . go on like that forever. I always thought we would get married.'

'Living together? We're not living together,' Dexter said indignantly.

'We're . . . *sleeping* together!'

He threw up his hands. 'I suppose you're going to hold that against me too. Every little thing I say or do.'

April stared at him. 'It doesn't mean anything to you, does it?'

He smiled then, intimately, and she almost recognized him again. 'Of course it does, honey,' he said. She recognized his tone, but this time she understood it, for the first time. It was the sleepy-cat, purring tone, the happy tone, the pacifying tone, but there was nothing in it of love, and April wondered how she could have listened to it for over a year and never noticed that. All right, Dexter didn't love her. The enormity of it was such that she could not comprehend it, and so she put it at the back of her mind. Perhaps he could not really love. It was not for her to understand. He wanted to be with her, that was all that mattered. That was a form of love. If it was all Dexter could manage she would live with it and be grateful for even that.

'I won't talk about marriage any more now,' April said falter-ingly, trying to pacify him. 'We'll talk about it another time.'

'There's nothing to talk about.'

'When are you taking your vacation?'

'I thought I'd take it at the end of the month,' Dexter said. 'Now I think I'll take it next week.'

'What are you going to do?'

'I don't know.'

April almost said, You said you might go to Europe, but then she stopped herself. He might jump on her again. Instead she said, 'I've always wanted to go to Bermuda. A girl in my office went there on her – last June, I mean, and she said it was marvelous.' She waited for him to give some sign that things were just as they had been before, that he was taking her with him.

'I don't know where I'm going to go,' he said.

'I saved my vacation,' April said. 'I have two weeks. The same as you.'

'I might take a month and go to Europe.'

It was like having a tooth drilled, after a while it hurt so much you didn't really notice it any more, you rode along on the crest of the noise and the pain and forgot what time it was or where you were. 'Not alone?' April said.

'If I can get some girl to go with me I won't go alone,' Dexter said. He walked into the dressing room and began combing his hair in front of the mirror. April could see him through the open doorway. She remembered the first time she had ever come up to this apartment, that summer so long ago, when he had peered into the mirror in that same posture after he had tried to kiss her. And how many times since then she had watched him combing his hair after he *had* kissed her, and made love to her, so that by now the simple act of combing his hair had for her a great and sentimental importance. She wondered whether she would ever again be able to watch a man combing his hair, stooping in front of a mirror, without this same mixture of happiness and misery.

'I met a girl at a party last week,' Dexter said casually. 'I might ask her.'

'A . . . girl?'

'Yes.'

'You'd take a strange girl?' April cried.

He was bent over the mirror, trying to press the wave into his hair with two stiff fingers. 'Well, I'd take her out for a while first, of course, to see if we liked each other.'

'How can you take another girl?' It was more a cry of pain than a question, all sorts of thoughts were revolving in her head.

'Well, I can't take you,' he said, as if it were perfectly reasonable. 'You'd try to turn it into an elopement. You'd have a miserable time telling me how *long* we've been going out together, how much of your time I've wasted.' Was it actually true that he sounded hurt and sorry for himself? 'If I've wasted so much of your time already, I think it's only fair that I stop right now.'

'Oh, Dexter!' April said. 'You stop picking on me like that. I never said you wasted my time. I just mentioned how long we've been going together because I feel it's a bond. Now you stop talking like that . . . please, darling.'

'I mean it,' he said. He came out of the dressing room straightening the points of his pocket handkerchief.

'You'd start going out with another girl?'

'As many of them as I can find.' He sounded actually pleased with the sound of the idea. 'Then *none* of them can say I wasted her time for a year.'

'And what about me?' April asked in a small, frightened voice.

'I've invited you to dinner tonight. I'm still available.'

'And . . . tomorrow?'

'You'd better make a date with somebody else.'

Afterward, when she was alone in her apartment, April remembered every word. Everything Dexter had said to her returned, relentlessly; and her own answers, which seemed so logical and intelligent and loving, and which he had not seemed to understand at all. They had had dinner, or at least they had sat opposite each other while Dexter ate and she fought back the tears and pushed the food around on her plate. She couldn't even drink a cocktail and get drunk, nothing would pass her throat. She had kept her eyes fixed on his face, trying to understand him, to reach him, to find out why whatever they had had together had shattered so suddenly and terribly, beyond repair. Whatever she saw on that face bewildered her. It was closed off from her, under that mask of poise Dexter had perfected through years of the proper schools and the proper older acquaintances and countless introductions to strangers. He could not completely control his voice, so that the charm and smoothness did not quite extend to his tone. She could tell when he spoke that he was uncomfortable, although he insisted on keeping the conversation to inconsequential things. It was the longest and worst meal April had ever sat through in her life, and yet it was also the shortest, because Dexter had made it perfectly clear that he would not see her again.

'I think it's easier this way,' he said. 'A clean break. Then we won't drag it out and keep squabbling. I want to break it off here.'

'Please . . .' April said, 'wait until after Thanksgiving. Please. I can't bear to spend a big holiday alone. I'll go home for Christmas, but Thanksgiving . . .'

'That's two months!' he said indignantly.

'That's not so long.'

'No,' Dexter said. 'Now.'

She could not face the office the next day, she called in and said she was sick. That was not untrue; she was sick. When she looked at her face in the mirror she looked like someone who had been drowned and beaten and kept awake for four nights. Her skin was pale white with reddish blotches, her eyes were red rimmed from crying and her lips bore purple tooth marks where she had bitten them. Her throat felt raw. She could not lie on her bed because then the thoughts came pouring in, so she paced the floor, still dressed in the dress she had worn for cocktails and dinner the night before. At eleven o'clock she called Dexter at his office.

'Who is calling, please?' his secretary asked.

'Miss April Morrison.'

'I'm sorry, Miss Morrison, Mr Key isn't here.' She really did sound sorry, perhaps she knew. April called him at his apartment and let the phone ring ten times. She called him again at his office at twelve, and at three, and at four and four-thirty. Every time the secretary sounded sorrier. In between these calls April called him at home. There was never any answer. Then she knew at last why his secretary had sounded so sorry. Any sympathetic woman would feel badly when she was talking to another woman who was obviously terribly upset and she knew she had to tell a lie.

19

In the late fall Caroline Bender realized that she had been going out with Paul Landis for a year. She did not feel sentimental, the way she would about an anniversary. She was only surprised that she had been seeing him for so long without feeling any differently toward him, except perhaps more at ease, as one always is with an old friend. She had never gone out with a boy steadily for such a long period of time except for Eddie, and she and Eddie had been in love. It's a mark of endurance, Caroline thought, rather pleased with herself – but *whose* endurance, I wonder?

She mentioned their anniversary to Paul the next night at dinner. He seemed much more moved than she had been. 'This calls for a celebration!' he said, looking happy and excited, and promptly ordered a bottle of the best champagne.

Drinking her champagne and looking at Paul thoughtfully over the rim of her wide glass, Caroline couldn't help thinking, He'll never forget his wife's birthday or their anniversary. It was a comforting feeling. And yet, it hurt a little, because she felt she could never bring herself to love Paul enough to marry him, and so she would miss out on a lifetime of thoughtful little gestures. She was realizing already as she came to the end of her second year in New York that thoughtfulness like this was hard to find. There were men like Dexter Key, whom she hated for what he had done to April, all good looks and charm and loving himself so much that he didn't even bother to be subtle about it. There were the dozens of utterly mismatched blind dates she had been inflicted with in the past two years, a sentence at hard labor starting with the words (usually uttered by some nice older woman who hardly knew her or the boy) 'I know a nice young man for you to meet.' These amateur match-makers seemed to think that the mere fact that Caroline wore a skirt and the man wore pants was enough to make them want to hurl themselves into each other's arms. And there was the majority, the so-so dates, the young men who didn't particularly care about her or she about them, but who continued to call her once in a while for dinner or drinks because they too were marking time. It was nice, in the face of all this, to be with someone like Paul, who really cared about her, and she had known girls who had married men like Paul for that very reason and because they wanted so badly to be married.

More and more lately, during these dreary months, she had found herself thinking of two things. One of them was Eddie. If I had married Eddie, she kept thinking, I would be happy today. I wouldn't be putting up with any of this. But then the other thought came in: I wouldn't have this wonderful job either. Caroline knew in her heart that if she had the choice today she would still throw away her job in a minute for life as Eddie's wife. Or she could continue to work for a few years. Eddie would be proud of her, he would like her to work if it was what she wanted. Paul would too, she supposed, but he was always so wrapped up in his own work and his legal cases that he seemed to feel her work was a little game, especially since he had glanced through two or three of the Derby books and had stated flatly that they were for idiots.

'We have to go somewhere special tonight,' Paul was saying, 'since it's our anniversary. It's too late to get theater tickets. Why didn't you tell me before?'

I didn't think it was that important, she wanted to say, but instead she smiled and shrugged. 'I'd just as soon go to the movies, Paul, really.'

'Nonsense. We'll go to the Blue Angel.'

She sat in the dark club watching the show, her hand in Paul's. She had a collection of matchbooks from extravagant places, dropped here and there on tables in the dingy apartment she still shared with Gregg. They made it look as if she lived a gay, mad life. What a typical picture for anyone from out of New York:

career girl's apartment, stockings drying over the shower rod, clothes flung helter-skelter in the rush to get to the office on time, to a date on time, a scrap of cheese and some canned orange juice in the icebox, perhaps a bottle of wine there too, wads of dust lying under the studio couch because you couldn't clean except on weekends and sometimes not even then, and all those brightly colored matchbooks with names of well-known eating places, so that even if one managed only two good and sufficient meals a week one could still light one's cigarettes for the rest of the week with the memory.

The apartment that had once seemed so exciting now seemed too small to Caroline. The walls seemed to be closing in. She longed for a separate living room and bedroom so that she and Gregg could each have some privacy. But she wasn't ready yet to live all alone, because she couldn't afford alone the kind of apartment she liked, and because there were lonely times when she was glad for a roommate to confide in. And also, with Paul it was safer. He would never be the kind of man who would try to sleep with her unless she herself first made it clear that she did that sort of thing, but after a year he was getting to the point where sex with Caroline was something very emotional to him, and she tried to avoid that as well as she could. It was easier lately to lie and say, Gregg has company tonight and I think they'd like to be alone, or, Gregg went to sleep early tonight, and thus keep their physical contact confined to a brief kissing session in the hall. Paul lived with his parents, and so he had no bachelor lair to lure her to. It was strange, Caroline thought, rather amused, he was so conventional about planning every step of their evening to conform to gracious living that he still, at twenty-six, had the conventional attitude that one necks at the *end* of the evening. No cocktail hour embraces for him, no ride to the beach on a summer day and a feverish sprawl behind a lonely dune. You kissed the girl in her apartment after you had wined and dined her. It was rather like a bargain. And by its very regularity and predictability his love-making had lost all its attraction for her and almost seemed an obligation.

She liked him, she really liked him, and she wanted to be good to him. But what could she give to him? Her company, of course, was the first answer, but her twice-a-week company was both a satisfaction and a frustration to him. She knew he would rather see her this way than lose her, that he took out many other girls and had not fallen in love with any of them. She and Paul had all the outward ease with each other of old friends but very little of the communication. True, when she told him of Miss Farrow's latest harassment she never had to stop to tell him who Miss Farrow was, and he was always sympathetic. He knew Caroline's likes and dislikes to the point where he could order for her in restaurants, and he often said, 'Oh, you don't want the duck, do you? You had that last week.' But these elements in their relationship were more important to Paul than to her. A waiter who knew her well could tell her she'd had the duck last week. But no one but a man she could love could look into her heart and know what she was thinking and show it by his answer to something she had said.

So what then could she give him? Love? Sex? Perhaps some other men would think she was a bitch, she thought, for keeping their relationship on such a semi-pristine plane for so long. And perhaps others would think she was just the kind of innocent virgin girl they had been looking for. Whatever Paul thought about it was a mystery to her. He kept his feelings well hidden. Or, perhaps, Caroline was guiltily beginning to realize, his feelings had been there all along, in his eyes, but she had deliberately kept herself from seeing them.

When the show was over Paul paid the check and they walked for several blocks in the fall night air that was just beginning to turn chilly.

'Are you cold?' he asked, peering at her in the dark. 'You look cold.'

'No, I'm fine.'

'Are you sure?'

'Yes.'

For some reason, tonight his solicitude annoyed her. Was it because he really was clucking over her too much or because she disliked herself for not feeling more grateful? If she had loved him, how happy she would have been that he cared if she was chilly or not! This way her only thought was: I can take care of myself. It was the first time she had felt that way, independent, withdrawn. In her mind's eye there floated the image of a manuscript she had left half read on her desk at five o'clock when she left to meet Paul. It had been an engrossing novel and right now she wished with all her heart that she could know what was going to happen next in it. She should have taken it with her, then she could have curled up in bed and read the rest of it before she went to sleep.

'I can give you my coat,' Paul said, 'if you're cold; or we can take a taxi.'

'Let's take a taxi,' she said. A taxi would be much quicker than walking, and soon she would be home. She was suddenly so depressed she could hardly talk.

She paused at the doorway with her key in the lock. 'May I come in for a minute?' Paul asked.

She didn't care. Let him come in, let him go home, what did it matter? Depression was like a companion, she could almost talk to it. Paul hadn't gotten past the front door in over a month so now that too was becoming a pattern. In the past few months her whole life had become a pattern, predictable, the same.

'Come on in,' she said.

She turned on the lights, and Paul helped her off with her coat and hung it in the closet. 'Would you like a drink?' she asked.

'Yes,' Paul said, quite pleased. 'Scotch and soda, if you have it. And make it light, I've had enough tonight already.'

I must have too, Caroline thought; I feel so tired. She rummaged about in the kitchen. 'I'm sorry, we're out of soda. Will water do?'

'Fine.' Paul settled himself on one of the studio couches and lighted a cigarette. He reached over to the bedside radio and turned it on, moving the dial until he found a program of continuous classical music. She could tell he was digging in for a good long stay, and the knowledge made her feel even more depressed. She didn't want to make pleasant conversation and then allow herself to be kissed for fifteen minutes. She wanted to send him away and turn out the lights and get into bed with her head under the pillow and cry.

She didn't know why she did it, but she made him a very strong drink. The glass was halfway filled with Scotch and three ice cubes before she put the water in. It looked good so she made the same for herself and carried both into the room and sat beside Paul on the studio couch. 'Cheers.'

'Cheers,' he repeated. And then, 'Ouch!'

'Too strong?'

'It's all right,' he said. 'But I'll have to teach you how to make a drink.'

'You always know how to do the right thing,' she mused. 'Don't you?'

'I can make a better drink than you can,' he said happily. He was in a very good mood tonight, the exact opposite of her own. He reached out and ruffled her hair. 'Come sit nearer to me, I feel lonesome.'

Instead Caroline moved farther away. 'I feel lonesome too,' she said. She tried to keep herself from sounding melodramatic, but the very utterance of the words made her lonelier than ever.

'Then come sit over here.'

She was sitting on the very edge of the studio couch, her hands clasped together on her knees. She shook her head. 'Talk to me.'

'All right.'

She couldn't help smiling at that. 'At least you didn't say "What about?" Most people say "What about?" when you ask them to talk to you.'

'You have to give me credit for being more original than that,' Paul said.

'Do you ever get depressed?'

'Sometimes.'

'And what do you do about it?'

He shrugged and took a sip at his caramel-colored drink. 'I just go to sleep if I can. I only get depressed when I'm overtired from working too hard.'

'You know,' Caroline said, 'sometimes when Gregg comes in

late I'm still awake and we sit up and drink milk and talk and talk and talk. I get a mental image of the clock and it's made out of butter and the hands just fall around it like knives. One minute it's two o'clock in the morning and the next time I look it's four-thirty.'

'She must be an interesting person.'

'Oh, she has a wonderful sense of humor, but it's not that. We're both very serious at three o'clock in the morning. We talk mostly about ourselves and – believe it or not – life.'

'And what do you two discover about life in the middle of the night?'

'Nothing,' Caroline said. 'That's the trouble.'

'Do you mind if I tell you something about yourself?' Paul asked.

'Not at all.'

'You take everything much too seriously.'

'I do?'

He had finished most of his drink and his diction was not quite as clear and precise as it usually was. 'What the hell have you got to be so serious about? Where is it all going to lead you? It's one thing to enjoy your job, every girl should have something to do until she's married, but you live with it every minute of the day. You take work home, you worry about office politics, you let Miss Farrow get you down. If you ask me, I think you'd like to have her job eventually.'

'I would,' Caroline admitted.

'For what? So that you can be just like her? A crabby bitch? The shadow of mine enemy.'

Caroline smiled. 'Do you think I show signs of all that?'

'You're much too ambitious, and the worst of it is, you're fighting with windmills. If you had talent as an opera singer or perhaps a painter or an astrophysicist or something like that, then I'd say it was unavoidable. An artist or a genius can't help doing what he does. But you're knocking yourself out for that third-rate little publishing company.'

'It's hardly little,' Caroline said, hurt.

'Do you honestly think you're doing a job that some other girl couldn't step in and do just as well five minutes after you've left?'

'As long as we're being nasty tonight,' Caroline said, 'you're hardly Clarence Darrow. But that doesn't prevent you from living with *your* job twenty-four hours a day and talking about it whenever you're not in the office or bent over some work at home. There are boys in law school right this minute preparing to take the bar exams, perhaps to take away your potential clients a year or two from now.'

'That's different,' Paul said.

'Why is it different?'

'This is my career. It's an integral part of my life. What am I going to do if I don't do this? Starve or become a playboy, depending on my economic situation. Neither prospect appeals to me at all.'

'It's exactly the same with me,' Caroline said indignantly. 'What am *I* going to do? Sit home in Port Blair and polish my nails and wait for a husband? This isn't the nineteen-hundreds. A girl has to do something.'

'You could get married if you wanted to,' Paul said.

She sipped at her drink with intense concentration, trying not to say the wrong thing. It was easy enough for him to say that; she seemed popular, there was nothing wrong with her. Nothing except that there was no one she loved.

'With a little push,' Paul went on, 'I would marry you myself.' The tone was bantering and sentimental both, the words were slightly slurred from the strong drink she had given him. But even drunk, Paul Landis could never be anything but precise and intelligent and self-protective, Caroline realized. He was waiting for her to make the move. If she made a joke of it he would too, if she told him she had always loved him he would fall on his knees and propose. How easy it would be, Caroline thought, and how easy everything would be forever after.

'You're not ready for marriage,' Paul said finally when she had not answered. 'I guess you're too happy living the way you are.'

Happy? Caroline thought. *Happy?* Oh, my God, it's that I don't *love* you.

'You're still thrilled with your girls' dormitory existence,' Paul said. 'But you'd better watch out. Getting to like it too much can turn it into a trap.'

'All right,' Caroline said. She was too tired to argue, too bone weary to try to break her way through this incredible evenness that hid and protected whatever were Paul Landis' true feelings. Or perhaps what she saw of him on the surface actually was what lay inside too. Perhaps he really was Bermuda Schwartz. He was good and kind and contented to the point of smugness, and maybe he had a right to be. She looked at her watch and stood up. 'It's awfully late.'

He stood too. 'I was just leaving. I have to be at the office early tomorrow.'

They walked to the door of her apartment, she staying a little away from him so that he could not reach out and put his arm around her. 'Thank you for a wonderful evening,' she said.

'It was my pleasure.'

At the door they stopped. Paul took her by the waist with both his hands but she turned her head away so that they ended in an embrace but not a kiss. Paul kissed her on the side of her face and she put her head against his shoulder. 'I have a fierce headache,' she murmured into the cloth, wondering whether he would ever accept such a lie. 'I guess it's the hang-over I deserve, but a few hours early.'

He did not release her. 'I just want to keep my arms around you for a minute,' he said, almost gruffly.

Caroline put her arms around Paul's waist and they stood there like that for a moment, leaning against each other. He needs tenderness too, she thought, he must. Everyone does, even Bermuda Schwartz with his hat and gloves. Oh, Paul, I wish with all my heart that I could give that tenderness to you, and that you could give it to me, and that it would be enough.

He moved away from her finally and gave her a little pat. 'You feel wonderful,' he said lightly, 'even for a thin girl.' He picked his hat up off the chest of drawers. 'Next Saturday,' he said. 'I'll call you before. I've inherited two tickets to the opera, my parents are going to Europe.'

'That will be lovely. Good night, Paul. Sleep well.'

As she shut the door she could hear Paul's jaunty footsteps going down the stairs. He was actually whistling. I envy him, Caroline thought, for being busy and content and for finding refuge in Things. His best girl rejects his proposal of marriage; he thinks how nice it will be to go to the opera. Maybe I should try to be more like him. Tomorrow at the office will be better. Tomorrow something good will turn up in my life. When things are darkest, something always does.

What turned up the next day was something Caroline could never have thought of even in a daydream. She was in her tiny office when Miss Farrow came in with an armful of manuscripts that were so dusty and split on the edges from rubbing against their rubber bands that they looked as if they had been shunted around for months.

'You'll have time to read these, won't you?' Miss Farrow said. She put them on Caroline's desk without waiting for a reply.

'What are they?'

'Some of mine. I'm cleaning out my backlog.' Miss Farrow paused and smiled, a small, cold smile with more of smugness in it than happiness. 'I'm leaving on Friday.'

'Leaving!'

'There'll be a memo going around to that effect.'

Caroline didn't quite know what to say. How nice? I'm sorry? The first thought that entered her mind was that Miss Farrow had been fired, but she knew that was impossible. The next thought was that Miss Farrow had found a more comfortable job, but that seemed almost as ridiculous. She finally compromised on: 'This must be quite a shock to everyone.'

'I don't like to leave in such a hurry and leave you all up in the air,' Miss Farrow said. 'And I finally trained my new secretary too. But it can't be helped.'

'Where . . . are you going?' Caroline ventured.

The smile widened. 'I'm getting married. My husband is moving his plant to California, so of course I have to leave Fabian.'

'How exciting!' Caroline gasped, not quite able to grasp it all at once. 'I certainly wish you all the luck in the world.'

'Thank you.'

'When are you getting married?'

'Friday or Saturday. Probably in the country.'

Miss Farrow looked different somehow, softer. Or rather, not as hard. She even looked less suspicious and less frantic. Then suddenly Caroline realized what part of the change was. Miss Farrow was not wearing her hat. Her red hair, pulled back in a chic neat chignon, gleamed under the overhead lights. Caroline felt a rush of warmth for her. She was leaving, the monster was going away. Now at last she wasn't someone to be afraid of and dislike, she was only another woman, whom a man found feminine enough to want to take for his wife. Caroline stood up and held out her hand. 'We'll miss you,' she said.

Miss Farrow's hand was cool and slim, with sharp long nails. 'I'll write once in a while from California,' she said, smiling. 'But I'll see you around before I leave.' They shook hands, like two men, and Miss Farrow went out. Caroline picked up the first manuscript from the pile she had left.

'Why, that old rat!' The date on the blank comment sheet was five months old. And it was a Western. Caroline looked through the other manuscripts in the stack. No wonder they had looked so shop-worn. They were all five and four months old, and they were all Westerns. Caroline knew that Miss Farrow hated to read Westerns as much as she did. But at least I read them, Caroline thought indignantly, I don't hide them!

At half past four Mr Shalimar's secretary telephoned and said he wanted to see her. Caroline took a hasty look in her compact and walked quickly down the hall. Mr Shalimar was seated behind his huge desk, busy with papers. She had not seen him for over two months, except for passing in the hall, and he too seemed to have changed. He looked smaller, less authoritative, less frightening. There was really no one in the office who was afraid of Mr Shalimar any more, they all thought of him as a rather pathetic, lecherous old man, and perhaps by this time he knew it. The story of his behavior at last year's Christmas party had spread immediately afterward and had given courage to those typists and filing clerks who had had similar experiences with him in the past, so that eventually every girl who had been pinched or kissed by Mr Shalimar had come forth, whispering and giggling, to add her story to the office gossip.

'Ah, Miss Bender,' he said, almost eagerly. 'Sit down. Here, next to me.' He gestured to a chair and Caroline took it cautiously. 'I hardly ever see you any more,' he said. He smiled at her, and added coyly, 'You must be avoiding me.'

'No, no, not at all. I've been working very hard.' And she added coyly, to keep up the spirit of the act, 'That's what you want, isn't it?'

'All the same, you should come in to see me once in a while,' Mr Shalimar said. 'I like to know what my favorite editors are doing.'

Caroline did not quite know whether to feel suspicious or pleased. This behavior was strange, to say the least. She said nothing.

'Have you found any exciting new books for us?'

'I'm reading a manuscript now which may turn out to be something.'

'Good,' he said, 'good. Keep at it. Keep turning them out.' He picked up a typewritten sheet of paper from his desk. 'You know of course that Miss Farrow is leaving us.'

'Yes.'

'We'll be sorry to see her go. She's a good editor.'

'Yes,' Caroline said.

'I had thought at first of getting in a new editor to take over Miss Farrow's authors, but then it occurred to me that there are several bright young editors right here who could do the job just as well.' He reached out and handed Caroline the sheet of paper. 'Here is a list of Miss Farrow's authors and the manuscripts some of them are working on. I'm turning them all over to you.'

Caroline's heart turned over with happiness. She took the paper as if it were a rare original document and looked at it. Miss Farrow's authors! Some of them were the pick of the crop. 'Thank you,' she said.

'You'll have to work hard,' Mr Shalimar warned. 'You'll have to keep a watch on what each of these authors is doing, encourage them, write to them if they haven't done anything for us for a while, edit their manuscripts, even listen to their troubles.'

'I'd love that!' But already, through the radiant glow, her mind was clicking away. 'I'll need an expense account to take them to lunch.'

'You'll get it.'

'The same as Miss Farrow's. We don't want them to think they've been handed down to an assistant, that will insult them.'

'Hers was very small, though.'

There he goes, Caroline thought, trying to cut corners. What a liar! 'I know,' she lied in turn, 'she told me what it was.'

'Well, then, of course you'll get the same.'

'Thank you.' She looked down demurely, gathering her courage, and then looked up at him. 'I guess since Christmas is very close I'll be getting some kind of raise in accordance with my promotion. I'd like to ask for twenty dollars a week. I know that isn't as much as Miss Farrow gets, but it seems a fair compromise.'

'Oh, I don't know about a raise,' Mr Shalimar said. 'After all, this new job is quite an honor for you. You'll be getting something, of course, but I wouldn't count on twenty dollars. The company isn't that rich.'

The old bastard, Caroline thought. Now I know why he thinks the 'bright young editors' can do Miss Farrow's job just as well. Half as expensively is what he means. 'I hope you'll keep my request in mind, though,' Caroline said. She stood up. 'And thank you again. I'll try to do a good job.'

'Come see me sometime,' Mr Shalimar said, waving.

Back in her office Caroline read the list of authors excitedly. When Paul had said last night she wanted Miss Farrow's job he had never dreamed she might actually get it. *She* had, but of course it had been a dream. Her pique at Mr Shalimar's financial ruses was gradually fading. She would do a much better job than

Miss Farrow had – anyone could – and then she would get the extra money. And she already had the expense account. She was a real editor, like Miss Farrow, like Mike. A *real editor!*

20

There is something very trying about holidays in a large city, perhaps because everyone feels obliged to be happy. In the country, in a large household, there are preparations for Christmas for many days before, children hang up decorations, trees are trimmed, and some people even make their presents instead of buying them in a department store. Everyone draws together and there is a fine feeling. In the impersonal city, in New York, people who are originally from other places yearn to go home where holiday means family and people they love. Those who stay because they have no family or because they have been invited to enough Yuletide cocktail parties to tip the scales in favor of the lighted fortress huddle together as the crucial days draw near, drinking and laughing and shutting out old memories, as one stops listening to nursery rhymes at a certain age, and the sophisticates among them exclaim to each other, Oh, I *hate* Christmas!

As Christmas drew closer and the old year died slowly in a blaze of lights April Morrison could not decide what to do. Should she go home? She was so grief-stricken after her rejection by Dexter and so embarrassed to face all the relatives who had been told to expect a fall wedding that she wanted to stay in New York and hide. And then, too, in New York was Dexter Key, somewhere, doing something, living and perhaps, finally, accessible. Despite her unhappiness she could not help but be thrilled by the lights along Fifth Avenue, the choirboys high on top of Saks with voices that actually sang in the evenings, the huge tree at Rockefeller Center with its enormous luminous Christmas balls, the tree attached to the front of the Lord and Taylor building made of hundreds of little light bulbs. And the store windows! The skaters that whirled mechanically on circles of mirror ice, the princesses and the angels and the fluff and the tinsel and the music that played until all hours of the night while people slowly filed by, held in by velvet ropes, peering into the lighted windows, stuffing freezing hands into their pockets and listening to their children exclaim with joy. April loved all this with all the delight of a tourist's heart, but it also saddened her because when she finally went home to her apartment her little tree looked so lonely and artificial on the bridge table and there was no one she loved to look at it with her.

She knew that on Christmas Eve Dexter's parents held a huge open house. They invited all their friends and many of Dexter's friends. The year before she had not gone, she had been in Colorado. But she knew where they lived and she knew what she was going to do.

Maybe it was a crazy thing to do but she didn't care. Knowing she was going to do it made her feel happy for the first time since Dexter had left her. When she dressed on Christmas Eve in her most beautiful dress her hands were shaking. She had had her hair done, she had taken twenty minutes with her make-up. She looked, she thought, like Cinderella going to the ball, and perhaps she was. The prince, at any rate, would be there.

She went to Dexter's parents' house in a taxi, so as to be sure not to muss her hair. She arrived at a quarter to eleven. It was late enough so that no one would notice her entrance and if they did they would be so full of Christmas punch they would be glad to see another pretty girl. She was trembling, happy and excited and frightened all at the same time. A burst of noise greeted her when she stepped out of the elevator. There was a huge fat wreath pinned to the Keys' front door and the door was locked. April smoothed her hair and rang the bell.

A maid opened the door, a thin little maid in a shiny black dress with a tiny white apron. She had evidently been hired only for this occasion because she looked at April blankly, liked what she saw, smiled timidly, and said, 'Come in. Ladies' coats this way.'

April walked quickly behind the maid, looking around. It

seemed to be an enormous apartment, with huge high-ceilinged rooms and expensive-looking French furniture and many mirrors. One of the rooms, the den, had coat racks lined up in it. The maid hung April's year-old beige cashmere coat between a brown mink and a black seal. 'Go right into the living room,' she said and darted away, leaving April alone.

So this was Dexter's parents' house. She felt as though she loved everything in it because they were things that were close to him. Perhaps this den was the room he had used as a child. She walked toward the noise and the press of guests, glancing through half-opened doors as she went. There was a room with a double bed – perhaps his parents' room. And a guest room, or was that one his old room? She loved them all, she wanted to run inside and look at all his former things. Instead she worked her way through the crowd to a table set with a great crystal punch bowl and accepted a cupful from a uniformed butler. Next to the punch table was a tall Christmas tree, reaching right up to the ceiling, covered with ornaments and piled up to its lower branches with elaborately wrapped presents. It was like the tree her family had at home and it made her feel more at ease and more hopeful about the outcome of this whole evening.

She looked around for Dexter. At first she did not see him in this mob of merrymakers, and then she did, tall and dark and frighteningly familiar against the drawn white silk curtains of a window across the room. He had a glass in his hand and he was talking to a girl who was much shorter than he, so that April could hardly see her over the heads of the crowd. Dexter, she thought, oh, Dexter. She only wanted to stand there, invisible and unnoticed, and look at him, terrified of being hurt by him again and longing to keep that face she loved in her sight forever.

Her hand was trembling so much that she almost spilled her punch on her dress. She drank it to get rid of it, hardly tasting the sweet fruity taste. It had liquor in it, gin or something. Maybe that's what I need, she thought, and went to the table for another, turning her head several times to keep track of Dexter. He seemed set, he wasn't going to move away for a while. He was drinking a highball, not punch. April wanted to sneak up and confront him, smiling and looking as if nothing had happened between them, but she was afraid to take a step. She held out her cup for more punch, smiling instead at the butler, who smiled back and said, 'Yes, indeed!' as if he was glad to have wooed someone away from the bar and the stronger liquor. The punch was strong enough for April. She felt a warm glow and she was beginning to relax, and as she did her yearning for a word from Dexter became unbearable. She pushed her way toward him.

'Hi,' someone said. She looked up, dreading any interruption. It was a friend of Dexter's, a boy with a white nothing-face and short brown hair.

'Oh . . . it's Chet, isn't it?'

'That's right. How're you, April?'

'Fine,' she lied, smiling nervously and wondering how to get rid of him.

'I haven't seen you since this summer,' Chet said.

She remembered him more clearly now, he was the boy who had always seemed to be making vague passes at her when Dexter wasn't looking. She'd never been sure whether he liked her or was just a wolf, or if he knew about her and Dexter. Now she didn't care, she only wanted to get away from his polite conversation and get to Dexter.

'Are you here with someone?' Chet asked.

'I . . . no . . . yes.'

'No. I was invited.'

'No, yes?' He was grinning at her.

'No. I was invited.'

'Well, I'm alone too,' he said happily. 'Can I get you a drink?'

'Not right now, thank you. I have to see someone.'

'Dexter?'

She looked at him, open and startled. 'Why?'

'Well, you two used to be good friends.' What was that, a grin or a leer?

'We still are,' April said, 'and I want to say hello to him since he's the host. I'll see you later.'

He held up a hand. 'I'll see you if you don't.

She moved toward the window, keeping her

Then she was right in front of him, so close that s

his aftershave cologne. It was a faint scent but it hit her

ally that it almost staggered her. 'Dexter,' she said.

He looked down at her. There was absolutely no ex

on his face to give away his feelings at that moment, not ick,

not surprise, not annoyance, not even inadvertent pleasure.

'Hello there,' he said. He paused for a moment and then turned

to the girl he was with and introduced them. 'Ruth Potter, April

Morrison.'

'How do you do.' The two girls looked at each other for an

instant, sizing each other up. Ruth Potter was small, with a round

face and a bright green dress. She seemed satisfied after a moment

that April was simply another cocktail-party room circulator and

not competition, and so she smiled and said, 'I'll see you later,

Dexter, Bunny will kill me if I don't make obeisance,' and moved

on to another group.

'Who is she?' April asked.

'An old friend.' Dexter was already starting to move away. 'I have

to get another drink.'

'Are you surprised to see me?'

'What do you think?'

'I . . . haven't seen you for a long time.'

'How are you?' he asked finally, like someone remembering his

manners.

'Oh, Dexter,' April whispered. 'Oh, Dexter . . . I've been so sick.

You don't know.' Her eyes filled with tears and she had to fight to

keep her voice from breaking. She didn't want to make a scene

right here, that wasn't what she had come for.

'What's wrong?' he asked. For the first time he sounded slightly

concerned.

'It's so terrible,' she whispered.

'Well, what is it?' He was even more concerned now.

'I haven't been able to sleep or eat or anything. I lost ten pounds.'

'*Why?*'

could hardly answer. She knew what he expected, he wanted her to say she had some disease, he seemed to be waiting for catastrophe. Nothing less than catastrophe would satisfy him now because he had been aroused and he was upset. She realized it too late, but there was no going back.

'What is it?' Dexter repeated.

'I miss you so dreadfully.'

'Oh.' His expression of curiosity and concern turned to annoyance. 'Is *that* all?'

She touched his wrist, trying to take his hand. 'You're the only man I ever loved,' she whispered. 'You were my first love. I love you so much. Please give me another chance.'

'For what?' he asked. He shook his hand away from her touch with a swift reflex action, as a cat shakes off the hand of an annoying human being who is trying to pat him.

'We could start again, we could see each other. I'll never mention marriage to you. Please just see me. I want to talk to you . . .'

'What's there to talk about? I'm not going to talk about you and me.'

'We used to talk about so many things.'

'And they're all said.'

'Dexter . . . don't you love me at all?'

'Are you going to nag me about that now?'

'Please tell me.'

Dexter looked around furtively. 'Are you going to make a scene in front of my friends?'

'Can't we go somewhere and talk? Just for a minute. The den . . .'

He looked at her with obvious impatience. 'All right.'

He walked ahead of her, smiling at guests who greeted him along the way, and April followed him blindly, pushing people out of her path. They went into the guest bedroom and Dexter shut the door. 'Now what do you want to say?'

She could not talk, she was crying. She wanted him so desperately to take her into his arms, even stroke her hair, do something to show that he cared for her if only as another person who was crying her heart out and wishing she could die. But he did none of these things, he simply stood there holding his empty highball glass and watching her.

'What's the matter?' he asked finally.

'I call you and you don't answer the phone,' April sobbed. 'I just want to hear your voice, I wouldn't even care if you didn't ask me out. I can't bear not to be with you. You've gotten to mean so much in my life, I can't bear it without you. Everything reminds me of you.'

'What good would talking on the phone do?' Dexter asked. 'You'd only get around to asking me to see you and I'm not going to do that.'

'Why?'

'I wish I'd brought a drink,' he said, 'I can't stand here carrying on this stupid conversation without a drink. This is a party. What are you trying to do?'

'Dexter,' April said, 'will you tell me one thing? Tell me truthfully and I won't bother you any more.'

'What is it?'

It was the moment, the terrible moment that should never have happened and could never have been avoided. 'Did you ever *really* love me?'

Dexter looked at her for a moment and then shrugged. 'I never really thought about it,' he said.

What else could she say? It was all over. He had forgotten or he was frightened or perhaps he was telling the truth. It did not matter. He did not love her now and he was busy forgetting everything he had said to her because it had happened so long ago. Everything was over.

'Thank you,' April said softly. She wiped her eyes with her handkerchief and blew her nose. 'I just wanted you to tell me.'

'I'm going back to the party now,' Dexter said. 'Fix yourself up and come on back and meet some of my friends. Have a few drinks. You might as well have a good time as long as you're here.' He walked to the door and opened it.

'Dexter!'

343

'What?'

'I just want to tell you something. I'll always love you, as long as I live.'

'No you won't,' Dexter said calmly. He walked out and shut the bedroom door behind him.

When April emerged from the guest bedroom half an hour later she looked like a changed person. She had washed her face and put on fresh make-up and combed her hair. But it was the expression that made her look most different. She had seen it in the bathroom mirror and it had surprised her. The smile was fixed, the nostrils pulled a little from the effort, the eyes were bright and round, like those of a doll. She looked enough like a stranger so that she could evaluate her looks almost objectively. She's a pretty girl, April thought of her face in the mirror. She's hard looking, though, she looks a little reckless. She looks like a girl who does nothing but go to parties and drink and flirt and laugh and laugh and laugh.

She walked out of the bedroom with her head held high and went straight to the bar, where she had two straight Scotches. It was funny, the taste of liquor had always seemed unpleasant to her but tonight it tasted good. She hadn't had dinner, so she ate a cherry and an olive from two bowls on the bar. That took care of dinner. She wasn't looking anywhere because she didn't want to see Dexter, she just drank and smiled.

She felt a warm hand on her arm. 'I knew I'd see you,' Chet said. 'May I join you?'

'Of course.'

'What are you drinking?'

'Scotch.'

'Smart girl. That punch is a waste of time.'

'Lots of things are,' April said brightly. 'So we just look for something better.'

'You are right,' Chet said. 'You are right.' He put his hand on her waist.

'Do you have a cigarette?'

'Right here.' He lighted it for her. She had perhaps smoked four cigarettes in her life but she drew on it deeply without inhaling and felt better.

'Thank you,' she said.

'Refill?'

'Love it.'

They clicked their newly filled glasses together and April tossed her head, her hair swirling about her face, and smiled at him. He put his arm around her waist. 'You're such a fun girl,' Chet said. 'I'm sorry we never got to know each other better.'

'Why, is it too late?'

'Is it?'

'When it's too late to have a good time,' April said brightly, 'you might just as well give up and die.'

'I'll drink to that.' He did. So did she.

There was Dexter with Ruth Potter again, walking past the bar. April saw them as two Dexters and two Ruth Potters. Her face felt hot. Dexter was avoiding looking at her but she knew he was aware of her. Let him think she didn't care. Her smile was so fixed it felt like a grimace.

'It's hot in here; isn't it?' Chet said.

'Terribly.'

'I can't even hear myself talk.'

'I can't either.'

'Let's go downtown to one of the better bistros and usher in Christmas Day with a glass of hot grog,' Chet said. 'Do you have to visit relatives tomorrow?'

'I have no relatives in New York.'

'Good. I don't have to visit my family until four o'clock. We'll have plenty of time to nurse our hang-overs.'

'It'll be my first Christmas Day in New York and my first hang-over,' April said. She laughed.

'And your first date with me.'

She went to the den to get her coat, and Chet waited for her at the front door. She tried not to think of anything as they shut the door to the apartment behind them, only of when she would get another drink and how much nicer it would make her feel. Chet sat very close to her in the taxi and she pretended he wasn't there. But she felt the warmth of him and it was comforting to feel the warmth of another human being even though he hardly existed for her. There was a buzzing in her ears.

'Merry Christmas,' Chet said. He put his arms around her and began kissing her, with her head against the back of the taxi seat. Her eyes were closed and the cab was going round and round and she hardly knew what she was doing. She had the feeling he was slobbering on her chin, but what did it really matter? His hand on her chest bone just above the cut-out neckline of her dress felt very cold.

On New Year's Eve at nine o'clock Mary Agnes Russo DeMarco
was dressing to go out to a party. 'Zip me up, honey,' she said,
turning her back to her husband Bill.

He did, with effort. 'You're getting fat,' he said affectionately.
They both beamed at each other. She was pregnant, the baby was
expected in the summer, and she just wanted to eat and eat all the
time. This would probably be the last time she could squeeze herself
into this party dress, but she didn't mind. She already had a wardrobe
of maternity clothes and she could hardly wait to put them on.

'Honestly,' Mary Agnes said, 'I never thought Dotty and Bo
were going to get around to giving this party. I thought we were
going to be stuck without anything to do tonight.'

'We could have given a party,' Bill said.

'I guess so. But after all the money we spent on the wedding
and our honeymoon it wouldn't have been much of a party. We
have to save now, you know.'

'I know,' he said. And they beamed at each other again.

'I can't imagine New Year's Eve without a party,' Mary Agnes
said, 'can you?'

'Uh-uh. How many people are they having?'

'I think about twelve.'

'Are they having champagne?'

'I hope so,' Mary Agnes said worriedly. 'I just can't imagine New
Year's Eve without champagne. Can you?'

'No.'

'Maybe we should bring them a bottle,' Mary Agnes said. 'Do
you think so?'

'Yes . . . just in case.'

'Can we afford it?'

'Sure,' Bill said. 'Just one bottle. After all, it wouldn't be New Year's Eve without a bottle of champagne.'

At eleven o'clock on New Year's Eve Gregg Adams and David Wilder Savage were sneaking out of a party that was going on full force. They shut the front door of their host's apartment softly so no one would hear them and ran down the hall to the stairs, hand in hand. 'Shh,' David said.

They reached the first floor, panting. 'Why are people always so insulted when you try to leave their parties?' Gregg asked happily.

'Because they're so bored when there are only a few people left; then they have to talk to each other.'

'Oh . . .' She laughed and they ran to a taxi, which took them to David's apartment. He lighted a fire in the fireplace and put a chilled bottle of champagne and two crystal champagne glasses on the table in front of it. He put a stack of records on the phonograph and sat beside Gregg on the couch.

'Now,' he said, 'we can welcome in the New Year in peace.'

Gregg was holding his hand with one hand and with the other she was fingering a tiny gold heart she wore on a fragile chain around her neck. David had given it to her for Christmas and she had never taken it off her neck since that day, not even to take a bath. She would never take it off, she was thinking, until she was married to him or to someone else. She had wanted an engagement ring desperately, but of course he was not the kind of man who would present her with an engagement ring, and so he had done the next best thing: given her a sentimental present that could be taken either as significant or as nothing. A heart meant love. But a tiny golden heart could also be only a piece of jewelry, and perhaps only time would tell her which it was supposed to be.

'What a perfect New Year's Eve,' Gregg said, sighing. 'I hope fifty-four will be just as happy. Or better.'

'Better than perfect?'

'You never know,' Gregg said, 'until it happens.'

At eleven-forty-five on New Year's Eve Barbara Lemont and her mother were in their living room listening to the radio. They had listened to crowds of people waiting for the New Year halfway around the country, in Crystal Palace ballrooms and Blue Twilight lounges and Hilton hotels, and now they were listening to the horn-blowing and revelry in Times Square. *In just fourteen minutes the gold ball will go up the Times Tower*, the voice of the announcer said, *and when it reaches the top it will be nineteen fifty-four!*

'Why don't you turn on the television,' Barbara's mother said. 'We can watch the people.'

'Do you want to?'

'Sure. It's New Year's Eve, isn't it? We'll listen to the radio *and* the television.'

Barbara switched on the television set. 'It'll be murder,' she said.

'I don't know how those silly people can go out there and get trampled on and call it fun,' her mother said. 'I'll bet there are a lot of drunks in that crowd.'

'I guess so.'

'And purse-snatchers,' her mother added cheerfully.

Barbara sighed. It didn't matter so much that she didn't have a date, it would only have been with someone she didn't care about anyway. New Year's Eve was such a long evening with someone dull, everyone felt he had to stay up late as a matter of principle. Soon it would be twelve o'clock and then it would be morning and she could forget all about this ordeal for another year. Where was Sidney now, what was he doing? Did he ever think of her? He probably thought she was at a party having a good time with some eligible man, if he thought of her at all. She had wondered so often lately whether he still thought of her, although she had tried to put him out of her mind.

'Cheer up,' her mother said. 'Lots of girls don't have dates tonight. I'll bet you're not the only one.'

'I don't mind.'

'Next year will be better. You'll see.'

Next year . . . Barbara thought. I wonder whether I'll still be thinking of Sidney. No one carries a torch for that long, not even an idiot like me. I wonder where I'll be next year and who I'll be with. It seems as though every New Year's Eve that you sit alone or go out with someone you hardly know or can't bear, you think of all the other New Year's Eves you've done the same thing, and it seems as if it's endless. Sidney said something like that once, he said when things are bad it seems as if they've always been that way. Oh, Sidney, if I could only call you up and have you cheer me for five minutes. It would make all the difference in the world. Or would it? Would it really?

At one minute to midnight, the last seconds of nineteen fifty-three, when the gold ball had started traveling up the Times Tower and all over the city people were reaching for champagne glasses or for their companions and preparing for the hearty wishes and round of kissing, someone at a party in the East Thirties reached out and turned off all the lights. 'Hey,' someone else cried, 'turn 'em back on! I can't find my date!'

Everyone laughed and the lights were switched on again. Caroline Bender was standing in front of a Christmas tree with Paul Landis. 'One minute,' he said, looking at his watch.

She smiled nervously and looked elsewhere. What time is it in Dallas, she wondered.

'Midnight!' someone cried. 'Happy New Year!'

'Happy New Year,' Paul said quietly. Everyone around them was in embrace, kissing each other to welcome in the new year, some of them taking advantage of the moment for all it was worth. Paul looked a little embarrassed with all these people around, and he took hold of Caroline's shoulders very lightly and leaned down to put his lips on hers chastely and briefly. But the contact was too much for him and he put his arms around her and pressed her to him.

Her eyes were shut. Eddie, my darling, she thought, willing her thoughts across the entire country to wherever he might be, Happy

New Year, darling. I still think of you. Remember me, just for this one minute. Remember me.

She broke away from Paul's arms and lips as gently as she could. 'Happy New Year, Paul.'

'Stop necking, all you kids,' their hostess cried gaily. 'Especially you old married ones. Shame on you. We can eat now. Caviar! And more champagne coming up.'

'Shall we?' Paul asked Caroline. He held out his arm and she took it and they walked together to the buffet table, skirting their way around one couple who were newly married and evidently didn't care at all whether there was caviar or not.

At half past four on New Year's morning, which was still New Year's Eve to some people, April Morrison was leaving El Morocco with a young man named Jeffrey, who was a friend of Chet's, who was a friend of Dexter's. She was more than slightly drunk and she tripped as she tried to get into the cab. Jeffrey, who had sobered somewhat in the chill air of early morning, took her arm quickly and they fell into the taxi together, laughing and clutching each other, and rode that way all the way across town to her apartment.

'May I come up?' he asked, but he was already halfway up the first flight of stairs and April did not even have to answer. They sang and laughed and hushed each other as they climbed the stairs, and stopped on each landing to hug and kiss.

'We look like two bears,' April said, 'with our coats on. I can't get my arms around you.'

'We'll soon remedy that.'

In the apartment she went directly to the bridge table, which was now a bar. 'Look!' she cried, holding up a Scotch bottle. 'It's empty. What happened to it?'

Jeffrey thought for moment, seriously. 'Somebody drank it,' he said at last.

'I know who!'

'Who?'

'Me! This afternoon.' It seemed very funny and she laughed and laughed. 'No,' she said, 'it was yesterday. Yesterday afternoon.

When I thought I wouldn't have a date for New Year's Eve. Before you called. I was so depressed.'

'I'm glad I called,' he said.

'So am I.'

He took off his coat and dropped it on the floor and April did the same. He was a good-looking boy, she thought; not really her type because she liked dark men like Dexter, but good-looking anyway. This was only the third time she'd gone out with him and she had been as surprised as all get out when he'd called and asked for New Year's Eve. She wondered whether Chet had told him anything about the two of them, and at first she had worried about it, but Jeffrey hadn't been hard to handle. Chet had. It made her rather sick to her stomach to remember what she had done with Chet, and that was why she didn't see him any more. Now that she looked back at it she wondered what she had ever seen in Chet and how she could have done it. But she wasn't going to think about it any more. It was over.

Jeffrey was looking around the room. April was glad she'd cleaned it up, her clothes were hung away in the closet and her bed was neatly put back into the wall. It looked a little like the living room of a three-room apartment, there was the kitchen, there were the two closed doors; why, he might even think she was rich. She hoped he did. Maybe he would think more highly of her than Dexter had, he wouldn't think she was a little hick. He thought she was simply a friend of Chet's and a former girl of Dexter Key's. Why, she could be anybody.

'*Now* we're not bears,' Jeffrey said. He advanced toward her with open arms.

'There's still some gin,' April said quickly.

'I don't want gin.'

'I do.'

She poured the gin into a glass with an unsteady hand and ran away from him into the kitchenette to pull a tray of ice cubes out of her icebox and rip up the lever. The cubes rattled into the sink, and April snatched three of them and dropped them into her glass. The gin spattered up onto her dress.

'Oh,' he said, 'you've messed your dress.'

He was trying to wipe off the dampness with her kitchen towel and put his arms around her at the same time, and April was trying to put the glass of gin up to her mouth. She managed finally and took a large swallow, fighting to keep it down. She'd never had straight gin before, but it wasn't bad, it was rather like a Martini. Jeffrey kept trying to kiss her and she kept turning her head and trying to get at the gin, and finally they compromised and she would let him kiss her and then he would let her take a swallow from her glass until the gin was all gone.

'Ahh . . .' he murmured, 'drop that damned glass.' He took it from her hand and put it on the drainboard.

'Who are you?'

'Jeffrey.'

'Do you love me?'

'I adore you.'

'Really?'

'Yes.' He was trying to unzip her dress.

'I don't love you,' April said.

'You don't?'

'No. I hate you.' She didn't say it with animosity, she simply said it.

'That's all right.'

'Is it?'

'Yes,' Jeffrey said. He kissed her. 'It's all right.'

'Don't bite.'

'No.'

'I hate you,' April said again, pleasantly.

'All right.'

She was cold without her dress. 'Ahhh . . .' he sighed, and lifted her in his arms. It was like a scene from a love novel, April thought dizzily, the dashing hero lifting the heroine, carrying her to a satin-covered bed. Jeffrey turned his head, looking for the bed. There was none, nor was there a couch, but there was a door. He headed for it, carrying April in his arms, and when he was close enough to the door he reached out one hand and turned the knob and pulled it open. April closed her eyes, her arms wound tightly around his neck so that she would not fall. 'Darling . . .' he murmured in her ear and pulled down the in-the-wall bed.

He knew what that door was all along, April thought, he wasn't fooled at all. The only way he could have known was that Chet must have told him. She was so humiliated that she wanted to get right up out of bed, but it was too late; and so she kept her eyes closed tightly and summoned up the feeling the gin had given her, the feeling that it didn't really matter because life was so much fun, so much fun.

22

Spring. Everything is softer, the air is soft with a reminder still of cold and promise of the warmth to come, the landscape is softened with new tiny pale-green leaves. Girls from offices on their lunch hours linger in the patch of spring sunshine that falls on the sidewalk in front of their building, they don't want to go back in, they'd rather walk in the park. Perhaps some of them do. They lunch on hot dogs from a white wagon and stroll down paths between bushes of frothy yellow forsythia and feel their hearts fill with an indescribable feeling: happiness, hope, poignance, impatience. In Rockefeller Center workmen are setting up tables where the skating rink used to be, under the great statue of Prometheus, and in the park there is the sound of children's roller skates where there used to be the silent slip of blades. There is something very evocative about children roller-skating in the springtime, it seems to tie all the generations together in the stream of life. Some things never change. The typists on their lunch hours remember when they used to skate on the sidewalks in front of their houses, or in the park, like these children, and it seems such a short time ago. They remember the scraped knees, how it felt to fall, and the freedom of speed when they got up to try again, and the exciting, tooth-rattling feeling of metal wheels rushing over rough concrete. They are old enough now to have children of their own, and perhaps in a year or two or three they will. And some spring not so far away their own children will be swooping down the paths of the park on a Sunday afternoon, skating through the tunnels and calling out to hear the sounds of their own voices echoing back to them.

Barbara Lemont's daughter Hillary was four years old that spring of 1954. She herself was twenty-two. One could never be quite sure if they were sisters or mother and daughter when she took Hillary walking in the park. They looked exactly alike, straight light-brown hair pulled back behind the ears, Hillary's in two pigtails, Barbara's in a barrette, small slight bodies, calm gentle faces. They both wore gray coats that spring, with white pearl buttons, and Hillary carried her first handbag, infinitesimal, made of imitation red patent leather, just large enough for her doll-size handkerchief and her toy lipstick.

Barbara was quite successful for a young career girl, with her two columns published every month with a by-line. She went to cocktail parties given by cosmetic companies to introduce a new shade of lipstick and nail polish, and by chemical companies to introduce a new fiber, and by perfumeries to show off a new kind of perfume and cologne. She ate fried codfish balls on toothpicks and tiny sausages and drank Martinis and watched tall, thin models take baths in colored bubbles or stroll about in weird abbreviated costumes, for which they were paid ten dollars an hour and for which she was paid nothing. She met many male buyers and writers who were middle aged and married and exceedingly bored with these parties and often were not quite sure why they had been invited. Some of them asked her out for dinner, but she always refused. She met career women in their thirties and forties who always dressed like the fashion pages of the magazines they worked for and seemed much less bored than the men. And she met several girls her own age who wore dark-green nylon stockings and a great deal of eye make-up and carried little notebooks, who looked about furtively and excitedly and often accepted the dinner invitations of the older men whom Barbara had refused. It was a world where Barbara had finally achieved a toe hold, and where she was accepted and even recognized, but where she herself felt she only half belonged. Because at the end of the parties she went home, and home was not a garden apartment with a red telephone and three giggling girls and a casserole supper by candlelight, but a walk-up filled with the worn, respectable furniture of twenty-five years of living, with a child's tricycle in the middle of the living-room floor and a television set that blared out a housewife's futile dreams on 'Queen for a Day.'

She still thought of Sidney Carter, at night when she was tired and could no longer censor her thoughts, or sometimes when she was in the crowded elevator after lunch, filled with male executives and the scent of gin, all of them bound for other floors and other lives and all of them oblivious of her. She could imagine his routine, and imagining it brought her a certain comfort. He's eating lunch now, she would think, or, he's on the train now, reading all those newspapers. She was not so sure about the evening train, and that hurt. She wondered whether he was having cocktails with a woman, a sophisticated, older career woman who had had many affairs and would be fascinated by but never fall in love with a Sidney Carter.

That spring Barbara's husband Mac remarried. She was not quite prepared for the feeling the news gave her: shock, fright, pleasure because she really wanted him to be happy, but most of all the knowledge that a period of her life was over forever. He telephoned and asked if he could fetch Hillary and introduce her to his wife, and Barbara's first reaction was one of panic. *She's all I have*, she thought. But then she realized that Hillary had been living with her for almost all of her four years, and that Hillary loved her, and so she said, 'Yes, Mac. Come over.' He evidently thought it would be bad taste to introduce his wife to Barbara as well, and Barbara did not suggest it. She did not think she could face meeting the wife of a man she had once loved, it would remind her too much of Sidney. So on a Sunday morning Mac arrived at the apartment and took Hillary by the hand and led her out to the street where his wife was waiting in their car by the curb, and Barbara had the strangest feeling: that she was a stone in the middle of a wildly rushing river, stationary and buffeted, always the same, while life went by and changed all around her.

On the first really warm spring day, when automobile sounds came in through the wide-open windows, two things happened. Barbara remembered it afterward as a very strange day, because in the course of four hours she changed from believing in nothing to believing that everything in life was good. She ate lunch at her desk because she had a great deal of work to do, and then she suddenly decided she could not bear another moment of air conditioning on a fine spring day and so she opened her window and leaned out over the sill looking at the people and taxis down below, like colored specks, and the office buildings blocks away, misty in the afternoon warmth. She breathed deeply and her heart began to pound. And then all of a sudden she was crying, not with tears but a kind of dry, straining contortion, throat aching, mouth open without sound, eyes tightly shut. She was shaking all over, because it was spring, because it was warm, because she was alone, and because it seemed at this moment as if she could never bear another instant of her life. It wasn't anyone special she was crying for, she had gotten over that, it was simply that she was shaken with a need to give, to love, to expand with the warmth of every living thing in the changing season, and no one seemed to care. When the telephone rang she hardly heard it, and finally she turned as if in a trance and picked the receiver up.

She didn't know why she had answered it, because she knew she was going to hang up in an instant. It was curiosity that made her answer, that was all. 'Hello.'

'Barbara . . .'

'Oh . . .'

'Barbara . . . it's Sidney.'

'Oh,' she said again. She sat down, holding the receiver in her two hands.

'I didn't think you'd be in,' Sidney said. 'I thought I'd take the chance.'

'How are you?' she said, amazed at how well her voice was holding up, not betraying her feelings at all.

'Wonderful. How are you?'

'Fine.'

'I was wondering,' he said, 'have you had lunch yet?'

'Lunch?' she repeated stupidly.

'I know it's the last minute. I just had a business lunch date broken and it's the only day I have free this week to do whatever I want. So I thought I'd call you.'

'I'm surprised,' Barbara said.

'Could you have lunch with me?'

She was trembling. 'Yes,' she said, her voice very steady, 'I'll meet you downstairs if that's convenient for you.'

She waited for him in front of her office building, as she had those two evenings so long ago and she wondered whether he would think she had changed. She had no idea why he had called all of a sudden but she would not let herself analyze it. All she knew was that one moment she had been leaning out a window feeling like the most insignificant speck on earth and now she felt as if something extraordinary was about to happen to her. She tried to think of the worst thing that could possibly happen, so that she would not be disappointed. He doesn't want me to write the column any more. That was pretty bad. It was also unbelievable.

He stepped out of a taxi and he looked so completely unchanged that it frightened her. She was back in that moment to last summer, and nothing had changed at all. She knew she still loved him, that she had never stopped loving him, and that frightened her the most.

He walked over to her and smiled, holding out his hand as one does to a business acquaintance. Not knowing what else to do, Barbara shook hands. 'Hi,' Sidney said. 'You look exactly the same.'

'Do I?' She was smiling, terrified, so intent on what she would say to him to hide her feelings that she almost did not have any feelings at all.

'Do you want to eat outside?'

'Yes.'

They began to walk toward the place that had been the skating rink in winter and now was an outdoor café with small tables and umbrellas. 'You look happy,' Sidney said, glancing at her as they walked, 'or I should say, exceedingly content. Your life must be agreeing with you.'

'I like my job,' Barbara said. 'It's very exciting.'

'You look like a girl who's in love. I hope you're not just in love with your job?'

'I don't think I'm that type, really,' Barbara said lightly. She shrugged. 'Maybe I'm just in love with spring. That happens.'

'I haven't seen you for such a long time,' Sidney said.

They walked down the steps to the outdoor café and found a table next to the fountain that spurted from the statue of Prometheus. 'This is nice,' Barbara said.

'What would you like to drink?'

'A Martini, please.'

'I haven't seen you for such a long time,' he repeated. 'I thought you'd be engaged by now. I used to look in the papers sometimes.'

'Did you?'

He nodded.

'Well, I'm not.'

'You're in love, though.'

She smiled, as if it didn't matter in the least. 'No, not today.'

The waiter arrived with their Martinis, and Barbara and Sidney smiled at each other and sipped at their drinks and smiled at each other again, like idiots. Barbara felt as if she were going to faint.

'I missed you,' he said finally.

'Not very much.'

'*Very* much.'

'I missed you too,' she whispered.

'Barbara . . .'

'Why did you call me?' she asked.

His voice was so casual it was almost as if he had said, 'I'm going to Florida for my vacation.' He said, 'I'll be divorced in two more weeks.'

'Divorced . . .'

'Those things happen.'

'I guess they do.'

His voice was still casual but very gentle. 'My wife's going to remarry after the divorce. Someone we've known for years. Those things happen too. I wanted to tell you that so you wouldn't feel uncomfortable; you have a way of feeling uncomfortable about the oddest things.'

'My husband remarried last month,' Barbara said. 'Spring must be marrying time.'

'Yes.'

'That's funny,' Barbara said. Hold on, she told herself, hold on to yourself, don't fly apart. This isn't the time, you don't even know if it will ever be the time again. She kept looking at him, carefully, to see if she was saying the wrong thing, to know when to stop. How could you expect someone else to go on feeling the same way you had for all those months? It was too much for any rational person to hope for. 'Do you have any special plans?' she asked casually.

'For what?'

'For the spring. For summer. For people.'

'Yes. In a way.'

'Oh?'

The waiter came over then, brandishing two menus, and Sidney waved him away. Barbara leaned forward, her hands clasped tightly in her lap so he would not see how they were trembling. 'Such a long time,' Sidney said.

'It was a hundred years ago and it was yesterday,' she said.

'For me too.'

She tried to keep her voice detached, as if she were discussing a love affair that had happened between two other people. 'Sometimes I used to think it was a shame I felt the way about you that I did, because it's so much worse to lose something special than never to have it at all. And then I thought . . . it's better just to have had it.'

'You sound as if it's over.'

'No,' she said, 'no, it isn't. For me at least. I don't think it is.'

'I used to hope you would start to dislike me,' Sidney said. 'I thought I was doing you a favor. Then I was afraid you did dislike me.'

'I'd never dislike you.'

The waiter came over again, insistently, because it was the height of the lunch hour and it was crowded. 'Another drink, sir?' Sidney nodded impatiently and the waiter whisked up their empty glasses and went away.

'Oh,' Barbara said. 'Hold my hand.'

He did, instantly, and something that had been holding them apart seemed to break away with their mutual touch so that each clung to the other with both hands, and they looked into each other's face with a look that was pained and showed the beginning of amazement. Suddenly Barbara didn't care any longer if she said the wrong thing or not. She blurted it out and as she did she could hear her voice thicken in her throat and she didn't care about that either. 'I love you,' she said. 'I've always loved you. Don't hurt me again. I'd just gotten over it and now it's all back, just the same. If you care about me tell me now, but don't make me wait any more and don't make me guess. I never want to have to guess about anyone again.'

He was holding her hands so tightly that she could feel his pulse through his fingers. 'You'll never have to guess about me again,' he said, and he sounded almost as if he were the one who was asking for the favor. 'I love you too.'

She said it again, because it was such a warm, beautiful feeling to be able to say it, 'I love you.'

'I love you,' he repeated softly.

'God, let's get out of here. I'm going to cry.'

'Don't you dare.'

He stood up, pulled out Barbara's chair, and dropped some bills on the table. As they left they nearly collided with their waiter, who was carrying a small round tray with their fresh drinks on it and who looked very vexed. 'We never seem to finish a meal together,' Barbara said, laughing.

'I know.'

'What do you want to do?'

'Look at you. Talk to you. Hold you. What do you want to do?'

'The same.'

'It's been so long,' he said again.

'Yes. And all the time I thought it was I who was missing you.'

'No, darling,' Sidney said. 'Do you have to go back to your office this afternoon?'

Barbara shook her head.

'Won't they mind?'

She smiled up at him, winding her fingers in his, feeling him return the pressure immediately, as he always had, as she knew now he always would. 'No,' she said. 'And I don't care if they do. I don't care if I never go back to my office again.'

23

It was Caroline's third summer at Fabian and she felt as though she had been there for ten years. She knew the summertime routine by heart: the hot sleepless nights, the escape to air-conditioned offices where one often caught a summer cold, the relaxed, desultory pace, the planning for the two-week vacation (made rather frantic because you knew it was the only vacation you would have for another entire year). She had gotten the small raise Mr Shalimar had promised her and she was now making ninety dollars a week. She knew that was only five dollars more than Mr Shalimar's executive secretary made, and sixty dollars less than Miss Farrow had received for the same job, and although she tried not to, she knew she felt resentful. Although she had never been materialistic and had never been poor enough to feel the fright of poverty but only its small annoyances, Caroline was beginning to realize more and more that in the business world one's ability was judged by the amount of money one made. There was always a great deal of secrecy about raises at Fabian, but you always found out, and if you knew that someone else had gotten a larger raise there was a certain amount of jealousy. It was like not winning a prize, and you knew you had to wait until the following Christmas before you could try again.

She had her own secretary, a girl of eighteen named Lorraine, who had just been graduated from Katharine Gibbs and looked as if it had been only a year or two since she had taken the braces off her teeth. Caroline was startled to find how young this girl seemed to her. She was so young, so eager, so innocent, so anxious to make good, the way Caroline herself had been only three years before.

Through this girl's eyes Caroline saw everything differently. Mr Shalimar was an austere and famous editor, April was her ideal of the girl from out of town who was now glamorous in New York, and Caroline herself was 'so lucky to have that marvelous job.' Caroline wondered secretly how long it would be before Lorraine became jealous of her, accustomed herself to the exciting new work, and began to wonder why she herself couldn't do exactly what Caroline was doing and just as well.

April, who had been shifted around from boss to boss during her three years in the typing pool and as Miss Farrow's secretary, had finally been given a minor publicity job. She liked it because it gave her more independence and more money and it was interesting. She seldom managed to come into the office in the mornings before ten o'clock. Caroline knew that April went out nearly every night, and it seemed as if every month she had a new romance, someone who telephoned her at the office every day and took her out to cocktails and to dinner.

'He's crazy about me,' April would say, rather flattered but completely unaffected in any other way, and then after a few weeks she would be talking about someone else who was crazy about her. Caroline wondered whether the reason April always seemed so unaffected by these attentions was that she knew underneath that the men were not really in love with her at all. She smiled frequently and brightly, without warmth, and covered up the circles under her eyes with a lighter shade of powder base, and spoke in a quick patois that was composed of all the newest expressions and affectations. If it was fashionable among the supper clubs to speak like a bopster, that was how she spoke; if the fad was trade expressions from the theater, then April knew them. She was having an education.

Caroline spent nearly every summer weekend at Port Blair, lying on the second-story terrace outside her bedroom window dressed in a towel, or at the beach. On Saturdays Paul Landis would drive up in time for lunch, go to the beach with her, and take her to a restaurant for dinner and then to the movies. Their Saturday routine was always the same, and although it was pleasant and certainly more interesting than sitting at home with her parents, sometimes she would feel she couldn't bear to do it one more time and then she would lie and tell him she had another date. Once in a while April or Gregg would come up for the weekend or for one day of it, and if it was a Saturday Paul would take out Caroline and her friend. He liked April and Gregg because they were Caroline's closest friends but he always seemed a little superior about them, as if he were sorry for them.

'She just doesn't want to settle down,' he would say about April, as if she were a giddy debutante. 'I don't know if one man could ever make her happy. She gets tired of them so quickly.'

Gets tired of them? Caroline would think, remembering Dexter. Or just can't handle them? She remembered a conversation she had had with April one weekend that summer, a frightening conversation and one that had made her surprised and sad. It had been a hot night in June, and she and April had been sitting in her back yard in the dark with the porch lights turned out so as not to attract mosquitoes and a small citronella candle burning in a glass on the grass beside them. It was very still. Through the back windows Caroline could see the maid drying the last of the dinner dishes and through the side windows of the house next door she could see the images on a television screen. She had not had a serious talk with April for a long time.

'When I remember myself as I used to be when I first came to New York,' April said, 'I just can't believe it. What an innocent I was! Remember when I was planning to marry Dexter?'

'Yes,' Caroline said.

'I even tried on wedding dresses.'

'I know . . .'

'Can I ask you something?'

'Of course,' Caroline said.

'Do you sleep with Paul?'

'Paul? No. My goodness, no.'

'Doesn't he want to?'

'I don't know,' Caroline said thoughtfully. 'I suppose he must, in a way. But in a stronger way he doesn't.'

'He wants to marry you, doesn't he?' April said.

'I'm pretty sure he does.'

'Do you think you would marry him?'

'I don't know,' Caroline said wistfully. 'I don't think I ever could.'

'Because of Eddie?'

Caroline thought for a moment. 'No. I can't spend my whole life in mourning for Eddie. I wouldn't marry Paul because of Paul, no one else.'

'You can't spend your whole life in mourning,' April repeated sadly.

'I meant that for you too.'

'I know.' April sighed. 'It's not that I don't think I'll ever find another love, I know that's not true. It's just that the way I felt about Dexter, the things I did, the fool I made of myself – I can't forget that. I don't think I ever will forget it. It hurts me now to think of it.'

'Anyone has a right to make a fool of herself if she's really in love,' Caroline said. 'There aren't any laws. But you have to realize everyone else does it too, and forgive yourself. That *is* a law.'

'Whose law?'

'Caroline's law,' Caroline said.

'Do you really believe that?' April asked softly.

'I have to I try to, that is.'

'You were in love with Mike Rice for a while,' April said, 'weren't you?'

'Yes. In a way.'

'Do you know what Dexter said to me?' April said. 'It was the last time I ever spoke to him, that night when I went to his parents' house and tried to get him back. The last words I ever said to him were: "Dexter, I'll always love you, as long as I live."' Her voice was so low Caroline could hardly hear it, but clear and sad, like the voice of a child making a confession. 'And Dexter said to me: "No you won't."'

'He's more experienced than you were,' Caroline said. 'Maybe he knew.'

'That was the night I made that terrible scene,' April said. 'I cried and cried. I didn't have any pride at all.'

'Girls do that,' Caroline said. 'Maybe I would have made a scene with Eddie if he had told me goodbye instead of writing to me about it.'

'And then I started going out with all those other boys,' April said. 'Do you remember Chet?'

'Yes . . .'

They were silent, each thinking thoughts that existed only in the dark of night when they were alone, or alone with a friend who was close and dear. Caroline could hear the crickets chirping in the grass. 'Will you tell me something?' April said.

'Mm-hm.'

'I'll tell you if you tell me. We'll count to three and then show each other how many fingers. Then neither of us will have to say it.'

'Say what?'

'How many boys we've each slept with.'

It was strange, here in the dark where she and April could barely make out each other's faces Caroline was not in the least embarrassed. She felt sorry for April, though, because April's voice was so young and clear and quiet and because she knew April's love affairs must be bothering her very much to make her bring them up in this way, to have company, to have an understanding friend, to make her feel less alone.

'All right,' Caroline said.

Each put a hand behind her back, in a fist. Caroline put out one finger from her fist, for Mike Rice. 'Ready?'

'One, two, three, go!'

They held out their fingers in the light from the citronella candle. Caroline held out one finger. April held out four. Neither of them said anything for a moment.

'Oh, I feel terrible,' April said softly. Then she smiled. 'Who was yours?'

'Mike.'

'Really? I kind of thought it was.'

'Who were yours?'

'Dexter,' April said. She took a deep breath. 'And Chet, you know him. And . . . Tom Banks, that boy who used to fly me to Long Island in his private plane. And Tom's friend Walter, the one who was producing that off-Broadway play. I only did it once with him, one night when I couldn't get away from him any longer. *Oh!*' She put her hands over her mouth, and her eyes above them looked pained and terrified. '*Oh! I forgot someone!*'

'You forgot . . .'

'I must have wanted to put it out of my mind, I forgot it completely. Jeffrey. He was a friend of Chet's. I remember it all now, it was New Year's Eve.' Her voice was frightened. 'That makes five.'

'It's all right,' Caroline said, 'it's all right.'

'I forgot,' April said. 'How could I forget? It must have been such a dreadful experience. I just forgot it. I remember now . . . he went right to my in-the-wall bed. He knew just where the bed was. I remember I was so embarrassed. Oh, Caroline . . .'

'It's all over,' Caroline said. 'It was a long time ago. Six months.'

'*How could I ever have forgotten a thing like that?*'

We've all changed, Caroline thought that night, and later in the office she thought it again. Two and a half years, more than half of a college education. It's inevitable that something must happen. She was sorry for April, and she wondered whether or not she should also be sorry for herself. Certainly she herself could not go back either, but would she want to? She was still the same girl Mike Rice had described two years before, sitting on the rock between two decisions of two different ways of living, but now life and the things that had happened to her had emphasized those differences. Nothing was simple any more, not belief, not satisfaction. Even month by month she was more unsatisfied, wanting more out of her career, wanting to get ahead, to make more money, to have more responsibilities and to be recognized. It was the same with people. She would never again be awed and frightened by a Mr Shalimar, but on the other hand she would never be romantically impressed by a Bermuda Schwartz. It was like taking taxis. At sixteen if a boy took her from one place to another in a taxi she had been impressed by the luxuriousness and sophistication of it, but two years later if he wanted to go by bus instead of a cab she had been vaguely annoyed. It's easy to see what's happened to April, Caroline thought, but can anyone see what's happened to me? What's happened to me is invisible, but so is a pane of glass, and if you try to break through it you get hurt.

Mr Shalimar had received two postcards from Miss Farrow, one from California and one from Hawaii where she was vacationing. His secretary brought them around from desk to desk to show the girls, as if all of them had once been very fond of Miss Farrow and would be glad to know that she remembered them. It was a kind of sorority, with admission assured only after you had gone. Now that Miss Farrow was no longer there to make everyone feel uncomfortable she was actually spoken of with affection. It amazed Caroline. Mary Agnes and Brenda were also members *in absentia*; Brenda had handed in her resignation on her first day of morning sickness and Mary Agnes had continued at her desk until the end of her sixth month of pregnancy. No one had ever heard from Brenda again, although the girls who had been there as long as Caroline and April still spoke of her on occasion, with amusement. Remember Brenda, they would say, the girl who had her teeth pulled out when she got engaged? As for Mary Agnes, she was given a baby shower on the day she left, and when her son was born she sent a tiny blue announcement depicting a stork carrying a bundle, to be passed around among her friends at the office. And one day at the end of July she appeared.

'Hi,' she called. 'Anybody home?'

'Well, if it isn't Mary Alice!' said Mr Shalimar heartily. He hadn't really known her too well.

Mary Agnes was wearing a rather matronly looking navy-blue dress but otherwise had changed not at all. She was as thin as ever, and Caroline remembered that Mary Agnes had been the only girl she had ever seen who had actually looked flat chested in a maternity dress.

'How are you, Caroline?' Mary Agnes asked, looking around Caroline's office appraisingly. 'Anything new?'

Caroline tried to think of something Mary Agnes might find

exciting. 'I'm going to meet John Cassaro on Friday,' she said. 'We want to try to have him endorse a book he's going to star in for the movies. Then we'll run a band with the endorsement on it across the front cover.'

'He's in *New York?*' Mary Agnes said.

'He lives here, you know, when he's not making pictures,' Caroline said.

'No kidding. I always liked him.' Mary Agnes lowered her voice as if she were going to say something scandalous. 'You know, you don't usually think of a comedian as sexy, but I always thought he was the sexiest thing alive.'

'You and a million other girls,' Caroline said, smiling.

'Well,' Mary Agnes said briskly, and broke into a huge smile. 'Look what *I've* got!'

She opened her purse and took out a white paper envelope, and from it she took a sheaf of snapshots. 'Here's my *baby!*'

Caroline took the offered pictures with a mixture of interest and apprehension. One was always obliged to sigh and chuckle over the beauty of every single baby picture, no matter how many, and no matter how unattractive, and she had always found it rather embarrassing. But Mary Agnes' baby was a pretty one, from what Caroline could see of the round little face, round little eyes, and frilly bonnet, and so it was easy to cry, 'Oh, how cute!' over the first four or five nearly identical snapshots and cluck over the rest.

'Those are the latest,' Mary Agnes said proudly, tucking them back into her purse.

'They're darling.'

'He drinks his whole bottle. He's a regular little glutton.'

Caroline smiled.

'I knew you'd want to see them. He's so good. He sleeps the whole night through already, except for his ten-o'clock feeding.'

'That's wonderful.'

'I didn't mind getting up, though. It's so hot in the summer I hardly sleep anyway. We've got an air conditioner in the baby's room and next week we're going to put one in ours. A cousin of Bill's knows someone who can get it wholesale.'

Caroline nodded.

'Who do you think he looks like?'

'Who?'

'The baby. Who else?'

'I think he looks like you,' Caroline said. She'd already forgotten what the baby looked like.

'Really? I'm flattered. Most people think he looks like Bill's father. Of course, you don't know Bill's father. But that's who he looks like. Except around the eyes. He's got my eyes.'

'That must have been what I was thinking of,' Caroline said.

'Well, I'm going to go show April. I bet she's dying to see the pictures. Where is she? I couldn't find her.'

'Down the hall and turn to your left,' Caroline said. 'She has her own office now. She's been promoted to doing publicity.'

'That's nice.'

'Would you like some books before you go?'

'Books?' Mary Agnes said. 'I don't know. Have you got anything good?'

Caroline gestured to the bookcase. 'Take anything you want.'

Mary Agnes glanced at the bookcase without moving. 'Oh, I don't think so. Thanks just the same. Well, I'll be seeing you. So long.'

'Goodbye,' Caroline said. 'Thanks for showing me the pictures.'

'You're welcome.'

When Mary Agnes had gone triumphantly down the hall to find April, Caroline felt relieved because she had a great deal of work to do, and then suddenly she found herself filled with an emotion which she could only recognize as envy. Mary Agnes knew what she was going to do tonight; she was going to be home with her husband and baby. She would not go to an empty apartment and wait for the telephone to ring, and put a few records on the phonograph (not sad ones, because they would be dangerous) and feed the cat, and finally make a sandwich because it seemed silly to cook and set the table for oneself. Perhaps, if she thought about it at all, Mary Agnes might have a fleeting stab of envy for Caroline, because Caroline would be eating an expensive lunch at Moriarty's with an author, and because on Friday she would be meeting Mary Agnes' favorite movie star. But at the time she would be thinking of Caroline and John Cassaro, Mary Agnes would be sitting in front of her television set, with her husband, in a home, and John Cassaro would be an image on a screen for a moment, someone who did not really quite exist except in daydreams. 'Caroline is lucky,' Mary Agnes might say to Bill, 'she has such an interesting job.' And she might even turn to him and ask, 'Do you think I'm boring, honey?' But she wouldn't mean it for an instant, and her husband wouldn't even know what she was talking about. Boring? Half of his heart, the woman he loved? How could she be boring? Was life boring, was breathing boring, was serenity and calm and hope for the future dull?

I could have all that, Caroline thought, with Paul. But then she knew she couldn't. She was not Mary Agnes and she never had been. Was it because she was now more demanding and lived at a more acute level of awareness, or because she was simply not in love? A person was good and kind and steadfast and perfectly presentable, and yet for some perverse reason you could not love him in return. Although Paul did not know it, it was as disturbing to her as it must have been to him. *But I'm going to meet John Cassaro.* Her heart turned over like an adolescent's. She had liked John Cassaro ever since she had been a teen-ager sitting in a dark movie theater enraptured with the romantic substitute for the boys who were still too young to take her out. But on Friday she was not going to meet him as an adolescent admirer, she was going to meet him as an editor and a woman. She was old enough now to be of interest to him, and he was not too old to be of interest to her. Maybe this was only a daydream, in a more realistic vein than the one she had had at fourteen, but she could not help having it. She was to be at his hotel apartment at eleven-thirty in the morning. She would have preferred to arrive late in the afternoon, the cocktail hour was more suggestive of personal relationships. But eleven-thirty in the morning was better than nothing. And it would give her something to think about until Friday, and that was the most important of all.

As it turned out, she had something else to think about before Friday, something that nearly turned her private office world into a turmoil. On Wednesday afternoon at three o'clock Caroline saw Mr Shalimar returning from lunch, walking down the hall arm in arm with Amanda Farrow. Miss Farrow – or Mrs whatever her name now was – had a shiny walnut California suntan and she wore a sleeveless black linen dress to show it off, with an armful of clanking golden bracelets. She looked expensive and polished and somehow worried. When she passed Caroline standing at the doorway of her office Miss Farrow glanced at her but did not even nod in recognition. She's back in New York, Caroline thought, I wonder why. Is it for a visit or for good? She hoped Miss Farrow was only visiting and did not want to come back to the office; things had just started to be peaceful without her. Half an hour later Mr Shalimar called Caroline into his office.

'Sit down, Miss Bender,' he said, folding his hands on the desk top in front of him. He looked more assured than he had the last time Caroline had been in his office, and that worried her, because she knew Mr Shalimar was only self-assured when he knew he was making someone else uncomfortable. 'Well,' he said. 'How is the work going?'

'Fine,' Caroline said, smiling.

'You getting along all right?'

'Yes, thank you. Everything's just fine.'

'Not too much for you, is it?'

'Too much?'

'I only wondered. I don't see you very often. You just stay in there in your little office all day.'

'That's because I'm working,' Caroline said. 'There are four books being completed this month that I have to edit, and I always try to keep up with the unsolicited pile just the same. You've always said that every one of us should consider the unsoliciteds as much of a responsibility as the established authors, because that's where we find the new blood.' And Miss Farrow never bothered, she thought, hoping he would remember.

'That's right,' Mr Shalimar said. He cocked his head at her as if it had just at that moment occurred to him. 'Miss Farrow was in a while ago, I forgot to tell you. Did you see her?'

'I saw her pass by,' Caroline said.

'She's going to be living in New York again.'

'Oh?'

'It's too bad,' he said, 'her marriage didn't work out. She's getting a divorce. I guess she just couldn't keep away from us, eh?'

Caroline smiled nervously.

'You know,' he said, 'Miss Farrow was with us a long time.'

'Does she want to come back?'

'Well, that's what I wanted to discuss with you. I don't know what there is for her to do. You've been doing a good job with her authors and I don't like to start upsetting things just when we have them running so smoothly.'

For the first time Caroline realized what he had been leading up to and she began to tense with resentment at the unfairness of it. 'My authors *like* working with me,' she said, trying to keep her voice low and calm. 'You know they're all happy, and you've been happy with my work.'

Mr Shalimar cleared his throat. 'You have a great deal of work to do, now you know that,' he said, as if he were chastising an unreasonable child. 'Don't you think you could spare a few?'

'*Spare a few!*' She could no longer control herself, her voice broke with emotion. 'Authors are people, and sensitive ones at that. You can't just push them around from editor to editor. And what about me? Miss Farrow *left*, and I've been doing a fine job, you told me that. If she comes back she'll take all my authors, one by one, and I'll be a reader again. You know that's true.'

A faint smile crossed Mr Shalimar's face. 'You're very young to be an editor. You know you've been lucky. You don't have Miss Farrow's years of experience and yet you have her job.'

All right, you sadistic bastard, Caroline thought. If it's war, then it's war. 'I don't have her years of experience,' she said, 'that's true. Neither do I take three hours for lunch, nor do I come in to the office at ten o'clock, nor do I leave at four, nor do I polish my nails at my desk instead of reading manuscripts. I don't send my secretary out on fool's errands to department stores when she's getting fifty dollars a week to type office correspondence. There were a lot of things going on here that you perhaps didn't know about, but I'll tell you if I have to. I hope I won't have to.'

Mr Shalimar's smile broadened. 'I know about them,' he said.

'Then how can you suggest that you'll give half my job to her?'

'I want to be fair.'

'Fair? Fair to whom?'

'We have to be fair,' he said again, and then Caroline realized. Bossart had put him up to this, but whether Bossart wanted Miss Farrow back or was simply making the gesture and looking for a good excuse to tell her she could not return, Caroline could not figure out. She tried to calm herself enough to think quickly and clearly. Of course Mr Bossart didn't want Miss Farrow back, she was bad for the company. He was an executive, after all, above everything else, and he could sleep with her on his own time if he wanted to. Miss Farrow had left of her own accord, she had made it easy for him. Caroline's heart was pounding. I'll make it easy for him too, she thought, if that's what he and Mr Shalimar want.

'I know you're satisfied with my work,' she said calmly. 'I feel that the company owes me something too. I haven't asked for a great deal of money, I know I get much less than Miss Farrow did. I've been willing to wait and to do my best. But if you take away any of my authors I'm going to leave.'

Mr Shalimar raised his eyebrows, but Caroline could see that despite himself he looked pleased. He did not say anything.

She stood. 'I guess that's all,' she said, 'unless there's anything else you'd like me to do. There's a manuscript I'm trying to finish before five o'clock so I can give you the report to take home. Your secretary said you'd like to have it.'

Mr Shalimar tilted back in his swivel chair and crossed his feet on the desk. It was the first time Caroline had ever seen him do this, although April had told her he did it often in private. 'Oh, yes,' he said, 'I would.'

She turned to go.

'Caroline . . .'

'Yes, sir?'

He chuckled. 'Sir. Don't be so formal. You've been working here a long time. I wouldn't start cleaning out my desk if I were you. I'd get rid of everybody else in the office before I'd let you get away.'

'Thank you.'

'We'll have a drink together one night,' he said. 'You let me know when you're free.'

'I will. Thank you.'

She left, shutting the door behind her, and she could have run down the hall with joy. It would be a cold day in hell before she would have a drink with Mr Shalimar alone, but he didn't know that. And it really didn't matter. For the first time Caroline realized how much they needed her here. She was a good editor and they knew it. And she was so good that she was above office politics and secret knifings and social intrigues. She would never know whether or not she had been close to losing her position five minutes ago in Mr Shalimar's office, but her few moments of panic had shown her how much her work here really meant to her. It had started out as a stopgap, but now it had become a way of life. It gave her a sense of value and of belonging. Perhaps that, besides ability, was what made her so good at the job that they could not now afford to lose her.

On Thursday afternoon she did something she had not done in years. She bought two movie magazines to find articles about John Cassaro, and read them, wondering how much of the idolatrous, sugar-coated prose was really true. 'John Cassaro – The Lonely Man,' one of the pieces was entitled. There was a picture of him, the gaunt face and incredibly sexy mouth, the bright eyes that managed to be piercing and guileless at the same time. These magazines always like to tell the 'true story,' that a clown was sad – what else? How could a clown be happy, it would be too simple. And, of course, that a man who had a reputation as an off-stage great lover and scourge of chorus girls was really withdrawn and lonesome. Nevertheless, despite herself, it gave Caroline a strange kind of thrill to read this, as it must have given thousands of girls all over the country. He's lonely, they would say to themselves, no matter what a wild life he leads, he's never found the one girl who could understand him. After all, those chorus girls in Las Vegas, those starlets in Hollywood, they may be much prettier than I am but they only care about their careers. They probably think about themselves all the time, not about *him*, about the secret problems he could confess to them if they were really understanding. In the movies, in the magazine stories, the girl who tames the heel is the extraordinarily good girl, the white-collar and scrubbed-faced office girl who hasn't been anywhere.

'Why don't you get a copy of *Unveiled*?' Lorraine said. 'They had a piece on John Cassaro a few months ago. Do you want me to go downstairs and get it for you?'

'Yes, please,' Caroline said, thinking how already this girl was trying to anticipate her every demand in her anxiety to get ahead. Lorraine went quickly out of the office, and Caroline looked after her, trim in her new, conservative cotton dress, and she thought, Oh, God, I'm getting just like Miss Farrow. There's nothing about this girl not to trust, she's just a nice girl, and she wants to please me. If at this stage in my career I have to be afraid of an eighteen-year-old newcomer, then I'm nowhere. But she could not help wondering whether it would always be like this now because that was the way things were.

Lorraine was back in three minutes flat. 'Thank you,' Caroline said, taking the magazine, which had already been opened and folded back to the article she wanted.

'Not at all.'

'Good grief, how can they print such garbage?'

There were several murky photographs showing figures skulking about in shrubbery, and one good picture of a luxurious Las Vegas hotel. There was a photograph taken in a night club at a different time showing John Cassaro sitting with a pretty girl and looking into her eyes with a foxy smile. It had probably been a publicity date, but *Unveiled* didn't say that. The article was entitled, 'The Night the Virgin's Mother Knocked on John Cassaro's Door.' It went on to tell, without actually saying anything, that a twenty-one-year-old girl had been madly in love with her movie idol and had been drinking with him in his hotel suite when her mother and her rejected twenty-two-year-old boy friend had invaded the premises, finding (the magazine finally admitted) nothing. But by the time you got to the end of the article and groped your way through the leering, sneering prose it had been written in, you would think that there had been all manner of obscene orgies going on.

'I couldn't figure out,' Lorraine said, 'whether they had been doing anything or not.'

'Neither can *Unveiled*,' Caroline said disgustedly. 'They get their pictures from old newspaper files and movie magazines and make up half their scandal at their editorial meetings.'

'Can they *do* that?'

'They're doing it.'

'Somebody's going to sue them someday,' Lorraine said.

'For what? Read this. They *were* in Las Vegas and they *were* in his room together. They could have been playing Old Maid, and the article never said they weren't. But it was so damned sarcastic all the way through that it was just like being insulted with every line without his ever having anything to say he was insulted about.'

'I don't care,' Lorraine said indignantly. 'I'd go out with him in a minute if he asked me. Wouldn't you?'

Caroline smiled. 'It would be a good way to get hurt.'

'Hurt? Why?'

'Just take my word for it. I've been doing some research on the subject. He has quite a reputation, *Unveiled* magazine or not. He never takes a girl out more than once.'

'Well, one date isn't long enough to get hurt,' Lorraine said.

'With him, it evidently is.'

Lorraine opened her eighteen-year-old eyes wide with shocked delight. 'You mean . . .'

'I don't know,' Caroline said, trying to put an end to the discussion. 'I wasn't there, and so I don't know.'

But she saw Lorraine smiling to herself as she went about her typing and filing, and Caroline wondered whether even this level-headed and ambitious young girl was thinking secretly that if she ever went out with John Cassaro she would be the exception. Girls always think, 'I am going to be the exception,' Caroline thought; it's a weakness of the species, like a collie's tiny brain. She herself had often heard that John Cassaro was supposed to be an unforgettable lover, but somehow she felt that even to dwell on this possibility in her mind was rather cheap and childish. He was a real person, with a private life, and she was going to meet him that way in less than twenty-four hours, not as an imaginary bedroom partner but as a business contact. To think of it any other way would be bad for her, she knew that, whether he thought of her as a girl or not.

But that night she washed and set her hair, and in the morning she took a great deal of care with her make-up, telling herself that it was all for the good of Derby Books. She reached his hotel at exactly eleven-thirty and when she rode up in the elevator she wondered whether the elevator man knew where she was going. As she rang the bell to his suite she was thinking, Who's John Cassaro? Nobody. But she was overtaken with fright.

She had expected a sinister oriental houseboy, but Cassaro opened the door himself. He looked exactly as he did in his photographs, a little older perhaps, a little thinner. He was forty, she knew, but a very young forty.

'You must be Caroline Bender,' John Cassaro said.

'Yes.'

'Come in.'

He was wearing a navy-blue silk dressing gown and actually had a silk scarf tucked around his throat. It was exactly as she had imagined he would look in the morning. As she followed him into the living room, Caroline realized to her surprise that he was much taller than she had expected him to be. Perhaps because of the delicate bones of his face she had expected him to be small, but he was not, he was nearly six feet tall.

The living room was air conditioned, as was the entire suite, and it had a piano in one corner. It was a huge room, with pale carpeting and pale walls, and the blinds were opened to the brilliant summer sunlight. At one end of the room there was a door leading to a large terrace, and beyond the terrace wall Caroline could see the city sky line. I must remember everything, she thought, to tell Gregg and April.

'Would you like some coffee?' John Cassaro asked.

'That would be lovely.'

'I just got up,' he said.

There was a coffee table in front of the sofa, with a hotel coffee service set upon it. Caroline had somehow expected a fat manager to be sitting in the corner chewing a damp cigar, or some hangers-on with vague jobs, or a maid or a butler, but there was no one. He's all alone, she thought. How odd. He's alone with me.

'So you're from that lousy Fabian Publications,' he said abruptly. 'I didn't realize until yesterday. You publish *Unveiled*.'

'I'm with Derby Books,' Caroline said. 'I read that piece of garbage they wrote about you in *Unveiled* and I thought it was disgraceful.' She said it calmly, without vehemence, and he smiled a little.

'I don't pay attention to that stuff,' he said. 'But it seems ironic that Fabian Publications expects me to do them a favor after what they did to me.'

'I know,' Caroline said sympathetically, 'it seems unfair. But the promotion of the book will help the promotion of your picture, and that's the important thing.'

He did not touch his coffee but lighted a cigarette and got up from the sofa to pace up and down the room. He seemed nervous, and Caroline knew it was not because of a decision about an endorsement for a paperback novel, because that meant nothing to him; his nervousness went deeper than that. It was a part of his personality. Somehow she felt sorry for him. His voice was so familiar, like the voice of an old old friend, and yet it was the voice of the celluloid untouchable. The telephone rang then, and he answered it, in a kind of guarded growl.

'Yeah . . .'

She poured cream into her coffee and stirred it, trying to pretend she was not there. John Cassaro was speaking and listening, holding on to the receiver at the full length of its cord and pacing about in a circle like an animal on the end of a chain. She had never seen anyone talk on the telephone in such a way, as if every instant he was not moving impatiently was an instant wasted. He finished the conversation finally and came to stand over her.

'Are you a writer?' he asked.

'No, I'm an editor.'

'Do you like it?'

'Yes.'

'You look so young.'

'I'm twenty-three.'

'That's young, isn't it,' he said, 'to be an editor?'

'Yes, it is.'

He stood there above her, looking down at her for a moment more, and in that instant Caroline knew instinctively that all the stories she had heard about him were true. His voice that had made millions laugh and yearn at the same time still bore some of the intonations of his slum boyhood, his face and body had the hard wariness of someone who has fought for years to be where John Cassaro was now. She knew as he looked at her that if they knew each other better he might be capable of asking her to do any mad thing: run away with him, go on a brief but gigantic spree; and that it would be exactly the kind of thing that someone like her would find strange and significant and romantic, and to him it would mean nothing at all. They were complete strangers, and yet his look said, We know each other perfectly well, don't we? And she had to admit that it was true. She had never felt more conventional and limited and ordinary in her life.

He gave her a small smile and sat down on the sofa beside her. 'Cigarette?'

'Thank you.'

After he had lighted their cigarettes he sat snapping the lighter on and off, staring into the flame. Then he put the lighter on the table. 'All right,' John Cassaro said. 'What do you want me to do for you?' His eyes widened a little, just a flicker, but Caroline noticed it. She bent over her handbag.

'I have the endorsement right here, which I happened to write myself,' she said, not looking at him. 'I thought I'd save you the trouble since you're being kind enough to take the trouble to do it at all. If you like it, then just sign it here at the bottom and that's all there is to it.'

He took the piece of paper from her hand and read it quickly, all business, all personal wariness again. 'You wrote this?'

'Yes.'

'Do you have a pen?'

She handed him one, already uncapped. He leaned over the piece of paper on the coffee table, pushing aside the coffee cups, his lips clamped around his cigarette. He x'd out a word, wrote another in its place, and then wrote his signature in large, flowing letters at the bottom.

'Thank you,' Caroline said. She had her head tilted, looking over his shoulder at what he had written. He had simply changed an adjective, a small thing, but it was better his way. 'And thank you for the improvement,' she said with a little smile.

When he turned his head to look at her his face was only an inch or two from her own. She had the weirdest, most unreasonable feeling that he was going to kiss her, like some corny scene from a movie, and all of a sudden her heart turned over and she realized that if he were capable of such a thing it would be neither weird nor corny at all. She moved away from him quickly.

He did not move but sat there looking at her. 'You can send the thousand dollars to Boys' Town,' he said.

'That's very kind of you. I'll have the treasurer send it in your name when I go back to the office.'

He looked at his watch. 'I have to go downtown to a rehearsal. Why don't you make yourself a drink and then I'll drop you off on my way.'

'All right. Thank you.'

'Make me one too.' He stood and started for the bedroom. 'I'll be right back.'

There was a large bar next to one wall with every kind of liquor imaginable and an assortment of glasses. Caroline poured herself a Scotch and water and then stood there not knowing what to do because he had not told her what he wanted. She gathered up courage and called out to the closed bedroom door, 'Do you want Scotch?'

'Yeah.'

She made one for him too and then carried hers over to the door to the terrace. She could tell from the heat sizzling on the white stones outside that it was turning out to be a mean day. But in here it was cool and expensive, with white carnations in a vase on the end table and the best Scotch on the bar and well-trained hotel servants ready to arrive at a moment's notice with anything John Cassaro could ask for. He was going to a rehearsal, he had dozens of friends and millions of admirers, and yet he had asked her to wait and have a drink with him when it was she who should be grateful to him for signing the endorsement. He wasn't even being paid for the endorsement, since he had told her to send his payment to charity. Besides, what was a thousand dollars to him? He made two million dollars a year.

He came up behind her without a sound, dressed in a light linen business suit. 'Do you want to go out on the terrace?'

'Oh! Yes . . . I would.'

He opened the door and they stepped outside together. It was very hot but so high up that there was a small breeze blowing. There was an awning with two chaises under it and a glass-topped table, and a potted plant four feet high. A white pigeon was sitting on the terrace wall, cooing. 'Look,' Caroline said, pointing. 'He must be lost.'

'That one? I have him trained. He drinks Martinis.'

She laughed. 'It's so beautiful here.'

John Cassaro was leaning on the terrace wall, drinking his Scotch. 'You can see the ships from here, see?' he said. 'That's the *Ile de France*. You'll see it better in a minute. It's twelve o'clock.'

'I hate all ships that go to France,' Caroline said.

'Really? Why?'

'I was in love with someone who went away on one and never came back to me,' she said lightly. And as she said it she suddenly realized for the first time that she did not really mean that about hating the ships, that Paris was no longer a word that hurt, and that she was saying this to John Cassaro simply for something to say to him to prove she was a girl who had been in love.

'How come he never came back?'

'Got married.'

'She must have been Helen of Troy,' he said, glancing at Caroline.

She smiled.

He set his nearly full glass on the terrace wall. 'Now watch, the pigeon's going to come over to it and drink it,' he said. 'Don't make any noise.'

'I thought he liked Martinis,' Caroline whispered.

'Scotch before lunch. He needs a clear head or he'll fly into a windowpane.'

They stood there, side by side, elbows on the top of the terrace wall, looking out of the corners of their eyes at the pigeon. It cooed, ruffled its white feathers, and waddled slowly over to the glass of Scotch, taking gingerly steps with its toothpick legs. Then with a rustle of wings the pigeon swooped down on the glass, dipped its head over the rim and drank, poised, flapping and evidently thirsty.

'That's impossible!' Caroline whispered. 'I don't believe it.'

'He's half hummingbird.'

'Nobody will believe me. I'll tell them I was here with John Cassaro watching a pigeon drink Scotch.'

'Why not?' John Cassaro said. 'They believe everything else.' He looked at his watch again. 'We have to go.'

Walking through the hotel lobby with him, Caroline was very conscious of the glances of other people. They all recognized him, and they probably thought she was John Cassaro's latest girl. The mystery girl. He took her arm to help her into the taxi and it was just like the grip of any one of a hundred boys who had taken her out in the past eight years, and yet it was different. It was entirely different. Why should it be this way, Caroline thought, it's unfair. A hand is anatomically nearly exactly the same as any other hand, and yet one has the power to make me want to draw closer and another annoys me so I want to brush it away. I don't know him, he's nothing to me, he's just a celebrity I've heard of. This was not love, this was not Eddie, this was not even a friend she was deeply fond of. And yet at that moment if John Cassaro had chosen to kiss her she knew she would have responded with a passion that she had not felt since her romance with Eddie Harris. It was the first time she had ever realized that, despite everything she and her friends had believed and had told each other, there was such a thing as sheer animal sex appeal with nothing more sentimental between two people than magnetism, and it made Caroline feel so uncomfortable and vaguely guilty that she could hardly think of anything to say to this man all the way to her office.

The cab drew to the curb in front of the statue of Atlas. 'Thank you,' Caroline said.

He smiled at her from the depths of the taxi. He's just another man, she thought, just another man in a tan suit on a summer day, but she knew she was staring at his face. 'Good luck,' John Cassaro said.

She stepped out of the cab and walked into her office building, not daring to turn and look back for fear he might see her and think she was impressed by him. And then she thought, How foolish. I should have turned and waved. It might have done some good. *Good for what?* If I'm lucky I'll never see him again.

It was nearly twelve-thirty and girls were streaming out of the building in pairs, and groups, going to lunch. They all looked the same somehow: hot, surprised at the swift blast of heat after their air-conditioned tower, hungry, a little wilted, glad to be released for an hour to chatter and relax. Some of them were pretty but most of them weren't, and none of them was so beautiful that you would turn around to look at her twice. Perhaps one in a thousand would have a life that would draw notice in ten years, and very few of them really cared. But all of them had their daydreams at times, and perhaps sometimes the daydreams included a date with John Cassaro. So why shouldn't mine? Caroline thought. I'm no different, really, except that I've met him, and I don't think that's going to make that much difference. Daydreams are harmless and they *do* make a great difference; sometimes all the difference in the world while you're waiting for something real and good.

The next day when Paul came up to Port Blair Caroline made him sit through a double-feature movie with her, and then at one o'clock when he tried to kiss her she pleaded exhaustion from the late hour and the day of sun at the beach, and fled to her room. For the first time since her first date with Paul she felt as if she had escaped from him and was glad to be alone and free again. The last thing she thought of when she fell asleep was John Cassaro feeding the Scotch to the pigeon and she remembered the shape of his hand as it curved around the glass. Paul had stayed overnight so he could go to the beach with her the next day, and as Caroline watched him sitting on the porch in the morning reading the Sunday papers and working the crossword puzzle like a member of the family, she had a sense of unreality, as if she were living in two worlds simultaneously. At ten-thirty April telephoned her from New York.

'Caroline! Guess who just got married!'

'*Who?*'

'Barbara Lemont – you know, my friend. She eloped with Sidney Carter from the Carter Agency. He's the one she's been madly in love with for a year. She just called me. They went away for the weekend and got married.'

'That's wonderful!' Caroline said.

'You should see him, he's so handsome, and he's the suavest man I ever met.'

'He must be old,' Caroline said.

'No. He's forty. That's not so old, do you think?'

'No,' Caroline said, thinking of John Cassaro, 'it can be the best age.'

'She's such a nice girl,' April said. 'I'm so glad for her. She's going to quit her job and stay home to take care of her little girl.'

'And live happily ever after . . .' Caroline sighed. 'How come a man like that didn't get grabbed up before?'

'He just got divorced.'

'Maybe those are the ones to look for,' Caroline said. 'But it's a long look.'

'I don't know,' April said wistfully. 'I don't know anything any more.'

'What's all the excitement?' Caroline's mother asked after Caroline was off the phone.

'A friend of April's and mine from the office just eloped. Barbara Lemont; I told you about her.'

'Oh, yes, the one with the child. Who did she marry?'

'Sidney Carter. He's forty years old and wildly successful – he's the head of his own advertising agency. And April says he's very handsome.'

Her mother clucked with what Caroline realized to her surprise was sympathy. 'Well, poor girl, she'd have to marry an older man. Who else would support her child?'

'But we think she's *lucky*,' Caroline said.

'She's very lucky. A young girl with such a big child. She's lucky to have gotten someone at all.'

'I agree,' Paul said.

You would, Caroline thought. You would.

24

Summer is tourist time in New York, and they come by the hundreds, streaming into the hot city by Greyhound bus and train and plane and private car, in their white shoes and light summer clothing, with their cameras and their suitcases and their saved-up spending money, and their dogged determination to ignore the heat that rises from the blinding pavements and to do everything. By everything they mean Radio City Music Hall, and Times Square at night, and the UN and the Automat and a hansom cab ride and some Broadway shows. Some of them have never been to New York before, and they stay at hotels that native New Yorkers may never have set foot in, where trucks rumble outside their window and neon lights blink in, and after a week or ten days in a certain ten-block area they go home and say, Well, New York is a fine place to visit, but I certainly wouldn't *live* there. And others may bear with them letters to friends of friends or distant relatives, and they will stay with them in the Bronx or Flushing or Jericho, and make their daily pilgrimage to the heart of the city, and they say, Well, New York certainly is *big*, but I don't know why they say it's unfriendly. And others, who have a great deal of money to spend, stay at the Plaza or the Waldorf or the St Regis, and go to the hit musicals with tickets that cost fifty dollars a pair, and dine at the Colony and the Brussels and Le Pavillon, and drink at the Harwyn and the Little Club and the Starlight Roof, and when they go home they say, Once a year is enough for me, I couldn't stand the pace!

In the summer of fifty-four, in the middle of August, a young man named Ronnie Wood came to New York City for a visit, his first. He had an Argoflex camera in a tan leather case slung over his shoulder and he wore a pale-gray Dacron suit, the kind that you can wash out yourself in your hotel room, and in his battered canvas flight bag he had the name and address of a girl named April Morrison, whose mother was a friend of his aunt's back home in Springs, Colorado. He was five feet nine inches tall and he had wavy brown hair that fell over his forehead when he moved his head, and inquisitive dark eyes, and he stammered a little when he was nervous and with people he did not know. He did not know April Morrison.

The first day he arrived in New York he checked into a hotel near Grand Central Station and walked to the UN building, where he took pictures of the flags flying and the glittering architecture, and could not get a ticket to get in to watch the General Assembly because the tickets for the day had already been allotted. Then he walked across town to Broadway and looked at all the shooting galleries and pizza stands and movie marquees, and he looked at the girls from the offices out on their lunch hour and he took some more pictures and he wondered whether any of those girls could be April Morrison. He knew she worked somewhere in the Fifties, and after he had eaten a lunch of a hot dog and a paper cup of coconut milk from a Broadway stand he walked over to Fifth Avenue. It was ninety degrees in the sun that afternoon, but Ronnie Wood was only mildly uncomfortable. He was much too excited to be uncomfortable.

He saw two boys in shirt sleeves, so he took off his suit jacket and tossed it over one shoulder, holding it with two fingers, as he had seen Gary Cooper do in the movies. He had started to carry his jacket that way years ago when he had had a brief ambition to be an actor, and now it was an automatic mannerism. He walked to Rockefeller Center, looking at the people and into store windows, and when he came to the statue of Atlas in front of a huge office building he set his camera and squinted up at it. There was New York, exactly as it had always seemed to him it ought to be. Enormously tall, impersonal buildings, with the personal touch of a work of art. That girl, April, worked right around here some-place.

He decided to call her and he looked around for a drugstore. There was none in sight. He walked for fifteen blocks without finding a drugstore, and by then he had given up. He went back to his hotel and took a shower and lay on his bed in his underwear. It was ten minutes to five. On an impulse he decided to call her at her office anyway and see if she would have dinner with him. He hoped she wasn't a dog. It would be a heck of a thing, Ronnie Wood was thinking, to have dinner with a dog the first night that he was in the exciting city he had always wanted to see.

'As a matter of fact,' April Morrison said, 'I am free tonight. But just for cocktails. I could meet you in front of my office at half past five.'

He liked her voice, it had a breathless, sexy quality. It was a *whispery* voice. 'All right,' he said, trying not to stammer. 'I'll have on a light gray suit.'

'So will I,' April said. She laughed. 'See you soon.'

He didn't have the faintest idea where to take a girl for cocktails before dinner in New York but he supposed she would know. She had sounded sophisticated. *I'm free . . . just for cocktails.* Well, all the better. His first night in New York he wanted to be with a girl who was as sophisticated and New Yorkish as anything in the world. He was already imagining what she would be like. Somehow, Ronnie had the feeling, this girl would not be a dog at all.

He saw her, standing in front of the statue of Atlas, her hair blowing in the slight evening breeze that had come up. It was going to rain. Her hair was very golden in the lowering late day, with touches of red in it, short and blowing and bright. She *did* have a gray suit on, made of something silky and thin, so that he could see the curving outlines of her body. And she had a beautiful face. When she saw him approaching her she smiled at him.

'April?' he said.

'Hello, Ronnie Wood.'

'I'm glad to meet you,' he said, beginning to stammer again. 'I'm glad you could make it tonight.'

She put the tips of her fingers on his arm, lightly. 'We'd better go somewhere quick before it rains. Do you have a favorite place?'

'Me? No . . . no. I thought . . . I'd leave it to you.'

'We'll run and duck into the Barberry Room.'

They ran, and arrived breathless and smiling at each other. The first drops of rain were just starting to fall as Ronnie pushed open the glass door. They found a table in the back. 'Wow,' he said, 'it's dark in here.'

'You'll get used to it.'

'What would you like to . . . drink?'

'A vodka Martini. With an olive.'

'A vodka Martini. With an olive,' Ronnie repeated carefully to the waiter. 'Make it two.'

'Well,' April said. 'Have you been in New York long?'

'Just since this morning.'

'And what have you seen?'

'I walked about twenty miles,' he said. 'Or it's beginning to . . . feel that way.'

'My goodness,' she said. 'You're certainly ambitious.'

'Yes,' he admitted.

'I used to do that, when I first came to New York,' April said. 'I would walk for miles. I even got lost. Have you been lost yet?'

'I don't think I'd know,' he said. They both laughed.

April lifted her cocktail glass. 'Cheers,' she said brightly.

'Cheers.'

'And here's to a good vacation for you.'

'It's starting out that way already,' Ronnie said.

'Tell me something about yourself,' she said. 'What do you do?'

'I'm going to go into business with my father back home. Real estate. I just got out of the Army.'

'In Korea?'

'No. I was lucky. I was in Germany.'

'Really? I've never been to Europe.'

'One leave I had, I flew to Rome,' he said. 'It was beautiful. A beautiful city. I never did get to Paris, though.'

'Maybe you'll go back sometime.'

'I'd like that. It would be a great place for a honeymoon.'

Was it his imagination, or were her eyes filming over? She looked for an instant as if she were going to cry. Then she smiled at him. 'Can I have another drink?' she asked brightly.

'Sure . . . waiter! Two more . . . uh, vodka Martinis. Please.'

'I like them much better than regular Martinis,' April said. 'You can't taste that gin taste. I used to like gin, but then one morning I woke up with a dreadful hang-over and I never could bear the taste of gin again.'

'You shouldn't drink so much that you get a hang-over,' he said. 'You should be more careful.'

'My goodness, you sound like my father.'

'I'm sorry . . .'

'It's all right,' April said. She smiled at him. 'Most girls like to have a man who worries about their health.' She sipped at her Martini and looked at him over the rim of her glass. 'I do. I don't care a bit about my health when I'm left to my own devices.'

'Well, you should,' he said. When he had seen her standing there in front of the statue of Atlas she had looked to him like everything a New York girl should be: sophisticated, leggy, beautiful and very poised. And now she had flashes when she seemed to him just like a reckless little girl. Somehow he liked her better this way. 'I won't let you drink too much tonight,' he said. 'I wish . . . you'd have dinner with me.'

'Maybe I can.'

'You tell me where you want to go. I'm the stranger.'

'That will be fun.'

'Do you want me to . . . tell you some more about myself?'

'Yes,' she said very interestedly, 'do.'

'Well . . . I wanted to be an actor for a while. In fact, I was going to go to dramatic school on the G.I. Bill, but I finally talked myself out of it. I guess you have to have a certain temperament for acting, a lot of confidence in yourself as the commodity you're trying to sell, and I figured I would do better selling real estate.'

'Isn't that funny! I wanted to be an actress for a while. That's why I came to New York.'

'Really?'

'But after I'd been here for a while I gave it up. That's why I'm in publishing. At least it's in the arts.'

'It sounds fascinating.'

'Oh . . . it's fun.'

'I think that's the important thing,' Ronnie said, 'to do what you like.'

'Do you like selling real estate?'

'I don't know yet. If I don't, or if I'm no good at it, I'll find something else.'

'You have a lot of courage,' April said. 'Most boys just get into a rut and stay with it for the rest of their lives.'

'Well, I don't want to be a drifter. I certainly don't want to be that. But I'm still young enough so that I can try for a while to find what I'll do best.'

'How young?'

'Twenty-four,' he said.

'That *is* young.'

'Why? How old are you?'

'Twenty-three,' April said.

He laughed. 'You sound like an old lady.'

'Sometimes I feel like one,' she said lightly.

'Please have dinner with me.'

'I'll have to break my date.'

'Could you? I mean . . . would you?'

'Yes,' she said.

Ronnie reached into his pocket. 'Here's a dime for the phone.'

'It's all right. The waiter will bring a phone to the table.'

My God, he thought, I thought they only did that in the movies. But the waiter came and plugged a telephone in next to their table and April picked up the receiver and started to dial. Then she put her hand over the phone and cut the call off.

'Tell me something,' she said abruptly.

'What?'

'Are you lonesome?'

'Lonesome? Why?'

'I just thought you might be,' she said. 'Your first night in New York and all.'

'I guess I am,' Ronnie said slowly. 'I hadn't really thought about it. But if you don't have dinner with me I *will* be lonely, I know that.'

'That's all I wanted to know,' April said. She lifted the receiver again and started to dial, and while she was waiting for the number to ring she turned and smiled at him.

25

On a night in mid-October, when the first frost came to the outlying suburbs and people began to remember how nice it was to stay indoors by their hearth or television set, cozy and warm, Gregg Adams was in David Wilder Savage's bedroom going through his bureau drawers. She worked at it furtively and quickly because he was in the shower, and as long as she could hear the sound of the water she knew she was safe. She had no inkling of what had prompted her to do such an outrageous thing, except that he was occupied and she was here, and suddenly a compulsion had overtaken her *to find out*. What she was going to find out, she had no idea. But he had been a mystery to her for so long, with his self-contained and apparently self-sufficient life, that she felt if she could only find some secret thing of his, some letters, some photograph, anything, then she could understand him better. She had toyed with the idea that he was an ordinary person, that there really was no mystery about him except in her own mind, but then she had rejected it. There must be an answer hidden somewhere; life was not that simple.

At the bottom of the middle drawer, under a pile of clean white shirts, Gregg found several envelopes. They looked as if they had been tossed there, not hidden, by someone who was untidy rather than secretive. She listened for a moment to the sound of the shower and then opened the envelopes. One contained a photostatic copy of David Wilder Savage's birth certificate and his passport. She looked at these, especially the passport picture, and she was sorry she had not known him then. Even those years that he had lived and worked and traveled and been in love without her made her jealous.

Three of the other envelopes contained letters, and one held photographs. She looked at the photographs first. They were all of the same person, a young man whom she did not know but who looked definitely familiar, and then Gregg realized who it was. It was Gordon McKay, David's friend, who was dead. They were merely snapshots that could have been taken anywhere, two taken indoors and therefore hard to make out, one outdoors in the country, and one with a girl. Gregg wondered who the girl was and whether she had meant anything to David as well as Gordon, and why she was in the picture. That was the trouble with spying, you never could ask for an explanation of what you had found out.

She turned to the letters. They were to David, and the signature was 'Gordon.' Her heart was pounding as she smoothed out the folded sheets of paper, and she resented Gordon McKay furiously for having such a tiny, illegible handwriting that she would hardly have time to make it out. The first letter was an account of a trip, and it was funny. She almost laughed aloud at some of the descriptions but caught herself in time. There wasn't anything odd in saving a letter like that, it was something you would want to save. She skipped over some of the obviously innocuous passages to the end. No closing salutation, no love, just 'See you soon – Gordon.' She opened the second letter and began to read.

She had the sense that someone was standing behind her. She had no real reason, simply that sixth sense that makes a cat's fur rise and a human being feel a disturbing prickling at the back of his neck. She turned. David Wilder Savage, wet and naked except for a towel, was standing not five feet away from her with his arms folded and an expression on his face of inconsolable fury. He did not say a word, or move, he simply stood there and watched her. Behind him, from the other room, Gregg could still hear the sound of the shower turned on full force.

'What are you doing here?' she asked stupidly.

'Playing Gregg,' he said. He walked over to her then and took the letters from her hand. They slipped from her cold fingers into his, and he glanced at them and put them back into her hand and closed her fingers around them. He still did not speak and she could not think of anything to say. She stood there and watched him, trying to think of some excuse, some joke to make it all right again, while he very methodically and grimly opened each drawer of the dresser and took out everything that was in them, in handfuls, and tossed clothes and papers and miscellaneous articles to the floor at her feet.

'Are you crazy?' she asked finally, shakily.

'Here,' he said. 'I'm making it easier for you. You can look at everything. Would you like me to clean out the top of the closet?'

'Stop it,' Gregg cried, frightened. 'Stop it!'

'I don't want you to miss anything,' he said.

She was knee-deep in a tangle of clothing – socks and shirts and underwear, and even his leather jewelry box, which he opened first so that the cuff links and tie clips that were inside spilled out. He finished emptying the bureau drawers and then he turned and walked back to the bathroom without a word and slammed the door. Gregg was so humiliated she did not know what to do, and she was filled with love for him. Poor man, he was completely innocent and hiding nothing. She shouldn't have gone through his things, it must have annoyed him terribly. She would put everything back neatly where it had been before and then he would forgive her. As she put back his clothes Gregg cheered up a little. She was rearranging everything so neatly, folding some things and making room for others, that he would be glad, after all, that this had happened. She could tell him she had been trying to do this in the first place, for a surprise, and that she had come upon the letters by accident and had been tempted by them. That was it! He'd believe her.

The shower had stopped and a short while later David himself emerged from the bathroom, fully dressed in clean clothes. Gregg had just finished putting everything away. He ignored her, walking around her, and looked at his watch.

'I'll give you five minutes to finish investigating and get out of here,' he said calmly, 'and if you're not out then, I'm going to throw you out.'

'Why?' she cried. 'Why?'

'You don't know why?'

'No! I was just trying to clean out your dresser drawers for you, make them a little neater. For . . . a surprise,' she finished lamely.

'I have a maid for that,' he said.

'Well . . . I just wanted to . . . do something for you.'

'And did you find a lot of things? Did your sick little inquisitive mind find all kinds of secrets? Did you discover that I have twelve pairs of black socks and ten pairs of gray? Do you know that I keep my torn handkerchiefs at the bottom of the pile instead of throwing them out? Did you find my expired driver's licenses and some old letters and photographs that I forgot to put into an album? And are you satisfied?'

There was nothing else to say. 'Please forgive me,' Gregg said.

'Why do you have to do things like that?'

'I don't know . . .'

'I don't know either,' he said. 'And I just don't care any more. I'm tired of the sight of your face. I can't stand to see it any more. I want you to go away.'

'You can't really mean that if you have to ask me to go,' Gregg said. 'If you really hated me you'd try to throw me out.'

'Hate you? I don't hate you.'

'Then forgive me. I'll never do it again.'

'I keep telling you, I don't want to have to forgive you. I've forgiven you for a thousand things – invasion of privacy, neurotic mistrust, insensitivity, selfishness. It isn't just *this*, tonight. This is only the very last thing. Why do you think I crept up on you? Because I'm getting to be like you, in a way; I'm beginning to have hallucinations about you. I want you to get out of this house, as a personal favor, like a big girl.'

'Don't be mad at me,' Gregg said. 'I'll go sit in the living room and then after a while you come in and we'll pretend the evening just started. We'll just start all over again.'

'Come on,' he said, 'like a big girl.' Why, he actually sounded as if he were soothing someone who was deranged. 'Come on,' he repeated. He went to the closet and brought out her coat. 'Here's your coat.'

'Are you throwing me out?'

'Yes.'

Gregg felt so sick it seemed as if there was hot blood in her eardrums. 'You can't throw me out,' she said, 'it's early.'

'Here's your purse.' He looked at it as he held it out to her. 'It's pretty,' he murmured.

'You've seen it before.'

'Did you have gloves?'

'I don't want to go home!' Gregg said. Her voice rose in her fright at the utter lack of emotion on his face. Anger was something she could cope with, she would only have to soothe him, perhaps even cry, and he would be forgiving. But this complete calm and resolution was something she had never seen on David's face before. 'I don't want to go home! Don't make me go home!'

'I don't care where you go,' he said.

'I'll walk around the block and come back,' she suggested.

'I'm going to sleep now. It's late.'

She was afraid to touch him. 'What time will I see you tomorrow?'

'I'm busy tomorrow.'

'Well . . . when will I see you?'

'I never want to see you again.'

'Why? What did I do?' Gregg cried. 'What did I do?'

'You don't know, do you?' he asked. He actually sounded sorry for her. 'You really don't know.'

He stood there for a moment looking at her. There was pity on his face, as well as calm now. 'Kiss me . . .' Gregg whispered.

He leaned down without touching her with his hands and kissed her very lightly on the forehead. 'Be a good girl,' he said.

'I'll call you tomorrow,' Gregg said. She drew herself up to her full height and walked to the door. 'Good night.'

'Good night, Gregg.'

She walked out into the hall and he shut the door behind her. She could hear the soft click of the lock. She turned. There was his door, closed, and he was behind it. Behind it, moving about, still awake, was the most precious thing in her world. She stood close to his door, listening. She could hear faint sounds through his door, footsteps, the sound of a record starting on the phonograph, and they reassured her. She could tell what he was doing from these sounds of his routine, and it was almost as good as being there with him. He was alone, all alone. After a long while Gregg grew tired from standing there in one place in her highheeled shoes and she began to slip her feet out of her shoes one at a time and stand on only one, rubbing the aching toes of the other foot on her ankle. She looked about for a place to sit.

The stairway that led to the upper floor was just outside David Wilder Savage's door, and the wall it ran along was the outside wall of his apartment. In her mind she could see the layout of the rooms, and Gregg knew this was his bedroom wall. She climbed the stairs to a step near the top, just under the halfway landing and a small closed window, and sat there. The light bulb which illuminated the hall was downstairs, on the main landing for this floor, and up here in the gloom it was shadowy and still. She leaned against the wall and heard nothing. She had a moment of disappointment, afraid that the wall was too thick for any sound to escape. But then she heard footsteps and a thud that was frighteningly close. It was as if he had thrown something to the floor. She realized that she had not heard anything before because he had not yet entered the room.

How strange it was, and how intimate, to be here in the darkness, listening to those sounds of someone she knew so well and loved so much. She heard the closet door close as he evidently put away his clothes. He was going to bed. Poor thing, he was going to bed. She looked at her watch. It was ten minutes to twelve.

Very faintly, she heard him cough as he settled down in bed. God, you could hear everything. She heard the telephone ring beside his bed, and she sat bolt upright, straining to hear. She heard his voice . . . his voice . . . if he only knew how close to him she was, hearing everything. It was a business call. Gregg gave a sigh of relief. She only wanted him to go to sleep, to stay there all alone, separated from her by this thin, revealing wall, hers for the night. She heard him stop speaking, walk about the room, close another door. Then he came back and she knew he had gone to bed. For a long time there was no sound at all, and Gregg knew that at last he had fallen asleep.

She put her hand against the wall, palm toward where he would be. My darling, she thought. Soon it would be morning and then she could call him on the phone. She knew she could telephone him early because he had gone to bed early, and so she would not be waking him up. Everything would be all right. It had to be all right. He was right here with her and she knew what he was doing. It would be morning soon. At three o'clock in the morning Gregg left David's apartment house and took a taxi home and went to bed. Caroline was already asleep, breathing very quietly, curled up next to the wall. When Caroline's alarm went off at eight Gregg would get up too. That would be early enough so that David would not have had time to leave the house and escape.

It was only after a week had gone by that Gregg finally realized he had meant it. A week! It seemed like forever. She could hardly face the fact that it was only three days, then four, then at last seven. She called him every morning, early, often being answered by a sleepy voice that hardly seemed to know what she was saying. And he always hung up on her. 'I meant it, Gregg,' he would say. 'Stop calling. Goodbye.' She would call him right back and he would answer, innocently the first time, and then hang up on her. And when she would call him again his hello would be wary, and finally he would not answer at all. She got into the habit of telephoning him at night just to hear his voice, not answering his hellos, and then she would hang up on him before he could do it to her. She did not know if he ever realized these mystery calls were hers. She called him at dinnertime to see if he was out or at home, and at nine to see if he had stayed home for the evening. She called him after midnight to see if he had returned. But telephone calls told her nothing, for he could have been there all the time with another girl. If he was alone, if he was possibly suffering despite his firm refusals to give her another chance, then she wanted to know it. So a week after the night

David had told her goodbye Gregg left her apartment at one in the morning and went to his.

She went furtively up to his floor and crept to her place at the top of the stairs. She hoped no one would decide to go home at this hour and accidentally find her; they might think she was peculiar. She huddled close to the wall, listening.

'Darling?' a voice said. It was a female voice, a light, sophisticated voice that would say 'Darling' and not mean it – and the man she said it to would know she had not meant it. Gregg stiffened, seeing waves of light flickering in front of her eyes there in the half-darkness.

'Mmm?' It was he, she could tell even by this one syllable.

'Which side do you sleep on?'

'This one.'

'Do you mind if I have it? I'm peculiar that way.'

Gregg was clenching her fists so tightly they felt numb.

There was affection in David's voice, but also an underlying touch of worry. 'Don't tell me you're compulsive? Just don't tell me that.'

The girl laughed. 'No, darling.'

Darling, Gregg thought. Bitch, bitch, bitch. Who did you sleep with last night? Somebody else you called darling? Or my David, my love? She was shaking with humiliation and grief, and hatred for this girl whom she did not know even by appearance, and she wanted to stand up and run away, down the stairs to the street, but she was powerless to move. She had to stay, to listen, to hear the worst and suffer the more for it, and never give him up no matter what it cost her in pain and even disgust with her foolish self. She heard sounds then, the beginning of love sounds, and she wished more than anything to faint. She felt as if there were a flame running from her throat to the pit of her stomach. She was shuddering all over, like someone who is about to retch, but she could not pull herself away from that wall and those familiar words and soft noises.

It was over at last and she heard footsteps and a door close and then later returning footsteps and footsteps passing them. Dirty pig, Gregg thought, using his bathroom, using his towels, using his bed, using *him*. Using my love, my beautiful love. I wonder whether he's going to fall in love with her.

It didn't matter, as long as he didn't fall in love with that girl. Gregg had to know. She would forgive him anything, as long as he was only using that girl's body and did not love her. She wondered whether there was a way to find out these things as well, whether there would be a way to see what went on inside that apartment instead of only to hear.

26

On an evening at the end of October Caroline invited April to dinner at her apartment. They met at the office at five o'clock and stopped on their way home at a grocery store, where they bought bread and cheese and ham for sandwiches, and chocolate milk and chocolate-marshmallow ice cream. They deposited their parcels in Caroline's kitchenette, and April took off her shoes and sat on the studio couch while Caroline took off her good office dress and hung it away and put on a pair of old velvet slacks and a sweater. She did not bother to make cocktails because neither of them ever drank when they were not out with men. She put some records on the phonograph and sat on the opposite studio couch, Gregg's bed.

'Where's Gregg tonight?' April asked.

'I don't know. She's been acting peculiar lately,' Caroline said.

'It's that David Wilder Savage thing.'

'I know . . .' Caroline lowered her voice, as if Gregg actually were hiding somewhere, under the bed or in a closet. 'She calls him up all evening long. And then at about twelve-thirty, just when I'm going to sleep, she leaves the house.'

'I thought he wouldn't see her.'

'He won't. I don't know where she goes. Well . . . I do.'

'Where?'

'You mustn't tell,' Caroline warned.

April's eyes widened. 'Of course not.'

'She'd be terribly embarrassed if she thought anyone else knew. But I had to tell you. It gives me the creepie-crawlies. She goes to his apartment house and she sits outside his apartment and listens.'

'My God!' April said. 'How come he doesn't come out and catch her?'

'There's a sort of side place where she sits. On the stairs. And the worst part of it is, she calls me up at the office the next day and tells me everything that went on.'

'Like, *girls?*'

'Yes.'

'Oh, God,' April said again. 'Poor thing. How can she do that? I never dreamed of doing that with Dexter.'

It was the first time in over a month that April had mentioned Dexter's name. Ever since she had met Ronnie Wood, the boy from home, she had been like a different person. They had gone out together every evening of his two-week vacation in New York, and when he had left he began writing to her every day. April had a resiliency even Caroline had never suspected. One day she had been a miserable girl with a false smile and little real interest in anything, and then suddenly she was in love, surprised at it herself, but not nearly so surprised as her friends were.

'What have you heard from Ronnie?' Caroline asked, to change the subject.

'He wrote to me again today,' April said.

'And how often do you still write to him?'

'Every day.'

'What do you ever find to write that much about?'

'Oh, thoughts,' April said. 'How I feel about things. I almost never tell him what I'm doing. I mean, what *do* I do? I don't go out or anything, and every day at the office is nearly the same. I send him books sometimes. He says he misses me.'

Caroline didn't want to ask the obvious question: What do you think is going to happen? She was afraid for April because she was always so full of hope and allowed herself to be hurt without ever thinking hardheadedly about anything, and yet, it had been two months, nearly sixty letters; it was incredible.

'You know,' April said, 'I keep looking between the lines of his letters for something to be wrong with him. Like, is he neurotic, or selfish, or a liar? But he seems so perfect I can't believe it. No neurosis at all. And he loves me.' Her voice was the same soft, clear voice that had told Caroline so many shocking stories of heartbreak not long ago, but now it had wonder in it and a kind of pride. 'It's amazing,' April said. 'He's *normal*.'

'Is he still working for his father?'

'Yes. He says he likes it. He's going to take another vacation at Christmas if he can get away, and he's coming to New York. He says he wants to see me.'

Caroline waited for the words she knew were coming next: 'We're going to get married.' And she expected them with trepidation, not because she mistrusted Ronnie Wood – although there were few boys she really trusted when you came right down to it – but because of April. April was always expecting so much, and the words 'We're going to get married' coming from April had a pathetic ring. She would have much preferred to hear April say, He's proposed to me. But April said neither, she simply smiled happily.

'I'm so crazy about him,' April said. 'I'd like it if he'd marry me. I think . . . *maybe* . . . I can get him to marry me. I wish he would.'

And that, Caroline thought, coming from April, is like anyone else being ten years more grown up.

It was fun to make sandwiches with April and talk about people at the office and about life and to notice how, as often as she could, April would interject a reference to Ronnie into the conversation. It was obvious that she was in love with him, but she seemed so much surer of herself than she had been with Dexter that Caroline's fears were nearly allayed. 'I didn't sleep with him,' April said, 'and I'm not going to when he comes to New York this time, either. He's very respectful. He didn't even try, he just kind of asked me if I'd come up to his hotel room one night and I said no, so he never asked again. I'm dying to, though; it's a real struggle for me not to. He's so darling, isn't he? Don't you think he's darling looking?'

'Yes,' Caroline said, although Ronnie Wood's looks were not the type that had ever appealed to her. He seemed so young and unsure of himself. He probably was just the kind of boy who would worship April, and Caroline certainly hoped so.

'You know,' April said, 'I saw Dexter on Saturday. I went to Brooks Brothers to buy my father some ties for his birthday, and Dexter was there buying a tie. He tried not to notice me, but then he really had to, so he said, "Hello. How are you?" And I said, "Fine, how are you?" And then he told the salesman he really didn't see any ties he wanted and he would come back some other time, and he ran away. It was such a strange feeling.'

'How did you feel about him?' Caroline asked.

'I don't know. I really didn't feel anything. I mean, I looked at him and I thought how if Dexter really tried he could have me back. After everything he did he could have me back anyway. And yet, I'm sure I don't still love him. I love Ronnie in a different way. I think I love him more than I loved Dexter. But it's different.'

'But Ronnie's such a good person,' Caroline said. 'And Dexter's no good, you know that!'

'I know . . .' April said thoughtfully. 'It's funny, I was thinking on Saturday how unfair it is that every girl's first love can't be the one who'll turn out to be right for her. Sometimes he's the worst person in the world. But there's always something about your first love – if you're old enough, I don't mean sixteen – that you can't forget. It's like suddenly, for the first time, everything's important because you're doing it with him. And then there are all the little things in the world that hurt for a long, long time, because you used to do them with him and you can't any more.'

'I know,' Caroline said.

'I wish Ronnie could have been my first love. He was right there, all the time, and neither of us had ever met each other. He was in college, and then I was in New York, and he was away in the Army . . . I guess it's just a question of timing.'

'But maybe if you'd met him before you wouldn't have fallen in love with him,' Caroline said. 'You might have been looking for different things.'

'Oh, I'd always have loved him!' April said. 'Any time. I know I would have.'

I think she really would have, Caroline thought.

'I'll wash the dishes,' April said.

'There's nothing to wash.'

'Well, let me do it.'

'I'll show you my new shoes,' Caroline said. 'Very dark gray calf, wait till you see.' She went to the closet and rooted around among the shoes, hers and Gregg's, on the floor, and a pillowcase full of dirty laundry which Gregg had forgotten to take downstairs to the Chinaman, and one of Gregg's skirts which had fallen off the hanger on the overcrowded rod. 'I never can find anything in this mess. I wish we had more room.' She found the shoe box at last, and picked up Gregg's skirt to put it back on its hanger. As she did, something fell out of the skirt pocket to the floor.

She picked it up. It wasn't 'something,' it was three cigarette butts, one with lipstick on it, an empty lipstick case, and a torn piece of a letter. She looked at this rubbish with distaste, shrugged, and put it back into the pocket of Gregg's skirt. But her hand felt something else which made her recoil, withdraw, and then, with amazement, reach in to take it out to look at it. It was two more cigarette butts ringed with a darker lipstick, a piece of a colored envelope, an empty matchbook from a restaurant and a black bobby pin. 'Ugh,' she said. Her shoes didn't seem important any more, and she put the box on the closet shelf.

She didn't know what made her think of it, perhaps the fact that the pillowcase seemed not full enough to contain laundry and did not have the odd bulges in it that crumpled towels made. Caroline knelt and gingerly opened the knotted top of the pillowcase and peered inside. 'Oh, my God!'

'What's the matter?' April asked.

'Look at this stuff.' Caroline carried the pillowcase out into the room and looked around for a place to put it. Not the studio couch, certainly, nor the dining table. She finally put it on top of the radiator. 'Look.' She held the top of the pillowcase wide open, and April bent over it, looking inside.

'Garbage!' April whispered. 'Where did you get the garbage?'

'It's Gregg's.'

'In a pillowcase?'

'The thing that really gets me,' Caroline said, 'is it's in *my* pillow-case.'

It wasn't really garbage, in the sense of what you find in a garbage pail; it was wastebasket refuse: a torn stocking, a piece of a stocking box with the size printed on it, an envelope that had held air-line tickets, some more bits of letters and bills and papers, discarded cigarette wrappers from two different brands, empty matchbooks and an empty vial that had contained a prescription, with the code number and name still in it, made out to a Miss Masson. Caroline and April stared at these things for a moment in bewilderment, and then Caroline hastily knotted the top of the pillow slip again.

'I'd better put it all back right away.'

'What is she doing with that stuff?' April asked. 'I don't under-stand.'

'I wonder how long this has been going on . . .' Caroline thought back to how long the pillowcase had been on the floor in the closet, but it was impossible to remember. Gregg had always been untidy, but even so, something as large as a half-filled pillowcase . . . It hadn't been there last week, that she knew, because that was when she had bought the shoes and put the shoe box on the closet floor in the corner.

'Cigarette butts,' April said. 'I mean, *cigarette butts!*'

'Those other things aren't much better,' Caroline said.

'Caroline,' April said, 'do you think Gregg is crazy? That's pretty peculiar, to collect all that stuff.'

'Maybe she just likes garbage,' Caroline said. The two of them looked at each other, and then suddenly it seemed very funny and they began to giggle.

'What does your roommate do for a living?' April mimicked. 'Why, she's a garbage collector. Only there's one thing wrong with her. She brings it home.' Their giggles turned into laughter and they gasped with mirth.

'I'm sorry,' Caroline choked, 'I can't go out with you tonight. I have to go and collect some garbage.' She wiped her eyes.

'I'll have to save mine for her from now on,' April said.

'No. She doesn't want *yours*.' Caroline's laughter faded, she looked at April again, and it wasn't funny any more. 'It's awful,' she said. 'Do you know that?'

'I know . . .'

'Whose do you think it is?'

'I don't know.'

'Yes you do.'

'Yes,' April said slowly, and her face was troubled. 'Yes, I do. Don't you?'

They talked for a while of other things, but their thoughts were on Gregg and what had happened to her, and finally they talked about that again. 'She told me everything else,' Caroline said. 'But she never told me this.'

'She was probably embarrassed.'

'I don't blame her.'

'It's *his*, isn't it?' April said.

'Who else's?'

'How does she get it?'

'She must wait until he dumps his rubbish. Or till his maid does, he has a maid. I know Gregg never gets into his apartment, she told me so.'

'Isn't that strange . . .'

'She must have a terribly low opinion of herself,' Caroline murmured, 'to do something like that. She must really think she's nothing, to make herself suffer that way.'

When April left, at eleven, Caroline was not tired. She was still thinking about Gregg and the garbage, because it was so curious, and because it depressed her. She had known eccentric people, but they were silly old middle-aged women and men whose friends talked and laughed about them behind their backs and who managed to live and get along despite their odd habits. But to have her roommate, the girl she had lived with and known for over two years, turn out to be so disturbed, was another matter. She could not comprehend it. None of us would do something like that, Caroline thought – not April, not me, nobody. If I told my mother she'd say, You can't live with that girl any longer, she's sick. And

April and I laughed, we thought it was funny. There must be a middle ground somewhere, between revulsion and amusement, that would tell us what's really the matter.

She slept finally, fitfully, but when Gregg opened the front door Caroline heard her in her sleep and woke up. Gregg turned on the light in the closet and began to take off her coat. 'Oh,' Gregg said, 'did the light wake you?'

'No,' Caroline said.

'I'm glad you're up. We can talk. Are you sleepy?'

'A little.'

'Well, you can talk for a while, can't you?'

'Yes . . .'

She sat up in bed and Gregg turned on the overhead light. Everything was in a glare, as it is when you first open your eyes to electric light after sleep. Gregg was standing in the center of the room, all white and gold and wraithlike, her face very pale in the white glare, her eyes dark-circled from too little sleep, her blonde hair long and unkempt and wispy around her shoulders. She was still wearing her coat, open, her hands in the coat pockets. And Caroline could see that the pockets were bulging.

'I found out who the girl was,' Gregg said. She sat down on the foot of Caroline's bed, and despite herself Caroline drew away a little. 'There are two girls,' Gregg said, 'but the second one he likes better, and she goes there all the time now. The first one doesn't go there any more. She had dark hair and dark skin, I know because she wore dark lipstick and had a black bobby pin. I found the lipstick on some cigarettes they threw away.'

So it's true, Caroline thought.

'The second girl is from out of town. Either that or she just got back here from a trip. She left the envelope from a plane ticket from California. I thought at first she was an actress, but then I found a bottle of pills with her name on it, and I can't think of any young actress named Masson, can you?'

Caroline shook her head.

'I called up the drugstore and said I was she and asked them to renew my prescription and I would call for it. But the druggist said it had codeine in it and he couldn't renew it without a new prescription. I think it was a painkiller, not a sleeping pill, because David has sleeping pills he could have given her. She takes pills for cramps when she has her period. I know that too, because I heard her say she had the curse. Isn't that funny – I know everything about her, what color lipstick she wears, how her voice sounds, what kind of cigarettes she smokes, how big her feet are, even when she has her period, and I've never seen her. And she doesn't even know I know.'

'Oh, Gregg . . .' Caroline said. 'Gregg, don't . . .'

Gregg was smiling, a tiny, cold smile. 'Do you know how I found out? Look!' She pulled her hands out of her pockets, filled with new evidence, more dirty things, and held them out tenderly, as if they were jewels. 'I'm going to sort them all out tomorrow,' Gregg said. 'I got them from his wastebasket. The maid puts all these things out in the back hall in a paper bag, and the janitor comes and takes it away. But lately he hardly has anything to take away.'

'Gregg,' Caroline said softly, trying not to say the wrong thing, 'what good is all this going to do? It's only making you miserable. Look, I can get you a job at Fabian for a while and you'll be busy and you'll meet new people, and you'll be making money, and then at Christmas maybe we can go skiing in New Hampshire or somewhere. You'll have enough money by then. This isn't doing you any good, this hanging on, this . . . *scavenging.*'

Gregg didn't seem to be listening. She had spread out the new evidence on her lap and was busily sorting it out, her tongue in the corner of her mouth, like a little girl who is fixing her doll's bed. 'Her first name is Judy,' Gregg said. 'I think he likes her a lot. His voice is different when he speaks to her – more tender. Isn't that funny . . . I know everything about her. I wonder if he's going to fall in love with her, I mean, really in love. I wonder what she has that I didn't have . . . I'm going to find out.'

27

In the beginning of November Caroline had a dream that disturbed her for days afterward. She was not quite sure whether she had been asleep when it had happened or half awake, so that it had the quality of a wish rather than a dream. The dream concerned Eddie Harris. He was so real, to every last detail, and so unchanged, that he seemed to be speaking to her from across the entire spread of the country, like some extrasensory perception. She could tell herself that it was natural to think and dream of Eddie at this time; holidays were approaching, times for parties, for family, for people to be with those they loved best, if they could. And what did she have? Paul Landis and a series of casual dates who were no more interesting than Paul and did not have so good a character. And a fading daydream of John Cassaro, a daydream she had finally decided was a joke on herself rather than an aid and support. But the dream of Eddie had been so real, his voice had spoken to her with such uncanny exactitude, that all the remembered feeling she had had for him returned poignantly and she could not shake it off for days. Caroline began to wonder whether perhaps it could be possible that Eddie had been thinking of her at that very moment, and that was why she had dreamed of him as she did.

He had been telling her he loved her. I always have, he was telling her; I finally had to face it. They had looked into each other's eyes and she knew it was true, their hands touched and they both knew they belonged together. But of course! Caroline thought when she awoke and lay in bed with her eyes shut, clinging to the last wisps of the dream. Why didn't I think of it before? It was so real and so strong an image that she felt as if she had been fated to find Eddie again and remind him of her existence.

The next day in the office Caroline thought of him from time to time all day, and when evening came the desire to write him a letter came to her, as if it were the most natural thing in the world. This is nonsense, she told herself, it's just something I want to do, so I'm making up all sorts of excuses for it. If I could ever find out where Eddie is, I'm sure he wouldn't answer my letter anyway. And I'd never know whether he got it and didn't want to answer, or forgot to answer because I'm nothing at all to him even as a remembered friend, or whether he didn't get the letter at all; and I'll always wonder and it will hurt me. Nevertheless, the next day she called Information and asked for the address of the Lowe Oil Company in Dallas, Texas, and wrote it down. Somehow she was sure he would be working for his father-in-law, in some bright public-relations way, because she understood Eddie well, even after all this time. He would have to work there. If he didn't, then she could never find him, because she certainly couldn't write to him at his home, even if she were writing out of curiosity and no baser motive.

It was curiosity, really, Caroline finally realized. It was three years since Eddie had broken their engagement, and many things had happened to her, so naturally she was curious to find out what had happened to him. The people who are part of our past and help to make our present what it is always stay in our minds, if only because we always wonder what would have happened if things had been different so long ago. Did he have children, had he changed, had he grown stuffy, as so many of the boys had whom she had known at school? Why shouldn't I write to Eddie, Caroline thought. I'm no danger to him, I'm just a curious friend.

So at the end of the week she finally wrote to him. It was a short letter.

Dear Eddie, she wrote, on the typewriter and on her office stationery. *It occurred to me that it has been three years since I saw you last, and since so many interesting things have happened to me since then I thought I'd write and tell you about them, and I hope that you'll write and tell me what's happened to you.* That sounded stilted and foolish, but Caroline could not think of any other way to put it. She reread what she had written several times and then tore it out of the typewriter and threw it away. *Dear Eddie, I was looking through my old college photograph album the other day and I came upon some pictures of you, taken years ago, and they reminded me of you. So here I am, a voice from the past, and an inquisitive one. So many interesting things have happened to me since I saw you last that I thought I'd write and tell you about them, and I am curious to hear what the years have brought to you.* Oh, God, that sounded as if they were both a hundred years old! How was it that she could write such fluent and intelligent letters to her authors but for Eddie Harris, someone who really meant something to her, she was nearly illiterate? She finally let it stand and went on to tell him of her job as an editor, trying to make it sound as if she had a great deal of prestige and led a gay, mad life taking well-known authors out to lunch and cocktails for literary discussions and guidance. She told him that she had her own apartment in New York, with an actress he might have heard of (making it sound as if he would have heard of the successful ingénue Gregg Adams if he kept up with the theater), and that she was having fun. *And how are you? Do you have any children? I remember you always played the piano so well – I hope you haven't given it up.* She signed it, finally: *As ever, Caroline.* 'As ever' was good, it could mean everything or nothing. She put the letter into an air-mail envelope before she could lose her nerve and addressed it to Eddie Harris at the Lowe Oil Company and marked it Personal. And now that she had been so reckless, and had gone to all this trouble already, she scribbled 'Please Forward' on the front of the envelope. At least she would know he had received it, at least she wouldn't keep buoying up her hopes with false excuses if he didn't write back.

She put the letter into her out box and watched the mailboy take it away. It was done. But it was not irrevocable, she could run to the mailroom right now and snatch the letter back and tear it up. Knowing that she could, she left the office immediately and went home, and when she got there, safely away from any sane thoughts of salvation, she began to think: It takes two days for a letter to get to Dallas. Say three, to be absolutely sure. And a week for him to answer, at the outside, and then three for his letter to get back to me. Two weeks. I won't think about it any more until two weeks from today.

There was a certain peace of mind in knowing that there were two weeks of no man's land, during which she could be neither hurt nor shocked nor disappointed, because nothing that could happen within those two weeks would be any fault of hers. Afterward she could begin to wait, and go to the mailroom before the mailboy could even bring around her letters, and berate herself, and wonder whether Eddie thought she had been trying to get him back. Afterward could come doubts, but now there was peace. Oddly, Caroline felt happier than she had felt all year.

On Tuesday afternoon John Cassaro called her at her office. She recognized his voice instantly but did not quite believe it. For a moment Caroline had the thought that this was some kind of an odd practical joke. But on the other hand, she had known, secretly, that they would meet again, and she felt so strange – aloof, away from him and his charm, able to take care of herself. The manuscript clerk came into Caroline's office with an armful of manuscripts while Caroline was on the phone and Caroline impatiently waved her away. The girl was a gum-chewing cow, she liked to wait around until you were off the phone so she could engage you in ten minutes of meaningless conversation about the manuscripts she was bringing.

'I didn't have any trouble finding you,' John Cassaro said. 'The operator knew right away who you are. She said, Oh, *yes*, Caroline.'

'Is that what she said? *Caroline?*'

'Mm-hm.'

She knew then that he was teasing her, and she liked him for it.

'Oh, I'm famous here,' she said happily.

'You must get more phone calls than anyone else around.'

'I don't know.'

'Hey,' John Cassaro said, 'my pigeon misses you. He's so miserable he's switched to Alka-Seltzer.'

Caroline laughed. 'That's a hang-over,' she said. 'You can't fool me.'

'Why don't you come on over and see for yourself?'

'Well . . .'

'Come on over after work and have a drink with me.'

My one date with John Cassaro, Caroline thought. Do I want it tonight? Or do I want it ever, at all? 'I can't,' she said lightly. 'I have another date.'

'Oh? With your boy friend?'

'I have no boy friend.'

'Then slough him off and come over to see me. He hasn't got a pigeon like mine. Hmm?'

I'll *bet* he hasn't, Caroline thought. 'I can't,' she said with more resolution.

'You *do* like him.'

'It's not a question of that. But if I stood him up and lied to him . . . then if I ever broke a date with you you'd never believe me.' Now what had made her say that? She didn't have anything at all to do tonight, except sit home and think of Eddie, and yet she'd said no to John Cassaro and then thrown out that hint that she'd like to see him another time.

'You're right,' John Cassaro said. 'You're a hundred percent right. You're a nice girl. Have a good time tonight.'

'Thank you.'

'Goodbye.'

He hung up first, and Caroline replaced the receiver slowly, realizing for the first time how nervous she was. Her hands were cold and she had an empty feeling inside, like being hungry. She tried to imagine what it would have been like if she'd gone to John Cassaro's hotel suite for cocktails. She would have been more nervous than she was now, and he would be stalking her, shooting charm at her like poisoned arrows, and the whole experience would have unnerved her. She didn't really mind that she had said no, even if he never called again. She was quite sure he would never call again. You couldn't hurt the pride of a celebrity like John Cassaro and expect him to take the chance of its happening again.

He was through with her, before anything had even started. *But Eddie might write . . .* And that was why she would have been so unhappy at John Cassaro's apartment, because her heart would have been elsewhere. She had to admit to herself at last that she was much more interested in whether Eddie still thought of her, so interested in it that she didn't dare even think about it.

Some mornings if Caroline came to the office ten or fifteen minutes late the first mail was already there, tucked under the leather edge of her desk blotter. It was easier that way, these last few days; she had one fewer mail delivery to wait for like a caged animal in her cubicle. Despite her resolution not to care, she was thinking a little, thinking that perhaps her letter had gotten there in only two days, and that he had written the day he received it. When she came into her office on Wednesday, at a quarter past nine, the mail was there, protruding out of the blotter's leather edge like a white fan. And one of the envelopes was made of blue tissue paper with red, white and blue air-mail edging around it. She snatched it, her heart pounding. The name and address were handwritten and even in the instant it took her to recognize the forgotten but familiar handwriting her eye had traveled upward to where the postmark said *Dallas, Texas.*

She could not find her letter opener, she slit the envelope with her fingernails, her hands shaking, careful not to tear the letter that was inside. She sat in her swivel chair and read, and as she did the shape of the letters that formed the words was so dear to her, so well remembered, so unchanged, that she almost couldn't breathe.

DEAR CAROLINE:

I was very happy to hear from you. I thought you must have forgotten all about me by now. Your life in New York sounds wonderful. It certainly has been a long time when you think of it – three years – longer perhaps for me than it has been for you. I haven't much to tell you. We have a daughter, a year old, named Alexandra, Sandy for short. I'm working for my father-in-law, doing something nongeological and nonexecutive, if you can figure out what that is. Sometimes I wonder if he can! We have a house in the suburbs, which even though this is Texas is only a half hour by car from my office. And we have a heart-shaped swimming pool, which has to be seen to be believed, and two enormous Dalmatian puppies, which also have to be seen to be believed.

I'm going to be in New York on business about the fifteenth of December, for a week. Could I call you at your office? I'd like to see you again, and if I told you it was for old time's sake that would only be half the truth. Perhaps we could have lunch together.

As ever,

EDDIE

Caroline reread the letter three times before she finally folded it and put it back in its envelope. What did he mean: It's been longer perhaps for me than it has been for you? That a long time makes one forget? Or that he had missed her more than she knew? She knew Eddie well enough to know that he would never write or say a mean thing, even inadvertently; he was much too clever. So he must have meant that it was a long time because he missed her. *He misses me!* And the other reasons that he wanted to see her . . . She put a piece of paper into her typewriter roller quickly.

DEAR EDDIE:

I'd love to have lunch with you in New York, so please do call me. This is my office number . . .

She had a calendar on her desk and she would begin to mark off the days. It was only a little more than four weeks to the fifteenth of December.

28

The incurable optimists are those who always say, Tomorrow will be better, and mean tomorrow literally, or at the most, next week. Those who are more practical, and more often right, think in long terms, like a year. April Morrison, who had never had a long-term philosophy of life, thinking only, I won't think about it today or else I'll suffer twice, was thinking for the first time in terms of measured change as she sorted and packed her belongings on the tenth of December. A year ago, she was thinking with awe, it was right before Christmas and I was the most miserable girl in the world. And today I'm the happiest.

The night she had gone to Dexter Key's parents' apartment to ask him if he would see her again seemed so long ago that now she could look at it right in the face, without cringing and without pain. It had been a mistake, as her whole alliance with Dexter Key had been, but a girl was entitled to make mistakes. She still thought of her relationship with Dexter sometimes as an alliance, some-times as a romance, depending on her mood, but occasionally when she thought of the things he had done to her she wondered how she could have been in love with him at all. She remembered how he had always said, It will be all right. Everything will be all right. She remembered especially how he had said it on the night she had told him she was going to have a baby. How happy she had been then, happy and frightened and really believing in the future. She realized now, dimly, that when Dexter said, 'It will be all right,' he was talking to reassure himself, not her. No matter what, she would never hold anything against him. She had needed him so badly, it had been her fault not to have understood what he was. And now that she had Ronnie, all the other was like a bad, sad thing that had happened to her years and years ago – and a lovely thing too in some ways, although April was beginning to have to strain her mind to look back and remember why.

With surprise she came upon several gin bottles under the sink, empty ones. She had never thrown them away and then she had forgotten they were there. The memory of other nights came back to her as she gingerly carried the empty gin bottles to the incinerator, nights that hurt her more to remember than any memory of Dexter Key. But all that was over, and eventually she would forget them too.

She had wondered seriously whether or not she should confess everything to Ronnie. He had come back to New York a week ago and they had seen each other every day, and held hands in the street like teen-agers, and talked for hours about themselves and their future as they sat at a tiny round table in an espresso place in the Village, and kissed wonderingly and lovingly in her apartment, and talked about how many children they wanted to have. And finally Ronnie had said, as if she had known all along, 'Here I am planning our family and I haven't even proposed to you officially. Wait . . .' And he took her hand in both of his and said, 'April, will you marry me?'

Happiness filled her chest and her throat, and her eyes filled with tears and she could not trust her voice to answer for fear she would begin to cry. So she nodded her head and put her cheek on his hand and then finally she looked up at him and said, 'Yes, of course I will.' They just sat there for a while, Ronnie with his arm around her and she with her head on his shoulder, and all April could think was Happy Happy Happy, like some silly refrain running around and around in her head. And then she began to wonder whether she should tell him about the other boys.

She owed it to him; he would find out anyway when they were married. She was terrified that he would find out. What would he think of her? He wouldn't know how many, but he would know there had been someone. But he was so happy, how could she possibly tell him? You couldn't just bring it up and say, 'Oh, by the way, since we're getting married, I thought I'd mention that I've had a lover.' What could she say?

She finally asked Caroline, because Caroline was the most sensible and compassionate girl she knew.

'You're a fool if you tell him,' Caroline said firmly. 'What do you want to do, hand him a knife and tell him to go cut his throat?'

'But to have a secret like that . . .'

'That's supposed to be a secret.'

'Ronnie trusts me. He sort of . . . idolizes me.'

'And he's going to have good reason to,' Caroline said. 'You love him, you intend to be faithful to him and make him happy for the rest of your life, don't you?'

'Of course!'

'Then what are you going to do, tell him you've been a bad girl and you have a guilty conscience? Don't you think he's slept with girls?'

'Oh, I'm sure,' April said. 'He was in the Army.'

'And would you want him to come and describe it to you?'

'Of course not!'

'It's worse if you tell *him*,' Caroline said. 'Believe me, it'll be worse. If you had met Ronnie two years ago none of those things would have happened to you. It's just rotten luck. You would have married Dexter if you could have, but he wouldn't. None of us is responsible for the wonderful people we don't meet; we're only lucky when we do meet them. He's interested in your life with him now, from now on, not what you did before he knew you. If you tell Ronnie about Dexter and those others I'll never speak to you again.'

'I won't tell him,' April promised.

'And you'd better start forgetting about them as fast as you can.'

'But . . .' April said. 'I . . . he's going to *know*. He's going to know when we're married.'

Caroline bit her lip. 'Your first time with Dexter,' she asked softly, 'did it hurt? Did you have to make him stop? Was there— '

'A sign?'

Caroline nodded.

April shook her head wonderingly. 'No,' she said slowly, rather surprised as she remembered that night as it had been. 'No. Everything was just fine.'

'Some people are lucky that way,' Caroline said. 'Go get married to Ronnie, and when I come to the wedding, see if he has a friend for me who's as nice as he is.'

'He couldn't have a friend who's as wonderful as he is!' April said happily. 'But I'll look!'

So now she was packing, saying goodbye to her apartment and to New York and to the job that she had never really liked enough to miss now. How strange it would be to lie in bed every morning until ten o'clock, and to be able to cut out recipes from the newspaper and make things that Ronnie liked, and to know that there was someone who would come home to her every evening, who would want to come home to her, who would direct himself to his home as a bird flies south in winter, instinctively, for warmth and love and the life he needed. Things that had never seemed so interesting before: tablecloths in store windows, embroidered sheets, silverware, now took on a great significance. She had looked at these household things when she had been in love with Dexter, but then it had been different. Dexter had his own apartment, with his own things in it, and when she had thought of marrying Dexter it had always been with the idea of moving into his apartment with him, into his sheltering arms, not the sharing of a home that she and he might build together. Would Ronnie like blue sheets or white, she wondered, and whichever he wanted he would have. You couldn't ask Dexter if he preferred blue sheets, he would only shrug and look annoyed because such talk frightened him. April realized for the first time that he had been gruff with her because he had been frightened.

The girls at the office had given her a going-away luncheon when she handed in her resignation, and for a few minutes there had been something unreal about having an office party all for herself when for three years she had been contributing and going to parties for other girls. Now she was the one with the corsage and the feigned surprise, and the grin of happiness which she didn't have to feign at all because she was so happy. She liked them all, all those girls, even the ones who had hardly spoken two words to her. How nice they all were to come to her luncheon and to make a fuss over her, and to give her a present. April had opened her present with misgivings, preparing her cries of delight as she untied the silver ribbon that had little paper wedding bells attached to it, because she knew from experience that the gift was usually some quite ugly thing that one of the typists thought was pretty. But it had been a white nylon nightgown, short and pleated, with little pink and blue rosebuds embroidered on the yoke, the most beautiful nightgown April had ever seen. She caught Caroline's happy glance across the table as she held the nightgown up for all the girls to see, and then she realized that it had been Caroline who had chosen it for her. Of course! Caroline knew just what April liked.

And Caroline had given her a going-away present of her own, to take back to Colorado, a square white leather overnight case with her married initials on it in gold and room under the make-up tray for her new nightgown and slippers. April ran her fingers over the tiny gold initials, A.M.W., as if she were reading braille. How wonderful they looked: A.M.W. So symmetrical. And so natural.

She locked one suitcase and began to pack her new case. Caroline would be here in a moment or two, to help her pack and say goodbye, and then Ronnie would arrive, and then they would get into his new bright-red station wagon and drive away. When April had heard that he had bought the new station wagon just to drive her back home in style, instead of in his dirty old jalopy, she had nearly cried again.

All over the city they were putting up the decorations for Christmas, the great tree in Rockefeller Plaza and the smaller trees along the center strip of Park Avenue. There was Christmas music in the stores where April had bought part of her trousseau, and it made her think of the Christmas before as well as the one to come, so that she felt both excitement and a faint, diminishing sadness. There would always be sounds and things to look at that had special meaning, and it was this meaning that made memories. But from now on all her memories were going to be good. April knew that. Her doorbell rang and she ran to answer it. It was Caroline.

'Hi,' Caroline cried, embracing her. 'You're nearly all done, what is there for me to do?'

'Just sit here and talk to me,' April said.

'Do you want me to hand you things from the closet?'

'Oh, thanks.'

'Look at this!' Caroline cried. 'Your new suit. It's beautiful.'

'That's for after the wedding. To go away in. I'll have to wear a coat over it, though, it's so cold in February. Look at my new coat, it's in the box there.'

Caroline opened the box that was on the table and exclaimed over the coat. 'Oh, it's lovely!'

'And did you see my at-home outfit? Isn't it silly?' April held it up, a pair of red velvet overalls and a white satin shirt.

'It's darling. When is your wedding dress coming?'

'They're doing the alterations at the store and mailing the dress to me at home.'

Caroline was standing at the window looking out at the winter garden below. 'Guess what,' she said, 'somebody's finally put Christmas decorations on that little tree out there. Poor thing, it hasn't any leaves on it and it looks so funny.'

April came to look over her shoulder. 'It's kind of a mangy little tree, isn't it?' she said, surprised. 'I always used to think it was so wonderful.'

'It looks worse in the winter.'

'I guess so. But this apartment looks awful too, look at it!' She turned around to face the room, holding her arms out wide. 'None of the dishes match, the silverware's tin, and look at that bed in the wall! Nobody has a bed in the wall any more, it's an antique. And do you know what? It had a broken spring in the middle of it that got to just kill me after a couple of years.'

Caroline smiled. 'Remember how thrilled you were with all of it when you first moved in?'

'I know . . . And do you know what I was thinking? After I go away, another girl will move in here in a week or two and she'll think it's all so wonderful, the way I did.'

'It'll probably be an old widow, on relief, with three or four tomcats,' Caroline said.

'No, it will be a girl, I know it will,' April said. 'It has to be another new girl, like I was. I wish I could leave her a note or something.'

'A note? What kind of a note?' Caroline asked, surprised.

'I don't know exactly,' April said. 'Just something that says, I know just how you feel. I wish someone had done that for me. Oh, well, it was only a thought.' She shrugged.

'I know what you mean,' Caroline said slowly. 'Nobody ever thinks that other people have exactly the same problems and thoughts that she has. You always think you're all alone.'

'Oh, I'm going to miss you!' April said. 'I'm going to miss you so much!'

'I'll miss you too,' Caroline said. 'More than you'll miss me, because you'll have Ronnie.'

'We'll write to each other all the time.'

'Of course.'

'Some people forget to write, like the girls I went to school with, but you and I won't forget. Will we?' April said.

'No,' Caroline said, and April thought she sounded a little sad and looked a little faraway, as if she really knew better. 'You and I won't stop writing to each other.' She cheered up then, and smiled. 'But I'll see you in only two months, at your wedding, and then in the spring when you and Ronnie go to Europe you'll have to stop first in New York.'

'We'll have a reunion,' April said happily. 'Just think, Caroline – Europe!'

The telephone rang then, and April answered it.

'Honey,' Ronnie said. 'Are you ready yet?' How dear his voice was, how gentle.

'All but one suitcase,' April said. 'Are you ready?'

'Yes. I'll wait around for five minutes and then I'll check out and bring the car around. Can I park in front of your house?'

'Sure,' April said, 'I've seen people do it.' The image of a long black limousine flashed through her mind, but she pushed it hurriedly away. Soon she would see a bright-red station wagon at the curb in its place, and then the new image would stay in her mind forever after. 'I'll see you soon, darling,' she said.

She was stuffing all her last-minute things into the last suitcase, running to look into the bureau drawers to see if she had forgotten anything, pushing a quarter-filled perfume bottle and some old letters into her already overcrowded purse. 'That's one thing about going by car,' she said, 'you don't have to be so organized.' She ran to the mirror to put on more lipstick and fresh powder, and then she was ready. She looked about the room. 'My gosh,' she said. 'This old dump. It's never *been* so neat.' It looked depersonalized somehow, stripped of all its character, and yet so many things had happened here that April hated to turn her back on this room without some sort of a goodbye. But she couldn't think of anything to do, so she just stood there at the doorway, surrounded by her luggage, and looked. First Barbara, she thought, and now me. We're all leaving this house.

The doorbell rang then and she turned to open the door for Ronnie. He walked into the room and bent down to kiss her on the side of the neck, a quick, instinctive gesture. 'Hello,' he said. 'Hello, Caroline.' He picked up a suitcase in each hand.

April picked up her overnight case and bent to lift the last suitcase. 'No,' Ronnie said, 'don't do that. I'll come back for it.'

'Up three flights of stairs? I should say not.'

'Quiet,' Ronnie said good-naturedly, and ran down the steps.

'He's so nice,' Caroline said. 'He loves you very much.'

'I know.'

They stood there smiling at each other, neither of them willing to say the preliminaries to goodbye just yet, and waited for Ronnie to return. He was back in a few moments and took the last suitcase and April's overnight case. 'Here we go,' April said, and shut the door to her apartment for the last time.

There was a chill in the air, but not an unpleasant one, rather the kind that makes you wonder why you never realized how much you enjoyed winter. The sun was shining, dazzlingly bright, catching the little bits of mica in the sidewalk and making them glisten so that if you were a young child or a dreamer you would catch yourself stooping every once in a while to pick up what your eye had mistaken for a jewel. Then you would straighten up again, embarrassed, hoping no one had noticed, but sooner or later you would only be taken in by that incongruous glitter once more. April felt the band of her engagement ring inside the finger of her glove and pressed her fingers against it. A narrow platinum band with a little blue-white diamond-cut diamond set in it. 'I want you to pick it out for me yourself,' she had said to Ronnie, 'and give it to me as a surprise.' So he had, and it had been exactly the shape of diamond she wanted. She had wanted only what he wanted for her, but somehow their tastes in big things were so similar that he always seemed to know what she liked.

He piled her suitcases into the back of his station wagon, beside his one. She had her new going-away coat in its paper box and handed it to him, and he put it carefully on top of the pile.

'Well,' Caroline said.

Ronnie held out his hand and Caroline took it. They shook hands warmly. 'You're April's favorite friend,' Ronnie said. 'I'm going to miss you too, even though we've just met. You'll have to come to visit us sometime.'

'Thank you,' Caroline said. 'Maybe I'll be able to.' She turned to April.

'Oh, Caroline,' April said. For the first time she realized it was true, she was going away, she was leaving New York and her friends here, and after she returned from Europe perhaps she might never come back again. You never knew. She might have a baby the first year, she would have other friends, you got tied up when you lived in a place . . . She kissed Caroline on the cheek. 'Goodbye, Caroline.'

'Goodbye, April. Have a safe trip. And happy . . . happy *everything*.'

'You too,' April said softly. 'I mean it. I hope you'll get what you want too.'

'Thank you,' Caroline whispered.

'Goodbye.'

'Goodbye.'

April went around to the other side of the station wagon then, where Ronnie was holding open the door for her, and she climbed in. The sun was so dazzling on the side window that she could hardly see Caroline standing there on the curb, except as a dark silhouette. April held up her hand and waved, and the silhouette waved back. She reached behind her then and snapped down the lock on the door. Ronnie settled behind the wheel and started the engine, letting the car warm up for a moment. He looked at April, and he did not say anything but simply smiled at her. She smiled back, and her throat nearly choked with love and happiness. 'Hey,' she said softly.

'What?'

'We're really going.'

'Mm-hm.'

She moved closer to him and put her hands around his arm.

As the station wagon moved through the city April looked out the window at all the sights that had meant so many different things to her during the past three years. How drab they looked in winter, and yet, they would always thrill her. Here was a part of the city she did not know, and here at last was the highway, flanked on one side by the cold blue water, deceptively sunny-looking in the bright day. She took one last look through the rear window at the skyscrapers vanishing behind them, and then she turned to look ahead and at Ronnie's capable gloved hands on the red wheel, and she did not think of or miss the city at all.

29

For people who have something in the present it is easier to forget the past, although you never wholly do so. When winter comes, spring is a vague memory, something looked back at with nostalgia, but winter is the here and now and requires all your energies. If spring were to vanish and there were nothing, an abyss, if that were even possible to imagine, then you would live with memories of spring for ever and ever or else become a part of the abyss itself. The same can sometimes be said for love, but not always. There are some loves that live on for years, inexplicably, although the lovers are parted and there is no hope that they may ever reunite except as polite and distant friends. Caroline Bender thought of all these things as she marked off the days on her desk calendar, waiting for the return to New York of Eddie Harris.

Will it be the same? she thought. Will it even be nearly the same? Now that the fifteenth was drawing closer, she was alternately cautious and filled with all the elation of a bride. It was ridiculous, she told herself, and yet, she had never felt this way before in her life, as though she were really not herself but some young girl waiting innocently and adoringly for the fulfillment of her dream. Then, at the times when her fears overtook her, she would brace herself for disappointment, for the discovery that Eddie was, after all, human and might turn out to be nothing more than the prototype of all young husbands, bringing out baby pictures, chattering about his work, telling her how he had taken up golf. The image made her blood run cold. She remembered how, when they were in college, when she and Eddie had been in love, they had read *Tender Is the Night* together, and she took the book from her shelf in her apartment and read it again. There was a scene in it of reunion between a married man and a girl he had loved years before, a reunion that ended not in poignance but in something even more upsetting: dull lack of interest. They had both changed, and when they met again they had a brief, unloving affair and drifted apart, not really minding, not really aware of what they had missed. If that happens to me and Eddie, she thought. Oh, no . . . And yet, perhaps it would be merciful. She would be delivered from him, from his spell, and she could go on to the future, whatever that was. If she were to find that Eddie aroused only indifference in her, then wouldn't it be better, not worse? It would be sensible, and she wouldn't even know it was happening. She would just pick up her life again and say, Well, that's that. The thought made her want to cry.

At the bottom of her bureau drawer, under her sweaters, she had her college photograph album, put away out of sight because it contained so many pictures of her and Eddie together with their old friends. And beside it, in a silver frame that was tarnished black by now, was an eight-by-ten photograph of Eddie. She took them out now, for the first time since she had moved to her apartment in New York, and she looked at them. She was almost afraid to look at Eddie's first; she looked at herself. How much younger she had looked! More tender, with tender, undefined features, the face of a very young girl. She thought she was prettier now, she had more style. She wondered whether Eddie would think she had changed much. And Eddie? His face leaped up at her, so familiar, so beloved, that involuntarily Caroline reached out her fingers to touch his lips and stroke his cheek. She loved him so. If she could only kiss him. No wonder she had hidden the pictures in the dresser; to look at that enlargement every day would have broken her heart.

But now, for a little while, she could face it again. She put the photograph album on her coffee table and the silver-framed picture on the top of her dresser. *Eddie*. His presence seemed to fill the room. And as Caroline looked at the photograph she remembered for the first time in almost two years exactly how his voice had sounded, every tone and accent of it, as if she had spoken to him only that morning: slightly husky, soft, a voice almost in his throat, with that indefinable quality known as sexiness, and always full of humor.

She remembered his voice making plans for both of them, and that hurt. She could repeat his words to herself, thinking how they might come true, but underneath they hurt her. To have believed so unquestioningly in something that had meant the world and then to find that it simply did not exist was a frightening thing.

There were the phonograph records they had played together, which she had always been afraid to play again just for herself. They were old seventy-eights, and when Caroline put the first one on the phonograph she was struck at first by how different it sounded, distorted, far away. But then the melody hit her, and everything came back so rapidly and with such force that she rose to her feet and began to walk about the room, dancing a little to the music, thinking of Eddie and herself three years ago and almost holding out her hands to him. Her lips moved as she spoke to him, half in the words she had said to him when they had listened to those records and had made love – but really love, *love*, not any sham of passionate strangers but a thing of tenderness and close-ness and great passion too, always with the words of love from each to the other – and half in the words that she would like to say to him now. It was a daydream in which Eddie was in the room, returned to her, and in this dream they both understood that noth-ing, really, had changed.

How quickly those shellac records were over, only a few tanta-lizing minutes and then you had to run to return the clicking arm. Caroline knelt by the phonograph and turned it off. Two more days. Two more days . . .

The next day she went to Saks on her lunch hour and bought perfume and cologne and bath oil, the same fragrance she had worn when she had gone with Eddie, and which she had never worn since. Opening the stopper at her desk, she was nearly taken with dizziness at the familiarity of it, a throat-catching scent of flowers and memories and former happiness that she felt sure could never affect anyone else the way it did her. Tomorrow. Tomorrow . . .

That night she went to bed at nine o'clock so that she would look fine in the morning, but she could not sleep. Perhaps he won't come tomorrow, she was thinking; perhaps it will be the next day. Can I bear it, to wait another day? I've waited so long already. But she knew that she would wait the day if necessary, or another week, or any time, since nothing could be so long as these sleepless hours in the last, anticipatory night.

Gregg came in at three, tiptoeing, and Caroline turned her face to the wall and pretended to be asleep. She would not, she could not, listen to Gregg tell her what new secret things she had discovered from sifting through David Wilder Savage's garbage. Not tonight. She liked Gregg, and she felt so sorry for her, but tonight of all nights, waiting, Caroline wanted to feel alone, untouched, pure, away from any talk of neurosis or heartbreak or aberration, so that she could wait for Eddie as Caroline, not the receptacle of someone else's sorrows, not a girl who had suffered and blundered in her turn, but Caroline whose heart was full of love and wonder and hope. The last thing Caroline remembered was the luminous hands of her clock at four, and then she slept.

She was in her office at nine and sat at her desk with her hands tightly holding the arms of her swivel chair, looking at the telephone as if she could will it to ring. She knew this was silly, he was probably asleep or not here yet, but she could not bear it. She tried to read a manuscript, but she found herself rereading the same paragraph four times and not getting any sense out of it, and so she put the manuscript aside. It wasn't fair to her authors, she might as well just sit and suffer. At a quarter to eleven her telephone rang. Caroline jumped, a startled, involuntary motion, and snatched up the receiver.

'Hello?'

'Caroline,' Eddie said.

That voice, that one word, were so close and familiar they made her begin to tremble. Her heart was pounding. 'Eddie? Eddie? Hello!' she said brightly.

He sounded relieved and his voice came pouring out of the telephone with more confidence, making her remember everything, bringing him closer. Her lips were almost touching the receiver as if it were Eddie himself. 'How are you, Caroline?' Eddie said and, not even waiting for her to answer, 'You sound wonderful.'

'How are you, Eddie?'

He gave a little laugh. 'I was up all night on the plane. I have red eyes and a black beard. Can you see me for lunch anyway?'

'Of course! What time? Where?'

'Twelve o'clock? Or would one be better for you?'

'No, twelve is fine.'

'Well, I'm at the Plaza.' He paused. 'I think it would be better . . . since it's been so long and I just want to talk to you without a lot of strangers listening in . . . could you meet me up here?'

'Yes . . .'

She pulled a pencil out of her pencil holder, spilling the entire supply in the process, and wrote down the number of Eddie's room. 'It's a suite,' he said, 'and it's down at the end of the hall. Just keep walking to your left when you get out of the elevator.'

'Yes . . .'

'I'll see you then,' he said softly. 'Twelve o'clock.'

'Yes . . .' And he had hung up.

How businesslike they both had sounded, Caroline thought. Plans, time and place. And yet, that lowering of the voice, his wish to meet her somewhere private, signified emotion, even over an impersonal telephone. She went quickly to the ladies' room, where she washed her face, although she had washed it only two and a half hours before, and put on fresh make-up: mascara, everything, lightly so that it looked very natural. She put more of the perfume at her throat and on her hair, although the scent of the bath oil she had bathed in that morning still lingered, and then she looked for the dozenth time to see if the seams of her stockings were straight. She must have combed her hair fifteen times at that mirror before she was satisfied with the result, although she realized wryly that even in getting in and out of a taxi the December wind would destroy what she had so carefully done. Eleven-thirty. She couldn't go back to her office, she felt too nervous.

She walked down the hall to the office that April used to have. It was funny, since April had left she still sometimes started toward that office, forgetting that it was empty, that April would not be there to speak to her and share her secret. Just because it made her feel better, Caroline opened the door to April's office and walked inside. There was the bookshelf of brightly colored paperback books, the desk completely emptied except for the office-issued blotter and pen-in-inkwell and calendar, and there was the coat rack on which she always used to see April's beige cashmere coat. If April were here they could talk, they could pass these fifteen minutes of waiting. Now Caroline just stood there, and then she turned and walked slowly back to her office and put on her coat and gloves and walked still more slowly down the hall to the elevator.

When she got out of the elevator on Eddie's floor at the Plaza it was only a quarter to twelve. Caroline hesitated, hearing the metal doors of the elevator click shut behind her. She could hover here or she could sit on the steps or she could take the chance and ring Eddie's doorbell. She bit her lip and walked slowly along the hall, reading the numbers, until she came to his, and then, timidly, she lifted her hand and rang his bell.

There was silence and then she heard footsteps, only one or two, as you hear when someone is just at arm's reach of the door-knob, and then Eddie opened the door. They each stood there in silence, looking at the other. He had not changed, he had not changed at all. His hair was still cut fairly short, a medium sandy brown. His face was freshly shaven, smooth and so handsome she realized she had forgotten quite how beautiful he was. He looked at her intently, almost stared, and then he grinned and said, 'Come in, Caroline, come in.'

He was wearing a dark-gray flannel suit with narrow lapels and a shirt with hairline blue and white stripes on it, and a plain dark tie. You noticed the suit almost as an afterthought – yes, it was gray – but what you saw first was the way he moved, the way an animal moves inside its coat. When he lifted his arm to help Caroline remove her coat she saw the arm and the hand with complete awareness, not the flannel sleeve, or the cuff beneath, or the cuff link, if there even was one. She was aware of all this dimly, trying to think of something to say. 'I'm a little early,' she said.

'I'm glad.'

'You haven't changed at all,' Caroline said.

'Neither have you.'

'You don't think I've changed?'

'Not a bit. I was afraid you would. I was afraid you'd look like those terrible women you see on Fifth Avenue, who always look as if they've just stepped out of the hairdresser's.'

'They probably just have,' she said, laughing. 'They go three times a week.'

'And bring their dogs, and strap them to the leg of their chair.' He was grinning at her, and then as his eyes met hers his smile faded and he reached out and touched her arm. 'Sit down,' he said. 'Sit down. I'm so glad to see you.'

'I'm glad to see you,' she said softly. 'Eddie.'

There was a window with sunshine pouring in and a tiny, dimly exquisite view of the park below through the transparent curtains. In front of the window was a love seat and a bottle of champagne in a silver cooler. 'I have champagne,' Eddie said. 'I thought it would be fun. Champagne for breakfast. Oh, but you've probably had breakfast, it's so late for you.'

She shook her head.

'Remember that Sunday at school when we went to the Ritz for breakfast and had champagne?' he said happily. 'I don't even remember what we had afterward.'

'Neither do I! I remember I was in the shower and you called me up and you said, "Let's have breakfast at the Ritz," just like that, on the spur of the moment, and I'd never been there except for dinner, and then only with my parents.'

'It was fun, wasn't it?'

'Yes,' Caroline said. 'I guess everything we did in those days was fun.'

'I remember everything,' Eddie said. His face was calm, but his eyes were sad, as if they were looking far back into the past. He leaned forward and pulled the cork out of the bottle of champagne, and it popped. 'It doesn't always have to pop, did you know that?' he said. 'That's a fallacy.'

'Really?'

He poured champagne for them both, into wide crystal glasses, and handed one to her. He lifted his glass and looked into her eyes. 'I guess I should say, To reunion.'

'That sounds like college alumni, Class of Fifty-Two,' Caroline said softly.

'Does it?' He looked into his glass quickly and drank.

'You're not sunburned,' Caroline said. 'Somehow I expected to see you with a tan.'

'Not in the winter. Remember that time we had a picnic on the beach?' he said.

'Revere.'

'Yes. And it was much too early so everyone was really shivering but no one would admit it.'

'And we ran up and down the beach to get warm.' Caroline laughed. 'But what a gorgeous day it was, everything so blue and white and sunny.'

'Just cold.'

'But somebody went swimming. It was you!'

'So it was,' he said. 'I remember now. God, how sorry I was when I got out there in that ocean, but I didn't dare admit it.' He looked at her. 'Oh, Caroline . . .'

Their eyes met, and Caroline felt as if she were going to cry. 'You never would admit it when you made a mistake, ever,' she said in a very small voice.

'That was a long time ago,' Eddie said softly. 'I was just a child then. It's only three years, but it's been much longer than that, really. Much longer than that.'

'That's what you said in your letter,' Caroline said. 'What did you mean by it?'

They were sitting side by side on the love seat and it was so narrow that if she moved only a few inches she could touch him. She wanted so badly to touch him, even to reach out with her finger and brush his wrist to know that he was really here with her at last, to feel anything of him that was permanent and his, that she could not help herself; she put forth her hand on the velvet cushion and touched the back of his hand. He turned his hand over instantly and closed his fingers around hers. 'What . . . did you mean by it?' she repeated breathlessly, her voice catching in her throat.

'That I missed you,' he said stiffly. With his free hand he lifted the bottle of champagne. 'Let's have another glass, it'll go flat if we don't.'

'We . . . ought to have champagne twirlers,' Caroline said.

'Those sticks with little fins on the end of them? Have you seen those? There's a woman in Dallas who has one she carries around in her purse, it's solid gold with a little diamond set on the tip of each fin, and when she stirs the champagne all the bubbles catch the light.' He grinned at her. 'It's like every bad joke about a Texas millionaire.'

'You still sound a little bit like a New Yorker just visiting there,' Caroline said. 'Is that how you feel?'

'In a way. Of course, I've made a lot of friends, and some of them are really wonderful people. You know, other . . . young couples.' His voice faded out on the last two words, as if he realized too late how the words would cut her. He covered her hand with his other hand. 'It *is* true, you know,' he said, softly, looking into her eyes. 'It's my life, it's the life I have. You've been having fun, haven't you? Is there anyone you're . . . serious about?'

'No,' Caroline said.

'I still have the letters you wrote me when I was in Europe,' he said. 'Isn't that funny? I couldn't throw them out, that was all.'

'I don't think it's funny,' Caroline said.

'No . . .' he said. 'It isn't funny. I read them sometimes, when I'm alone in my office with nothing to do. It's quite often that I have nothing to do. And when I read them I . . . I could kick myself for being so cruel to you, for being such a stupid fool. They were such sweet letters, so *good*. Everything about you as you really are is in those pages, so giving, always giving. And . . . I'd read each one when it came, and then I'd go to a party, or a dinner with some diplomats or ambassadors, or counts or something, and I'd think I was having such fun. The young man on his first trip to Paris.' He said it with such self-hating scorn that Caroline was filled with pity for him. 'I did everything I thought I was supposed to do. I even rode through Les Halles at four o'clock in the morning on a vegetable wagon. Remember that, in F. Scott Fitzgerald? The carrot wagon. Well, this one had carrots on it too, and Helen and I were tossing them around just like in the book, and singing songs, and we had a bottle of red wine – oh, God.' He let go of Caroline's hand and put his hands over his face.

'Eddie . . .'

'Have some more champagne, darling,' he said finally and reached for the bottle.

'Eddie, darling . . .'

'I missed you so terribly these past three years,' he said. 'I'd dream sometimes in the middle of the night that I was falling off a cliff, and I'd wake up suddenly with a jolt – did you ever do that?'

'No.'

'Well, it's frightening. And then I'd lie awake in the dark for hours and I'd have the terrible feeling that I'd lost someone, and I knew it was you, and you'd never care for me again, and we'd never be together again.'

'I love you,' Caroline said.

'Do you?'

'Always.'

She held out her hands to him and he took her into his arms. 'My darling . . .' she said. 'Darling . . .' At last she could touch him, at last, and she put her arms around his neck and stroked his hair, so familiar, so soft, and they kissed each other for a while with a fierce, frightened intensity, as if any moment they let each other go they might be parted again and lose each other as they did before, and to lose each other this time after everything that had happened would be more than either of them could bear.

He took his lips away from hers only once, to say, 'I love you, Caroline, I love you,' and then they kissed again for a long time, and finally he drew away and Caroline put her head on the place where his neck joined his shoulder, where she had always rested it so long ago. He put his cheek on her hair and then he brushed his lips across it. 'You always smell like those little flowers,' he said. 'Little sweet flowers, lots of them, not any special one.'

'It's the perfume I always used to wear.'

'I walked into a room once, it was at a party, and there was a girl there with that same perfume on. I went up to her, I don't know why, really, because I knew it wasn't you, but I touched her on the shoulder and she turned around; and it was terrible. It was like seeing someone else's face on a member of your own family.'

Caroline smiled and turned her head and kissed him.

'Let's run away,' he murmured. 'Let's run away somewhere. I don't know where.'

'Where?'

'Back to four years ago. Do you think we can do that? Make everything else disappear?'

'If we really try . . .'

He was stroking her face and her hair with his fingertips as if he was trying to refamiliarize himself with them, and then he put his arms around her and held her tightly. 'You're just exactly the same,' he said.

At that moment Caroline felt she really was the same. Nothing had happened to her during these three years, nothing of any import. She was Eddie Harris' girl, as she always had been, and the world was good. It was their world, because they loved each other, and they would take care of each other, each doing good things for the other, for ever and ever.

'Where will we run?' Caroline asked tenderly.

'I don't know. We can't really, except in our minds.'

'Why?'

'Because this is the world,' he said sadly.

You've changed, Caroline thought, and the realization hit her with pain, but only for an instant. Of course people didn't run away, but they made plans, and nothing that had been done in haste and childishness could not be undone some way. 'I didn't mean *really* run off somewhere,' she said, smiling at him.

He kissed her again and Caroline could feel her lips growing warm against his and she put her arms around him and let herself drown with love. After a while they drew away, but slowly, with one more kiss and one more. 'We have a whole week,' he said.

'Yes.'

'I love you so much, Caroline.'

'I adore you.'

Eddie sighed. 'I guess I have to feed you. I invited you here for lunch so you're going to get lunch. What would you like?'

'I don't care.'

'Chicken sandwich, filet mignon?'

She shook her head. 'Anything.'

He called Room Service, and while they were waiting for their lunch Caroline told Eddie about her friends in New York and her job and her apartment, about Gregg who collected garbage and April who had finally married a boy from home, and about the day she herself had gone to Mary Agnes' wedding and had pretended it was hers to Eddie. She told him all this briefly, making it all sound light and pleasant, except, of course, the part about Gregg, which was disturbing. It was like the old days together, sharing everything, and Eddie listened intently, holding her hand and never taking his eyes off her face. By the time the lunch came Caroline realized she was very hungry.

The waiter wheeled in a table covered with a long white linen cloth. The filets were juicy and garnished with watercress and covered by domed silver covers. But when Caroline had taken two or three bites she realized she could not get another one past her throat; she was too filled with excitement and happiness and love. She put down her fork and knife.

'I can't eat,' she said. 'I'm just so . . . excited.'

Eddie had not eaten either. He pushed his plate away. 'I can't either.'

'It's a shame, they're so expensive.'

'Does your cat eat meat?'

'Just chopped-up cat-food meat.' She laughed.

'Are you happy?'

'Yes. Are you?'

He nodded. 'Happy and sad.'

'Why sad?'

'Because you're so beautiful.'

'Why does that make you sad?'

'I don't know. I just said that. It doesn't make me sad, really. I'm glad you're beautiful. It makes me happy to look at you.'

'I love you.'

Eddie took her hand. '. . . you too.'

'We must never, *never* have to go through all that agony again.'

'No,' Eddie said.

When Caroline came back to her office at half past three she tiptoed past Mr Shalimar's closed door and went into her own cubicle. She sank into her swivel chair, exhausted with happiness and surprise and emotion. At five-thirty she would meet Eddie again and they would have dinner and spend the evening. She could not make any plans for their future; her mind was too full of everything that had happened to her today, from the first word Eddie had spoken. She only wanted to sit here in peace and remember it, go over everything he had said, every word of love and reunion and feeling, and remember how it had felt to kiss him and be held in his arms. But even now she could hardly remember his kisses, all she remembered was happiness and passion and love, obliterating anything as exact as the actual touch of his lips. She would have to notice everything more carefully tonight so that when she was home alone in bed she could remember, but she was quite sure that she would forget, again, to notice, because when she was with Eddie every abstract and rational observation fled.

She managed to leave her office at half past four so that she could rush home and change into her most beautiful cocktail dress for Eddie. She realized that this was the first time since she had been at Fabian that she had spent a day in the office doing no work at all. But one would have to be superhuman to work in spite of everything that was happening, Caroline thought, feeling a slight pang of guilt and then putting it out of her mind. She had waited three years for Eddie, he was her life, her future. What was fifty pages of a manuscript compared to that? She took another bath with the bath oil Eddie liked and put on her brand-new red chiffon dress with three floating layers of skirt. As she looked at herself in the mirror Caroline thought fleetingly of the image of herself she had shown to Paul Landis and the other boys through the years, the thin girl in the black dress, efficient and gracious and untouchable, always. And here she was, flushed with excitement, her skirts swirling as she moved, colorful and silky, leaving a trail of faint sweet fragrance. She was someone she remembered from long ago, and yet she was different, more self-possessed, more poised, and knowing, because she had once lost him, just how precious it was to have someone to love.

She met Eddie in the lobby of his hotel. 'You went home,' he said, looking at her dress admiringly. 'That's my favorite dress from now on.'

'Mine too, then,' Caroline said.

They walked out together into the cold, brightly lighted night, and as they walked down the wide white steps of the hotel Caroline was conscious of people glancing at them, as people always do who are passing others on a stairway. She knew they made a striking couple, because they were young, because they were both good-looking, because they were happy and in love. 'I couldn't do any work this afternoon,' Caroline said.

'I couldn't do much, I can tell you that.' He smiled at her. 'You take up all my thoughts. I had to go to see someone who has an office down near Wall Street, overlooking the river. You could see the ships go by, and he had two pairs of binoculars, so we stood there and looked out the window at the liners and the little tugboats. I was thinking about you, of course, and just then a ship from the French Line came by, all white and shiny in the sun, on its way to Le Havre. I felt as if somebody had walked on my grave.

I remembered how you looked on the pier, the last time I ever saw you, when we said goodbye.'

'How do you think I felt?' Caroline said softly. 'I've seen quite a few ships going away in my time, and they always reminded me of you.'

'We won't think about it,' he said, pressing her hand. 'We're together now.'

They were walking down Fifth Avenue and they stopped in front of Tiffany's, where the little windows were lighted for the night. The great steel doors were closed and locked, and behind the glass windows diamonds sparkled on dark velvet: a necklace like a waterfall, a ring with a round stone in it too huge to be believed. Caroline and Eddie stopped and looked into one of the windows, hand in hand, as lovers had stood before through the years, the ones who intended to buy and the ones who could never afford to but were just wishing. On a piece of velvet, under all that magnificence, was a platinum engagement ring with a small heart-shaped diamond set in it. 'Look,' Caroline breathed. 'I've never seen a heart-shaped diamond before.'

'I wish I could buy you that necklace,' Eddie said. 'All those diamonds. I'd drape it on you like the Queen of Sheba.'

'I don't want the necklace. I don't want to be the Queen of Sheba. I just like that little ring.' She laughed. 'It probably costs a fortune.'

Another couple strolled by them and stopped to look into the next window. They were an older couple, Caroline hardly noticed them. But Eddie stiffened. 'Go around the corner,' he whispered. 'Quick! Look in a window.' And he pushed her, not roughly, but with the insensitivity of haste.

Caroline was so startled that she let him push her, she walked to the corner and turned it, looking back over her shoulder once at Eddie. He was walking away, past the couple, and as he did they turned and greeted him and he stopped. Caroline looked into the window around the corner, and the diamonds and sapphires in it began to wink and shimmer at her as if they were five-pointed stars. She realized that there were tears in her eyes, but she did not quite know why she was crying. If they were people Eddie knew from Dallas, or old friends of his family's from New York, who knew he was married, perhaps he thought he had to hide her. He had, after all, something to keep secret – the fact that he was going to leave his wife for another girl, and so he must protect the other girl until the unpleasant separation had been accomplished. That was sensible. Why, then, did she feel so hurt, so frightened?

Eddie came up the street finally, from the opposite direction, walking briskly. He had evidently gone all the way around the block. 'I'm sorry,' he said, taking her arm. 'They're Helen's parents' best friends. I knew they were in New York but I had no idea we'd run into them. We'll have to be careful from now on.'

Caroline didn't know what to say. She let Eddie lead her past the Tiffany windows and down the street. She turned her head to look at him. He was so young, the outline of his profile was so perfectly made, unmarked by any of the signs that time and living eventually leave. His hand on her arm was warm and reassuring. He was so young, it was such a difficult thing for both of them. Changing one's life, especially with others to think about, was always difficult. But being separated from each other was worse, and he knew that too.

They went to a quiet little French restaurant on the West Side where Caroline had never been before. Eddie spoke to the waiter in perfectly accented French and ordered their food and wine. 'Do you like snails?' he asked. 'Or are you afraid of them?'

'No,' Caroline said, 'I like them.'

'Remember Locke Ober's?'

'Yes, of course.'

'I could afford to take you there about twice a year.'

'It's all so odd when I look back on it,' Caroline said. 'I remember things we did, and how much things cost, and I remember how impressed I was then, and I wonder, after all this time, if we went back and ate in all those places over again, would they seem so expensive?'

'Remember the two-dollar steaks at Cronin's?'

'Yes, and we could only afford those once in a while.'

'Remember that song we used to play in my room: "Someday I'll Find You"?'

'Over and over. I just couldn't sing it, though, the melody was too hard for me. But how I loved it! I still have the records, all of them, that we used to play.'

'I do too,' Eddie said. 'But I never played them any more, I couldn't.'

'Neither could I . . . until I got your letter. They made everything seem too close. You do still play the piano,' Caroline said, 'don't you? All that wonderful jazz? What a right hand you had!'

'I still play,' he said. 'Sometimes.'

'Oh, you should!'

'I play at parties. You know, I'm the guy who always wanders away just when everyone is getting drunk, and starts to run off a few chords. The shy one.'

'You were never shy!'

'It's a good excuse, though,' Eddie said. 'Shy or . . . feeling depressed; who can tell the difference from the outside?'

'Oh, Eddie . . .'

The snails arrived, cooked in their shells, in round silver platters with little hollows for each shell, and garlic butter sauce and silver tongs. But when the platters were set down on the table Caroline found that once again she could not eat. 'I can't,' she said.

Eddie laughed. 'Neither can I. Do you think if I stay here a whole week we'll starve to death?'

'We'll get used to each other,' Caroline said. 'It's all so new . . . it's all so . . . wonderful.'

They sipped at their wine and laughed and looked at each other and held hands under the table. 'It's new,' Eddie said, 'and yet you've always been a part of my life. I feel almost as if we're married. I feel as if we grew up together, you're the little girl I teased and played with and fell in love with. It's as if we'd spent our whole childhood together, in some funny way, and no one else can ever mean the same thing to either of us that we mean to each other.'

'I know,' Caroline said. 'I know you so well, I know you better than anyone in the whole world.'

'And yet, how old were you when we met? Seventeen? Eighteen?'

'Does it make any difference?' she asked tenderly.

'None, darling. None at all.'

'I'll never love anyone the way I love you.'

'I couldn't,' he said.

'What are we going to do?'

'I'll think of something,' Eddie said. 'You just listen to me.'

After they had dinner or, rather, after they had ordered several courses and tasted them and let them stand, they went to Caroline's apartment, where they sat on the studio couch and listened again to all the old scratchy Noël Coward records they had listened to when they had first been in love, and laughed over the photographs of themselves as they had been four and five years ago, and drank brandy, and found themselves quite quickly embracing again, kissing, clinging to each other, as if even to be an arm's length away was too much of a separation after these lonely three years. It was strange, although they had done many more intimate things than merely kissing when they were in college, each of them seemed afraid. They had been parted for so long that in a way they were timid with each other, but, most of all, the image of Eddie's wife stood between them, as if she was a problem that had to be solved and could not be thrust aside. He was like a visitor from another world, transitory, wanting to stay, assimilating slowly because part of the assimilation meant breaking the old ties. He probably thinks I resent her, Caroline thought with her eyes shut, her head on Eddie's shoulder. And I do. I hate her.

At eleven o'clock Eddie stood up. 'Darling,' he said, looking at his wristwatch, 'I don't want to, but I have to go. I promised some people I'd have a drink with them. They're the people I came here to see. Eleven-thirty was the latest I could put them off to, I told them I was going to the theater.'

'Oh . . .'

Eddie grinned. 'Tell me quick – the plot of a play you've seen that I can say I just saw, in case they ask.'

'I wish I could go with you,' Caroline said sadly.

'So do I.'

'This has been the happiest day of my entire life,' Caroline said, putting her arms around him. 'If I'd wanted to imagine it I couldn't have, it's been too lovely.'

He kissed her. 'I'll see you tomorrow too, and the next and the next. I'll call you in the morning. And we'll have lunch.'

'Yes.'

'And dinner.'

'Yes.'

'Why do people always congregate around food?' he said. 'Have you ever thought about that? They meet for cocktails, or dinner, or lunch, or coffee – always gathered together to gobble something.'

She laughed. '*We* don't.'

'No, we don't, do we? We must be antisocial.'

'Good.'

'I love you, Caroline.'

'I love you, darling. I'm glad you've come back.'

After Eddie had gone Caroline realized for the first time how tired she was. She was exhausted. More had happened to her in this long day than in any other single time in three years. As she washed her face she thought fleetingly of how wonderful it would be to be able to go along with Eddie when he went to see business acquaintances, as his wife, and not be left alone here to wait. It was so hard to be the outsider, the hidden woman. It was a role for which she was unsuited. But it wouldn't be for long, and soon she would be married to Eddie, and he would never have to hide her again. And meanwhile she would sleep, because tomorrow they would be together again, and that was more important to her than anything else.

They met the next day in Eddie's suite for lunch, and it was as it had been the day before. The same excitement, the same pounding of the heart preceded the moment he opened the door, and today there was something new: the joy of knowing in advance that everything would be all right. There had never been anything he could not say to her, even in the old days when he was worried or moody and did not want to speak to anyone else, and there had never been anything she could not say to him. But now Caroline was conscious of the unavoidable difference: there were two things of which Eddie could not speak, Helen and his daughter. She wanted more than anything to see a picture of his baby, and yet she was afraid to ask and afraid if she did he would show one to her. Eddie's child, who might have been hers instead. It would be a little like looking into a mirror of the future. The most Caroline could bring herself to ask was 'Does your little girl look like you?'

'Exactly, poor child.'

'Oh . . .' And she was sorry she had asked, because that hurt. She wished the child might have looked exactly like Helen, with nothing of Eddie in her face, so that she herself would not feel this strange, personal longing come upon her.

'I want to give you something,' Eddie said. 'Let's take a walk, do you want to?'

'Yes. What is it?'

'Something significant and permanent. I don't know what, exactly. Let's just walk and see what happens.'

They walked across Fifth Avenue, close together but not touching, and in the bright daylight of this crowded noon hour they might have been merely co-workers in an office who had decided to lunch together and were walking to a restaurant. The secret pleasure of knowing that they were on their way to do something infinitely more exciting and meaningful filled Caroline with joy. She could not stop smiling and she felt she might laugh out loud for no reason at all. She hardly noticed the people who hurried by them, everything was a blur except Eddie walking beside her. They walked past Tiffany's to Bonwit Teller and then Eddie stopped. 'I like this,' he said, and he led her inside. They wandered about for a while in the crowd of perfumed women shoppers, and finally Eddie stopped in front of the counter that sold the real jewelry – rings and bracelets and pins of gold set with precious stones. 'Quick – go over there,' he said, smiling, gesturing at the scarf counter across the aisle.

'What, again?'

'I want to surprise you.'

450

She was so happy she felt like a child again, with a resurgence of that long-vanished feeling that a present is magic. She could hardly resist looking at Eddie out of the corner of her eye as she pretended to be glancing at scarves. How handsome he was, how tall, how beautifully put together. It was simply unbelievable luck that everything about him should be so beautiful. She could not imagine how anyone else who noticed him there could help but see it too. And those other women would know that he was choosing a present for someone he loved, bent over the glass showcase so earnestly, with a look of pleasure on his face. There were rings beneath the glass where Eddie was leaning his forearms, plain gold rings and some with many stones. *Buy me a ring*, Caroline thought, shutting her eyes, as if she might wish it true. *It doesn't have to look anything like an engagement ring, a plain gold cocktail ring would be much better, and no one will know but the two of us until it's done.* Her finger almost ached, as if she had worn a ring on it every day for years and then suddenly lost it. *Please, a ring . . .*

She waited until Eddie came up behind her and touched her arm. 'I didn't wait to have it gift-wrapped,' he whispered. 'Let's go somewhere where I can give it to you.'

They walked back up the street to the park and then crossed the wide thoroughfare where taxis and private cars came swooping down around the corner, to become jammed in the noon-hour bottle-neck. There were a few hansom cabs waiting in front of the park, their horses blanketed and standing very quietly and patiently, steam rising from their breath in the chill air. It was easy to find an empty bench on a cold day like this one, and Caroline and Eddie sat close together while he reached into his pocket and handed her a tiny pasteboard box.

She pulled her gloves off and took off the top of the box. There was a layer of white cotton, which she lifted, and underneath, nestled in another layer of white cotton, was a very tiny gold heart on a fragile gold chain.

'Oh . . .' she said. She adored it because it was from him, and because it was a heart, and because he had chosen it himself, and yet she had the strangest feeling, as if she were almost afraid to touch it. It was the identical heart that Gregg had received from David Wilder Savage last Christmas, when what Gregg too had wanted had been a ring. Oh, but that was *silly*. 'Darling,' Caroline said, 'thank you.'

'Do you like it?'

'I love it.'

'I'll fasten the catch for you,' Eddie said. 'Turn around.'

He took off his gloves and she felt his fingers on her neck so that she forgot about the heart, and then he said, 'It looks pretty.'

She felt it with her fingers, at her throat, tiny and solid and reassuring. 'I'll never take it off,' she said. 'Never.'

That night they had dinner at another dark, obscure little restaurant, and sat for hours over cups of espresso coffee and talked in whispers while a fat, many-colored candle flickered beside them. Caroline was wearing a dress with a cut-out neckline, to show the golden heart. She was beginning to have a completely revised opinion of every dress she owned; they were either dresses that looked well with the gold heart or they weren't. She wore no other jewelry. Every now and then she would reach up to feel the heart with her fingers, to make sure it was still there, because it was very light and she could not feel the chain around her neck, and because knowing it was there made her feel that everything was in its place and right.

'I have to go to my parents' house for dinner tomorrow night,' Eddie said. 'They felt bad when I stayed at a hotel, and worse when I kept telling them I had to attend to crass commercialism instead of to them. They haven't seen me for six months; they came down to see the baby last summer. But I'll try to get away early and then I can meet you.'

If I were Helen, Caroline thought, I'd be invited too. 'I wonder whether they still remember me,' she said.

'How could they forget you?'

'And I can't even ask you to send them my regards. I wish I could.'

He didn't answer. 'I can get away by eleven o'clock,' he said then.

'Eddie, why did you stay at a hotel?'

'When I got your letter I thought, I hoped, you'd still care about me. It was more of a daydream, really. But I wanted to stay at a hotel in case things for some unlikely reason really were the same between you and me, so I could go my own way without anyone's trying to make social arrangements for me. The man I came to see on business wanted me to stay at his apartment, he has eleven rooms. I didn't have a hard time getting out of that. I told him it would hurt my parents' feelings.'

They went to Caroline's apartment later on in the evening, because Gregg was not there, and this time it was more familiar, as if she and Eddie were returning to their home. She switched on the overhead light and Gregg's cat ran to her, crying, and butted its head against her shin and ran around her feet, rubbing its sides against her ankles. Eddie bent down and picked it up, stroking its fur. 'Poor thing,' Caroline said, 'she forgot to feed it again.'

'I'll feed it,' Eddie said. He found a can of cat food on the shelf in the kitchenette and opened it with a can opener and emptied it into the cat's dish. Then he filled another dish with fresh water.

'You look so domestic,' Caroline said lovingly.

'It's a nice little alley cat.'

'This is our home, and that's our cat, and soon we'll lock the door and it'll be night outside, and in here we'll be warm and happy.'

'And safe,' Eddie said. 'And happy for ever after.'

They walked into each other's arms simultaneously, as though there were no other place in the room that could possibly exist for them. 'We'll be happy,' Caroline whispered. 'Happy . . .'

Not ever in her life before had she been so bewitched, so lost, as she was in these moments with Eddie. And even when she was away from him, as she discovered the next morning in the office, there was no thinking of anyone or anything else. She would think of a dozen things she wanted to say to him, and then when they were separated again for the routine of their business day she would think of a dozen more. Her mind was going in all directions at once, but at that height of awareness she had always felt when she was near Eddie. It was as if, with other people, there were several layers of apathy and fumbling noncommunication weighing her down, light but immovable, and then with Eddie those layers were stripped away, so that she would realize suddenly how limited her relationships were with everyone else. Every thought she had seemed important because he would understand, every idea important because he would be so quick to respond. No one had ever understood her as Eddie did, no one had ever known her so well. As she sat at her desk Caroline imagined what he was doing as he went about the city, meeting someone, talking, always expressive. She sat at her desk lost in thought, her fingers automatically feeling the tiny gold heart at her throat, waiting for their next hour of meeting, and nothing else had any meaning for her at all.

That evening when she waited for Eddie to come to her apartment after his dinner with his parents Caroline took her second bath of the day and put every dress she owned on the studio couch to see which one would be good enough for him to see tonight. How different it was to try to make herself look beautiful for someone she loved, it was more fun than almost anything.

When her telephone rang she picked up the receiver automatically, although she really did not want to make conversation with anyone who did not know any of this all-consuming, marvelous secret. At first she hardly recognized the voice at the other end.

'Well!' Paul Landis cried jovially. 'At last! I've been trying to get in touch with you all week.'

'Oh?' Caroline murmured. Her first reaction was one of annoyance, because he liked to have long conversations with her in the evening, and tonight there was nothing she wanted to say to him.

'You've been very popular this week,' Paul said.

'Yes.'

'Have you been having fun?'

'Yes.'

'That's good. I even tried to get you at the office yesterday, but you were still out to lunch.'

'Oh . . . yes.'

'Three-hour lunch hours,' Paul teased. 'I told you you were going to get to be like Miss Farrow.'

She didn't even have the energy to answer back. 'I was just getting dressed to go out,' Caroline said.

'Another date? My! I'd better get my bid in or you won't want to see me at all next week.'

'I can't see anyone next week,' Caroline said quickly. 'I mean, I'm already tied up.'

'What a shame. I thought we'd go to the very early show at a good movie on Wednesday night, when it isn't crowded, and then have a nice leisurely dinner.'

'I'm sorry. I already have a date.'

'Well, Thursday then.'

'I don't know.'

'When will you know?'

It had not occurred to her to ask Eddie when he was going back, she had been too busy being happy. But of course he would go back, he had to talk to Helen, he had to report on this business trip and make arrangements about his work. If he would no longer be married to Helen Lowe, Caroline was sure he would no longer be working at the Lowe Oil Company; it would be too embarrassing for all concerned. He might go back to Dallas on Wednesday night, or, at the latest, Friday.

'I don't know,' she said again.

'What's the matter? You sound in a fog.'

'No . . .'

'You must be tired from all those late nights. Why don't you stay home once in a while?' Paul said. He sounded a little jealous and a little sanctimonious. Caroline could not tell which feeling was the one he meant and she really did not care.

'It's the Christmas season,' she said lightly. 'You know how it is.'

'Yes, I guess so.'

'Besides, it's only been two nights. I don't know why you act as if that's so many.' She was beginning to revive enough to banter with him. This is Paul, she told herself, Paul, remember? Your friend. You like him.

'I suppose that's not so many,' Paul admitted. He sounded happier. 'But you're going to drink grog with me New Year's, aren't you?'

'What?' she asked vaguely.

'New Year's Eve again. We can't escape it. We'll share all our old regrets together.'

'Oh, Paul,' Caroline said gently, 'I haven't even thought about New Year's Eve. I've been so busy – my work and . . . friends from out of town. I don't even know where I'll be on New Year's Eve.'

'With me, I hope,' Paul said.

'Could you . . . call me next week? I can't talk to you any more now.'

'Oh,' Paul said, as if he had just figured out the answer to the problem that was puzzling him and now he felt secure again. 'Your date is there.'

'Yes,' Caroline said.

'All right. I'll call you at the beginning of the week. Save New Year's Eve and one evening before, too, so I can give you your Christmas present.'

'Yes.' Caroline said. 'I'll speak to you later. Goodbye.'

'Goodbye, butterfly.'

By the time she had replaced the receiver and walked across the room Caroline had forgotten Paul Landis' existence. As she dressed she pretended that this was really Eddie's home, and that he was coming home to her. And then she no longer had to pretend. It was true. When he rang the doorbell a little after eleven she ran to open the door. 'Hello, darling.'

Eddie stood in the doorway for an instant, dark spots on his lapels and shoulders where raindrops had fallen. 'It's raining,' he said. 'I don't want to get anything wet.' He wiped his shoes on the mat.

'It's all right, it doesn't matter.' She took his hand and led him into the apartment.

'What did you do tonight?' he asked, taking off his coat.

'I don't remember,' she said happily. 'Nothing much. Waited for you.' He sat on the studio couch and took hold of her hand. 'Do you want to go out somewhere?'

She shook her head. 'I don't care. Do you?'

'No. I want to be alone with you. I don't want to sit in bars.'

'Do you want some coffee?'

'No, thank you.' He had a rueful half-smile on his face. 'The strangest thing happened tonight. I was talking to my father after dinner, just the two of us, having a drink together in the living room, and he said, "Eddie, are things any better with you and Helen?" I said, "What do you mean?" And he said, "I could tell when we came to visit you last summer. I didn't want to say anything then, but I knew something was wrong."'

'And what did you say?' Caroline asked softly.

Eddie shrugged. 'I said everything was fine, of course.'

'You did?'

'I had to. I don't want to hurt any more people than I have to. This thing is between us, darling; I'm not going to involve my father.'

'I suppose you're right.'

'But he knew,' Eddie said. 'I can't fool my father. You know how smart he is. He just looked at me and said, 'I hope so.' That was all. But the way he said it I knew that he wasn't fooled.'

'It *is* strange,' Caroline said. 'Other people worrying about your life, thinking about it, and never really able to help.'

'He said something about you, too.'

'About me!'

'He said, "Remember Caroline Bender?" And I said, "Yes." And then he said the strangest thing of all. It nearly knocked me off my feet. He was turning his whisky glass around in his hand and staring at it like an antique appraiser, and he said, without even looking at me, "Sometimes I wonder what would have happened if you'd married her."'

'Oh . . .'

'I said, "So do I." And that was all.'

'So do I,' Caroline said softly. 'I wonder about it all the time. No, that's not quite right. I don't wonder. I know.'

'You and I *are* married,' Eddie said. His voice was as soft as her own. 'No two people could be more married in this world.'

'No.'

'I wanted to tell him about us. I wanted to, more than anything. But I couldn't.'

'I know.'

'I want to tell everybody.'

'So do I,' Caroline said. 'I can't bear to talk to people who don't know about us, it's as if everything else is just hypocritical small talk.'

Eddie smiled. 'I know.'

'Hear the rain? It's really coming down now.' They listened in silence for a moment to the sound of the rain pouring outside. 'Outside there's rain, and people making conversation, and telephones ringing, and a great stream of people who see us and speak to us and don't know anything about what's happening to you and me. And here we are, a whole world of love right in one room.'

'I know.'

'Your hair isn't wet any more,' Caroline said tenderly. 'It's all dry now.'

She stroked his hair and Eddie took her into his arms. For the first time she was really conscious of the feeling of his lips, so that she could remember them, gentle and soft and cool, and then warmer, and the skin of his face, smooth and cool and then warmer, familiar and remembered yet always new and a little surprising because try as she would she could never remember quite how pleasurable, how perfect, the feel of it really was. No matter how much she yearned for him when he was not there, when he was in her arms it was better, always better and always new. From the instant Eddie touched her and she touched him Caroline was no longer aware of the sound of the rain outside her window or of anything in the room. The lights were on, it was harsh and bright, but behind her closed eyelids she saw only a gold-streaked blackness, and when she opened her eyes she saw the beloved nearness of Eddie's face. When his gentle hands searched for the closing of her dress her own hands helped him, and when he slipped the dress away from her to the couch or wherever it drifted, she was conscious only of a feeling of freedom and relief not to be covered by all that unwieldy cloth. She could not be close enough to him, she held to him with her arms, hands, lips, knees, every part of her body that could be closer to his body so that they might dissolve together into perfect union.

'I love you, Caroline,' he whispered.

'Eddie . . . I love you, I love you.'

Closer, closer, and nothing could be more natural. The great pleasure was love, that Eddie was with her in her arms, as close as anyone could be, and then there was another pleasure, the physical one, almost unbearable because her heart was so full of love for him. He was murmuring to her and she to him, words of tenderness and passion, hardly aware what the words were, aware only of their meaning, not knowing what they were doing except as a great and consuming need to be closer and to give love and to share love, in every way.

They lay in each other's arms for a long time afterward, but neither of them mentioned what they had done. Caroline thought vaguely of saying something, but she did not want to spoil it with words, for what was there to say? She only knew that she was happy, and that she loved him more than ever, and that she had never felt so united with anyone before, in all her life.

He drew away from her finally and sat up. 'When does your roommate come back?'

'Who?'

'The actress.'

Caroline smiled. 'Oh, Eddie . . . I forgot she existed. She'll be back any minute. What time is it?'

He was still wearing his wristwatch. 'Nearly one o'clock.'

'Oh, then we have time.'

Eddie was dressing quickly, she had never seen anyone dress so fast. 'Get dressed, darling, hurry up,' he said.

Caroline could hardly even think. She watched Eddie with her eyes, unmoving, and then finally, like a sleepwalker, stood up too and put on her dress over her skin and rolled up her underthings and petticoat and stockings and put them into one of her bureau drawers. She slipped her feet into her shoes.

'Now we're so respectable,' Eddie said. He smiled at her. 'I love that dress too, and I hardly had time to look at it. You look as if you're all ready to go to a party. Look at yourself.' He took her hand and led her to the mirror that hung over her dresser and he stood there behind her, his arms crossed over her waist in front, resting his chin on the top of her head. Caroline put her hands over his. 'I like the way we look together,' Eddie said. 'We look as if we were intended to be that way.'

Caroline looked at their double reflection in the mirror. They looked like an old-fashioned daguerreotype – or, no, that was not quite it. She knew then what it was. They looked like a wedding picture.

When Gregg had come back and Eddie had left, Caroline lay in bed thinking of what had happened that evening. It seemed odd to be lying here on the same studio couch where she and Eddie had made love only a few hours before. It made her feel closer to him, as if he were still here with her instead of in his hotel. She thought of their love-making with awe, remembering. I'm glad I waited for Eddie, Caroline thought. And then she thought of Mike Rice. But it didn't really happen with him, she reassured herself; it wasn't the same. He can't spoil it for me, I won't let anything spoil it. Eddie was my only lover, and he always will be. With Eddie it was different, there was no thought of pain or of fear, but only love and closeness. She could never have believed that something so important as sleeping with someone could be so natural. There was no word even to describe it except Love, 'sleeping with' sounded so foolish.

She remembered the afternoon with Mike, long ago. It had been on this very same bed, and Caroline was sorry for that. She had thought of Eddie then, she had wanted it to be Eddie instead. But perhaps, she thought, if it hadn't been for Mike, I might never have had this night with Eddie, and I would have missed all that unshy and heartfelt giving. I wonder . . . But it didn't really matter why . . .

'Caroline!' Gregg whispered. 'Are you asleep? Can you talk to me for a while?' Caroline kept her eyes shut and she could hear the rustle of small papers as Gregg put something on the coffee table between the two beds. She knew what Gregg wanted to have a long middle-of-the-night talk about: her latest discovery; and tonight again Caroline could not bear to listen. She was too full of her own happiness and she could not break the spell.

She saw Eddie the next morning and then on all through the weekend. The weekend was the best, because she did not have to go to the office and they could have the entire day together. Eddie was always cautious about where he took her, he did not want anyone he knew to see the two of them together, and although it made Caroline feel a little resentful, she could not help but admit the logic of it. Scandal, any kind of scandal, was anathema to Eddie. In many little ways he seemed to have changed, or perhaps she saw him more clearly because she was older. He was imaginative and charming but he was conventional too, and conventional habits and appearances meant a great deal to him. Caroline was glad. At heart she was conventional too, affair with a married man or not. She could not even think of her affair with Eddie as 'An Affair with a Married Man' except as a joke, because she knew it was different. It almost seemed more natural for her and Eddie to be together than it was for him to be married to Helen. Caroline wanted nothing more than to be married to Eddie and to be conventional with him, to have young married couples for friends, to do the ordinary things that everyone else did and have fun doing it. She thought of Mike Rice once more during these happy days, and that was when she remembered his description of her as a little girl sitting on a rock between the call of two different lives. She had wanted to be conventional, he had said, but with an unusual person. She could never be a Mary Agnes. But neither could she be a Gregg, and hiding in one tiny restaurant after another began to make her irritable.

'When do you have to go back?' she asked on Wednesday afternoon.

'Day after tomorrow. I have to be home on Christmas Day.'

She tried not to feel the pain his words called up, but it was difficult. Christmas: family time. Eddie had to be home in time for

Christmas, not with her, but home. 'You know,' she said lightly, smiling at him, 'it makes me feel sad when you say that. I wish you could be with me instead.'

'So do I.'

'But you will be, next Christmas. I have that to look forward to anyway.'

'Oh, Caroline . . .' He looked so sad, something seemed to have come over his face, draining it of color. He lifted her hand to his lips and kissed it, and then he held it tightly.

'What is it?'

He shook his head and did not answer. He only held her hand more tightly, as if he were in actual pain and having something to hold on to made him more able to bear it. She could not look at him that way, unhappy, different. She could almost feel his pain herself, as if bands were constricting her chest, making it difficult to breathe. 'Darling,' she said again, 'what is it? Don't look that way.' She put her other hand on his wrist.

'When you touch me . . .' Eddie said. 'You're the only girl in the world who can affect me that way. It's . . .'

'I know . . .'

They were in a restaurant, finishing their coffee, and they stood simultaneously without another word, and Eddie helped Caroline to put on her coat. 'I won't go back to the office this afternoon,' she said. They went out to the street, and found a taxi, and went directly to Eddie's rooms.

There was no other place she wanted to be but close to him, as close as possible. 'Is this what a honeymoon is like?' she asked him afterward, laughing.

'I don't know,' he answered. 'Mine wasn't.'

'Oh, Eddie . . .'

'Well, it wasn't. I don't know, we just didn't seem to have much to say to each other when we were alone together. I felt as if I had to try to think of things to say. I would never, never feel that way with you. I think of things I have to tell you even when I'm not with you.'

'I'm the same!'

Twilight comes early at the end of December, and it was dark outside. 'Let's just stay here all evening and have a sandwich or something sent in,' Eddie said. 'I can't move.'

'I don't even want to move,' Caroline said lovingly, 'if it's anywhere away from you.'

They had only one more day together, after tonight, and happy as she was Caroline knew they had to make some plans together, discuss some of what would happen in the next few weeks, even if it would be unpleasant. 'You'll have to tell Helen,' she said. 'What will you tell her? Will you tell her about me?'

'She must never know about you,' Eddie said firmly.

'And how long will it take . . . to get −' she could hardly say it, but it had to be said − 'the divorce?'

He looked at her with a glance that was almost dramatic. Then he shook his head. 'Caroline . . . I can't . . . I *can't* get a divorce.'

'Can't?' She stared at him, frightened. 'What do you mean, you can't? Why can't you?'

He shook his head again, and on his face was that pale and tortured look that had hurt and mystified her at dinner. But now she knew what it meant. 'I can't,' he said. 'I can't. It would hurt too many people. It would be . . . the end of my life as it is now, everything, my work, my family, my friends, my home. I love my child, Caroline. I can't . . .'

At first Caroline could not believe what he was saying, and then suddenly she knew it was true. Or at least true at that moment. She could not believe it was true for ever. 'What about me?' she asked softly. 'What about hurting me?'

'I don't want to hurt you, darling. I couldn't hurt you.'

'Don't you think this will hurt me? Eddie, you're my life. You always have been.'

'I promise you,' Eddie said, 'I'll find some way before I leave New York. I will.'

'And you'll marry me?'

'I can't marry you, darling.'

'There is *no* other way,' Caroline said. There were no tears in her eyes, but her throat ached as if she were about to cry and she fought to keep her face placid. It was the first time she had ever tried to hide her feelings from Eddie, but she did not want to cry, she only wanted to understand and to reach him so that he would understand how she felt.

'Please don't think I'm going to marry you, darling. Please don't go on telling yourself that,' he said pleadingly.

'Did you know this all along?'

'Yes,' he said.

'You should have told me,' Caroline said softly, and then her voice broke. She could not say anything else because she knew if she were to open her mouth to speak she would cry.

Eddie laced his fingers together and looked at them, not able to look into her face. 'If anyone had told me three years ago that someday I would sit here and say to you that I love you more than anything in this whole world and yet I'll never marry you, I wouldn't have believed him. But I've changed. Things used to be simple then; you fell in love, you married, you wanted something, you took it. But they're not simple any more. *This* is the way life is, not the way I thought it was then.' He looked up at her finally, for the first time, and added quietly, 'And not the way you think it is now.'

'I was always the levelheaded girl whom everyone else told her troubles to,' Caroline said. 'But not now, not this one time. Not with you. And I know I'm right now, because I believe in you, I believe in *us*. Eddie, please don't make me stop believing in us.'

'There are a lot of things you stop believing in after a while,' Eddie said. 'Don't you think I'd be happier with you than I am the way things are now? Don't you think I want a wife I can love, whom I'm happy with?'

'You must be happier with her than you'll admit,' Caroline said. He shook his head. 'I'm not.'

'Then what is it you like? That safe, comfortable life? That heart-shaped swimming pool? That air-conditioned office with nothing to do? Those parties at the country club where you play the piano and feel nostalgic about me? Is that what you like?'

'Don't say that.'

'Is it true?'

'It's my life,' Eddie said. 'That's true.'

She was so hurt she could scarcely speak to him, she sat there immersed in pain and bewilderment, as if she were in a high temperature, and she could not even look at Eddie's face because looking at him made everything worse. She looked at the wall because it was cream colored and innocuous and bare and she waited for the pain to leave her as one waits for the crisis in a fever. But it did not leave her, and she did not know what to do.

'I can't lose you,' Eddie said. 'I'll have to think of something.'

'Think of me,' Caroline whispered. 'Please. Think of me.'

The next morning at the office she was still numb, but she was beginning to revive. Eddie would think of something, he had promised. Perhaps he would think of a way to have half custody of his daughter. She would even be willing to help bring up someone else's child, and she would love the child, if it would make Eddie happy and make him hers. It seemed so much responsibility, so many things she had not thought of, or had not let herself think of, but there must be a way, and if there was, Eddie would find it. In the hall she saw Mike Rice.

'Hey,' he said affectionately, 'I've been watching you lately. You look like you're in love.' He peered at her.

'I am,' Caroline said, trying to smile.

He was genuinely pleased. 'I knew it. He's a nice, young, eligible guy, isn't he?'

'. . . Yes,' Caroline said.

'I knew that too,' Mike said. 'I'm glad, Caroline.'

'Thank you,' she murmured, and then she moved away from him quickly before he could say anything more. She felt then that all avenues of escape were closed to her.

She met Eddie at his hotel at twelve. There was a cowhide suitcase, open and half packed, lying on the luggage rack.

Eddie took her into his arms. 'Do you love me?'

'Yes.'

'You really do?'

'Oh, I *really* do.'

'Everything will be all right then,' Eddie said, stroking her hair. 'We'll be together.'

'When are you going to leave?'

'Tomorrow afternoon on the five-o'clock plane. I'm packing now because I have to go out to dinner tonight with those same people. You'll come to the airport with me, won't you?'

'Yes,' Caroline said. 'Of course, darling. But what then? What about afterward?'

'That's all arranged. Could you be ready to leave New York in a month?'

'A month . . .' She could hardly catch her breath. '*Yes.*'

'You'll have to quit your job. You don't mind, do you?'

'No,' she said, 'oh, no.'

'I've found you a job in Dallas. It wasn't easy, but I was just lucky this turned up. There's a very wealthy, kind of eccentric man who's starting to write a book, and he needs an editorial assistant. You've had so much experience you'll be perfect for the job. I'll give you his name and address and you can write to him yourself right away.'

'It's all right,' Caroline murmured, her arms around Eddie's waist, her head resting against his chest. 'It's all right. I have enough money to stay there for a while, until we're married. I don't need the job.' She looked up at him. 'Unless, of course, *we'll* need the money. I'll be glad to work if we do.'

'Caroline . . . Caroline . . . you love me, don't you?'

'You know I do.'

'You know I can't marry you, I told you that. You know that, don't you?'

She drew away from him. 'What do you mean?' she asked, frightened and bewildered. 'Why do you want me to go to Dallas?'

'So we can be together, darling. Forever. Don't you want that too?'

'Together *how?*' Caroline asked, beginning to tremble with hurt and shame because she already knew what he meant and she could not quite bear to accept it all at once, it was too terrible.

'Together,' Eddie said. 'You'll take a little apartment, and you'll have this good job, and I'll come to visit you. You'll be near me, and we'll have lunch together at least twice a week – I can arrange that – and I'll get away to spend one or maybe even two evenings with you, and we'll speak on the phone every day, and sometimes we'll even be able to manage a whole weekend together. We can drive to the—'

'Lunch together!' she cried, interrupting him. She took a step away from him, as if she had suddenly found herself embracing, by mistake, someone who looked like Eddie Harris but really was only a stranger with an uncanny resemblance. 'One or two evenings when you've escaped from your wife and your respectable married friends? A *weekend*? And I'm to go on like that for ever and ever, alone, waiting for you, hidden? What do you want me to be?'

He was very pale. 'I want you to be with me.'

'When? When you're free for the evening?'

'Caroline, I'll see you nearly all the time, I'll see you . . .'

She didn't want to say it, not because of fear of hurting him but because to say the word would suddenly make it true, and that was almost too much to bear. But she had to say it, to face him with it, and to make herself know, for once and for all, that it was what he meant. And also, she realized, because even now she was hoping desperately that Eddie would deny it. 'You want me to be your mistress, don't you.'

'Don't say that,' he whispered. 'It sounds so ugly.'

'It *is* ugly,' Caroline said. She backed away from him even farther, longing at the same moment to throw herself into Eddie's arms and beg him to reassure her that it was not true, that he loved her, that this whole discussion was a hideous joke. And she took another step away. 'Is that what you meant?'

'It won't be ugly for us,' Eddie said quietly. 'We'll make it . . . different.'

'So that's your solution. That's your plan to make us both happy. And twenty years from now I'll still be sitting in that little apartment in Dallas, waiting for you to come and have lunch with me, waiting for you to come to make love to me in the evening and then go back to your wife; and I'll be forty-three years old and I'll never have had any children, or a real home, or someone to love me and care what happens to me – and all this because *you* didn't want to hurt anybody.'

Eddie didn't answer. He bit his lip and looked at her and then he turned away. 'You make me want to . . . cry,' he said.

'Do I?'

He nodded.

'I didn't do anything,' Caroline murmured. 'I only told you what you already know.' And then she found herself crying, uncontrollably, standing there in the middle of the room with her hands over her face, too miserable and stunned to move or sit down or run out of the room. Eddie was at her side in three steps, and held her in his arms, and when she could finally look at him she saw that his eyes were closed and that his face was wet with tears. 'Please . . .' she whispered, and then she could not say anything more.

'Don't . . .' he murmured. 'Don't, darling . . . I love you, I do . . .'

'What is it you love so much that loving me doesn't make any difference?' she asked. 'I just want to know that.'

He did not answer, and then she knew.

She went into Eddie's bathroom after a while and washed her face, but she was too tired to put on any make-up and she really didn't care. She walked slowly back into the living room and sat on the love seat where they had sat the first time they had met again in this room, and she folded her hands tightly on her knees and tried to breathe slowly and quietly without sobbing and she could not think ahead to what she would be doing even an hour from now.

Eddie sat down next to her without touching her and looked at her sadly. 'Will you think it over?' he asked. 'Don't say yes or no now, just think it over. You can tell me tomorrow morning when we meet. Please just think it over, for me.'

She couldn't answer.

'Caroline? Will you?'

'All right,' she said at last. 'I'll think it over.' But she knew even then it wouldn't work, that she couldn't live the way he had planned. And yet, to live without him after they had been together again was like a second death. She looked at Eddie. Even now, in spite of what he had done to her, she loved him. This person who had asked her to spend her life as his mistress wasn't Eddie, it was some cruel mad stranger, she told herself. It had to be. But she knew it *was* Eddie, and this was the way Eddie liked to say the world was. 'You look so dramatic,' she said, sighing. 'You have such a dramatic look on your face.'

'I do?'

She smiled at him weakly, because she still loved him, and because her heart opened up to him every time she looked at him or heard his voice, no matter what he had revealed about himself. 'Yes.'

He smiled too, then. 'I don't mean to.'

'I know you don't.' Her voice was very gentle and full of love.

'I'm thinking about how it will be to go back there tomorrow night and know that no matter how long I wait you'll never come to me. I can't bear that.'

'But you will bear it,' Caroline said gently. '*I'll* be the one who won't be able to bear it, I'll be the one who'll slowly die inside.'

'If you won't come to me,' Eddie said, taking her hand at last, 'then I'll come here next summer for a visit. I can do that. I'll stay for a week, and we'll be together then at least.'

'Twice a year?' she said. 'Am I to live for that?'

'Perhaps you will come to Dallas.'

She shook her head. She touched his fingers with the fingers of her other hand, stroking them, running her fingers along the back of his hand and the inside of his wrist, because at this moment he was hers, to touch, to love, to hold, to familiarize herself with for all time. 'Do you want to know the difference between you and me?' Caroline said. 'I'll tell you. You'll go away tomorrow and you'll go back to Helen and your friends and your job and your good, contented life, and I'll stay here. And in five years you and Helen will take a trip, maybe to some romantic place like Rio de Janeiro. And one night in Rio you'll be in your big expensive hotel and it will be the dinner hour, and while your wife is getting dressed you'll go downstairs to the bar. You'll buy a drink and you'll take it outside on the terrace with you, because there's always a terrace. And you'll be looking out at the beautiful tropical night and listening to music from inside the bar, and you'll sip at your drink, and then you'll think of me, and you'll feel pleasantly sad. That's all. Pleasantly sad.'

Gregg Adams, sitting in the shadows at the top of the stairs outside David Wilder Savage's apartment, looked like a child of twelve or fourteen who is still afraid of the dark. Her knees were drawn up to her chest, her arms were clasped about her knees, and her blonde hair hung down around her face as a schoolgirl's does. She shimmered a little in the midnight shadows, pale white face, pale white-gold hair that caught the reflections of the tiny overhead bulb like a firecracker giving off sparks, and a pale tan raincoat. She was cold in her raincoat and now she couldn't remember why she'd put it on instead of her winter coat. She hadn't even known she was wearing it until she found herself skirting a patch of ice on the curb in front of David's house and discovered she was shivering in the night wind. She remembered now also that she had forgotten to eat dinner, but she didn't really care about that because she felt too ill to be hungry. He was in there, in his apartment, with the girl.

She heard music, turned up high, as it always was. You could hear it dimly through the bedroom wall if you rested your cheek against the outer wall, even though the hi-fi set was in the living room. Next to the place on the wall where she leaned her face someone had written something. It was a scrawl, written with crayon. It said, 'I hate Johnny.' For some reason Gregg thought that was funny, and she smiled, closing her eyes. I hate Johnny. Who hated Johnny? A girl probably, Gregg thought. Some girl whom Johnny had mistreated, or perhaps only ignored. I hate Johnny, she said to herself happily. I hate David. No, I love him, I love him. I hate Gregg.

She opened her eyes instantly when she heard the sound of unsteady footsteps. Somebody was coming up the stairs, and her heart began to pound. Who would be coming here at this hour, after midnight? A drunk probably, or something worse. She shrank against the wall, hoping that whoever it was would not notice her and would go right by.

Go away, she thought, go away, go away. If she thought that hard enough, whoever it was would leave. Go away, I hate you. Leave me alone. Go home. But she saw the top of a round white head, streaked with sparse, straight black hairs, coming up the flight of stairs below, and she heard the sound of footsteps and labored breathing. The head moved from side to side as its owner's body moved from side to side, and she heard the soft thud of an arm or hip striking the rail. She knew even before she smelled the whisky that the man was drunk.

He reached the landing and stood there for a moment, panting, before he started up the stairs to where she was sitting. At first he did not see her. He was of medium height, but he looked very tall because she was curled up in a little ball trying to hide, and he was almost as wide as the stairway itself. His coat hung open and so did the jacket of his suit, and his sleeve was torn as if he had already fallen once, perhaps in the gutter. She saw his face first, a white, rather stupid face, his mouth hanging open with the effort of catching his breath. There was a smudge of dirt on his cheek. Then he started up the stairs toward her, holding tightly to the rail, and suddenly he noticed her and stopped.

'Hey . . .' he said.

Gregg didn't answer.

'Hey! Hey you, girlie!'

Her heart was hammering so hard she saw red streaks in front of her eyes. Get away, she thought, get away, get away from me.

He started up the stairs again, but this time he was coming toward her because he knew she was there. What could she do? Run down? Run up? *Run somewhere!* He was only four steps away from her now and his waist was on the same level with her eyes. She saw his white shirt, containing his huge stomach like a parachute, and the beltless trousers below it. There was one button holding the trousers together above the zipper, and the edge of the fabric had turned over from the tightness of it, showing the white lining. Gregg stared at that white lining with fascinated horror, and at that zipper, and it was as if she were a little girl again, staring at strange men in the street after the first time she had discovered that they were different from little girls. Get away from me, she thought wildly, get away, get away . . . rapist!

'What's the matter?' he asked. 'You lost your key?'

She hardly heard him. She jumped to her feet and tried to push her way past him to go down the stairs, to get to David's apartment, to escape. She could feel that great, immovable, cloth-covered body blocking her way and could smell his breath. 'Move,' she sobbed, elbowing him away, slipping past him in the little space that was left between him and the wall, and as she did her foot missed the step below and she groped for it, feeling the sickening lurch of lost balance as she started to fall. She did not know if it was his voice or her own she heard crying out. All she felt was the world coming up at her, the world turning inside out, inside her own throat, inside her head, as she clawed for a railing, a hand, anything that was not there.

'Well,' Paul Landis said happily. 'This was really a pleasant surprise. I'm glad you called me tonight. I was just sitting there, trying to unwind from my hell of a day at the office, and I can't think of a better way of spending the evening than with you.'

Caroline smiled at him but she did not answer. She was tearing up lettuce for salad because it gave her something to do with her hands, but she was hardly aware of what she was doing. Eddie was having dinner with those people now, she was thinking, and soon he would return to his hotel and go to bed. Perhaps he would have a difficult time falling asleep because he would be wondering whether or not she would say yes tomorrow. As for her, she wondered when she would ever be able to fall asleep with ease again.

'How do you like your steak?' she asked. 'Rare, don't you?'

'As rare as possible.' Paul said. 'Can I help with anything?'

'No. You just sit there. Have another drink.'

She finished making the salad and put the steaks into the broiler and then she went to sit on the studio couch opposite Paul. She lighted a cigarette and put it out almost immediately because she could hardly taste it.

'Can't I make you a drink?' Paul asked.

'No, thank you.'

'I'm glad you're cooking me a dinner,' Paul said. 'I haven't eaten here for a long time.'

'My cooking is no treat, believe me,' Caroline said. She lighted another cigarette.

'It is to me.'

She smiled weakly at him and put her cigarette out in the ash tray. Smile, speak, react, go on living, she told herself. First you'll have to tell yourself when to do it, then it will finally become automatic, the way it used to be before this afternoon. People go on living, they have to. She was glad she had asked Paul to come over, because she needed someone who really liked her to be with her. Paul was comforting. Perhaps if she were to cry on his shoulder and tell him all about Eddie he would not be comforting, he might tell her it was her own fault. He might never understand. But in any case she could not take the chance, nor did she really want to. What had happened to her today was her own problem, and she had to cope with it alone. As for Paul, he was her friend, and he was here for dinner, and he would keep her from thinking too much. For that she was grateful.

'I'm glad you were home when I called,' Caroline said.

How grateful he looked! It hurt her to see how his face lighted up when she said that, and she felt fonder of him than she ever had before. He only wanted to be good to her, in all the accepted and respectable ways, and it would give him pleasure. 'I brought your Christmas present,' Paul said, reaching into his pocket.

He handed her a small package, wrapped in department-store Christmas paper. 'May I open it now?' she asked.

'I want you to.'

She opened it, and inside, nesting on a layer of white cotton, was a large rectangular gold charm, marked like a calendar for December, with a tiny ruby set on the twenty-fifth. 'Oh, it's beautiful!'

'You have a bracelet for it, I've noticed it,' Paul said.

'I do. I'll have this one put right on.'

'I really bought it with an ulterior purpose in mind,' Paul said.

'What?'

'I thought perhaps the date might have more significance than merely another Christmas.'

If you only knew, Caroline thought. I hope to God I never again have another Christmas like this one has turned out to be. 'Really? In what way?' she asked.

'Something sentimental.'

'I've got to turn the steaks,' Caroline said quickly. She stood up. 'I'm sorry to interrupt you, dear, but I know you hate them well done.'

'You're very domestic, do you know that?' Paul said.

'I am?' She was bent over the broiler, turning the steaks, and she did not look at him. The smoke from the sizzling meat made tears come into her eyes, or perhaps it was something else that did.

'You really are.'

She came back to the couch and sat there, looking at her Christmas present. It was so thoughtful of him, and so extravagant, the way Paul always was. Her only thought was: He shouldn't have spent all that money. But she knew he enjoyed doing it for her, and that made her feel a little less guilty about not caring more for the sentimentality of his present.

'What I meant by sentimental,' Paul went on, looking at her closely, 'was that I thought perhaps this year you would have something special to remember this Christmas for.'

Her heart turned over and there were tears in her eyes now. Stop talking, she thought. Please . . .

'What I mean is,' Paul said, 'I'd like to . . . well, I might as well get out with it, and say it.' He smiled, a little self-consciously. 'I never was a trial lawyer, so I'm no good at speeches. I'd like this Christmas to be the day you and I were engaged to be married.'

'Oh, Paul . . .' Caroline said gently, and she shook her head.

'Don't say no,' he said lightly. 'You don't know what a good catch I am.' And he smiled at her so she would know he was only making light of it because it really meant so much to him.

'You are,' she said. 'You are. You'll make some girl very very happy.'

'Why not you?' he asked, still smiling. 'You're my favorite girl. You're the only one I really care about making happy.'

'You do make me happy,' she said, trying to match his light tone and not able to look at him. 'But I don't want to get married.'

'Yes you do.'

'Someday, yes. But not right now. I'm . . . not ready to get married right now.'

'Don't wait too long,' Paul said.

She smiled up at him, able to meet his eyes at last because this last comment had hurt her enough to overcome the guilt she felt at having turned him down. 'May I still keep my Christmas present?'

'I should say so. Maybe it will make you change your mind. You still have one whole day until the twenty-fifth.'

'I'd better look at those steaks,' she murmured, and fled to the stove.

Paul had brought wine besides the Christmas present and they had it with their meal. She put a record on the phonograph, a loud jazzy one that would in no way remind her of Eddie. She had taken his picture off the dresser and the photograph album off the coffee table. But she did not need anything to remind her of Eddie, she was numb with bewilderment and unhappiness and she felt as if there were a little motor in the top of her brain that she could not turn off, no matter how hard she tried. She needed all her efforts simply to respond, to speak, to answer, to act alive for Paul. She was two people: the Caroline who asked him if he would like more wine, would he like regular coffee or expresso, and the Caroline who was clinging to these simple thoughts as a last desperate refuge, lest the motor in the top of her brain explode.

'I was working on an interesting case in the office today,' Paul said. 'There's a corporation in the Bronx . . .' Click, the motor turned off his voice. He went on talking, telling her of his case, and the motor attended to certain functions, such as: Smile, Nod, Clear the table, Bring an ash tray, Smile, Nod . . . And all the time she was so numb with pain that she was only aware that she had cleared the table when she saw her hands bringing dessert plates.

After dinner they sat on the studio couches again and drank a great deal of coffee, or at least Paul did, while Caroline sipped at hers and watched him and listened to him speak when she could concentrate on it, and stood up once in a while to change the record on the phonograph.

'Oh, you have Noël Coward!' Paul exclaimed, looking over her shoulder. 'Play that. I like it.'

'I'd rather not,' Caroline said. Her voice was soft and faraway in her own ears. Had she really answered, or only imagined herself speaking? 'Let's play this one.'

'You look tired,' Paul said.

'Tired? I guess I am.'

He looked at his watch. 'Would you believe it? It's after twelve. I've really started to relax now. Don't you feel relaxed?'

'I guess so,' she murmured. She was so tense that she had pains running down her back, and when the telephone beside the bed shrilled she jumped and gasped.

'Your boy friends certainly call at odd hours,' Paul said pleasantly.

Eddie . . . she thought. Oh, Eddie . . . She was almost afraid to answer the phone, afraid that if she did, when she heard his voice she would start to cry. She knew it was Eddie, it had to be.

'Hello,' she said. She could barely manage the word.

'Caroline?'

It wasn't Eddie, she didn't know who it was. 'Yes?'

'This is David Wilder Savage.'

'Oh . . . How are you?'

'Can you come over here right away?' he said. 'Something's happened to Gregg.'

Paul came with her uptown to the address David Wilder Savage had given her. It was a walk-up, and parked by the curb in front of it were a black police car and a long ambulance. There were two men taking a stretcher out of the ambulance, and Caroline hurried into the house before they had even started in and pressed frantically on the buzzer.

'The door's open,' Paul said, and put his arm around her as he led her in.

She ran up the stairs, with Paul trailing her. She did not know what floor David Wilder Savage lived on, but as soon as she saw the crowd of people clustered on the landing she knew. She pushed her way through them. Gregg was lying on the floor at the foot of a flight of stairs, and she looked unconscious. A policeman took hold of Caroline's arm.

'What happened?' Caroline cried.

'Don't touch her,' the policeman said. 'She's dead.'

She couldn't believe it, she just stared at him, and then at Gregg. 'She's not dead!'

David Wilder Savage was standing in front of his half-opened door, dressed in a bathrobe, and there was a girl standing partly behind him looking troubled. That was all, troubled. She was wearing a bathrobe too. 'This is Miss Adams' roommate, Caroline Bender,' he said to the policeman.

The policeman loosened his grip on Caroline's arm, but he did not let go entirely, as if he was waiting to see if she was going to do something desperate. 'I'm sorry,' he said.

'Gregg?' Caroline said softly. 'Gregg . . .' She knelt down beside Gregg, who looked as if she were only unconscious, and then she saw the odd, bent way her head fitted on her shoulders. Her soft blonde hair fanned out on the floor, over the dirt that was there, and where people had walked with their shoes, and without thinking about it Caroline reached out toward her.

'Don't touch her!' the policeman said, pulling her back.

'Don't let her lie there like that,' Caroline said. 'It's so dirty there.' And then she began to cry, because she realized that Gregg didn't know or care whether it was dirty on the floor or not.

There was a man standing leaning against the wall. He looked gray and sick and as if he would fall if he were not using the wall for support. 'She fell right down,' he murmured. 'Right down. She just ran right down the stairs and fell down.'

'It's all right,' the policeman said. 'We know.'

'Right down . . .' the man repeated, as if he were stunned. 'Right down those stairs. I thought she was locked out.'

Two interns came up the stairs with a stretcher, and the crowd moved aside. There were the two policemen and some people who were in nightclothes and were evidently neighbors, and the man who had witnessed the scene; and David Wilder Savage and that girl. He had his arm around the girl now and he did not say a word. Paul put his arm around Caroline. 'Don't look,' Paul said softly.

Caroline couldn't help looking. She watched as the interns put Gregg's body on the stretcher and carried it away, down the stairs, very gently, as if she were still alive. Someone had put a sheet over her, and Caroline had the wild, illogical feeling that if they didn't take the sheet off Gregg's face she would smother. But Gregg was dead . . .

'Somebody has to call her family,' Caroline said. She looked at David Wilder Savage standing there in his bathrobe with his arm protectively around that girl, as if he were married to her, and suddenly, although she knew it was not his fault, Caroline resented him. 'I don't know where they live,' she said, looking pointedly at David. 'They never wrote to her, and Gregg didn't say. Somebody has to find her family.'

'We'll find them,' the policeman said.

'It's somewhere in Dallas,' Caroline said.

'They'll find them,' Paul said gently. 'Come.'

Caroline was still looking at David. He had not said another word, and his pale face was controlled; a little unhappy, a little shocked, but mainly controlled. The girl beside him looked bewildered. She was young, in her early twenties. That's Judy Masson, Caroline thought suddenly, as if she actually knew the girl. It gave her a strange, queasy feeling. Don't you *care?* Caroline wanted to cry out to them. 'Is that all now?' David Wilder Savage asked.

'Yes,' the policeman said. He was writing in a little notebook. 'You can all go home now.'

Home, Caroline thought. She let Paul lead her away, feeling his gentle, capable hands on her shoulders. She didn't even say good-bye, but then as she started down the stairs she looked back once and saw David Wilder Savage leading Judy Masson back inside his apartment, protectively, and closing the door. Nobody cares about anybody, Caroline thought; we could all die, and who would care? Does anybody *really* care about anybody? When she found herself in a taxi with Paul she put her head on his shoulder and let the tears come out of her closed eyes, and she was grateful for his comfort. Who am I really crying for? she wondered. For Gregg? For myself? For every girl in the world who wanted someone to care?

'We'll go to your place,' Paul said.

She hardly heard him. I wouldn't listen, she was thinking, when Gregg wanted to talk to me in the middle of the night.

When she was in her apartment – the apartment she used to share with Gregg – Caroline let Paul take off her coat and then propel her gently to the studio couch. She lay down and he took off her shoes and put her coat over her like a blanket and poured out a little glassful of brandy. 'Drink this,' he said. 'I don't want you to think about it any more tonight.'

'You're like a nurse.'

She drank the brandy and he knelt down on the floor beside her bed and stroked her hair. 'You can't stay here tonight,' he said.

'No . . .'

'Do you want to come to my place? My parents are home, it's all right.'

She shook her head. 'I want to stay here.'

'I don't think you should.'

'Will you stay with me?'

He looked worried for a moment and then he smiled. 'I will if you like.'

'I don't want to be alone,' Caroline whispered.

He was still stroking her hair, gently, hypnotically. 'I don't want you to be alone,' he said very softly. 'I want to take care of you. You'll never have to be alone.'

Her eyes were closed. She hardly knew what she was saying. All she knew was that she didn't want to be like Gregg, she didn't even want to be like Caroline, she didn't want to be alone. 'Do you love me?' she asked. 'You've never said so.'

'Yes,' Paul said. 'I love you.'

'Very much?'

'Very much.'

'I want somebody to love me,' she whispered.

'I love you.'

'Do you still want to marry me?'

'Yes.'

'I want to marry you, too,' Caroline said.

Paul rose to his feet and sat down on the studio couch beside her. He put his face next to hers, his cheek against her cheek, and did not say anything for a moment. Then he said, 'I'll make you happy.'

'I know you will.'

He turned his face and kissed her on the mouth. She did not move. Happy, she was thinking, happy . . . It was what she had said to Eddie. She tried not to think of it, but only to smooth out her mind as you smooth out the sheet on a rumpled bed and not to think of anything but Paul and how he would take care of her and cherish her forever after. 'You'll be glad,' Paul murmured. He kissed her again, gently, as one might kiss an invalid, and yet she could feel the pulse beginning in his lips and she tried to keep her mind blank and smooth.

Paul lay beside her on the narrow studio couch. There was just enough room for the two of them if they lay close together. He did not disturb the coat that covered her but put his arm around her waist over the coat and held her to him. 'Caroline . . .' he said, and he kissed her mouth again.

Eddie, she thought, and she fought to keep the thought out of her mind. This is Paul, my fiancé. My fiancé. He loves me so much. And I'm so fond of him, so very fond of him. I love him. She kept her eyes shut as Paul kissed her again with more feeling and then she felt his hand moving the coat aside and touching her shoulder. She did not move, or even dare to breathe. His hand moved to her waist and the bones of her ribs just beneath her breast and she still did not move. She tried to think of how much she really cared for Paul; he was so good, so kind, so right.

'How do you feel?' he asked.

'Fine,' she whispered.

'Let's get married as soon as possible,' he said. 'We've known each other so long. I've waited for you so long.' His hand touched her breast and she knew then what he meant. *Eddie!* she thought.

It came into her mind like a scream, so loudly and desperately that she wondered if Paul himself had not heard it. Oh, please, she thought, please God, make everything be all right.

She opened her eyes and looked at Paul. He was leaning on one elbow, with his other hand beginning to stroke her breast, and he was looking down into her face, smiling at her tenderly. She realized then that he had taken off his glasses and folded the earpieces back neatly behind the lenses and placed them on the coffee table next to the bed. She had never seen him without his glasses before, and it startled her a little because he looked so naked without them. His face was so close, so undressed, there was something so intimate about it, all white and half blind with the preparations for love. This is how he'll look when we're married and he goes to bed with me, Caroline thought. She was suddenly overtaken with a wave of nausea and fright and she sat up quickly.

'What, darling?' he asked.

She had her hands over her face and was shaking her head. Eddie, Eddie, Eddie, she thought, and she knew then that it would be no use to try any longer with Paul.

'Please,' she said. 'Oh, please. Go home now.'

'Don't you want me to stay? I'll sleep on Gregg's bed, or even in the chair if you like.'

'Please go home, Paul. Don't worry about me. I'll be all right now.'

'Are you sure?'

'Yes.'

He stood up and put on his glasses again. He smiled, completely unaware. 'Would you like me to tuck you in before I go?'

She shook her head.

'You go to sleep. I'll call you tomorrow morning.' He was smiling down at her. 'And Caroline . . .'

'Yes?'

'Save Monday lunch hour. We'll go for the ring.'

She shook her head but she did not answer. She could not bear to tell Paul tonight. I'll tell him tomorrow, she thought; on the telephone.

When Paul had left she stood up slowly, like someone who is first testing his unsteady legs after a long illness, and walked to the door. She locked it. Then she walked back to the dresser and opened the drawer where she had hidden Eddie's framed photograph and she took the picture out. It wasn't a very good likeness, it was too formal. Eddie looked much better than that. But it was all she had. She set the photograph on top of the dresser and looked at it for a while. Tomorrow she would have to get some silver polish and shine up the frame.

How long she sat on the edge of her bed staring off at nothing she did not know. She could call Eddie right now, or she could not. He would meet her tomorrow and she could say yes to his plan, or she could not. She did not even try to make a decision, she simply sat there, and she tried not to think of anything at all. Her mind that had been so active she could not shut it off, when Paul was making love to her, was now completely stilled. It had stopped working at last, she had managed to turn it off. The little motor had run down.

She did not even feel like crying. She had cried, and it was over now. She was through with crying, numb, drained, dead. I'll sit here forever, she thought tiredly, and never think again. Everything will be easy that way. Never think, never move. If tomorrow never comes and I never have to speak to Eddie again, I can go on. But Eddie's face, his voice, his words, the meaning of the question she dreaded, tore her with so many conflicts that she could not think about them. She could not say yes and give up her life to live only a poor part of a life forever after. That would be more painful than anything that could ever happen to her now. She knew only one thing, dully, that she never wanted to feel as hurt again as she had in these past hours, when the hurt was so great that her mind rebelled and could not register it any more.

The telephone rang four times before she answered it, although it was only inches from her hand. 'Yes,' she said.

'Caroline . . . is it really you?'

'Who is this?'

'Can't you guess?'

'I don't want to guess.'

'It's John Cassaro.'

'Oh,' she said. She paid a little more attention now, because his call was a surprise. She felt nothing, but she was surprised, and that at least was something. 'How did you find me?' she asked.

'There's a great American institution known as the phone book. You made it this year, baby.'

She smiled, despite herself. 'I guess I didn't think of that.'

'I must have waked you up,' John Cassaro said sympathetically.

'No . . . What time is it?'

'One o'clock.'

She looked at her watch. It was twenty-five minutes to two. Well, what did it matter? 'Do you always call people in the middle of the night?'

'My friends I do.'

'Oh.'

'I didn't wake you up, did I?'

'No,' Caroline said. 'You didn't.'

'I get lonesome at night,' John Cassaro said. 'Don't you ever feel that way?'

'Yes.'

'What's the good of getting another phone call in the daytime when you're busy? It's the night hours that are the bad ones.'

'Yes,' Caroline said again. She was beginning to feel a little better. She didn't believe a word John Cassaro was saying, they were obviously lies, and yet they happened to be true too.

'Nighttime is a waiting time,' he said. His voice was low and intimate over the telephone, an after-midnight voice, from one person who is alone to another. 'What are you doing, Caroline?'

'Now?'

'Yes.'

'Nothing,' she said.

'Are you dressed?'

'Yes.'

'Do you have a suitcase and an evening dress and a bathing suit?'

'Yes,' she said, perplexed.

'Then put them all together and take a taxi to my hotel. I'll be waiting for you downstairs and I'll pay the cab. We're going to Las Vegas for Christmas.'

'Who's "we"? Not me,' Caroline said. But she was surprised to find herself smiling at the impudence and madness of this man. He sounded a little impish too, as if the Las Vegas trip was an idea he had thought of only this instant on the telephone with her.

'"We" consists of you and me and four of my friends. Don't worry, we're going to take a regular plane. It leaves at four-thirty, so you'd better hurry up.'

'Las Vegas . . .' she said.

'You don't have to work tomorrow. It's Christmas Eve. I'll get you back in time Monday morning. Now tell me something. Do you have something better to do on Christmas?'

'I . . . don't know.' He was actually trying to persuade her, in his way; John Cassaro, who could have nearly any girl he wanted if he would only ask. Why did he care whether she went or not? He could find a dozen girls once he got there. She still didn't trust him, but it pleased her that he wanted her particularly to go, even though she knew she had no intention of going.

'What better thing are you going to do tomorrow night?' he asked. 'Hang up your stocking with that guy?'

'What guy? And don't be so fresh.'

'That guy you wouldn't break your date with the last time I called.'

'I don't even remember who it was.'

'I do,' John Cassaro said. 'I remember your dates better than you do. What a girl you are.' His tone was so pleasant that she could not quite get angry with him. He was teasing her, he wasn't insulting her, and the difference in his tone showed the difference quite clearly. She wanted to hang up on him because he had called her at such an inconsiderate hour, with such a disrespectful request, and yet, somehow, she couldn't. Because his voice was amused and reassuring, and when she listened to it she thought of things like 'What shall I say to him now?' and it was fun, and when he made her spar with him this way she was only half aware

486

of her loneliness and pain, as if providence had sent someone to divert her.

'I don't know . . .' she said. 'I've never been to Las Vegas.'

'That's why you should go. Do you like to gamble? I'm lucky.'

'I'm sure.'

'I want you to meet my friends,' he went on. 'You'll love them.'

John Cassaro is begging me, she thought. Maybe he really likes me. I guess that's what all the girls thought: John Cassaro likes *me*, and then they never saw him again. But I'm being offered three whole days. That ought to mean something. And at the back of her mind Caroline knew it meant nothing, that she was rationalizing, because at this moment John Cassaro's carefree and fascinating and unexpected voice was miraculously capable of cheering her up. 'I'm kind of glad you called,' she said. 'I was depressed.'

'So was I. What's the good of being depressed?'

'No good, I guess.'

'You're right. Listen,' he added, 'if you want to be depressed in Las Vegas it's all right with me. Brood yourself to death. I don't care. But I'm willing to make you a little bet you won't be depressed from ten minutes after you hit that plane.'

'I won't?'

'Want to bet?'

'You told me you're lucky at gambling,' Caroline said.

There was a pause and she heard the click of a lighter, and she knew he was lighting a cigarette. Suddenly she saw him in her mind: the angular face, the piercing and guileless eyes, that mouth with its corners turned up just a little and now with a cigarette in it. Knowing what he was doing made her see him clearly, and she wondered whether the room was brightly lighted or dim and what he was wearing and whom he had been with before he called. 'I am,' he said.

'Lucky?'

'Mm-hm.'

'I need luck,' Caroline said. 'Everything has been pretty terrible lately.'

'I can't promise you'll be lucky,' John Cassaro said. 'But at least you'll have a good time. Sometimes I think you need all the luck in the world just to do that.'

'Tell me something.'

'What?'

'Are you prowling around on the end of that telephone cord?'

'What?'

She smiled, although he couldn't see her. 'Nothing. Never mind.'

'Hey, Caroline . . .'

'What?'

'Come on over.' He hesitated. 'Please.'

Something inside her fluttered, very gently, like a leaf falling to the ground. She hardly felt it. But it gave her the strangest feeling.

'It will take me a while to get organized,' she said.

His voice was more intimate, pacifying, almost affectionate. 'I don't mind. We'll all wait.'

'All right,' she said softly. 'I'll be there.'

She hung up and looked around the room as if she had never seen it before. She was going to get out of here, get away, escape, the sooner the better. John Cassaro would be waiting for her, and he would make her laugh, and he would make her think about other things. He was a clown, he was funny, he was charming, and so attractive that she might even notice it. He could not stop her from remembering, even from thinking, but he would help. He would divert her. He might even save her.

If anybody *knew*, she thought, alarmed. My parents would be appalled. But she had gone so far from them in these three years, her life as it was and as they had hoped it would be were so different, that she could never hope for them to understand. She could not turn to her parents and tell them how she felt this minute; she would have to recite to them her whole life history before she could do that, and even then they would never understand. She could not turn to anyone. April was gone, Gregg was gone, they were all gone. All those girls she had known, gone like shadows, Mary Agnes, Barbara Lemont, girls in the office, girls from home, all gone. And I'd better pack, because I'm going to Las Vegas!

Gregg's cat walked silently out of the bathroom and rubbed its side against Caroline's ankle as she packed. She bent down and picked it up, cuddling it to her face, kissing its soft fur, thinking of Gregg. Her fingers could feel the vibrations of its throat as it purred. 'Poor cat,' Caroline murmured. 'Poor baby cat.' She remembered how Eddie had carefully filled its dishes with fresh cat food and water, and the pain began again. Somebody would have to take care of Gregg's cat now. She kissed it. 'Nice little alley cat,' she repeated, in Eddie's words, and set the cat down on the floor. She went to the kitchenette and opened two cans of cat food. She'd heard somewhere that cats know how to pace themselves when they eat; you could leave enough food for three days and the cat would eat just enough each day. She put the food into two dishes and left two dishes of cold water and one of milk. Eddie had liked the cat. She would have to take care of it always, from now on.

32

On Friday afternoon, the day before Christmas, Eddie Harris checked out of the Plaza Hotel, took his suitcase from the bellboy, and waited on the sidewalk for a taxi that would take him to the airport. He looked at his watch several times, because he was nervous, because he would barely make his plane, and he wondered whether he would have time to call Caroline one more time. He had telephoned her when he woke up that morning, hoping she could come to have breakfast with him, but she had not answered. He had let the telephone ring much longer than was really necessary, and then he had asked the operator to try again. It had occurred to him as he was finishing his orange juice that of course she had been in the shower, and so he had called her again. There had been no answer. Damn it, he had thought, what's the matter with that girl? Don't tell me she went to the office? So he had called her office, not really angry with Caroline but annoyed at himself for having been stupid enough to forget that she might have gone to the office even though today was Christmas Eve.

'I'm sorry,' the operator said, 'there's no one here today.'

'Well, isn't there a night number or something? Can't you find out if she's in her office anyway?'

'I'm sorry, sir. I'm only the answering service.'

If Caroline had gone to the office, Eddie realized, she would have telephoned him. He thought perhaps she might be asleep, but no one he knew could sleep so deeply that an insistent telephone ringing twelve times would not awaken him. He called her again at noon, and at three. By that time he had to leave or miss his plane, and so he left.

To save time he took a taxi to the airport instead of to the terminal, and when he arrived he discovered that he had fifteen minutes to spare. He checked his suitcase through and then he walked to the nearest telephone booth and called Caroline again. At least he could say goodbye to her. As he listened to her telephone ringing far away, unanswered, it occurred to him for the first time that she might be sick. Perhaps she had been taken by an appendicitis attack in the night, or had been hit by a car on her way to his hotel this morning. Those things sounded ridiculous, but they did happen. Or perhaps, Eddie was just beginning to realize, she was there all the time, in her apartment, but did not want to speak to him.

He didn't want to wonder about it now because he knew that wondering would not do him any good. If something had happened to her, which was extremely unlikely, then he would discover it, and if she were angry at him, then he would find that out too. He had learned through the years that it did no good to waste hopeless conjectures on things you knew nothing about. You would always find out in the end.

He went to the cigarette machine and bought a package of cigarettes, glancing at himself in the mirror on the front of the machine. It reminded him of the night he and Caroline had looked at themselves in the mirror in her apartment, after they had made love. How beautiful she was! He wanted her that instant, with a physical sensation that struck him with the speed of lightning. He walked slowly to the gate that led to his plane, looking around, as if for some reason Caroline might have decided to come to the airport by herself and would just be rushing through the door, breathless, to throw herself into his arms. But he knew she wouldn't come, and he sighed, and he tried not to wonder where she was.

He remembered that he had nothing to read on the plane and so he turned around once more and went to the news stand, where he bought an evening paper and several magazines. In his seat, Eddie glanced at the headlines on the top half of the folded newspaper and turned it over. He tried to concentrate on it. The government was having some kind of vendetta against scandal magazines, and it was about time too, Eddie thought. On the lower half of the front page there was a photograph of John Cassaro with a girl. He had just been handed a subpoena to appear in court to testify.

Something about the girl made Eddie look twice. She was beautiful, with dark hair and a very white face, and large eyes that looked terrified. He realized that to him she looked just like Caroline. Perhaps from now on every girl would look like Caroline. He smiled, and read the caption under the photograph. *John Cassaro and Fabian editor.*

The story was in the column alongside. It didn't hit him right away, he glanced at it first simply to see who this Fabian editor was. Then he wasn't smiling any more.

With Cassaro in the plush Pharaoh Hotel was pretty Fabian editor Caroline Bender, 24, who works for the company that publishes Unveiled. *Asked by a reporter if Miss Bender was gathering further material for another* Unveiled *story, Cassaro swung a punch and had to be forcibly restrained by two of his friends. Cassaro described her later as 'an old friend.' Miss Bender refused to comment or to pose for photographers, and locked herself in her room, which is next door to Cassaro's.*

Christ! Eddie thought. He couldn't quite believe it still, it was like knowing someone was a few blocks away from you and suddenly discovering that he wasn't there at all, he was on Mars instead. What would make her go off with Cassaro?

The engines stopped racing now and then started up again as the plane began to rush down the runway. Eddie sat in his seat, strapped in by his seat belt, and stared at the picture of Caroline. It was Caroline, all right. Even in the photograph you could see that she had light-colored eyes, blue. He remembered how blue they were, and he remembered how her eyelids looked when they were closed, and how dark and thick her lashes were. God, she was *sleeping* with that guy! What would make her do a thing like that? Eddie looked more closely at the photograph. She was wearing a dress with a V neck and at her throat he could see the tiny gold heart he had given her only last week. She was still wearing it. She was wearing it when she went away with Cassaro.

He couldn't figure out what made girls do what they did. All right, John Cassaro was a celebrity, but Caroline knew lots of celebrities, that was her business. She was no movie-struck schoolgirl. She was a good, sensible, intelligent girl, gentle, loving. Loving . . . Eddie swallowed. He felt a little sick. The *No Smoking* sign had gone off so he lighted a cigarette and dragged on it deeply. Over the wing he could see the ground, far below, the skyscrapers like scale models on a table. Loving . . . She said she wouldn't come to Dallas with me, and then she went off with John Cassaro. Caroline . . .

I guess, Eddie thought, I never really knew her as well as I thought I did. Three years is a long time. I thought I knew everything about her. She was the girl I'd loved for such a long time, and I thought I really knew her.

He folded the newspaper. He didn't feel like reading any more. When the stewardess came down the aisle he would ask her for a drink. That was one thing about flying first class, at least you could get good and stiff. And soon he'd be home. Tomorrow he'd have Christmas with Helen and the baby. He'd bought Helen a mink jacket, the first really expensive present he'd ever bought any girl, and tomorrow it would be her surprise. She'd be very excited. *My wife*, Eddie thought. It was a good feeling to be able to give your wife a fur coat, even if it was only a jacket. It was like knowing you were on your way. You could see the future, planned, secure, getting better and better as the years went by. It was funny, but now that he was on his way home he missed her.

'Miss . . . Could I have a Scotch on the rocks? Make it a double.'

He'd never be able to figure it out about Caroline. He wasn't even going to try any more. You never knew what a girl was going to do, and once she'd done it you could never find out a logical reason why because she probably didn't know either. John Cassaro! One of the most notorious bedroom athletes in Hollywood. Christ! She'd be famous now herself, the girl who was with John Cassaro in Las Vegas. Eddie shook his head.

You're well out of it, buddy, he told himself. Maybe you're lucky.

Things wouldn't have worked out any other way, you were just too romantic. Now you know how things stand. You made the choice. And it was the good choice. Sometimes life *is* simple – sometimes, just when you think it never will be simple again.

He just wanted a decent book to read ...

Not too much to ask, is it? It was in 1935 when Allen Lane, Managing Director of Bodley Head Publishers, stood on a platform at Exeter railway station looking for something good to read on his journey back to London. His choice was limited to popular magazines and poor-quality paperbacks – the same choice faced every day by the vast majority of readers, few of whom could afford hardbacks. Lane's disappointment and subsequent anger at the range of books generally available led him to found a company – and change the world.

'We believed in the existence in this country of a vast reading public for intelligent books at a low price, and staked everything on it'
Sir Allen Lane, 1902–1970, founder of Penguin Books

The quality paperback had arrived – and not just in bookshops. Lane was adamant that his Penguins should appear in chain stores and tobacconists, and should cost no more than a packet of cigarettes.

Reading habits (and cigarette prices) have changed since 1935, but Penguin still believes in publishing the best books for everybody to enjoy. We still believe that good design costs no more than bad design, and we still believe that quality books published passionately and responsibly make the world a better place.

So wherever you see the little bird – whether it's on a piece of prize-winning literary fiction or a celebrity autobiography, political tour de force or historical masterpiece, a serial-killer thriller, reference book, world classic or a piece of pure escapism – you can bet that it represents the very best that the genre has to offer.

Whatever you like to read – trust Penguin.

read more
www.penguin.co.uk